More advance prai*bation*

"If David Sedaris were cas.... ...y Loman, it might sound something like *Probation*. Andy, a sharp-tongued traveling salesman, gives us the life events that led to his being taken away in handcuffs, and the hilarious and agonizing self-inquiry that follows. Snarky yet profound, it is a bold examination of the destructive effects of a life spent in the closet, reported with a Carolina twang."

—Vestal McIntyre, author of *Lake Overturn*

probation

tom mendicino

KENSINGTON BOOKS
www.kensingtonbooks.com

KENSINGTON BOOKS are published by

Kensington Publishing Corp.
119 West 40th Street
New York, NY 10018

Copyright © 2010 by Tom Mendicino

"I Love Rock N Roll"
Written by Jake Hooker and Alan Merrill
© 1982 Finchley Music Corporation
Worldwide Print Rights Controlled by Finchley Music Corporation.
All Rights Reserved. Used by permission of Finchley Music Corp.

"The Grand Tour"
Words and Music by George Richey, Norris D. Wilson and Carmol Taylor
© 1974 (Renewed) EMI Al Gallico Music Corp. and EMI Algee Music Corp.
Worldwide Print Rights Controlled by Alfred Publishing Co., Inc.
All Rights Reserved. Used by Permission of Alfred Publishing Co., Inc.

All Kensington titles, imprints, and distributed lines are available at special quantity discounts for bulk purchases for sales promotion, premiums, fund-raising, educational, or institutional use.

Special book excerpts or customized printings can also be created to fit specific needs. For details, write or phone the office of the Kensington Special Sales Manager: Attn. Special Sales Department. Kensington Publishing Corp., 119 West 40th Street, New York, NY 10018. Phone: 1-800-221-2647.

Kensington and the K logo Reg. U.S. Pat. & TM Off.

ISBN-13: 978-0-7582-3878-8
ISBN-10: 0-7582-3878-9

First Kensington Trade Paperback Printing: April 2010

10 9 8 7 6 5 4 3 2

Printed in the United States of America

For Rachel Klayman and Casey Fuetsch,
who have been indispensable

*A life is not important except
in the impact it has on other lives.*

—Jackie Robinson

Playlist

"Oh Playmate, Come Out and Play with Me"
(Saxie Dowell)

"Nancy (With the Laughing Face)"
(Jimmy Van Heusen/Phil Silvers)

"*The Patty Duke Show* Theme"
(Sid Ramin/Bob Wells)

"Overture to *The Magic Flute (Die Zauberflöte)*"
(W. A. Mozart)

"Last Dance"
(Pete Bellotte)

"Surrender"
(Rick Nielsen)

"You're the First, the Last, My Everything"
(Barry White, Tony Sepe, and Peter Radcliffe)

"Let's Pretend We're Married"
(Prince)

"Mame"
(Jerry Herman)

"White Christmas"
(Irving Berlin)

"What I Did for Love"
(Edward Kleban/Marvin Hamlisch)

"People Will Say We're in Love"
(Rodgers and Hammerstein)

"Snowbird"
(Gene MacLellan)

"I'm a Believer"
(Neil Diamond)

"Top of the World"
(Richard Carpenter/John Bettis)

"The Most Beautiful Girl"
(Norris Wilson/Billy Sherrill/Rory Bourke)

"Cracklin' Rosie"
(Neil Diamond)

"Well . . . All Right"
(Buddy Holly)

"You Never Can Tell"
(Chuck Berry)

"The Grand Tour"
(Norris Wilson/Carmol Taylor/George Richey)

"We're Gonna Hold On"
(George Jones and Earl Montgomery)

"Sweet Jane" and "Head Held High"
(Lou Reed)

"Kiss Me on the Bus"
(Paul Westerberg)

"Girlfriend"
(Matthew Sweet)

"Casta diva"
(Vincenzo Bellini)

"Love to Love You Baby"
(Donna Summer/Giorgio Moroder/Pete Bellotte)

"Help!"; "Ticket to Ride"; and "If I Fell"
(John Lennon and Paul McCartney)

"Love Me Tender"
(Vera Matson/Elvis Presley)

"I Love Rock N Roll"
(Jake Hooker/Alan Merrill)

"Suspicious Minds"
(Mark James)

"Little Saint Nick"
(Brian Wilson/Mike Love)

"Blue Christmas"
(Billy Hayes/Jay Johnson)

"Between Us"
(William Reid)

"Buddy Holly"
(Rivers Cuomo)

Priest

My lawyer knew what he was doing when he dressed me for my sentencing. He insisted I buy a new shirt, a button-down oxford, and new khakis, both two sizes too large. My neck barely anchored the collar, and my belt was useless. Outside the courtroom, he undid the knot in my tie and ordered a quick, sloppy Windsor. "Good boy," he said, "pants and shirt straight from the dryer. Loafers run down at the toe." I had done as I was told and slept in my blazer. "Pathetic." He laughed as he led me into the courtroom.

Just as he predicted, the judge took pity on me, a big, forlorn old boy, so ashamed of my transgressions that it was obvious I was unable to lift fork to mouth these days. I blushed when addressed by the Court. His Honor recognized something familiar in me. A face he might pass on the golf course or at the wine and cheese reception on opening night of the new season at the Performing Arts Center. A face he was startled to see from high atop his bench, out there, adrift in a sea of teenage carjackers in nylon shell suits and crystal meth pushers with frizzy, gray ponytails. A blazing blue Brooks Brothers shirt surrounded by agitated jumping jacks who couldn't sit still and pockmarked cactuses who dozed on the courtroom benches.

Probation. One year of counseling, no more arrests, and your record will be expunged. Next case, the People of the State of North Carolina versus . . .

My record.

Can they really expunge my record? I ask my lawyer. How do I know there won't be some ominous criminal sheet stamped RECORD EXPUNGED dogging me for the rest of my life, forcing me to explain I've never been convicted of molesting children or raping old ladies?

Well, he says, you can always just pay the fine, forget about the counseling, and spend the rest of your life explaining why you were giving a blow job off Interstate 85 one hot summer night.

He's got a point.

My counselor lives with three other priests in an old Queen Anne in Charlotte where he sees his private patients. I give myself plenty of time to find the place and arrive forty minutes early for our first session. He's in the driveway, washing a restored 1966 Mustang convertible, stripped to a pair of running shorts, wet black hair plastered to his chest. I introduce myself. Andrew Nocera. The criminal degenerate. He shakes my dry hand with his wet one and tells me I caught him with his pants down, literally, and excuses himself.

I wait in the study, listening to the clock mark off the minutes. I finger the silk place marker in the missal on the desk and flip through epistles and gospels, hoping to stumble across a passage to enlighten me about my predicament. Maybe Jesus, dozing on the crucifix on the wall, would have a few words of encouragement if I could rouse Him from His nap.

My counselor saunters into the office. His biceps rip against his shirt sleeves and his neck muscles bulge under the Roman collar. Is it Andrew or Andy? he asks. He tells me to call him

Matt. I tell him I'm old-fashioned and prefer to call him Father McGinley. Not necessary, he says.

"How are you?"

"Fine."

"Just fine?"

"Fine."

"Really?"

He sees me staring at his hands—the wide span between his outstretched fingers, the balls of his fingertips, the sharp black hairs, the clipped cuticles, and the flat buffed nails. He folds these anointed vessels together and waits for me to speak. Why am I entrusting my carcass, and maybe my immortal soul, to a Black Irish linebacker with a passion for emery boards? My lawyer was skeptical when I told him the counseling arrangements my mother had made. He was afraid of testing the judge's benevolence, knowing the distrust of papists that persists in the glass and steel cities of the New South. He warned me about deep-rooted suspicions that the Romans would connive to circumvent the Court's interest in my rehabilitation. No self-respecting judge was going to let me off with a few sprinkles of holy water.

But this time my lawyer was wrong. His Honor never raised an eyebrow. The Reverend Matthew J. McGinley, S.J., M.D., has an unrestricted license to practice medicine in the state of North Carolina, is fully certified in his specialty by the American Board of Psychiatry and Neurology, is credentialed for reimbursement for his services by every major health plan, and is well known and respected by the Court for his work with the abused and damaged boys of the juvenile detention system.

And so, with the imprimatur of both Church and State, those well-tended digits are going to peel me like an onion. We're going to get to the bottom of this. We're going to find a rational, scientific explanation why a nice-looking, respectable, barely middle-aged man with a wonderful, loving wife and a glowing future—a man with a mortgage on a beautiful town house with a marble foyer and a stainless steel kitchen, his-and-hers fully loaded sports utility vehicles parked in the garage, linen and alpaca and cashmere stacked in the closets—would drop to his knees in a piss-soaked and shit-stinking toilet and take some burly, sweaty garage mechanic's cock in his mouth.

Peel an onion and you find it doesn't have a core.

He asks about my new career.

"Job," I correct him.

"Do you like it?"

I tell him I sell display shelving to retail shops.

"Well, then you must know how to talk despite the fact you've given me every indication otherwise."

"Nope. I just open the catalogue and point."

"What would you prefer doing?"

"Sleeping."

"Why?"

"Is this where you start asking me about my dreams?"

"I'm not a Freudian."

"Well, then aren't we supposed to be talking about my unhappy childhood?"

"Do you want to talk about that?"

"No."

"What do you want to talk about?"

"Let's talk about work."

"Do you like selling?"

"No."

"Why? Don't you like talking?"

"No."

"What do you like?"

"I like listening. You and I should exchange seats. You talk and I listen."

"Doesn't work that way."

"Figures. Too bad. I'm a good listener. I measure and they talk to fill up the space."

"What do they talk about?"

"Nothing interesting. Sales are down, wholesale costs are up, rent is up, shoplifting is up, help is impossible, my husband hasn't fucked me in three months . . ."

"That isn't interesting?"

"Nope. You ought to see them. Dry skin and Hostess Ho Ho asses."

"You sound angry."

"Why would I be angry?"

"I don't know. Do you have anything to be angry about?"

"No."

No, I think, nothing at all. It's a wonderful life. Here I sit on a Friday night, straight from the airport, Johnny Walker Black on my breath, sticky armpits and stinky socks, itchy scrotum (please, not crabs again!), facing a weekend of transcribing measurements onto order forms. I'll wake up tomorrow just before noon, dreading the Saturday phone call from the Vice President for National Sales who's a born-again Christian and spouts *Praise the Lord* when I give him the weekly sales total. He'll say a little prayer that next week's totals are even better and remind me he's signed me up for a motivational forum at the Greensboro Holiday Inn next month. Oh, by the way, he reminds me just before signing off with heartfelt *God Bless*, there won't be a deposit to my checking account until the checks I've collected clear. Come Sunday, I'll hide in bed as long as I can and then it will start all over again on Monday. I'll leave my mother's house before dawn because Shelton/Murray Shelving and Display doesn't reimburse for parking and the long-term lot is halfway to South Carolina. I'll take a bite of a dry apple Danish and stare into a paper cup of coffee not hot enough to dissolve the non-dairy creamer, pacing the boarding area because the flight has been delayed again. . . . Hey, it's a wonderful life!

"Isn't the travel interesting?"

"Flying to Beaumont, Texas, or Lansing, Michigan, isn't what I'd call travel."

"Well, what would you call it?"

"Geographic displacement."

"Come on. Where are you coming from tonight?"

"Memphis."

"Tell me about it. Beale Street. Graceland. The Peabody Hotel. You must have seen something interesting."

"Am I allowed to smoke?"

"Tell me something interesting you saw and then you can smoke."

"Hmm. I saw an old lady at the airport tonight. She looked pretty brittle, with one of those old-lady humps on her back, but she was dressed pretty hip. Elvis T-shirt, sweats, black sneakers, Velcro wallet dangling from a string around her neck. Her husband helped her settle into the seat. Then he tucked a paper napkin under her chin and handed her an ice cream cone. She licked it and offered him a bite. Nope, he said, it's all for you."

"How did that make you feel?"

"Don't get old!" I laugh.

He hands me a silver cigarette case and offers me an unfiltered French cigarette. These priests sure know how to live.

"Is that really how you felt?"

"He's going to die soon. I saw it in his eyes. He knows he's gonna die and she'll be shipped off to a nursing home. He knows she's gonna spend the rest of her life waiting for him to walk through the door. And he's never gonna come."

What I don't tell him is that I locked myself in a toilet stall and cried.

The doorbell is ringing. "Shit," he says, "excuse me for a minute." I hear him talking in the hallway and then the screen door swings shut. I smell hot grease and tomatoes, oil, and pepperoni.

"I ordered this hours ago and it's just getting here. You eaten yet?"

He disappears, returning with napkins and two bottles of Coca-Cola.

"This is one occasion when it isn't bad manners to talk with your mouth full."

He eats like a bear, folding a slice in half and shoveling it into his mouth. He nods at me, his cheeks bulging with pizza dough. He washes it down and grabs a second. A pepperoni ring flips into his lap. He swallows a mouthful and says, "Tell me a story."

"About what?"

"About you."

"I don't know any stories."

"Why are you here?"

"You know why I'm here."

"Tell me about it anyway."

"I got caught sucking a cock at a rest stop on the interstate."

"Start at the beginning."

"I was lying on the couch, drinking scotch, staring at the television, watching a meaningless ball game on the West Coast. American League. I hate the American League. My wife had gone up to bed around eleven and I went outside for a smoke. I saw a light go on next door. My neighbor's son was home from college for the summer. He started to undress for bed. He pulled off his shirt and sniffed his pits. He yanked down his pants, then his shorts. His pecker was already at half-mast. I saw him take one stroke before he turned off the light."

My best efforts to make him blush or wince are wasted. He just stares at me, chewing on a slice of pizza.

"I waited a few minutes before I went back in. The room was so close I couldn't breathe. I was suffocating in my clothes. I turned off all the lights and stripped, lying on my back on the sofa. I tried to concentrate on the game, as if I gave a damn about the Oakland Athletics. All I could think about was that kid, sound asleep in his bed, snoring, smile smeared across his lips, dreaming of big tits and pink nipples. At two o'clock, I knew I was never going to fall asleep so I jumped up and pulled on my pants. If Alice woke up while I was gone I'd say I'd run out for cigarettes."

He licks the grease from his fingers and carefully dries them with the napkin.

"Why don't you start at the very beginning?"

I don't know how to respond.

"I take it that wasn't the first time you'd done something like that?"

I laugh. "Well, I knew exactly where to go, didn't I?"

"Then tell me about the first time you did something like that."

I hesitate. "Time's almost up, isn't it."

"We've got a few minutes."

"Well, why is it important?"

"I don't know that it is."

"Then why do you want to hear about it?"

"Because you want to tell me about it."

Funny thing. He's right. The state of North Carolina can call it therapy. He and I know it's confession.

"There's a fine line between the two. . . ." he says.

But I didn't say anything. . . . God, these fucking priests, reading your mind. . . .

"No. I'm not a mind reader. Just been doing this a long time. Go on, then."

"Okay. I was eighteen. Grown. At least I thought I was. Jesus, I thought I was hot shit. Hair parted down the middle;

long enough that it broke across my shoulders. Drove the old man crazy. He bitched about it a lot but never threatened to banish me from his room and board. Maybe he was afraid I'd take him up on it."

"Why do you think he didn't do that?"

"Actually, I think he had started to like me. You see, he'd kept his distance since I was young, really young, like maybe five."

"That's a common pattern among homosexual men."

His words are a punch in the gut. He assesses my reaction. It is the first time in my adult life I have ever been referred to as a homosexual man, at least to my face.

"Some believe that the male parent, by some instinct, begins to sense an otherness about the son at around that age. And he begins to withdraw, physically, emotionally. The father doesn't understand his discomfort with the child; the son doesn't understand why he is being abandoned. If you believe this theory . . . But now our time is really up."

"You call me a fag and then tell me time's up!"

I'm practically shouting. I can hear my voice shaking. This son of a bitch doesn't play fair. He offers me the last piece of pizza and shoves it in his mouth when I decline. Through the mush of dough and sauce, I make out the words "next week."

The Great Pretender

Step right up, folks.

Welcome to the greatest show on earth.

What you have here works. But there's always room for improvement. What works can always work better!

This used to be easier. I don't remember a lead ball swinging from my tongue.

Yes, ma'am. Yes, sir. And by the way, that truly is a lovely dress you're wearing today, Mrs. Cleaver.

No, I haven't sunk that far. Yet.

Competition. It's the name of the game. Too many retail outlets all selling the same things, the same brands. Look at these Maidenforms you've got here. How many places in town can you buy these? A dozen? A hundred? A thousand?

I have to remember to customize the sell at this point for the size of the city I'm in. The problem is *remembering* the city I'm in. Which airport did I fly into this morning? They all look the same.

Remember. It's not Maidenforms you're selling. It's you. You are your brand. And your space tells the customer who you are.

This is where the architect or the space designer or, God forbid, the interior decorator, intervenes, determined not to lose control, to put me in my place, remind me who I am. Just the fucking salesman. Sorry, the manufacturer's rep. I'm supposed to take the dimensions and answer questions. The "space" belongs to them; it's their prerogative. They are the artists. The sales boy should stick to describing the durability of the wood chip veneer.

I've studied my adversaries. I know all the types.

The neurasthenic aesthetes of indeterminate gender, swaddled in black turtlenecks regardless of the season, swooning over lighting concepts.

The foppish, overweight homosexuals with pinky rings and liquor on their breath, dropping fey hints, trying to figure out if "I am" and if "I'm available."

Worst of all are the tweedy first wives of captains of industry, barely sublimating their bitterness, castrating every male in sight, adding penises to their trophy belts.

Don't fight 'em outright, my Born Again National Sales Manager advises me, but you gotta resist them. You only have a couple of hours to score. Stay focused. Remember who's paying the bills. And if Miss Snotty Designer convinces the client later that *it's all wrong*, well, the deposit's been collected and there's no refund on custom jobs. Remember, it's war out there and Shelton/Murray Shelving and Display intends to win!

He makes it sound so easy. Why is it so hard? Is it because I'm tired? Is it because I don't care?

I don't care? How could anyone not care about products like these!

Be a part of the revolution in slatwall! Don't waste a precious inch of selling space! Make your walls work for you! Cost-efficient and durable! Powder-coated steel frame construction means it's lighter and easier to install and eliminates unsightly aluminum brackets!

Make a bold statement!

Create the environment of your imagination!

Differentiate your product!
Build brand identity!
Reinvent your image!
Shelton/Murray Shelving and Design doesn't just sell slat-wall.
We create solutions.
Yes. I can do this. I can do it well. I can be the best. The early verdicts are in. The Born Again National Sales Manager is pleased. Praise the Lord!

I just have to remember to be careful. Keep my hair combed, my shirt freshly pressed, and a stash of breath mints close at hand. Never let my rancid nights poison my days. Stay upbeat. Smile until my face hurts. Keep up the act. I ought to be able to pull this one off. Years of experience, a lifetime of lying, have prepared me for this. Oh yes, I'm the Great Pretender.

And if I truly hate this job so much, why do I dread Friday afternoon and the flight home? The thought of my mother, smiling, self-consciously *not intruding*, strikes terror in my heart. The flight attendant disapproved when I ordered a third scotch, sniffing at me as if I was just another pathetic middle-aged failure. The flight was full of them, overweight losers, moving their lips while they read the editorial page of *USA Today*, circling their wish list in the Air Mall catalogue, punching out sales memos on their laptops.

Don't lump me in with them, I wanted to tell that waitress in the sky. No way. I'm different. And I have the arrest record to prove it.

I congratulated myself on resisting the temptation of a former Big Man on Campus gone slightly to seed stroking his penis in the restroom in Terminal B. I dutifully kept my Friday appointment with my counselor and managed to feign enough enthusiasm to please Mr. Born Again Saturday afternoon. Now it's Sunday morning. I pull the sheets over my head and inhale the fabric softener. I close my eyes and dig into the familiar soft spots in this old mattress. "Andy?" I burrow deeper, hiding from her wake-up call. "Andy, are you awake?" The rhythm is so familiar I count to ten and whisper along: "Rise and shine."

"I'm up."

"Good afternoon, grumpy." She goes back down the stairs. I want to sleep, but Sunday dinner can't be ignored. The kids next door are playing Marco Polo in the pool. A lawnmower chokes on a stone. A motorcycle backfires. Farberware clatters downstairs and my mother is singing her kitchen song.

"Oh, playmate, come out and play with me. . . ."

The furniture in my room is scaled for a ten-year-old. The dresser mirror cuts me off at the chin. The monster models and Mickey Mouse and the Hardy Boys have never been consigned to attic or garage or trash. Two storage boxes of baseball cards are in the closet. The worn old chenille bedspread is as thin as a sheet. It's only temporary, I tell myself.

"Coffee's on the burner. Dinner in an hour," she calls. I pull on a pair of boxers and go downstairs. She offers to slice ham for my breakfast. I shake my head no and crumble a biscuit into my coffee. She makes a face, like she always does when I exhibit white-trash habits. I take a second biscuit and she tells me I'm going to spoil my dinner. She's making stuffed pork chops, my favorite.

I decide not to shave. Then I change my mind, not wanting to disappoint her. We're eating in the dining room and she's set a lovely table. I want to do something thoughtful so I clip a late-season bud from her rosebushes and place it on her dinner plate, a small gesture I know will please her. She kisses me on the cheek, as happy as if I'd bought out Tiffany's, and asks me to say the Catholic grace (she still calls it that almost forty years after converting to marry my father in a proper church wedding). I lie and tell her everything is delicious. She forgets things now, like salt, or she'll salt twice. All I taste is the stain-less steel flatware. I empty the pepper shaker over my food when she goes for hot biscuits. I do the arithmetic of mortality, counting the number of pork chops the future still holds. I clear my throat and chirp, telling her sure, I'll have a second.

We never talk about why I'm here. I'd called her from exile, a thirty-bucks-a-night motel near the Greensboro airport, drunk and crying, spilling my guts. The next morning I was on her doorstep. Every picture of my wife had already disappeared from my mother's home. Her only comment was it's a crying shame when things don't work out and we should be grateful we hadn't started a family yet. I moved in, nowhere else to go, nowhere else I wanted to be.

She paid the fine and the lawyer, suggested a priest for the counseling, made the arrangements, and never mentioned it again. My father-in-law was also my employer. He contested my application for unemployment benefits and won. He made sure that no North Carolina furniture manufacturer would hire me, but I got work soon enough with the help of an old fuck buddy who worked in facilities for the national department store chain that is Shelton/Murray's biggest account. It beats being put on the payroll of Nocera Heat and Air, the company my mother inherited after my old man died.

I never get personal phone calls. The only mail addressed to me is from divorce lawyers. I sleep through my days off. At night, my mother and I watch old movies on the cable channels. Saturday nights we go to the golf club for dinner. Over time, she is reacquainting me with each and every member. They look embarrassed, mumbling about how little I've changed. She won't allow anyone to excuse themselves until they have shaken my hand and welcomed me home. The strain shows around her mouth. I know that she and my sister Regina have had words, arguing about my "situation."

I imagine my sister is feeling triumphant, gloating over my

sudden, ignominious fall from grace. I should be sympathetic. I understand it's always been difficult, no, impossible, competing with the little prince. Her life would seem to be a success by any measure, at least if no one looked too deeply or asked too many questions. She has a thriving real estate business and the marriage to the golden boy, a bronze medalist in the giant slalom who's become the most successful contractor in south Florida to have never been indicted or slapped with an IRS tax lien. The perfect couple lives in an umpteen-square-foot hacienda in Boca Raton's most exclusive gated community. Yet none of it seems to satisfy her. Something lives on, a nagging resentment from our childhood, nurtured by her stubborn refusal to accept that there is one competition she can never win, not even after bearing the three children who ensure that the DNA, if not the family name, will endure for another generation. My little sister, precious Gina, loved as she may be, can never depose the firstborn son.

And much to Regina's chagrin, my mother refuses to see my hobbling back to the nest as a failure. She says it's absolutely wonderful having me home. She's happy to have someone to talk to. About my niece and nephews, about the neighbors, about the recently deceased and the long dead. About everything and everyone but me. Which suits me fine.

We're very comfortable here in the zone between questions left unasked and answers never offered. She's made peach cobbler—my favorite—and serves it piping hot with vanilla ice cream. I squeeze it into mush like I've done since I was old enough to lift a fork. My mother sighs and tells me that my youngest nephew does the same thing. We're so much alike she finds herself calling him Andy.

Dustin is his name. His goddamn mother practically willed him into being a little fairy by calling him that. Boys need names like Bob or Bill or Mike. One syllable. Not something that's a synonym for Tinker Bell.

The both of you always have an answer for everything, my mother says, both of you too smart by half. That's not the only resemblance she sees. He's quite the sissy and refuses to touch a ball or a bat. A lonely little kid who does all the voices for his action figures because none of the boys want to play with him. She laughs, telling me some wiseass comment, wry beyond his years, he made to his mother about his favorite television actress. I grunt and squirm, trying to conceal that the obvious parallels make me uncomfortable and that the kid's fey mannerisms, his refusal to blend in, his insistence on being different, embarrass me. I resent her obvious agenda, her assumption that I, of all people, should be sympathetic, willing to reach out and support the boy. Why him? Why aren't I expected to forge some special relationship with his rough-and-tumble older brother, who's showing the first signs of sullen adolescent rebellion, or his little sister, prosecutorial in her insistence that all things go her way? But for my mother's sake, I feign a little interest, assure her he'll turn out all right.

I've promised her I would mow the lawn. She fusses it's too hot, wait until the cool of the evening. She says I've just eaten. She's right, so I just lie down in the grass. She's at the kitchen window, listening to Sinatra, meaning she's thinking of my father, missing him, while she tackles her greasy pots and pans. I light a cigarette, hoping the nicotine will revive me. But my arm is heavy with sleep and the cigarette drops from my hand. The last thing I remember before drifting off is the hiss of grass scorched by the ember.

Charade

La Crosse, Wisconsin, doesn't have a lot to offer after ten P.M. There's the late-night talk shows or basic cable or, as a last resort, the Million Dollar Movie if the opening monologue and tracking weather patterns in Timbuktu don't strike your fancy. I doubt that a million bucks pays the catering bill on a movie set these days, but tonight's feature presentation is a classic. *Charade.* They say Cary Grant was a big old homo. It may be a matter of common knowledge in our enlightened times, but the very idea is blasphemy to my mother. When I was a child and did something chivalrous like open the car door or help her with her jacket, she would tell me I was her own little Cary Grant. Little did she know.

The more Audrey Hepburn bats her eyelashes—well, not exactly bats, more like flutters—the more standoffish he seems. He seems fixated on her flat chest. Maybe it's wishful thinking that he'll pull the cashmere over her head and discover she's really a little boy. You can hardly blame him for not wanting to jump her bones. Let's face it. She's not exactly the type of babe to make Woody Woodpecker spring into action. Elegant, chic, thin, European, yet no more threatening than the All-American

Girl Next Door, she's an ideal most men are indifferent to, but many women aspire to be.

Including Alice. Granted, an alabaster icon seemed an unlikely idol for my freckle-dusted wife. It's hard to imagine Alice posing for the *Breakfast at Tiffany's* poster with a three-foot-long cigarette holder dangling from her lips. Givenchy would have blanched at her ample Irish hips. Alice is more Kennedy than Hepburn, with an open, toothy grin rather than a sly smile, incapable of seeming coy. Her angular beauty is of a different sort, not coarser, but certainly more substantial. And her graceful gait is more athletic, more suited for racing down the soccer field than descending a staircase in a designer gown. One thing they do share is a soft voice, without harsh edges. Alice's is bit deeper, but, whatever talents Hepburn may have had, she couldn't touch Alice when it comes to singing the mezzo parts of a Bach cantata. All in all, stand them side by side and I'd choose Alice. Hands down.

I know this fucking movie by heart. This one and the musical with Fred Astaire and, of course, *Tiffany's*. Please, please, please, just one more time, Alice would plead and I had to concede, quid pro quo for forcing her to suffer through countless evenings watching chain-saw attacks on nubile flesh. This motel bed feels so fucking empty without her. That's the hardest thing for me to accept. No more long nights buried under a mountain of down, drinking wine and eating popcorn, watching movies and falling asleep in each other's arms. This is better than sex, Alice would say.

Maybe what she meant was that it was better than sex with *me*.

No, she didn't think that, not my Alice. She's not clairvoyant; she isn't a psychic. I was determined to never give her any reason to question or doubt me. I was a good husband, or at least I tried to be. I studied the arcs of her moods, armed and ready at the slightest hint of discontent or restlessness with surprise trips to Paris and tickets to the Metropolitan Opera and newly issued gift editions of classic cookbooks. The price tags didn't matter to her. A Cracker Jack prize would have done the trick. The clouds would disperse, the threat of showers would pass, and the forecast was bright and sunny again. And I did my duty in the sack, even going above and beyond it with the occasional gold medal performance, scoring a perfect ten. What else could all that sound and fury, all that rutting and humping, signify but the sincerity and depth of my desire?

Desire.

What a fluid concept. Would Mr. Webster, Mr. Funk, and Mr. Wagnalls say I desired her? Of course they would. I desired her during the comfortable silences on the long drive to my mother's home. I desired her on those happy evenings spent playing board games at the kitchen table. I desired her as I fell into a deep sleep while she lay propped against her pillows, captivated by Audrey and Cary. I even desired her, at least something about her, on those nights when she would fall asleep first and, tortured by insomnia, I would mute the television, silencing the sirens of the police drama or the explosions of a war epic. I desired her even though I didn't stroke her shoulder or roll her toward me and wake her with a kiss and stiff penis but, instead, would slip quietly out of the bed and take solace in the dungeon of the Internet, sometimes only staring at the lurid images, sometimes engaging in cybersex with another bored and restless suburban husband in some remote corner of our great nation. And I desired her when I slid quietly back under the covers and finally fell into dreams of citrus groves inspired by the conditioner she'd used on her hair.

And I desired her even more when I woke in the morning and heard her singing softly in the bathroom. I would open my eyes to watch her brush her hair. She would squint at the image that stared back from the mirror as she carefully tinted her lips and dabbed color on her cheeks. Lying there, her side of the bed still warm, I desired her, maybe not like the Continental lover my family name would lead you to assume I might be, but in a quiet, sort of British way, sneaking off to the kitchen to steep a cup of Earl Grey for her and being rewarded with an affectionate kiss on the cheek. *This is better than sex.* Damn right, Alice. Anyone can fuck you, but where would you ever find anyone else to serve up such a heady brew of tea and sympathy?

Only once did she take a pass, after we "lost" the baby. At first, I assumed it was a reaction to the brutal shock of the D and C and that it was only a matter of time until her hormones restored her body to equilibrium. But a month passed, then another, and she remained beyond my reach, a distant buoy bobbing on the surface of a placid but unnavigable lake. I would hear her talking on the telephone, jovial and lighthearted with her sisters and her girlfriends. Her shoulders would grow stiff if I approached her from behind and gently touched her. A slight edginess, probably noticeable to no one but me, would creep into her voice. I would rub her neck, trying to persuade her to relax, but her muscles would resist me and she would burrow deeper into her conversation until, defeated, I would walk away. I would hear the tension recede from her voice as I walked out of the room.

She carefully avoided me, keeping me at a safe distance, studying me. She was subtle as always, never cruel, rejecting every attempt at physical intimacy as kindly as possible. Yet her reticence was lethal as Kryptonite, leaving me powerless to assure her that all was well and good in our little kingdom. For the first time, I felt as if I could lose her. *Nothing, nothing*, she would say, when I asked if anything was wrong. *I'm fine*, when I suggested she was fatigued, that a checkup and maybe blood work might be a good idea. Finally, I said we needed a change, to get away. Spring had been cold and wet and Rome might be pleasant, or maybe Santa Barbara. She looked up from her dinner plate and gave me an indulgent smile.

"Not this time, Andy," she said.

I sat there, exposed. And, assuming the game was finally up, I found the nerve to ask the question I was afraid to have answered.

"Do you still love me?"

"I'm still here, aren't I?" she said.

I should have known better than to make the fatal mistake of asking one question too many.

"Why?"

She stood and picked up her plate, her appetite lost.

"Because I don't give up that easily."

We made the trip to Santa Barbara after all and, over time, her faith in my gestures of love and affection seemed renewed. One night, not that many months ago, we sat on the deck, reading in the soft, extended daylight of midsummer, tropical bossa novas spinning on the disc player. I looked up from my book and saw her staring at me. She hadn't aged a day since college, at least not in the fading light. She could have been that quiet, determined college girl who summoned the courage to join me, uninvited, while I tugged my hair and struggled with *Absalom, Absalom!* at the cafeteria table. What's up? I asked, and she grinned self-consciously.

"I was just thinking."

"About what?"

"That it's good to be friends."

"Yes, it is."

Damn, how this night has slipped away. Audrey and Cary are in the final clinch, about to embark on the happily ever after. Oh shit. I hadn't remembered how this fucking thing ended. I'd forgotten Audrey's last words.

Oh, I love you, Adam, Peter, Alex, Brian, whatever your

name is. I hope we have a lot of boys and we can name them all after you.

Goddamn it. It would all have turned out different if I had been more like Cary Grant. The son of a bitch was never stupid enough to do it in a public toilet and, if he did, he was smart enough to never get caught.

Mama's Boys

His wide shoulders span the narrow aisle between the peep booths. He's tall and carries a lot of weight. His belly is Jell-O but, all in all, he's packed too solid to be called fat. He's still wearing his work shirt. *Duffy Donlan* is embroidered above the pocket. Is that really his name or is it the logo design for the Looney Tunes fashion collection? He sees that I'm smiling and sets off in hot pursuit, following me through the maze. He's no Cary Grant and this little cat-and-mouse chase through a dirty book store on the west side of Cleveland is hardly a romp through the streets of Paris. But it's fun being the prey instead of the predator for a change and I slide into an empty booth, leaving the door ajar. He hesitates, then slips inside to join me.

The booth is tiny and he's a big man. He fumbles for quarters. Somehow, he manages to drop a few coins into the box while getting my shirt unbuttoned and my pants to my knees. There's no room to do anything but rub against each other. My nose is buried in his armpits and I work my arms around his waist. He kisses me and finishes off on my leg. I resist the affection in his hands. The attendant is swabbing out the next booth and the potent disinfectant kills any thoughts of romance.

The booth feels enormous after he leaves. I drop a few more

quarters. Someone jiggles the knob of the locked door, trying to get in, smelling cum on the floor. Every few minutes the door rattles again. When I run out of quarters, I head for the parking lot.

A couple of old men smoking in their cars wink and smile as I pass. A rusty Chevy Impala with the hood propped open is parked next to my rental. Duffy Donlan looks up from the engine. His battery has died and none of these pricks will give him a jump, afraid his battleship will suck all the juice from their Toyotas and Hondas. I can hardly blame them. How would they explain it to the little woman if they had to call for a ride home from the parking lot of the Aphrodite Adult Emporium and Video Arcade, conveniently open twenty-four hours, seven days a week? *Gee, honey, just thought I'd surprise you with a two-headed dildo for your birthday next month.*

Unburdened by such worries, I offer to give him a hand and help him string his battery cables between our engines. The Impala sinks closer to the pavement as he crawls behind the wheel. The motor flutters, then dies. He says thanks anyway and is startled when I say, "No problem, Mr. Donlan." Your shirt, I tell him, pointing to the pocket.

I don't know what comes over me but I offer him a lift home. Maybe I'm charmed by his goofy name. He asks where I'm from and what I do for a living as he guides me through residential Cleveland. He's on the maintenance crew for Otis Elevator, eighteen years and counting. I tell him I travel around the country selling display shelving. The travel part intrigues him. He knows how many miles Cleveland is from Charlotte. He's never even been to North Carolina but he studies the Rand McNally while he eats his cereal. He says he'd never been anywhere but Ohio and Indiana and Virginia until last summer. He doesn't count West Virginia because he drove straight through without stopping. But in July, he flew to Alaska for six glorious days. The sun never set. He hasn't made it to the wilderness yet, but he has a promise of a maintenance job in an office building in Anchorage.

There's a For Sale sign in front of the wood shingle house where he lives with his mother. He insists I meet his dogs. Four nervous huskies with meat on their breath are trotting behind a chain link fence. He introduces me to Wolf Larsen, the Malamute Kid, John Barleycorn, and Buck the Third, who rattles the gate with his enormous paws.

"I take it you like to read," I say, amused by the names of his dogs.

"I like to read about Alaska," he says, shyly, assuming I'll think he's stupid because he still reads boys' adventure novels. There's no reason to tell him I had a son, never born, named after Jack London.

He invites me inside for a cup of coffee. It's after two o'clock and I have an early flight. An unpacked bag waits at the hotel and my body aches for sleep. But his loneliness appeals to me for some reason, another grown man living with his mother. The tiny mudroom at the back door isn't much bigger than the peep booth and smells of cat litter and wet garbage. I watch him padding around the damp kitchen in his stocking feet, spooning instant coffee into plastic cups and waiting for the kettle to boil. He's nervous because the conversation is trickling away and he's afraid I'm going to get up and leave. He rips open a bag of chocolate cookies, bribing me to stay.

He asks if I'm a Catholic. I deny it. He tells me he's a lay deacon at his parish. I remember the holy medal dangling from his neck. There's probably a box of breaded fish sticks in the freezer, waiting to be thawed for Friday's dinner. He asks if I'm cold, it's pretty nippy for this time of year, and spikes the coffee with Canadian Club. The furnace roars and heat swells in the room.

The whiskey is cheap and burns my throat. I put my hand over my cup when he offers a refill and he tops off his own. It's warm and I'm sleepy and Duffy feels like talking. For all his size, he has a boy's voice, a lovely tenor that's pleasing to the ear. By his third shot of whiskey, he even has a hint of a brogue.

"I'm going north for the dogs, really. No, that's a lie. It's for me. I can't wait to see the winter. The ice. I'll be thirty-nine this Christmas. I don't suppose I'll ever settle down now. Nothing to keep me from going. Sweet Jesus." He blesses himself. Either he's a little drunk or he's more comfortable with me.

"I'm talking about her like she's already gone. Poor thing." He nods to a room above the kitchen. "She's had last rites twice now."

She used to be his mother. Now she's nothing but a shell with a big wet hole where her left breast used to be. She's on morphine, and all that's left to do is keep her comfortable and check for bedsores. He describes her clinically, without emotion. Duffy Donlan has no feelings for women, not even his mother.

"It's been hard on her since my dad passed." He pronounces *dad* the Irish way, with a silent "d." I follow him into the dining room. He wants to show me the photographs on the sideboard. He points to Dad, a beautiful cocky young man with wild black hair, wearing an Eisenhower jacket.

"He died when I was twelve," he says.

Someone clears her throat, announcing her presence. A redhaired woman with pale milky skin is standing in the doorway, a Botticelli in wire-frame glasses. She's as modest as a nun, hiding her skinny bare feet under her nightgown.

"Teresa, the ghetto cruiser disappointed me once again and my friend Andy here gave me a lift home. Andy, my sister Teresa."

"Good night, boys," she says with such a wicked stress on the word *boys* that I'm embarrassed by the dirty implications in her voice. Duffy ignores her.

"She's pissed that the house is all mine. Her dago husband's last job was managing a Kentucky Fried Chicken." *Didn't he hear me when I told him my last name?* "It lasted all of three weeks. That was four years ago. She's playing nurse, trying to make me feel guilty and give her a share of what I manage to get for this dump. I probably won't even be able to sell to whites. Fuck her."

I pick up a formal family portrait in somber black and white. Duffy, about sixteen, is standing behind his seated mother, his hand resting on the back of her chair. Seven younger Donlans surround them. The mother has a long Katharine Hepburn neck and that same arrogant stare. All her children are striking, with arresting eyes.

"Teresa, you've met. Maureen was the great beauty. She's in Vegas now. A cocktail waitress and the mistress of the owner of a GM dealership," he says. Duffy feels compelled to share the history of every sibling in the photograph, the common theme being his sacrifices for all the younger Donlans. His nobility is suffocating. It's creepy, his playing house with his mother and being a daddy to her children. There's something discomforting about a grown man sleeping under his mama's roof, eating the food she cooks.

He asks about my family. Nothing extraordinary, I say. "Any more of that whiskey left?" I ask to avoid admitting what he and I have in common.

"I thought you'd never ask," he says.

The bright kitchen feels like walking into daylight after the mausoleum of the dining room. I settle back on one of the hard chairs. He says we'd be more comfortable in the basement. He's fixed it up real nice, with a huge sofa, thick carpet, and a wide-screen TV. I'm comfortable right here, I say, no intention of being lured into his lair.

"Is there anyone special in your life?" he asks.

"Yes," I say, a blatant lie.

"You're lucky," he says.

"How about you?" I ask, already knowing the answer.

"No. Not anymore."

"What happened?"

"He got scared. He's a transit cop. Divorced. Buddy's his name. He has custody of his teenage son, so we had to spend all of our time here. My mother really liked him. He knew how to talk to her, never looked bored when she complained. I met the kid when he came over to watch the Super Bowl. I was careful, really careful, watched what I said, not dropping any hints. But the kid asked too many questions once they were home. Buddy said we'd have to cool it, at least until the boy moves out of the house. He still calls, asks after my mother. He's going to be a pallbearer at her funeral. Does your mother like your friend?"

"Yes. Yes. Very much," I say, completely comfortable with lying.

"You sure you don't want to go downstairs?"

"Yeah, I like it up here."

"It's a shame you live so far away."

"I don't always plan on living in Charlotte," I say, surprising myself.

"I bet you'd really like Alaska."

I tell him I'm a Southern boy, so terrified of ice and snow I won't even touch a Popsicle.

"You ought to try it. Come up. You have a place to stay. That would be great. I never meet anyone like you."

You never meet anyone like me? Count your lucky stars.

"Then again, you already have someone in your life."

Right, Duffy Donlan. I'm taken. And even if I weren't, how could we run off together, live happily ever after, until death do us part? Don't you see we have a little problem here? Whose mother will we live with? Yours or mine? Or maybe we could pack them up together, the four of us in a cottage with a white picket fence.

"You're really nice," he says, taking my hand.

You don't know the half of it. I'm nice, the nicest guy in the world. Ask anyone. They'll line up around the corner, starting with my wife, my sister, my father-in-law, all eager to testify on my behalf. On second thought, we probably shouldn't ask them. Let's ask my mother. *I solemnly swear it's the whole truth and nothing but the truth that my son has sacrificed his own happiness to take on the burden of his poor widowed mother. . . .* Wait a minute, Duffy, that's your mother on the witness stand, not mine.

You know and I know you haven't made any sacrifices. It's you who ought to be thanking her for providing the excuse to hide from yourself and the life you were born to live. While you're at it, thank her for helping you become an achingly lonely man who grasps at the slightest act of kindness, like a ride home on an unseasonably cold late-summer night.

"Hey," I say, "I'm really not such a nice guy."

"Yes, you are."

Who knows? Maybe he's right. And if he is, why am I being cruel, denying him a few minutes of warmth in his paneled and carpeted playpen in the basement? Why am I denying myself the opportunity to allow someone to touch me with affection instead of scratching me to satisfy their own itch?

"So," I say, clearing my throat, "it's really late and we're getting a little drunk. Maybe we ought to go downstairs and stretch out on that sofa for an hour or two, rest our eyes."

Bad timing. The front door opens before he can answer. Cold air precedes the crepe-soled footsteps. The wall clock says five fifty. Duffy looks over my shoulder and smiles.

"Cold out there, ain't it, Nancy?"

She works the arms of her coat onto a hanger.

"It's going to get a lot colder before summer rolls round again. Did you pick up the syringes like you were supposed to? What, no coffee made?" She picks up his cup and sniffs, clicking her tongue.

"Honestly, Duffy," she says, laughing. "Am I a nurse or your nursemaid?"

"Go on up to her. I'll put the water on."

Nice to meet you, she says even though we haven't been introduced. Duffy gets up and fills the electric percolator with water.

Nancy is only gone a few minutes. He holds his breath when he sees her. Perspiration glazes his face and drips from his chin.

"I'm sorry, Duffy. I'm so sorry," she says.

I don't belong here. I'm a stranger, embarrassed by the intimacy of the moment. He blinks twice and blesses himself.

He reaches for his wallet and hands the nurse a twenty.

"Go have a nice big breakfast at Shoney's. Take an hour. Take two. I'm going to have one more drink. I'll be asleep when you get back. Wake Teresa then. Tell her it just happened. Just don't let her wake me. Let her call the others. I don't want to listen to their shit."

He gives her a big hug.

"There, there. Don't be sad. You did a terrific job." She hugs him back and, turning to leave, gives me a hug too. I don't know why. I take the shot of whiskey he offers and extend my condolences.

"Thanks," he says. "Jesus Christ, it's hot in here." He strips off his shirt, soaked with sweat. The house is close to the airport and the first takeoff of the morning rumbles overhead.

"I have a plane to catch."

"I know. I know. Too bad. Here, take this."

He scribbles his phone number in Cleveland and the address of an office building in Anchorage. "I'll be there by next April at the latest. Come out. You really should come out."

He walks me to my car. He throws his arms around me when I go to shake his hand. His skin is on fire. It feels like he wants to squeeze the last breath from my chest.

"I'd love to fuck your brains out," he whispers in my ear.

I back out of the driveway and he runs back to the house, doing a surprisingly nimble one-handed jump over the gate. The dogs are all over him. I roll down the window. Halfway down the block, I can still hear them howling at the dying moon.

I take the piece of paper with the phone number from my pocket, intending to toss it out the window. Something stops me and, at a red light, I fold it carefully and slip it into my wallet. I know I'll never use it. Still, I want to keep it. Who knows? Maybe some night when I can't sleep, when I'm tossing and turning in the single bed in my mother's house, I'll think about picking up the phone and calling.

Hey, Duffy, remember me? The guy who thought he could never be as pathetic as you?

Another Peter Parker

"No, Matt, I did not make up the name Duffy Donlan. I swear."

"Why do you sleep with men you don't like?"

"I did not *sleep* with him. And who says I didn't like him?"

"Did you like him?"

"He was all right, I suppose. I didn't really get to know him."

"Are you interested in knowing him?"

"No. Not really."

"Then why did you keep his number?"

"I don't know."

"Why don't you call him?"

I stare at him, no less astonished than if a bare-assed Santa had just dropped down my chimney and was waving his furry caterpillar in my face.

"That's ridiculous. He lives in fucking Cleveland."

"You think it's ridiculous to call and say it was nice meeting you and to ask how he's doing? I bet he'd love to hear from you."

I'm sure he would. I doubt his phone's ringing off the hook. He probably gets as many calls as me. None.

"I wouldn't know what to talk about."

"What do you talk to other people about?"

"Shelton/Murray Design Concepts!" I bellow in my best carnival-barker tones. "Tomorrow's retail spaces today! Bold! Stimulating! Effective!"

"Why don't you cut the crap?"

"Whoa, that doesn't sound very professional to me," I say, feigning shock.

"You're avoiding the question."

"I am not. Here we are, having a pleasant conversation and you have to go all aggressive on me."

"I'm the one who's aggressive? How would you describe that little sales pitch?"

I know where you're going with this and, buddy boy, ain't no way you're going to coax the words *passive-aggressive* from these lips.

"Let's try it again," he says. "What did you talk about with Alice?"

Hearing her name, *Alice*, spoken in this suffocating room, is unbearable. For the past six weeks, he's barely alluded to her. I've never properly introduced the two of them. He knows nothing about her; she's a complete stranger to him. It's disgustingly presumptuous of him. He's taking liberties, dragging her into this sordid little exchange.

"I can't believe you would ask me that," I say—no—hiss, angry enough to want to smash his head against the floor and crush his smug face with the heel of my shoe.

"Why?"

He peels the foil from a Hershey's Kiss, pops it in his mouth, and tosses a candy to me. He must think he's Pavlov and I'm his goddamn poodle. I swat it with my fist and watch it sail over his shoulder.

"You're comparing some fucking hookup who came on my pants in a peep-show booth to my wife!"

"Your ex-wife, Andy," he says, not unkindly.

"Not yet!" I shout.

"So I take it the circumstances of your meeting somehow make him unworthy?"

"No," I say, hesitating. "Yes," I admit.

"Why do you pursue these sexual encounters if they make you unhappy?"

"They don't make me unhappy."

"Okay. Distressed. They distress you. Fair enough?"

"Fair enough."

"Then why?"

"Because I'm horny. Because I have a huge sex drive. Because I need to do it."

"Do what?"

"Have sex."

"Does it need to be this kind of sex?"

"What do you mean? As opposed to what other kind of sex?"

"How often do you masturbate?"

What an asshole you are, I think.

"Why does the question embarrass you?"

I stare at him in disbelief, as if anyone would need to ask such a question.

"Come on. We've been seeing each other, what, two months? You haven't spared me the details of your colorful little adventures. No, I'm not being judgmental. Just accurate. Isn't this sudden modesty just a little bit inconsistent?"

"That's where you're wrong," I retort. "Admitting you jack off is admitting you're a loser."

"So you don't masturbate because it would make you feel like a loser?"

"I didn't say that."

"Then what did you say?"

"I said no one wants to admit they jack off. How often do *you* masturbate?"

"I ask the questions here," he says.

"See? You use the therapeutic relationship to avoid having to answer the question. You've got the perfect excuse for not admitting the question embarrasses you."

"Fair enough."

Actually, once the question is raised, hostility gives way to curiosity.

"I mean, uh, *can* you masturbate?"

Matt throws back his head and howls.

"Let's see," he says, holding up his right hand and wanking the air. "Yep, I guess I'm still capable of making a fist and jerking off. Seriously, what do you think?"

I honest to God don't know. It was a sin when I was a kid, something that had to be confessed before you could take communion.

"Christ, I remember the humiliation after I'd progressed from impure thoughts to impure deeds. That fucking Father Gillen . . ."

Matt laughs.

". . . he was stone deaf. I almost jumped out of my skin when he screamed *Keep your hands off that thing!* I almost fucking died when I had to face all those pious ladies waiting to confess, one of whom was, of course, my mother."

Matt thinks this story is hilarious. Wouldn't have figured him to have a trite, situation-comedy sense of humor. Roll laugh track.

"So you haven't answered my question," I say.

"I thought I did."

"No. About whether it's still a sin."

"Not in my book."

"It's not your book that counts. Christ, what do they teach you in the seminary?"

Not a smart move to challenge him.

"What about your book?" he asks. "What's a sin in your book?"

Funny that it's taken me until now for me to realize who it is Matt reminds me of. It must be all this talk about sin. It explains a lot, maybe everything. It certainly explains my escalating pulse that first evening I pulled into the driveway and saw him stripped to his skivvies, well, his swim trunks, damp from the hose spray and glistening in the brilliant sun. It explains why I've been so resistant to him, fighting a natural impulse to draw close, become intimate, not physically (not that I would mind, but I know better than that), but emotionally, beyond the boundaries of our "therapeutic relationship."

You look alike.

You walk alike.

At times you even talk alike.

I could lose my mind.

When Fathers are two of a kind!

"I just figured out why I don't like you."

"Why?" he says, surprised, maybe (and this could be my imagination and some wishful thinking) a little hurt.

"You remind me of someone."

Father Timothy Hovis. The substitute priest sent by the Diocese of Charlotte to tend the flock of St. Matthew Parish while Father Gillen recovered from the first of a series of increasingly debilitating strokes. Tall, dark, chiseled, only one generation removed from County Mayo with an athlete's build and a cleft chin that looked like the thumbprint of God. He was only a few years out of the seminary and still enthusiastic about his vocation, serving the Trinity and the Church as passionately as he followed his beloved Red Sox. He was a man's man and a priest's priest. I almost burst with pride when he singled me out for praise in his *pawk-the-caw* Beantown accent: *Well, Mr. No-*

cera, it sure helps a homesick Boston boy to hear a good dago name like yours.

"Are you going to tell me who?"

"Some priest."

"That's it?"

I'd fought the old man tooth and nail. This time he was insistent. My mother's gentle persuasion—*Why, Tony, maybe we should wait another year when he's a bit older*—would not prevail. She must have known it was hopeless to oppose his will. One of the very few possessions he'd brought from Philadelphia was a formal black-and-white portrait of him and his best-loved brother, only a year apart in age, solemnly staring down the photographer, dignified beyond their years in their crisp white cassocks. Goddamn it. I was going to be an altar boy too, even if it killed me.

I thought it would. I shrank in terror whenever old Father Gillen barked at me to pay attention. I cowered in the presence of the other boys, my mortal enemies, wounded by their sneering disdain. And then one Sunday morning, Father Tim appeared. Even the old man was impressed by my sudden commitment to my sacred duties. I volunteered to serve at seven o'clock mass two or three times a week. I offered to do double duty on Sundays. Anything to spend a few precious hours with Father Tim.

"Just some priest," I repeat.

"I suppose you ought to tell me why you dislike him so much since I'm guilty by association. Or by reminiscence, to be accurate."

"It's not what you think."

"What is it I'm thinking?"

The sordid. The reprehensible. The predictable sad tale of predators and innocence betrayed.

"It wasn't a big deal," I say, regretting introducing the subject.

"Well, it obviously wasn't a small deal."

"He was a jerk."

"Why?"

Actually, Father Tim was perfect. Father Tim could do no wrong. Father Tim was my inspiration. We loved the same black-and-white movies, Karloff and Lugosi. He made me a Red Sox fan, much to the chagrin of my Philadelphia loyalist father. I'd decided to follow him into the seminary. I spent endless hours lost in reveries of the Adventures of Father Tim (mysteriously unmarked by age) and Father Andrew (all grown up), together conquering the world for God, inseparable, the closest of friends.

One Sunday morning he showed me and Billy Davenport the Boston College class ring he'd been left by his recently deceased father. I, who knew Father Tim so well and could sense his pride in his inheritance, was effusive in my praise. Only a true friend would know how important that ring was to him. So it was the ultimate betrayal, a stinging slap in the face, when, after Mass, I overheard him mimicking my high-pitched, effeminate voice for the amusement of Billy Davenport.

Oh, Father Tim! It's gorgeous!

"Ouch," Matt says, genuinely touched by the pathos of it all. "I'm sorry."

"You didn't do anything."

"I'm still sorry that someone made you feel that bad."

I was made of stronger stuff than you might know, Matt. Sure, I bawled my eyes out once I was alone in my bedroom. But I adamantly refused to ever serve another Mass despite the old man's threats of medieval forms of punishment. It took his apoplectic promise I wouldn't be able to sit for a week to force me downstairs to speak to Father Tim, who'd taken time from his busy schedule to persuade me to reconsider. No, sorry, I said, politely, but firmly. He bent down to put his arm around my shoulder and asked the question in his most empathic voice.

Was it something one of the other boys did? No, I answered truthfully, pulling away from his arm as if it were a red-hot branding iron.

"Shame seems to be a recurring theme in your life," Matt concludes.

No kidding.

"What about you? Aren't there things you're ashamed of?" I ask.

"Of course."

"So, do you masturbate?"

"Oh, for God's sake," he sighs, exasperated. "Well, I'll tell you this much. If I did, I wouldn't be ashamed of it. Time's up. Same time next week."

I stand up and, session over, extend my hand, offering a gruff good night.

"I bet Father Tim would be impressed by that firm handshake today." He laughs.

It happened, of course, over a period of years, the awkward ones, plagued by pimples and blackheads, wet dreams and inconvenient erections erupting at the most embarrassing times. But it felt like a sudden metamorphosis, a revelation, a mutation as startling and unexpected as the magical transformation of Peter Parker after being bitten by the radioactive spider. It seemed as if overnight I towered over my mother and stood facing my father, staring eye to eye. Dark hairs spiked through my pores. My voice dropped several octaves, rough as gravel, loud and harsh. A musky scent, like the old man when he rolled out of bed in the morning, followed me from room to room. The changes mystified me, as if some creature, weird and wonderful, had possessed my body. I stood in front of my mirror, studying this stranger for hours, fascinated by his thick eyebrows and the stubble growing on his chin. I could make his small but impressive biceps flex simply by squeezing my arm and force his chest to swell by swallowing a deep breath. I ran him through his drills, teaching him to squint like Steve Mc-Queen, grunt and mumble like Bronson, intimidate like Dirty Harry, how to stand, walk, even how to throw a punch.

An ancient speed bag, its black leather worn to dull gray after years of pummeling by my father, still hung from the basement ceiling. When I was small, I would sit on the steps, mesmerized by the hypnotic beat as my old man pounded at his frustrations, jabbing and punching with blinding speed. The bag had been neglected for ages, waiting for the day I would stand and confront it, determined to make it sing. My first swing missed and I struck the wall with my fist. Determined not to let it conquer me, I read every library book on the shelf on boxing training, studying the simple line drawing instructions on how to stand, where to hold your elbows and fists, the motion for a circle punch, how to throw a jab, where to find the belly of the bag.

My arms and shoulders ached for days and my fingers were swollen and bruised. But pain and frustration wouldn't stop me from mastering the bag. I bought a pair of cheap Everlasts to protect my hands.

Left, left, left.

Right, right, right.

Jab, strike.

Left, right, left, right.

Pow, pow, pow.

I descended into my dungeon every afternoon and punished the bag for every slight and insult, real or imagined, for all the frustrations and humiliations of the day.

Left, left, left.

Right, right, right.

Jab, jab.

Strike, strike.

Pow, pow, pow.

Da-dum-dum-dum.

Da-dum-dum-dum.

I knew my old man was standing on my old perch on the steps, watching. I picked up the speed, controlling the bag with a skill that surprised even me, making it sing with a voice it feared had been lost forever.

Pow, pow, pow.

Da-dum-dum-dum.

Da-dum-dum-dum.

I ended with a flourish, a magnificent punch that rattled the ceiling.

I dropped my fists and turned to confront him.

"Good speed," he said, obviously impressed. "Let me show you how to use your shoulders to get a little more power."

I pulled off my gloves and wiped my forehead.

"No, thanks. I'll figure it out myself," I said as I brushed by him on the steps, gloating over this long-awaited opportunity to reject him even though the taste of revenge was far less sweet than I'd always dreamed it would be.

A Short History of Masturbation

Matt, you think I've got no willpower. You think I'm weak, unable to resist temptation. It's nine o'clock in the evening, early, very early. Atlanta's a big old city with lots of big, horny men on the prowl. It's hump night and the boys are out there looking to hump. But I'm going to prove you wrong, you sanctimonious son of a bitch. Who knows what I'm passing up just to make a point? I see they're filming a movie in town, with you-know-who, that big, big star, the one who joined that whacked-out church after they threatened to out him and ruin his career. I'll bet tonight's his one opportunity to slip out unnoticed by the Grand Pooh-Bah of the Celestial Congregation and prowl the underbelly of gay Atlanta. I bet I'm his type, that he'd be all over me, begging to be my love slave, promising to please me like I've never been pleased before.

But no. I'm going to lie flat on my back and pound my prick until I squeeze it dry, fantasizing about the best fucking orgasm I'm never going to have.

They kept up the house and the lawn, minded their own business, and that's all that matters, my father always said. You couldn't ask for more in neighbors. But when my mother suggested inviting them to a holiday party, he put down his foot with an emphatic no that made it clear the matter wasn't up for discussion.

Mr. Marion Wright and Mr. Lesley Sax lived in a Victorian pile that lent dignity and a sense of history to the hapless split levels and ranches surrounding it. Mr. Wright and Mr. Sax had never restored the house since, unlike its contemporaries, it had never fallen into disarray. Rather they had preserved it and tenaciously held on to the original boundaries of a rolling lawn that dwarfed the others in the neighborhood. Mr. Wright's grandfather had built the house before the turn of the century. Mr. Wright's mother lived there from the day she was born until the day that God finally took heed of her son's many shaken-fist curses to the heavens above and struck her dead by inflicting a massive stroke. She claimed to never have slept a night of her life outside that house, insisting that she never even closed her eyes during her six-week honeymoon trip to Europe.

I remember the day Mrs. Wright was buried. My father threatened to whup my sister Gina and me for screaming and fighting in the backyard. Show a little respect for the dead, he warned. Late that night, I was awakened by the doorbell. I stood at the top of the stairs, behind my mother. My father told Mr. Sax to settle down and speak slowly so he could understand him. Then, barefoot and wearing only pajama bottoms, he left with Mr. Sax, closing the door behind them. My mother sent me back to bed and went to the kitchen to wait for him to return. An hour later I heard the front door open. I crept down the stairs and listened, safely hidden behind the kitchen wall.

Mr. Sax wouldn't let him call the police, my father told my mother. Mr. Wright had trashed his mother's bedroom, breaking furniture, shattering mirrors, ripping her clothes to shreds, tearing the curtains from the windows. The fat old bastard was curled up on her bare mattress, naked as a jaybird, sucking on the nozzle of a pistol. It only took a few sharp words from my father for Mr. Wright to hand over the gun. The goddamn thing wasn't even loaded. Mr. Sax got him into a bathrobe and my father forced shot after shot of bourbon into him until he finally passed out. Disgusting, the old man told my mother, just disgusting. I should have put the bullets in the gun for him. It's not like anyone would have missed him if he had shot himself. Well, I suppose Mr. Sax would have missed him, my mother countered. Jesus Christ, Ruth, my father said, the incredulous tone of his voice implying she was crazy.

After that night, Mr. Wright and Mr. Sax withdrew back into their solitude. I knew they were not real men like my father. The old man said Mr. Wright clipped coupons for a living. (I wondered how anyone could make any money snipping the newspaper to get ten cents off a carton of orange juice or a roll of paper towels.) And a good thing too, since he was a little "this way" (my father pursing his lips and waving his hand airily) and then there's all the goddamn booze . . . but then again, they mind their own business. When I asked if Mr. Sax had a job, the old man muttered under his breath and told me to go in the house and get him a can of beer.

Mr. Wright and Mr. Sax's lives didn't extend beyond the veranda. From the first warm spring evening to the last damp chilly night of autumn, Mr. Wright and Mr. Sax observed the world from the safety of their porch, Mr. Wright in an Adirondack chair, Mr. Sax in a rocker, a small table between them. Mr. Wright sipped a drink from a tall tumbler that Mr. Sax jumped up to refill each time Mr. Wright emptied it.

From the distance of our yard, you could see Mr. Wright's mouth moving, talking, talking, talking, as he jabbed Mr. Sax with the index finger of his free hand, making sure he didn't miss his point. Mr. Sax sat rocking, smiling and nodding his head, never saying a word. My sister and I, lying on our backs and counting the stars, heard Mr. Wright's harsh voice, slurring his words as he lacerated Mr. Sax for some imagined betrayal. The ending never varied: Mr. Wright stumbling out of his chair, Mr. Sax sweetly advising him to be careful, Mr. Wright slamming the door and locking it behind him. Mr. Sax would sit for an another half hour, rocking away, fingering the house key in his pocket and staring at the constellations in the sky, searching for his lucky star to thank for getting him through another day. Regina and I would mock him, mimicking his high, singsong voice—"Be careful!" "No, *you* be careful"—as we wrestled in the grass.

At age fourteen, my father put me behind a power mower and pointed me toward our lawn. Mr. Wright and Mr. Sax sat on their veranda, sipping away in the shade, amused by the struggle between a wiry kid and a six horsepower engine. I felt their eyes assessing me, lingering on my developing chest, Mr. Sax looking over the reading glasses resting on the bridge of his nose, Mr. Wright staring through the blue haze of cigarette smoke. One Saturday morning, Mr. Sax approached my father and asked if I would like to earn some extra spending money. The old man, determined I would repeat his up-by-the-boot-straps-through-hard-work-and-determination-Horatio-Alger story, negotiated the price. Ten dollars for my sweat and the wear and tear on his lawnmower. Five bucks extra if they wanted to set me loose on the boxwood hedges with a pair of clippers.

I acquiesced without argument, not knowing how to explain the queasy feeling in my stomach when I knew they were watching me. I refused to take off my shirt, not even when the temperature spiked into the low hundreds. Of course, Mr. Sax and Mr. Wright were perfect gentlemen, never advancing to remarks, let alone casual touching. Mr. Sax would bring me glasses of ice water or lemonade and, when the labors of Hercules were finished for another week, hand me my remuneration in a thick, cream-colored envelope. Lovely, just lovely, he'd say. I asked Gina why he couldn't just say good job or nice work. Because, stupid, she said, he's talking about you, not the grass.

Later that summer, Mr. Sax approached my father again. He and Mr. Wright were taking a short holiday (again, my father pursed his lips and flitted his hands, mimicking the conversation) and the guest house on Cape Cod refused to accommodate pets. Mr. Sax assured me Miss Hellman would be no problem at all. ("The fucking cat's a male!" the old man sputtered, disgusted.) He was as gentle as a lamb, the sweetest puss on earth. Just change the litter and make sure he had enough food and water. On the third day of cat-sitting duty, I persuaded my mother to take the Grand Tour. She oohed and aahed over each camera-ready tableau. A green velvet sofa with huge carved claw feet dominated the front room. Chairs with needlepoint seats and fierce straight backs were clustered for intimate conversation. Porcelain shepherdesses herded tiny crystal objects scattered atop the occasional tables. Spit-polished brass andirons waited for colder weather to return. Mr. Sax spent countless hours surveying his Master's domain, repositioning a hair here, an eyelash there, the perfect arrangement never quite achieved.

My mother and I wandered from room to room. But when we reached the wide staircase that led to the second floor, she hesitated, declining my suggestion we explore the rooms above. A troubled look crossed her face and she asked if I had been up there. No, I answered truthfully. She said she shouldn't have come here uninvited and for either of us to invade Mr. Wright and Mr. Sax's private rooms would betray their trust. She allowed herself one last indulgence, picking up a china plate to appreciate the delicate blue willow pattern. Imagine the holidays they once had in this house, she said. I tried to picture Mr. Wright and Mr. Sax as they sat down to dinner. Did they huddle together in one corner of the long table or sit at opposite ends?

And where exactly did Mr. Wright and Mr. Sax sleep? I would have to wait until Miss Hellman's next feeding to answer that question.

The cat sat at the bottom of the staircase, accusing me with his eyes as I climbed the steps. The windows were shuttered, letting in only thin strips of daylight. The first room was a bedroom, meant for guests, its closets and chests full of towels and linens. The second room was a study with walls of books and a prissy writing table with a full complement of expensive writing implements. The last room was for sewing, with an ancient Singer and baskets overflowing with spools of thread. Miss Hellman streaked across my feet, having decided it wasn't wise to let me wander these rooms alone.

He followed me up to the third floor. The door at the end of the hall was open; a huge canopy bed, mattress riding high above the floor, overwhelmed their bedroom. Books were neatly stacked on the nightstands on each side of the bed. A pair of reading glasses sat on one table. Mr. Sax's side of the bed. A cigarette case and silver lighter rested on the other. Mr. Wright's side.

The cat leaped onto the dressing table where he could watch my every move. I kicked off my sneakers and hopped on the bed. Giddiness overwhelmed me and I rolled from side to side, one minute Mr. Sax, the next Mr. Wright. Kiss me, you fool, I said, puckering and smacking my lips. Yes, *mon amour*, I said, hugging my ribs, a fourteen-year-old's idea of passion as inspired by crummy old movies. The cat licked its paws, bored by my childish shenanigans. I flopped on my back and threw my legs over the side of the bed. When I reached down for my sneakers, I saw them, a stack of magazines on the floor, nearly hidden by the dust ruffle, on Mr. Sax's side of the bed.

They sure as hell weren't *Life* or *Look* or *The Saturday Evening Post*. A chiseled figure flexed his enormous biceps on the cover of the magazine at the top of the pile. I knew I'd hit the jackpot, understanding for the first time the concept of "impure" I'd been taught in catechism. *Physique, a Magazine for Gentlemen*. I tossed them on the bed and raced through the pages. All the models had short crew cuts, clipped close to the skull, and every one was stark naked except for a little sock slipped over his penis, secured by a string around his flat hips. Dipping, stretching, flexing, stretching some more, looking right, looking left, looking down at their toes and up to the sky, always careful to keep that silk sock front and center. They made me think of my older cousin Bobby, who lived on a farm and who, that summer, had taken to strutting around his bedroom in nothing but his underpants, showing off his newly muscled chest and arms and legs and the bulge between his legs.

I dropped to the floor, looking under the bed for another stash. All I found was a pair of slippers with the heels stepped down. But the black-and-white magazines I found in the cedar chest at the foot of the bed made *Physique* seem as tame as *Weekly Reader*. The sailors didn't just pose alone in the sun. They sprawled in pairs on beds, on couches, on rugs. Black strips were burned into the photos to conceal their eyes. They had long flaccid dicks and balls that hung like weights in their wrinkled sacks. They smiled and reached out to each other, never actually touching. They had pimples on their asses, scars on their veins, and their arms were tattooed with Chinese dragons and bleeding hearts pierced by daggers.

I broke out in a sweat, my heart racing in my chest and blood pounding in my ears. My legs started shaking and I pressed my thighs together as tight as I could. My dick felt full, like I needed to piss, but better, warmer, more tingly. My hand, not even knowing what it was doing, yanked at my zipper and the cat looked up, surprised to find my pants down around my ankles. I rolled over on my stomach and rubbed against the mattress, not thinking about the men in the magazine but about Bobby strutting back and forth, remembering his smell, imagining myself on the floor with him, rubbing faster and faster, until I was so hard I was sure I would burst. I wouldn't, couldn't stop, and at the very last minute I panicked, realizing I'd lost control and nothing, not my gritted teeth or the hand squeezing the head of my dick, could stop me from pissing all over the bed.

Only it wasn't piss or anything like it. It was white and sticky; it must have been the stuff Bobby meant when he bragged about creaming the bed. It smelled like my socks after I wore them three days in a row. The cat pounced on the bed and sniffed at the dribble on the bedspread. I watched, appalled, as he licked it clean. I jumped off the bed and into my pants, anxious to get out of there.

That night at dinner, I couldn't look my parents in the face, absolutely certain they would realize something was different about me and interrogate me about what had happened in the few hours since breakfast when the old man had threatened violence if I kept flicking Alpha-Bits at my sister. I promised God I would never, ever, do anything like that again if He let me get away with this. And when He did, I climbed the stairs to Mr. Wright and Mr. Sax's bedroom the very next afternoon and every day up to the evening they came home.

Mr. Sax was delighted to find Miss Hellman healthy and happy and insisted I accept a ten-dollar tip on the twenty he had promised. August turned to September and then it was fall, Mr. Wright and Mr. Sax still watching me from the veranda every Saturday until the weather turned cold and the lawnmower went into hibernation for the winter. One thing changed, though, after they came back from their holiday. I started taking off my shirt, my adolescent chest glistening with sweat, compensation of a sort, or maybe bribery, for the stolen contraband hidden in a small footlocker stashed in the corner of my bedroom closet. If they ever missed their copy of *Sailor Tails* they never said anything.

This used to be a hell of a lot easier. And a hell of a lot more fun. I suppose I'm too distracted to really concentrate on imagining the big, big movie star riding my cock, shouting filthy names at me, ordering me to slap his ass as he bounces on my pole. Then again, lately I've been too distracted to concentrate when an actual live body is riding my cock, shouting filthy names at me, ordering me to slap his ass as he bounces on my pole. Fuck it, why not just read a good book, I decide, turning the pages of *Bang the Drum Slowly* until I drift off to sleep.

Homecoming

It's either this dump or the comfy linoleum of the Knoxville Regional Airport. One bounce on the bed makes me regret not spending the night on the terminal floor. I was damned lucky to get this sarcophagus. Every other room in town was booked a year in advance for homecoming weekend.

This was supposed to be a day trip. I flew in at nine. The manager of the emporium of Official, Authorized University of Tennessee Merchandise was emphatic. She would not, could not, make any decisions without the architect from Facilities who had been stricken by the flu that morning. I tried to persuade her she could at least *look* at the catalogue, let me take a few measurements.

"No, sorry," she said, perspiring in her Official, Authorized University of Tennessee Sweatshirt, size XXX-Large. "Facilities is very strict about these things. It will have to wait until he's back on his feet."

I would have sliced the fat bitch's brake cables if I'd known which car in the lot was hers. Now I'm stuck overnight in this backwater, on the hook for the cost of the counseling session I'd had to cancel with less than twenty-four hours' notice, all on account of a five-minute sales call. It's a beautiful autumn night, crisp and cool, the oaken hint of bonfires lingering in the air. It's hard to believe that only a few hundred miles away, raging thunderstorms have halted all air traffic into the Charlotte airport, stranding weary road warriors who just want to spend Friday night in their own beds. I don't have a bed to call my own so it's hard to call this a hardship. It's almost a blessing, in fact. When I called my mother with my traveler's tale of woe, she worried about me getting a flight tomorrow. Randy T. Olsson and his (third? fourth?) wife would be so disappointed if I couldn't make it to dinner Saturday night. He's been asking after you since you came home from High Point, she said, a harmless little white lie. Don't worry, I said, I'll be there, nearly dropping to my knees to beg Jupiter Pluvius to take mercy on me and summon a hurricane gale to spare me from an evening of forced small talk with Randy T, who, as the president of Nocera Heat and Air, had been receptive to the gentle suggestion by the sole shareholder, my mother, that perhaps I might appreciate becoming reacquainted with old friends my own age.

A scavenger hunt for essentials—toothbrush and paste, disposable razor, personal lubricant—takes me deep into the heart of Knoxville, probably the most improbable candidate ever for the site of a World's Fair. The town is teeming with alumni of all ages, drunkenly toasting Alma Mater and imploring the gods of the gridiron to deliver victory tomorrow. Not that it will really matter if the justification for excessive alcohol intake is celebrating a triumph or mourning a defeat.

I'm sitting at the bar of one those classic campus rathskellers, eating a hamburger and nursing a beer. A short woman, just shy of middle age and sporting a cascade of blond ringlets she should have cut years ago, sidles next to me.

"You shouldn't be here all alone tonight. Come over and meet mah friends."

She's a type I know all too well. The aging Party-Hearty Gal. Tri Delt, everyone else has. She's surrendered to her metabolism and forsaken calorie counts. She has to believe there's at least one man out there who's looking for a girl with a sense of humor and a head on her shoulders instead of a stick-thin, broomstick-up-her-ass debutante. She'd made sure there was no ring on my finger before she'd approached.

"Class?" she asks.

"I'm not an alumnus," I say.

"That's okay, tonight everyone's a Volunteer!" she says.

I might as well be a gentleman and help her caddy the drinks she's ordered to her table. Her friends eye me expectantly as we approach. I realize it's been a setup, sending Little Gloria Bunker up to the bar, all alone. The men stand and shake my hand. The women nod politely, squeezing their chairs together, clearing a space next to Little Gloria.

Andy, Andy, Andy, Andy Nocera, Andy, I repeat as I'm introduced round the table. I take my assigned seat, next to Little Gloria. They whisper among themselves, talking about me, giggling when they realize I know I'm the topic of conversation. They've been drinking since five; they're all a little toasted. The men make crude remarks; the women act offended. Someone belches and everyone pretends to be disgusted. I feel like I'm back in college. I guess that's what a homecoming is all about.

I got to the party a semester too late. The dormitory alliances and rivalries had been etched in stone when I arrived at Davidson after the Christmas break. The other freshmen had already overcome their bouts of homesickness and laid the foundations of their new world. No one was particularly interested in a newcomer, particularly one who was shy by nature, unsure of himself, not the type to approach a table and introduce himself, a coward who would never make the first move.

So I would find a seat alone, at the far end of the dining room table, and hunker down over a plate of macaroni and cheese and a pint of milk, pretending to be absorbed in the run-on sentences of William Faulkner while I counted the minutes until Friday afternoon when I could run home to Gastonia for the weekend. Later she would admit she'd had her eye on me since the day I'd arrived and that she never got beyond the first thirty pages of the copy of *The Sound and the Fury* she'd bought as an excuse to strike up a conversation with me that February night. (Valentine's Day, if memory serves.) And later still, she would admit she knew from that first night I was what she had been looking for.

A boy who had to be approached, who wouldn't speak until spoken to.

And who would then never shut up.

Alice Atkinson McDermott arrived at Davidson College with one ambition. To be different. Just being here was the first step. She'd made her stand, insisting on matriculating at this small, well-regarded liberal arts college—a spawning ground for communists and sexual libertines, in her father's certain estimation—instead of the small Catholic women's colleges her older sisters had been forced to attend. As formidable as those Amazons were, they, unlike her, hadn't had the good fortune to be born the youngest, the prettiest, and the favorite. And so her father, infamous among television-addicted insomniacs in both Carolinas as the King of Unpainted Furniture, finally conceded. On one condition. That Alice promised to attend Mass and take Holy Communion every Sunday. By the middle of Lent, I was attending with her.

But a month of Sundays and three dozen Sorrowful Mysteries of the Rosary wouldn't have fooled J. Curtis McDermott. He sized me up on first sight, at that tense Sunday afternoon brunch where I chain-smoked and refused to allow anything but black coffee to pass my lips. The simple fact that he hated me convinced her she was in love with her smart-ass, daydreaming little rebel. If truth be told, she would have preferred it if my armpits hadn't needed a good shellacking with an antiperspirant. But my sour apple presence certainly made an impression in the prissy little restaurant that served dessert cakes dusted with confectioner's sugar sifted over a paper doily.

But the body odor she mistook as an act of defiance was, in reality, the byproduct of sheer, abject terror. The overbearing pitchman on television, the King of Unpainted Furniture, was a soft sell compared to the Grand Inquisitor confronting me across the table. He was a massive, strawberry-blond Irishman with chiseled features, a barrel-chested Spencer Tracy with a seventeen-and-a-half-inch neck. He waved his hands as he spoke, inspiring irrational fears of the Boston Strangler's meaty hands gripping my neck. He bore down on me like a heat-seeking missile.

"Where are you from?"

"Gastonia."

"How do you spell your last name?"

"N-O-C-E-R-A."

I enunciated as slowly and carefully as a parent teaching a toddler the alphabet. Alice giggled, drawing an apprehensive look from her mother.

"I don't think I know your family," he said, suspicious of my origins.

"I have a cousin in High Point. Maybe you know him. Zack Vanzetti?"

Alice kicked me under the table, barely able to contain her glee.

"I don't think so. What parish does he belong to?"

"Alice says you're an English major," her mother interjected in a futile attempt to steer the conversation to neutral territory.

"I just don't understand that," he declared. "You've been speaking English since you learned how to talk."

"Actually, Daddy, Andy grew up speaking Bulgarian," Alice said, purposefully avoiding the pleading looks from her mother.

"I thought you were a wop?" he blurted, hypertension pumping blood into his cheeks.

"My mother was born in the Balkans," I lied, suppressing any trace of sarcasm in my voice.

"Jesus," he said, exasperated, turning to his wife for reassurance that North Carolina hadn't been infiltrated by communist agents from behind the Iron Curtain. "Are those people Catholic?"

I refused to let him pay for my meal, such as it was, and threw a couple of ones on the table when he wouldn't take my money. He wanted to have me drawn and quartered. His daughter would have married me on the spot.

That night we made love for the first time.

I was sprawled on the floor of her dorm room, flipping through her records in a futile search for Buddy Holly in the stack of Schubert lieder and Bach choral works. Try as I might, I couldn't appreciate the subtle beauty of Strauss's *Four Last Songs*.

"Let's listen to this instead," she said and I flopped on my back, swept up in the overture to *The Magic Flute*. She curled up beside me. I felt the heat of her body and could almost taste the peppermint on her breath. I stared at the ceiling and she touched my chin, gently turning my face toward her. I knew what I was supposed to do next. I closed my eyes and kissed her.

I knew she could tell I was a virgin. I could tell she wasn't, which made me all the more nervous. When she undressed and turned to show me her body, I realized I had never fantasized about how she looked naked. I stared at her breasts and her vagina. I knew I liked her, maybe even loved her. I knew I didn't desire her body. Funny thing about the body, though. It can respond to anything, anytime, even without the desire to possess.

"Shit," I said, pushing myself away from her. "We can't do this. I don't have any rubbers," I announced, not exactly regretting the reprieve.

"Don't worry. I'm on the pill."

I was awkward at first, but found my rhythm soon enough. I knew her moans were real. You can't fake a faker.

She made it easy for me, always careful not to be too demanding. She seemed genuinely impressed by the inanities that rolled off my silver-tipped tongue. I'd always been the listener, never the talker, and certainly never the center of attention. But there was something in Alice's deep green eyes, something about the way she'd nod her head, anxious that I know she absolutely, positively, one hundred percent, agreed with me, that compelled me to share my insights and announce my opinions. All of which, in hindsight, were the pathetically ordinary pronouncements of a self-absorbed undergraduate, the all-too-familiar polemics endured by long-suffering parents footing the bill to gild their (temporarily, they hope) obnoxious offspring with a liberal-arts education.

Alice insisted I go home with her one warm spring weekend. Their house made the Monument to Heat and Air where I'd grown up look like a shack. We arrived late Friday and were driving back to the dormitory by Saturday afternoon. The King had gone ballistic when he stumbled upon the copy of *The Militant, the Voice of the Socialist Workers Party* I intentionally left sitting on the toilet tank of the guest bathroom. Bellowing at the top of his lungs, he declared me guilty of treason. In my snidest, most condescending voice, I informed him it was perfectly legal to cast my vote against the oppression of free-market capitalism. And I then announced I could not spend one more minute in his house. Alice followed me out the door, triumphant.

Her mother came rushing toward us, pleading for a treaty or at least a temporary cease-fire.

"Alice, please, come back inside. He'll be miserable if he thinks you're mad at him."

"Well, I am."

"Alice, he loves you."

"And I love Andy," she announced, closing the door and telling me to start the car.

I knew she was mine forever.

Little Gloria Bunker can't accept that I can't stay for the Big Game tomorrow. The booze is flowing; everyone's loose and insistent on having a good time. She realizes she's going to have to be a *little* forward. After all, the night's not getting younger and my hands have yet to stray under the table. They're announcing last call, one more round, and the invitation to my room isn't forthcoming. She's shouting, thinking I'll believe she's just trying to be heard over the din. But I know she's hoping that her breath tickling my ear is what I need to get me started. Her friends are on the dance floor, flailing away to Donna Summer's "Last Dance," very consciously having decided to *leave us alone.* Little Gloria arches her back and takes the plunge.

"Would you like to stop by my hotel for a little while?"

She's mortified when I politely decline. She hates me for forcing her to declare herself, to put herself on the line, only to be rejected. I feel for her. I really do. But better to disappoint her now than later, when she's lying naked, ashamed of the body that's incapable of provoking the appropriate response in me. She couldn't know that I'm done with that. I've exhausted my ability to respond to a woman. I couldn't do it if I wanted to. And I don't want to.

I know what I do want. Knoxville's the big city in these ol' parts and it's a party weekend. Tucked in my pocket is a torn page from Damron's *Men's Travel Guide* promising a Young Crowd and Entertainment at the Annex, a Very Popular starred entry, a Private Club, serving after hours for Members Only. The parking lot is full and idiots like me are driving in circles, waiting for a space to open up. A couple steps in front of my car, forcing me to throw on the brake. It's Laurel and Hardy, a pair of clowns, parodies of masculinity in tight leather jackets and faux motorcycle caps, trailing cigar ashes as they wobble in their lace-up combat boots, as unsteady as two drag queens in stilettos.

"Good thing you're cute, baby," the taller one giggles, blowing me a kiss.

This is *not* what I want.

They disgust me, these preening mannequins, mocking everything I believe in. I made a mistake. I should have left with Little Gloria. I should give my old life another chance, if not with Alice, then with someone different, a new start, a fresh beginning. I don't belong here . . .

. . . but a parking spot miraculously clears and I'm standing at the door of the club, looking for a member to approach to sign me in as his guest.

There he is. The boy I've waited for my whole life. The boy I dreamed of being. Broad shoulders, open and friendly face, floppy hair, a wrestler, an Eagle Scout. He's Clark Kent, Wally Cleaver, and David Nelson all rolled into one.

"Sure," he says. "No problem. What's your name, in case they ask at the door?"

"Andy."

"Great. I'm Sam."

Sam. It's perfect. I'm gonna buy him a drink when we get inside. I'm gonna fight the urge to light up a smoke. I'll ask him to dance. Better yet, he'll ask me. We'll dance until they turn up the lights, then we'll end up in bed, fucking until the sun comes up, unable to get enough of each other. I'll even bottom if he wants. And I'll cancel my flight tomorrow so we can spend the entire day together, watching the game. Knoxville and Charlotte aren't that far. We can see each other every weekend. I can move.

A young fellow, lanky and good-looking, jogs toward us.

"Shit, dude, I had to park almost a mile away."

"Andy, this is Jason, my boyfriend."

"Hi," he says, shaking my hand.

"Jason, you sure you wanna do this?" my Sam asks. "It's getting really late and my parents are expecting us to tailgate with them tomorrow. I should just sign Andy in and we ought to go home."

But I'm already halfway to my car. I can't get away from them fast enough. I hate them, everything about them, if only for one brief and fleeting moment. I don't want to be a bitter old son of a bitch, steeped in envy. I'm glad they're happy. I really am. It's not their fault that I'll never know how it feels to tell the boy I've been waiting for my entire life to step up, shake a leg, get a move on, because my old man is checking his watch as he flips the dogs and burgers, telling everyone the party can't start until we arrive.

Randy T and the Long Red Snake

"Didn't you tell me once you were admitted to the University of Chicago?"

My counselor can be a bit unpredictable. I've thrown him a bone, sharing my little Tennessee adventure, expecting we'll spend our mandatory hour chewing on my rather promising attempts at insight. But instead, the motherfucker tosses me a curveball, a complete non sequitur.

"Yeah, so what? Don't you want to talk about my huge breakthrough on the night of the Volunteers pep rally?"

"I'm just curious. I mean, Davidson's a good school, but what made you give up such an amazing opportunity?"

"You're a real fucking snob, you know that?"

"I suppose it sounds like I am. But what I'm actually thinking is that it doesn't seem likely you'd be sitting here today if you'd made different choices."

"What makes you think I had a choice?"

"Everything's a choice."

"Yeah, well, it doesn't always feel that way."

The old man put me to work the summer before I was to leave for the University of Chicago. He'd done all right for himself, a big dago who came south with only his tool bag and the certification by Pennco Tech, courtesy of the G.I. Bill, of his proficiency in resolving the mysteries of the brave new world of HVAC. He took a chance on a hunch that the oh-so-genteel, seersucker-and-magnolia folk of Dixie would pay through the nose for the chance to sprawl spread-eagled in their underwear enjoying the frigid air blasting from their ceiling ducts. He was true pioneer stock, one of the trailblazers who conquered blistering sunlight and sweltering heat to make the Sun Belt safe for telecommunications empires and multinational insurance conglomerates in search of affordable real estate and cheap labor.

It made him a rich man. More importantly, it made him a shirt-and-tie man even if the tie was a clip-on and fastened to a short-sleeved dress shirt with a Knights of Columbus tie clasp. His kingdom was 4,500 square feet of partitioned office space and he commanded a fleet of twelve vans and an army of ten repair technicians, assorted clerks for payables and receivables, dispatchers, purchasing agents, and a timid young Catholic girl, handpicked by my mother to be his secretary.

And he had a son. To everyone within earshot, he bitched about my hair, my clothes, my eating habits, my new cigarette habit, my music, my this, my that. But after years of tension, after I'd won a state championship in the breaststroke, after I was named a National Merit Scholar Finalist, he needed to have me close, within earshot, within reach. He insisted I drive to work with him, long sweaty hauls to and from the dispatch office because Mr. HVAC refused to use the air-conditioning in his new Chrysler New Yorker because it was hard on the engine. I'd fidget while he fiddled with the dial of the radio, searching for the one low wattage station that played Sinatra, "King" Cole, and Sassy Vaughan instead of "that fucking shit-kicker shit." He filled the space between us with AM band static and his revelations about the crucifixion of Nixon, whom he'd loved, and the Democratic Party, which he hated for sell-ing its soul for the endorsement of the goons and extortionists that called themselves organized labor. His world had changed forever the night Ed Sullivan, *Ed Sullivan,* kissed that Supreme girl right on her big fat lips, defiling the sanctity of our living room. That's what he got for voting for Johnson in '64. Ronald Reagan would lead the nation out of the wilderness, you better believe it! Sometimes I'd respond with something vaguely "radical" to get a rise out of him. But it usually took every ounce of energy I could summon just to stay awake.

After two weeks of this torture, I accepted a job lifeguarding the rest of the summer. I told my father I was embarrassed, tak-ing his money for doing nothing, that the guys drew lots every morning, loser gets the old man's kid. I thought he'd have a stroke. He told me it was his fucking money and he'd spend it any fucking way he wanted and they were nothing but a bunch of fucking jealous bastards. And he was certain they were. But I knew they had never heard of the University of Chicago, couldn't even consider the possibility such a place actually ex-isted since it never had and never would appear in a bowl game or at the Final Four. And yet the old man bragged on, oblivious to the fact that they might have a hard time finding Chicago on a map if they were ever inclined to try, which they weren't since they only feigned interest, and a mild one at that, when the boss backed them into a corner at the vending machines and lectured them about my future as a world-famous brain surgeon who would probably win the Nobel Prize. All they saw when they looked at me was a wiry kid with pimples on his chin.

Starting that day, he doubled my wages and told the dis-patcher that, from here on in, I was assigned to Randy T. Ols-son, no ifs, ands, or buts. The dispatcher called over to Randy T and, reaching out to shake his hand, I was conscious of every crack in my voice, aware of my gangly arms, absolutely certain I was going to humiliate myself before the Great One. Someone more clever with words than I might have called my reaction a swoon. And, just like when he was a senior and I was a lowly sophomore, Randy T's eyes skimmed right over me, looking over the day's orders, barely registering my existence.

Randy T was one of the old man's trophies. Still famous throughout Gastonia, the Big Man on Campus, in fact, had never been that big. He was graceful and agile as they come, had an arm like a rocket, and was an inspiration for an avalanche of four-syllable adjectives and inspirational inanities from sentimental sportswriters as far away as Wilmington. His perfectly proportioned frame was a canvas of solid muscle. He had a face that, decades after graduation, would still bring a sigh when middle-aged women stumbled upon a high school yearbook packed in a box in the attic. He was a god descended from Olympus—all five feet seven inches of him.

Randy T had never made it beyond the first semester at the state teacher's college in the northwest corner of the state, the only place that had recruited him. The old man plucked him up and dropped him into an apprenticeship. The fact Randy T had real aptitude for the work was a bonus. The other technicians had to wear navy cotton duck Nocera Heat and Air work uniforms. Randy T had the old man's blessing to hit the trucks in a white wifebeater and jeans.

Randy T was into being mellow that summer. Maybe it was a reaction to the profound humiliation he'd suffered when he came home early one afternoon to find his bride of seven weeks buck naked in bed with his best man. More likely it was the prodigious amounts of marijuana he smoked. When the old man told Randy T to look after me, he shrugged his shoulders and said cool. He offered me one of his unfiltered Old Golds and said let's hit the road, coffee and bear claws five miles ahead.

Much to my surprise, on our third day together, Randy T asked if I wanted to hang out after work. He wanted me to hear the killer new Cheap Trick album; we could order in a pizza or maybe Mexican. I thought Randy T must have the life. Buddies to laugh at his stories, to roll his joints, to toss him another beer, to worship him. But long after midnight, when we were ripped on his homegrown pot and staring at some stupid shit on the television, I realized his phone hadn't rung all night. Randy T must have been lonely, nothing but his two toaster ovens, a coffee percolator, and a huge Mediterranean television/hi-fi console—his share of the wedding booty—to keep him company. Randy T was off chicks for the time being; he didn't even want to talk about them. He still loved his wife and wouldn't file for divorce. He was saving to buy a leather sofa to lure her back home.

Randy T and I stayed stoned the entire summer, watching television with the sound off and the stereo cranked, sharing his bong, falling asleep on his floor. I'd show up at home every few days to drop off my laundry and raid the kitchen for leftover lasagna and chocolate cake to take back to Randy T's. My mother fretted a bit about my random comings and goings, but the old man was thrilled I'd been taken under the wing of his young protégé and encouraged my newfound independence. He didn't care if I was out all night as long as Randy T delivered my sorry ass to work by eight o'clock every morning.

Randy T lived for rock and roll and hit the big arena shows when he could, but the closest big city was Charlotte and, back then, it was still just a puckered asshole on the South Carolina border. So every few months Randy T would head north to the university towns in the Triangle or to Richmond or, for the right band, all the way to D.C. itself. Which is where RFK Stadium was and where the Stones were playing the second week of August. But I was only eighteen, and as much as my father loved Randy T, hanging with him in Gastonia was one thing, the District of Columbia another. Randy T and I dug that the old man might not trust him to chaperon me in a city that was ninety percent colored to stand around with a bunch of drug addicts to watch a bunch of drug addicts. It's cool, Randy T said, we would leave Friday night after work, crash in Silver Spring with his brother who did something with drinking water for the government, get fucked up, pass out, wake up, get fucked up, catch the band, drive straight home, stayed fucked up all day Sunday, and roll into work Monday morning as if we hadn't done anything all weekend except take the truck out to fill the tank.

But on the big Friday afternoon, Randy T took sick. So sick that the lady at the last job of the day got worried and called the dispatcher. The old man drove out to the customer's house, panicking when he arrived to find Randy T mumbling incoherently, his forehead scorched and his glazed eyes dead. We raced to the emergency room and the staff took custody of Randy T, throwing him on a gurney and whisking him behind the curtains. The old man was rattled. He wanted me home, safe, but I stood my ground and insisted he drop me off at Randy T's apartment. I was stranded, no wheels of my own, completely baffled by the four-on-the-floor of Randy T's pickup. A few hits on the bong gave me courage. It was Kerouac time. Time for my own Electric Kool-Aid Acid Test. I stuffed the tickets, a pair of clean BVDs, a toothbrush and toothpaste, and a bar of Palmolive into a backpack and slipped a few joints into my socks. I cadged a ride in the parking lot from a lady I knew from the pool who was heading to the Publix out near the interstate. By three in the morning, I was north of Raleigh, shivering and cotton-mouthed.

The yellow eyes of a northbound tractor trailer emerged from the thick summer mist. The driver downshifted and the air brakes brought the big cat to rest. The engine purred, idling as the door to the cab swung open, welcoming me. A voice told me to toss up the backpack; a hand reached down to steady me as I mounted the cab.

He looked like Jimmy Dean, the country singer, not the actor, with big friendly blue eyes and a long, clean-shaven jaw. Cold for August, huh? he said. Where you heading? D.C., I told him, and he laughed and asked if I had an appointment at the White House. He offered me a bag of trail mix and a warm can of Pepsi-Cola. Stones concert, I said, trying to sound worldly and jaded, as if it were something I did every week. Cool, he said, the Stones are cool enough, but he preferred the real thing. He flipped the top of a cassette case filled with white boy blues—Michael Bloomfield, the Paul Butterfield Blues Band, John Mayall and the Bluesbreakers.

By the Virginia border, I knew he was a native of St. Louis which, according to him, was where the blues were born. He'd done seven semesters at Washington University, but dropped out because it was all bullshit, not real, not like this, barreling through the guts of America saddled to forty tons of steel and rubbing shoulders with the "real people," the tractor-trailer jockeys and mechanics and hash-house waitresses who held the answers to the mysteries of life. Once he had a little nest egg, he was going to Nashville to give Kristofferson and Waylon Jennings a run for their money.

I tried to embellish myself, trying on attitudes and experiences to make me seem worldly, experienced, someone who might interest him. I was surprised when he clucked with disapproval when I told him about Randy T and his stash of bongs and pipes. That shit will fry your brain, he said. Then he smiled and asked if it made me horny. Yeah, I said, sometimes it feels like I'm carrying a lead pipe down there. You oughta get Randy T to help you out, he laughed. Yeah, I said, distracted and exhausted by the chills riffing through my body.

He cranked up the heat to stop my teeth from chattering. He reached over and felt my shirt. You're drenched, he said. Then he put the back of his hand to my forehead and pointed to the bunk behind us. You're burning up. Hustle back there and get outta those wet clothes. Wrap yourself in the blanket and sweat it out before you get pneumonia.

I crawled into the bunk and peeled the clothes from my skin. He told me to retrieve the Band-Aid box tucked into one of his boots. I found a couple of joints and we passed one back and forth. He switched on the overhead light and asked what I thought of the artwork. He'd pinned a gallery of nudies to the walls of the bunk. Not airbrushed *Playboy* girls-next-door, but old, hard-looking babes with peroxided hair and black eyebrows. They had puffy tongues and long, dangling tits with tips like rotten pears. A girl in a double-page centerfold had dumped a can of beef stew between her spread legs. Stoned, I counted the little pieces of peas and corn in her pussy hairs. I was flat on my back and the Pepsi sloshed in my stomach. Go on, relax, do what you want, he said. Shoot anywhere, don't worry about it. I turned my head to tell him I was just going to crash and saw him pumping his long red snake.

I came as soon as I touched myself. Yeah, yeah, he said. He stared at me wild-eyed in the rearview mirror. Come up here and suck me off, he begged. I want to feel my cock in your mouth. His voice was harsh, threatening. I wanted to be home, in my own bedroom, safe. My head started throbbing and, trapped, with nowhere to run, I rolled over and escaped into a dream. I was floating in the surf. My neck was stiff; I couldn't turn my face away from the midday sun. I threw my arms across my eyes, trying to hide from the blinding white light. I heard a voice, then felt the heat of a body between my legs. He rubbed his cheek against mine, then licked my scorched face with his tongue, trying to cool me down. He found my mouth and tried to force it open and, when I resisted, he bit my neck, an affectionate little nip. I felt him lifting my legs and his cock searching for my ass.

He'd pinned me against the mattress. I tried to kick him

away, but my feet flailed over his shoulders. Hey, little buddy, relax. His voice was calm, gentle, but he pressed his forearm against my neck with just enough force to let me know how easy it would be to break it. When I started to cry, he kissed me and told me how easy this could be if I only just let it happen. Push down, he said, push, push like you're taking a big shit. The pain lasted less than a minute, just like he promised. I don't want to hurt your little cherry, he said. He kept his word, riding me slowly and covering my face with little kisses. I sank back into the dream, deafened by the sound of wave after wave of warm salty water crashing over me.

I opened my eyes to a white ceiling. The room was cool and clean. I turned my head on the pillow and saw a plastic bag of clear liquid hanging from a metal hook. My eyes followed the tube down to the white bandage on the back of my hand. I was naked, exposed, sandbagged in ice packs. I let my eyes drift back to the ceiling. I felt my lips crack and split when I whispered a single word. Mom. I fell asleep, my hand in hers, knowing she wouldn't leave the chair by my bed until I was safe again. Somewhere in the room, the old man was crying.

The hospital told them a trucker had brought me to the emergency room, delirious with a fever of one hundred and four. He'd said he found me half dead at a rest stop on the interstate. My mother always regretted he hadn't left his name and address so they could thank him for saving my life. The doctors said it was meningococcal meningitis. Randy T and me both. Highly contagious, spread by direct contact, coughing, sneezing, sharing unwashed eating utensils. I let them believe it. I knew it was a long red snake that had poisoned me.

I spent all of September and the better part of October recovering. Chicago was out of the question; a medical deferral postponed my arrival in the big city until the winter semester. The plan was to get a head start on the Great Books except that the Batman and Robin were more engaging than *Gilgamesh* and the epics of Homer cried out for a graphic edition, illustrated by the artists of Marvel and DC.

"You're still weak. Don't worry, your powers of concentration will return by the time you get to school," my mother reassured me.

But something lingered, a sense of dread that remained after the doctors confirmed the symptoms had resolved and I'd escaped without permanent neurological damage. I rarely wandered far from the Monument to Heat and Air, passing on the Clapton and Steve Miller Band tickets offered by Randy T. The promise of road trips and the lure of marijuana had led me to the cab of a tractor trailer, wrapped in a blanket and drenched in sweat. I preferred the solitude of my room, the lights ablaze through the night. I tossed and turned, sleeping fitfully, dreaming about endless stretches of empty highway leading to a dark strange city where no Dark Knight waited to protect me. The Joker of my nightmares looked suspiciously like a scarred and painted Jimmy Dean, mocking me as a coward, too sickly and weak to defend myself.

It seemed abrupt, a spur-of-the-moment decision, when I announced that Chicago seemed too cold, too far away, that college could wait a year, maybe two. Nocera Heat and Air's payroll could accommodate me while I decided what to do with my future.

"Like hell it will," my father announced, surprisingly calm and rational for a man prone to combustion and outbursts. "If you don't go now, you'll never go," he said.

"What makes you such an expert on higher education?" I snarled.

I'd always known I could infuriate him. Over the past few years, I'd learned it was easy to one-up him. But never before had I known I could hurt him.

"I know you think I'm stupid. You're right. I am. I know

I'm not smart like you. But listen to me. Just this once. I'm not telling you. I'm asking you. Please."

He walked away, defeated, his hopes and dreams for me having crashed and burned.

My mother waited until he'd left the room, then pounced, angry, accusing.

"All that man wants to do is help you. Why won't you let him do that?"

Words once used to protect me were now turned against me, as compelling as they had been when they'd vanquished my father ten years earlier.

All that boy wants is to be with you. Why can't you give him that?

Davidson College, close to home, familiar, an unlikely nest for predators and deviants, was thrilled I wanted to fill a space vacated by a first semester dropout. How different would it have all turned out if there had never been a bout of meningitis and a long red snake? Would I have blossomed in the Windy City or would I have been crushed like a bug by the profound thinkers nurtured in the intellectual hothouse of the University of Chicago? Maybe it all turned out for the best, my being cloistered in a humid, remote Southern outpost, my stature as the leading (and only) Trotskyite unchallenged, no one around to expose my limited comprehension of the vagaries of dialectical materialism. I sure did like to say those words, though. And the girl I would marry sure liked to hear them.

Diagnosis

I tell Matt I'm Humpty Dumpty and he's fucking with my head.

"That's my job," he says.

Okay, then, whose job is it to put me back together again?

He's not happy with me tonight. He says he sees a pattern here and asks if I recognize it. I shrug my shoulders. I shouldn't have told him about the "therapeutic" massage, complete with happy ending, in my hotel room in Orlando. He reminds me I'm on probation and the State of North Carolina wouldn't look kindly on commercial transactions for sexual release. He asks whether I understand the meaning of the term *self-destructive*. I tell him he's being melodramatic.

We move on to discussing medication. Or, rather, he's talking about something called SSRIs and I stop listening. Something behind his right shoulder is distracting me. A small abstract watercolor. Not abstract exactly, more geometric. Squares and pyramids strategically aligned by color. It has to be new. I've sat in this room every week since late last summer and never seen it before.

"Is that watercolor new?" I ask.

"What watercolor?"

"The one behind you. The one with all the shapes."

"No. Why do you ask?"

"No reason."

I scan the room searching for further evidence of my waning powers of observation. Desk, chair, sofa, crucifix. Those I remember. This paperweight, the Venetian millefleur, I remember that too. The psychopharmacology reference guide on the side table. That I haven't seen. That's definitely new.

"You aren't listening to me, are you?" he asks.

"Sure, of course."

Actually I stopped listening when he told me what I didn't want to hear. He's gone too far. He's overstepped his boundaries. He's diagnosing me.

Depression.

"Call in FDR!" I say.

"What?"

"I have nothing to fear but fear itself."

I think my stentorian Hyde Park mimicry is pretty funny, clever at least, but it doesn't get a laugh. He's holding a manila folder with papers attached by a strong metal clasp. A medical record. *My* medical record. I'm reassured by its brevity, just a few sheets of paper. It would be thick as the phone book if I were crazy. It had never occurred to me he was keeping a medical record. He's not my doctor. He's my *counselor*. That's what the State of North Carolina ordered. Counseling. I pay him a lot of money and he counsels me to stay off my knees in public toilets. That's the State's only interest in making me do this, to protect its upstanding citizens from stumbling upon acts of depraved perversion when nature calls while they're doing eighty miles an hour on its beautifully landscaped interstates. The State of North Carolina has no interest in *How I Feel.*

I tell him he has it all wrong.

"How so?"

I can't be depressed. Don't depressed people sleep all the

time? Lately, I can't sleep long enough to finish a dream, tossing and turning and twisting the sheets between my legs. Don't depressed people want to be alone? I'm constantly seeking out crowded rooms, noise, distractions. In fact, I crawl the walls when I'm alone, pacing, smoking, smoking, smoking. Aren't depressed people passive? Not me. It's easy to get a rise out of me these days. People stare at me from the safety of their own cars, shocked by my bulging veins and grinding teeth when we're crawling at fifteen miles an hour. Don't depressed people cry at the drop of a hat? Well, meeting one of the diagnostic criteria isn't enough. Besides, it's not as if I actually cry. It's just that I feel like crying.

"It's not a sign of weakness, you know," he says in his professional voice.

"And it's nothing to be ashamed of," he says.

"How would you know?"

Christ, I'm down his throat. He doesn't react. He's not startled, not taken back. He's *observing*.

"I know because it's a disease," he answers. "Just like hypertension and diabetes. I'm writing you a prescription."

"No."

"Don't be an ass."

He's slipping up. At least it shows he's not completely complacent about this.

"Sorry," he says. "Tell me why you don't want to try medication."

"I not only will not take them," I declare, sounding like a petulant five-year-old, "I'll never even get them. I'll never have it filled."

"You're not being rational. That's the depression talking."

That's the depression talking.

Where do they come up with lines like this? Do they teach them in medical school? Clever Diagnostic Quips 101?

"What are you feeling right now?"

"Nothing," I say. "I'm not feeling anything."

I'm lying. I'm feeling exhausted. Too tired to invest any more words and emotions in denying his diagnosis.

"You're always feeling something," he says.

"Okay, you win. I'm feeling depressed."

Maybe that will shut him up. The clock says only twenty more minutes until I'm released. I've let him win. Maybe he'll take pity and set me free early.

"Too easy," he says.

"What?"

"Too easy. How does depression feel? What does depression mean to you?"

"Abraham Lincoln."

"Excuse me?"

"Abraham Lincoln."

"Okay. You got me there."

"Abraham Lincoln. Diagnosed with depression one hundred years after he died. After he died, for Christ's sake. What does that tell you?"

Eureka. He's befuddled.

"I don't understand," he says.

"It's easy. Do you think one hundred years ago people walked away from the White House, shaking their heads and clicking their tongues, saying, 'Man, Old Abe, Honest Abe, he seemed a little *depressed* to me today'? Of course not. They'd walk out and say, 'Abe was awful quiet today.' Or, 'Old Abe seemed to be somewhere else.' Or, 'Abe was a little short-tempered, not like him to be that way.' The word *depressed* probably didn't even exist back then. Who invented it? Your buddy Freud? His buddy Jung? Hell, whoever it was, they got it wrong. Depression isn't a disease. It's a *description!*"

"So then tell me what it describes."

"Huh?"

"A description has to describe something, right? So tell me what it describes."

"You're playing fucking games with me."

"So why don't you play along? You're good at games."

He knows how to play to my vanity.

"I'll say *depression* and you say whatever comes into your mind. You've got one minute. I'll time you."

"Look, Matt," I say, "I'm not one of your juvenile delinquent pinheads. If you want to play a word association game, just ask."

"Sorry," he says sheepishly. He actually blushes.

He looks at his watch.

"Hold on. I need to smoke to do this."

"Go!"

I waste the first twenty seconds finishing a drag on my cigarette.

"... Okay. Depression. Black. Block. Box. Weight. Deadweight. Sink. Drown. Float ..."

I'm stuck on float.

"Float ... I see myself on my back, floating, bloated, bluish."

Dead. No, not dead. Just not alive.

"Time's up."

"How'd I do?"

"Great! You won," he says, clicking his pen.

"What did I win?"

"This."

He scribbles on the prescription pad and hands me my prize.

"You're going to take these, right?"

"Doctor's orders!"

At the door, he does something he has never done before. He hugs me. I'm too surprised to hug back.

"Everything is going to be okay," he says. "I promise."

Manipulative bastard. He knows just how to get to me. I had no intention of filling the prescription, let alone taking the damn things. But the hug has broken my resolve. I can't let him down. Spooky, I think as I drive away, I wonder if I'm becoming one of those creeps who falls in love with their therapist.

The Bride of Frankenstein

If I'd remembered tonight was Halloween I would have found some excuse to stay over in Davenport, Iowa. I could have called Matt to tell him I needed to cancel our session so I could take in the International Sofa Museum. What? They don't make couches in Davenport, you say? This great city must be famous for something! Agriculture? Okay then, I don't want to miss that exhibit of the world's largest ear of corn. Who would? Sorry. See you next week.

Instead I dutifully boarded my flight to Charlotte, only vaguely aware of the black crepe paper and orange twinkle lights draping the airport newsstand. Even the pumpkin on the porch of Matt's Queen Anne didn't set off any alarms. I made it through the hour—no breakthroughs, no new insights, another buck and a half that would have been better spent on a blow job from an Iowa farm boy trying to make ends meet. Afterward, I trudged home, grabbed a bottle of beer, kicked off my shoes, and flopped on the bed, ready to tackle the mail that accumulated during the week.

Let's see. Four envelopes from (who else?) the law firm of Dugan, Castor, and Mullen, LLC. One enclosing an invoice, the second several pleadings requiring review and signature, a third forwarding copies of correspondence from the enemy firm of McNamara, Kerrigan, Whiteside, and Greenberg, the gist of which is that I am a deceitful, repugnant lower form of life. The fourth, the bulkiest, is stuffed with mail addressed to Andrew Nocera, 12 Virginia Dare Court, High Point, North Carolina. Not much of interest. An alumni solicitation from Davidson College. A notice that my subscription to *Baseball America* is about to expire. (God damn it, Dugan, Castor, and Mullen, where are my back issues? What the hell am I paying you for?) Finally, at the bottom of the pile, is a letter from Kuperstein's Jewelers asking me to please contact them to arrange to pick up the inscribed gold bracelet ordered July 7. Failure to respond within the next thirty days will result in the forfeiture of my (substantial) deposit.

It was going to be a surprise, not a gift tendered out of obligation to observe a birthday, an anniversary, or a holiday. I was going to smack my forehead halfway across the Pont de la Tournelle, berating myself for, once again, forgetting something, something so important I'd even tied this thread around my finger to remind myself, see? What now? Alice would ask, rolling her eyes, exasperated, resigned to losing our reservation at Les Bookinistes because, as usual, I'd left my wallet on the dresser. This, I just remembered this, I'd say, handing her a small box tied with a white ribbon. I'd smile and wait for her to throw her arms around my shoulders, overcome when she discovers an eight-thousand-dollar piece of armor worthy of Wonder Woman, inscribed with the silly words of the Barry White song I liked to croak in her ear. *You're the first, the last, my everything.*

I can hardly afford to lose the four-grand deposit in my current circumstances, but I certainly don't have the spare cash to ransom the bracelet from those nasty Kupersteins. Ah well, easy come, easy go. Anyway, Alice might have raised a skeptical eyebrow, unmoved by sentimentality and a Gallic backdrop, suspicious of my motivations. Naw, I'm sure she would have grabbed my shoulders and covered my face with kisses, murmuring in French, thanking me, even though, lout that I am, I don't understand a single word of the language.

Goddamn it, go away, I mutter, irritated by the shrill, insistent bell summoning someone to the front door. I can't imagine who could be harassing my mother, who I assume must be in her room finishing dressing for a bridge game or a night at the movies with friends. I haul myself off the bed to investigate; I need another beer anyway. Halfway down the stairs, I hear my mother shrieking in joy.

"Oh Lord, I think you've just taken three years off my life!" she claims, thrilling the pint-sized Casper in a cheap, off-the-shelf costume.

"Boo!" he (or she) trills, turning to run down the walk.

"Be careful!" my mother calls. "When did you get home?" she asks, turning to me.

"A while ago. I came in through the kitchen."

"Well, welcome home."

"Do you want to go out to dinner?"

"I made lasagna. If you're starved, I can heat a piece now."

"Let's go out. It's my treat."

"It's Halloween, Andy! I wouldn't miss this for the world!"

Three little Jedi warriors and Yoda race to the porch. My mother is hopeless, not recognizing their costumes. She thinks Yoda is some kind of frog.

"*Star Wars*, Ma. They're characters from *Star Wars.*"

"How the hell would I know that?" she carps. "Obviously I could use your help here."

I'd like another beer but anticipate a gentle rebuke about setting a good example. But if I'm going to be roped into doing this, I ought to be given some slack.

"Just let me grab another beer."

The kids come and go in spurts. I tell my mother I don't remember Town Watch patrolling on Halloween and none of us ever wore silver reflecting tape over our costumes. Times have changed, Andy, she says, it's a different world now. Years ago, my mother would have known all the kids by name. The masks are pointless since they're all little strangers now. The costumes are disappointing. Only a witch or two, not a skeleton all night. Halloween belongs to Disney and Warner Bros. It's trademark protected.

"Andy, leave some for the kids," she scolds, catching me with my fist in the candy bowl.

"Ma, you could restock Wal-Mart with the candy you've got! Anyway, let's eat."

"Trick or treat isn't over."

"It will be if you shut the door and turn off the light."

"Andy, what's wrong with you?" she asks, chafing at my ir-ritability. "You used to love Halloween!"

Did I?

Like you said, Ma, times have changed. It's a different world.

Other boys collected Matchbox cars. For me, there were only the Famous Monsters of Filmland. And I was more than just a collector. I built my monsters with my own two hands from model kits.

My mother would cover the kitchen table with newspaper and I would spread out the airplane glue and little vials of enamel paint. I'd pick a time when I knew she'd be working in the kitchen. I wanted a witness to the creation. Patience, she'd say when I got too excited and tried to rush, you need to let the glue set and wait for the paint to dry.

My clumsy hands could attach the arms and legs to the trunk and mount the head on the neck. It didn't take a lot of skill to slap paint on the body. But the face needed her delicate touch. Wow, she'd say, this is the best one yet! She would promise to do a really good job so she didn't spoil it. My little heart would race as she very, very carefully, painted the eyes and the lips and the brows. When she was finished, my monsters looked just like the picture on the box.

The old man put shelves above my bed for my collection. I slept under their vigilant eyes. Frankenstein, Dracula, the Mummy, the Wolfman, the Phantom of the Opera, the Hunchback of Notre Dame, and Creature from the Black Lagoon. I loved them all. But there was a special place in my heart for my favorite. The Bride of Frankenstein. Regal, silent, austere, she was the most fascinating creature I'd ever seen. I never tired of watching her make her grand entrance in the last minutes of the movie, always hoping that this time, she would walk away from the rubble when the castle collapsed and escape into the horizon as the credits rolled. When I was nine years old, my mother asked me who I wanted to be for Halloween and I shouted, without a moment's hesitation, the Bride of Frankenstein, of course!

Our costumes were always her October project. That year, my sister was a chubby little Tinker Bell in tights and buckle shoes spray-painted silver. My mother spent a week turning chicken wire and cheesecloth into gossamer wings. My costume was simpler, several yards of muslin for the shroud and ACE bandages to cover my arms and legs. She bought a cheap wig at a discount store, shellacked it into a beehive, and painted skunk stripes at the temples. She gave me a chalk-white face and black brows and red lips. She drew raccoon circles on my face since nature hadn't blessed me with Elsa Lanchester's pop eyes. I looked in the mirror and saw the Bride of Frankenstein.

She took our picture and warned us one last time to watch out for cars and not to touch the candy until we got home. Regina was scratching and twitching, already anxious to shed her costume. The shoes pinched her feet, so she kicked them off and tossed them in her trick-or-treat bag, ruining her tights on the sidewalk. She approached the whole thing as a job, an annoyance to be suffered, the price for the payoff.

It was the best night of my life. I zombie-walked the streets, arms stiff, pointing straight ahead. I rotated my head counterclockwise, leading with my chin, doing all of the Bride's jerky robot bird moves. I let my sister do the talking when the neighbors answered the doorbell. Trick or treat, she said without enthusiasm. Then it was my turn, after the candy was tossed in the bag. I dropped my jaw and did a perfect imitation of her high-pitched squeal. EEEEEKKK! I was a hit. Everyone laughed and told me what a good Bride I made.

My sister shredded every vestige of Tinker Bell as soon as we got home. I stayed in my costume, wanting this night to last forever. We were upstairs in my room fighting over Milky Ways when we heard the old man's voice below. I couldn't hear what my mother was saying, but the tone of her voice was explanatory, conciliatory. Her words made my father angrier. He said she was responsible, that she indulged me, that he was the laughingstock of the neighborhood. The guy down the street had just accosted him in the driveway, taunting him about my performance.

"You know what they call him?" the old man screamed, so angry he was near tears.

"*Annie, ANNIE!*"

That's how I learned the difference between laughing with you and at you. I stood up and ripped off the wig. I tore it apart and stomped on the pieces. Gina looked up from her trick-or-treat bag, mouth full of chocolate and eyes full of wonder.

"I like your costume, Andy," she said. "It's better than mine."

She dumped her candy on the floor and stacked all the peanut butter cups, our favorites, in neat—for her—towers of orange and brown wrapping. I knew she would eat all hers first, the opposite of me, who saved the best for last, after the popcorn balls and hard candies and plain milk chocolate.

"Here," she said, pushing the peanut butter cups toward me. "You can have them."

The next morning she would crawl into her daddy's lap and he'd ask if she had a good Halloween. She'd say it was okay, but she didn't get any peanut butter cups, knowing he'd drive to the Piggly Wiggly and buy her an entire box.

"Is it broken?" she asked, looking at the pieces of wig on the floor.

"I think so."

"Mama's going to be mad."

"No, she's not."

"Yes, she will. She yelled at me for ruining my stupid costume."

It was the first time I understood the mother Gina knew was different from my mama just as her daddy wasn't my old man.

"Do you wanna play Clue?" she asked.

"Okay."

"You can be Miss Scarlet," she said as she pulled out the box. "I promise I won't tell."

Let's Pretend We're Married

Hot damn! What's the chance the station scanner would find this oldie but goodie pulsating down at the left of the dial? It's radio, of course, with the lyrics scrubbed squeaky clean, no forbidden words permitted, but not even the FCC can ruin this little seven-minute masterpiece. I intend to sing along to every syllable, even if means sitting in a parked car with the engine running while my counselor twiddles his thumbs, assuming some barely sublimated hostility is the only possible explanation for my chronic tardiness.

"You're in an awfully good mood for someone who's been sitting on a plane the last six hours," Matt remarks when I finally stroll into his office, still humming Prince's brilliant chorus.

"I heard a great song on the car radio tonight."

"What?"

"You probably wouldn't know it."

"Of course not. The only music I listen to is Gregorian chant."

"Are you serious?"

"No. Are you?"

Apparently my counselor has been following the career of

the Artist Formerly Known As since catching an early gig at First Avenue in Minneapolis. Well, la-di-da. This goddamn priest always knows how to put me in my place.

"So which song was it?" he asks.

"*Let's Pretend We're Married.*"

Why did I bring this up? The arched eyebrow and skeptical smile can only mean the simple act of enjoying a song is about to be infused with portentous analysis and provide him with a perfect segue to an inquisition into personal responsibility. Yes, I insist, I was always safe during my little extracurricular activities. Of course I didn't use condoms with Alice. Was he crazy? I might as well have branded *Unfaithful* on my forehead.

"Did you ever worry about passing along a disease?"

"I told you I was always safe."

"That's not the question I asked."

"Of course I worried about it."

"Did you ever think she suspected?"

And so on and so forth for the next fifty minutes.

Jesus Christ. I don't know how I'm going to survive missing a week of browbeating and emotional intimidation. Next Friday is the day after Thanksgiving and I have a reprieve.

"Have a great holiday," he says as I hand him the check.

Fuck you, I mutter as I walk out the door. What makes him such an expert on marriage?

Alice sighed and crawled into bed, a glass of chardonnay in hand to fortify herself for the challenge of plowing through the latest trade paperback selected by her book club to educate and edify. Fifty pages before lights out or else! I rolled on my stomach and grunted, too restless to sleep. I used to nod off at the drop of a hat. My wife would accuse me of narcolepsy and threaten to inject me with caffeine. That was another lifetime, before falling asleep meant having to wake up and crawl out of bed, shave and brush my teeth, put on my game face, convince the King of Unpainted Furniture I was obsessed with lumber prices and consumed with mortgage rates, higher rates equating a drop in residential home sales meaning fewer empty rooms begging to be filled with the affordable products of Tar Heel Heritage Furniture.

How the hell had I ended up a salesman? Worse yet, a *successful* salesman! The best goddamn salesman in the history of Tar Heel Heritage, better even than the King himself. Who would have believed I'd be a two-time runner-up for the national sales award by the American Home Furnishings Society? Who could have predicted I'd be recruited for a seat on the board of the North Carolina Furniture Association and chair its Government Affairs subcommittee, lobbying for protective tariffs on insidious foreign imports and testifying in support of legislation to decimate the right to collectively bargain?

It's all Alice's fault I've ended up tossing and turning in a bedroom in a suburban cul-de-sac, I thought, irritated by the dry, chafing sound of thumb against paper as she turned the pages of her novel. We should have parted ways when I started graduate school. She shouldn't have followed me to Durham and taken that job at the Montessori School, teaching music appreciation to the precocious offspring of Duke's junior faculty, being paid less than even my measly stipend from the Department of Comparative Literature. At least once a day, I would accuse her of resenting our shabby circumstances. She'd just laugh and say, "Not as much as you do."

"It's completely up to you," she said while I pondered her father's job offer. Always a pragmatist, he'd decided if Alice was going to be so goddamn stubborn, if she was going to insist he accept me, then at least he would co-opt me. I was floundering anyway, insecure among the pretensions of more impressively pedigreed academics, and highly susceptible to the power of suggestion. Curtis never missed an opportunity to make it obvious he questioned how a man could call teaching four hours a week "work." Alice assumed I had a choice. The King knew better. All he needed to do was impugn my masculinity and it was good-bye Duke and hello Sales. He made only one condition. No more living in sin. We slipped off to City Hall before he could initiate the tactical maneuvers that would climax with the Big Church Wedding.

Well, at least the job wasn't heating and air-conditioning. And the money wasn't bad. It certainly impressed the old man, who'd been exasperated by every decision I'd ever made, except for marrying Alice. He'd refused to contribute a single dime for me to lounge around at Duke and read paperback novels, but he insisted on fronting the down payment on the town house, not wanting to be outdone by that blowhard, the uncrowned King, J. Curtis McDermott.

I knew my wife would have been content living in a drafty old rental on the fringes of the campus of whatever liberal-arts college might offer me a tenure-track position. I was the one who'd made the very expensive, solid cherry sleigh bed we were lying in (literally and figuratively speaking, and definitely not a Tar Heel Heritage product). And Alice? She seemed happy enough to be married to the Senior Vice President for Sales and her career introducing the young scholars of the Greensboro Friends School to the glories of Wolfgang Amadeus. She hadn't changed much since college and still thought of me as a better-groomed edition of the obnoxious, smelly boy she'd married, with his torn flannel shirts and shaggy hair, his stupid record collection and dog-eared volumes of the literature of the South. She didn't even seem to resent that passion and spontaneity had been replaced with a purpose-driven protocol for procreation. We copulated on a strict schedule tethered to the time of the month and body temperature. Medical science was encouraging: *Millions of couples have conceived with a lower sperm count than yours, Mr. Nocera.*

"Why didn't you join the Junior League instead of that

damn book club?" I teased, distracting her from her assign-ment. "At least we'd get a discount on the cookbooks."

"Don't be a smart-ass," she shot back, smacking my arm with her book.

"Why do all these chick writers have three names?"

"I don't know. Why don't you ask them?" she laughed.

"Seriously. You put aside Dawn Powell to tackle the latest best-seller by Susan Moore Duncan? Look at these blurbs! 'A Radiant Achievement!' 'A Marvel of a Book!' Holy shit, Lucy Patton Kline says it's 'A Masterpiece!' Why are you reading this crap?"

Alice simply pointed to the television bleating at the foot of the bed and the busty coed in her underpants being chased by a masked maniac with a chain saw.

"It's classic morality play!" I protested. "Plus I'll know how to defend you if a serial killer breaks into the house."

"Andy, it wouldn't hurt you to pick up a book."

"I've read them all," I joked. "Be prepared. The *Hindenburg* is about to explode."

"If you fart in this bed I'm going to kill you."

"But you love me, don't you?"

"Against my better judgment."

"Come on, Alice. You'd never read this shit on your own. Why don't you quit that stupid book club?"

"They're a nice group of women."

"I thought you hated that one. I forget her name."

"Except for her. Anyway, February is my turn to pick."

"That's next month. I hope Susan Moore Duncan writes fast."

"We're going to read *Wuthering Heights*."

"Oh shit. I feel for you, sweetheart," I said, flipping the re-mote and flopping on my side to sleep. "They're going to make you pay for that!"

* * *

She'd carefully frosted a three-tier red velvet cake with my favorite cream cheese icing before coming up to bed. The sparkling wine was chilling and I promised I wouldn't forget to pick up the chocolate-dipped strawberries on my way home from work.

"So are you really going to discuss literature, or is this book club just an excuse to throw a Valentine's theme party? Are you serving anything other than sugar and alcohol?" I asked.

"Not now," she said, shushing me. "I only have a few pages left to finish."

I'd already seen the Biography Channel life of Vlad the Impaler, and nothing else on television was bloody enough to engage my interest. I flipped through a few pages of the new Reynolds Price novel and, bored to death, started making notations in *Lindy's Fantasy Baseball*, boning up for the draft in my rotisserie league. Alice sighed and closed her copy of *Wuthering Heights*.

"So, you finish?" I asked, having been successfully distracted from my deliberation on who to select for the Hot Corner.

"Yep."

"All prepared to lead the women of Virginia Dare Court on a safari to the heart of darkness?"

"Maybe."

"What's the matter?" I asked, slightly unnerved by the sad, faraway look on her face.

"I'm just thinking."

"About?"

"About a hundred years from now."

"We'll be dead."

"That's what I'm thinking about."

"Jesus."

"Don't you find it comforting? The thought of the two of

us, buried in a quiet church yard, lying side by side for eternity?"

"Shit, Alice. Maybe the book club should stick to Susan Moore Duncan."

"I'm serious."

I knew it wasn't the time for a wry aside, a sarcastic remark, an amusing joke.

"Come on, honey. Don't be morbid. We've got a lot of years before we need to worry about our final resting place," I assured her as I turned out the light. "Roll over."

She spooned into my body and I grabbed her hand and squeezed.

"I love you, Andy."

"I love you, too," I said as I drifted off to sleep.

The literary lionesses had been going at it since seven o'clock. The occasional shrill laugh wafted up to my hideaway. One flight below, red velvet cake was beckoning. Or what was left of it. Cupid wouldn't discourage sinful indulgence in empty calories on the eve of his feast day. The prospects of Alice saving me even a small, pitiful piece were dwindling. I yanked on my jeans and pulled a sweatshirt over my head. It wasn't as if I'd been banished to the bedroom; I didn't need a secret password to cross my own living room. I'd be damned if those harpies were going to polish off the last of my cake.

If I'd been expecting a hearty welcome, I would have been disappointed. Melissa from next door looked up and wiggled her fingers to greet me. Two young blondes, sisters if I remembered correctly, sat on the sofa gripping their knees, tense smiles threatening to crack their faces. Carolyn, Alice's colleague at the Friends School, was trying vainly to keep the peace. My wife didn't even acknowledge me as I pussyfooted to the kitchen. I recognized the tightly coiled posture of Alice in combat, poised to strike. Her nemesis had sucked the air out of the room, fueling her grandiloquent gestures with infusions of stolen oxygen.

A forlorn wedge of cake awaited me in the kitchen. Six dead soldiers, twenty-four dollars a bottle, were lined up on the counter. I was rooting in the fridge for milk when I heard Alice, slightly tipsy, go on the offensive.

"You have no idea what you're talking about! You're confusing love with raging hormones. A good relationship is based on compatibility, companionship, not on how many orgasms you have a night!"

Her adversary was an unlikely missionary of the gospel of base animal chemistry. Short and squat, her hair cut in a limp pageboy that accentuated her bulging eyes, she resembled an officious box turtle in Donna Karan eyeglass frames.

"Well, Alice, if that were true, we should all marry our hairdressers."

I faked a few snores, hoping I'd fool her into thinking I was asleep when she came up to bed.

"Are you awake?" she asked, ensuring that I was.

"Did you have a good time?" I asked, rubbing my eyes as if she'd roused me from a deep slumber. "The cake was terrific."

She was obviously agitated, unable to close her eyes and drift off to sleep.

"Do you want to watch some television?" Maybe the late-night chat fests might distract her.

"No. I think I'll read," she said, opening the copy of *Wuthering Heights* she'd brought to bed with her.

"I thought you finished that last night?"

"I did. I'm looking for something," she said, flipping through the pages. "Here it is. *Whatever our souls are made of, his and mine are the same.* You believe that's true, don't you?"

"Sure. Of course."

"You feel it, don't you?"

"What's brought this on?" I asked, feigning blissful innocence.

"I don't know. Sometimes I feel you're holding something back."

"Like what?" I asked, as if the idea was preposterous.

"I don't know."

"I'm not holding anything back," I assured her, still a half-truth since all the transgressions, the infidelities, the bald-faced lies wouldn't begin until sometime in the not-too-distant future.

The good husband I was, I knew it was the perfect moment for the cuddle, best appreciated without the necessity of a request. I sat up and banked my pillows and she snuggled against me.

"So what are the ladies reading next month?"

"Doesn't matter."

"Why not?"

"I'm quitting."

"I thought you loved the book club?"

"Maybe I'll start a new book club with women who want to talk about books instead of their pathetic sex lives."

"You mean they have sex lives?" I asked.

"I doubt it." She laughed. Or at least I thought she laughed. Maybe she simply snorted. "You know what tomorrow is, don't you?"

"Of course, it will be twelve years since the day we met. Hey, look at the clock! It's after midnight. It's officially tomorrow now. Happy Valentine's Day."

"Andy, if you ever stopped loving me you would tell me, wouldn't you?"

"Alice, I will never stop loving you," I swore, promising a celebration, dinner and a good bottle of wine, later that night.

* * *

"Andy, you're going to break the slats if you don't cut it out!" Alice chastised, but not too seriously. It was probably the bottle and a half of pinot noir we'd had at dinner, but she thought my ridiculous imitation of Prince performing "Let's Pretend We're Married" was hilarious. I cranked up the volume and strutted on the bed. Ooh-we-sha-sha-coo-coo-yeah! I loved that fucking song, a seven-minute orgasm, especially that nasty little refrain about wanting to fuck the taste out of that sweet little girl's mouth.

"Happy Valentine's Day! Come on, come on, dance with me, baby," I pleaded, pulling her up by her arms, the bed finally collapsing under the weight of a grown man and woman jumping on the mattress. We did it right then and there, with the Artist Formerly Known As serenading our coupling.

Several weeks later, I sat in my pants and socks, too stunned to finish undressing for bed, and she held my hand and told me our prayers had been answered. We were crossing a bridge and on the other side was a deeper intimacy, a family, the circle complete at last. Who could have predicted that all it would take after years of careful planning was one spastic little jig and broken bed slats to inspire one intrepid little sperm to take aim, blast off, and hit the target? Alice was sure the little tadpole swimming in a pool of her amniotic fluid was going to grow into a boy. After we backdated the calendar to determine the exact date of the miracle of conception, I insisted there was only one way to appropriately honor the Raspberry Beret Sorcerer who had succeeded where a legion of obstetricians, endocrinologists, and urologists had failed. Of course, there was the added benefit of a likely fatal myocardial infarction when Curtis was introduced to his new grandson Prince Rogers Nelson Nocera. My suggestion, needless to say, was summarily rejected and Alice started making a list of names, inspired by literary or musical icons, all of which I refused to consider. Yes, I remembered I was reading *Absalom, Absalom!* when we met but I just couldn't warm up to the idea of Faulkner Nocera. Dylan had become a cliché. I am being serious, I insisted: Johnpaulgeorgeandringo Nocera had a nice ring. Why would I ever agree to call our son Pynchon when I couldn't finish *Gravity's Rainbow?* Besides, I argued, everyone knows the rules. A boy's name should be one syllable with more consonants than vowels. Jack was the compromise, after London or Kerouac. Both great writers and great lookers.

"But what if Jack turns out ugly?" I asked.

"It doesn't matter."

"Don't you want the kid to be good-looking?"

"Looks aren't important."

"You thought I was good-looking when we met."

"I still do."

Oh, Alice, my sweet Alice. At best, I'm a six out of ten. The collision of Naples and Appalachia had yielded better results in my younger sister, proof that practice makes perfect.

"So looks *are* important?"

"Incidental. Sort of a fringe benefit."

"So what attracted you to me besides my beauty?"

"You were smart. You were funny. You weren't like other boys."

I didn't like where this was going. My wife chose me because I was "different."

"You were the first man I ever met who listened when I talked instead of thinking of what he was going to say next."

Thank God she hadn't fallen for me because I was a sissy.

"If you could change one thing about me, what would it be?"

"Ask me tomorrow. Tonight I'm perfectly happy."

"So you hope Jack will be a chip off the old block?"

"Your block," she said emphatically. "If he turns out any-thing like my father, we're going to have to trade him in."

The AFP was positive, "abnormal." Her serum protein lev-els were low. It's a screening, not a test, they assured us. No rea-son to get anxious yet. The chance of Down syndrome was one in a thousand, but an ultrasound and amniocentesis were rec-ommended just for our peace of mind. Modern medicine en-sures you'll never be blindsided by the left jab. There are no more awful surprises, no need to cry and curse your fate and fi-nally to resign yourself to the hand that's been dealt you. The tests confirmed the extra chromosome.

"It's your decision," I told her, thinking I was saying the right thing.

She was furious, angry at me. At herself. At the world.

"Don't put it all on me! How dare you make me take all the responsibility for this!"

"I mean I want what you want. Jesus, that's all I'm trying to say."

If only we hadn't shared the happy news with the world. After trying for so long, the three-month obligatory wait, the safety net, "just in case," seemed like an eternity. Living with your conscience, justifying, rationalizing, would be difficult enough without having to endure the judgment, silent or other-wise, of the morally absolute.

"We could tell our parents we lost the baby," I said.

"Why?" she countered. "If that's the decision we make, we should have the integrity to live with the consequences."

"I was just thinking about your father."

"If we decide to have this baby, it will be because it's the right thing to do. My father has nothing to do with it. I don't know why you even care what he would think."

Frustration, maybe even disgust, was creeping into her voice.

"Look, Alice, do you have the strength to raise this baby?"

"I don't know. Maybe. But I don't think you do."

I didn't. She knew it. It was an act of kindness for her to suggest that it was even a subject for discussion and debate. We left the question hanging between us, unresolved, until the calendar dictated that she couldn't wait any longer to make the appointment. We barely spoke as we drove to the clinic the morning of the "procedure." I asked if she was warm enough; she told me to turn left at the next light. I sat beside her as she signed the consent forms. She allowed me to kiss her on the forehead and, as the staff escorted her behind closed doors, I slumped into a chair, feeling nothing but relief.

I sat in the waiting room, a plastic bag of her personal items on my lap, the clothes she'd worn to the clinic, her watch and handbag. I was restless as a toddler, unable to concentrate on the words of the book I was reading (*The Southpaw*, an annual Opening Day ritual since I was fourteen), needing Dr Pepper and cheese crackers from the vending machine to pacify me. I knew she'd have the necessary quarters and dimes in her change purse and as I shuffled through the contents of the bag I found a medal and chain, carefully wrapped in her panties. The metal was black with tarnish, the impression of the Blessed Virgin worn and barely distinguishable. It must have been a talisman from her childhood, probably draped around her neck at her First Communion and not removed until late in her rebellious adolescence.

I knew then that whatever was happening in another room of the clinic was a mistake. Not a sin. A mistake. She'd made the decision, made it alone really, not trusting me to have the fortitude and patience to persevere through the struggles ahead. I should have assured her that I was up for the challenge, that little Jack would make us even closer, that I wouldn't, couldn't, ever abandon her, leaving her alone to raise our child. But I didn't. And if she had resorted to prayer, it hadn't been to ask for forgiveness for what she was about to do. Once she'd made the decision, she would have been absolutely certain it was the right one. She would have been praying for hopeless causes, the baby and me.

I never saw that medal again. It was consigned to its secret hiding place until the next crisis or tragedy when she would retrieve it from safekeeping, seeking the comfort of feeling it resting on her chest. There was no religious awakening in our household, no sudden appearance of Mass cards or scripture tracts. Over time, life seemed to return to normal. But sex gradually became an afterthought, a ritual to mark a special occasion, a birthday or anniversary, or another stop on the carefully planned itineraries to Europe or Mexico, scheduled between breakfast and an afternoon shopping spree. I'd guiltily initiate foreplay when I suddenly realized it had been weeks, no, months, since we'd last made love.

The rift between us, once opened, could never be completely sealed. We never actually made the decision to stop trying for another baby, but we never really committed to continuing the effort after the abortion.

I'm nursing my second, no, make that third drink, building a nice buzz as I sit alone at the Carousel, watching the clock on the wall. I've driven by here thousands of times; the place has been a notorious gathering place for "fairy nice guys" as long as I can remember. Father Matthew McGinley really got under my skin tonight, dredging up all these damn memories. Dreading the prospect of my first major holiday as a (disgraced) single man, I called my mother from the parking lot, pleading early holiday air-traffic delays ("Flight's not due in until almost midnight. Yes, I remembered to call the psychiatrist to cancel.") as if spending a few hours sitting in a gay bar still necessitated an elaborate alibi. Of course, the reality of the Carousel is far more benign than the sinful den of iniquity of my imagination. The owners haven't redecorated since the heyday of *The Brady Bunch,* and the plaid carpet and faux paneling have all the charm of a suburban rec room. So much for the maxim that all gays have good taste.

"Where's the jukebox?" I ask.

"Sorry, buddy, it's broken," the bartender apologizes. "But the deejay starts spinning in an hour."

The bartender plops another beer in front of me; the guy at the end of the bar has bought me a drink. I turn toward my benefactor and offer a nod of appreciation without acquiescence. He raises his glass and smiles. He seems friendly enough, not bad-looking, a bit scruffy, my type, actually. He'd be a real possibility if it weren't for my state of mind tonight. In the mood I'm in, he looks slightly ridiculous, a grown man in a Carolina Tar Heels Basketball hoodie.

"Tell him thanks," I say to the barman.

"He says thanks, Harold," he bellows.

"You're welcome," Harold shouts back.

I look away quickly before he reads an invitation to join me in my eyes.

It's pushing toward eleven. The Carousel is starting to get crowded. Mr. Tar Heels Basketball is lingering at the end of the bar. Friends greet him and he laughs, too loudly, intending to get my attention. I understand the message being delivered. *See? I'm not a freak, a criminal, a psycho. I've got friends who are happy to see me. Don't be frightened. I'm a normal guy. Smile. Strike up a conversation.* Protocol demands I buy him a beer if I order another drink. I'm thirsty. I don't want to go home. *Hey, bartender, one for the road, and send one to Hank—sorry, Harold—at the end of the bar.*

"What's your name?" Harold asks, challenged by his friends to walk over and introduce himself.

"Andy," I say, trying to suppress my irritation at having my space invaded.

"Sorry, I didn't mean to bother you," he says, contrite, his overture rewarded by my obvious lack of interest.

"That's okay," I say blandly so as not to encourage him.

"I just wanted to thank you for the beer. Have a nice Thanksgiving," he says.

"You too," I mutter, turning away.

The Carousel is starting to hop.

"So what do you think, Blue Eyes?"

The snaggletooth sitting next to me insists I join the debate.

"Streisand or Midler?"

"Streisand or Midler what?"

He rolls his eyes as if the question—and the answer—is obvious.

"You must be one of those queens who can't think beyond Madonna," the snaggletooth sneers, dismissing me from the conversation.

"Yeah, that's me, all right," I snarl, firing up a cigarette.

I wish I was still married.

It's time to hit the road. I swallow the backwash in my beer bottle, preparing to do penance for my bad behavior. Harold's back is toward me. I touch his shoulder, expecting he'll turn and sneer, revenge, after all, being sweet.

"Sorry for being so rude earlier. It's been a long week," I apologize.

"No problem," he says, smiling. "You come here often?"

"Not really."

"We'll try it again next time." He laughs. "Gimme a kiss."

Why not? I give him a friendly peck and slip out the door.

The temperature's dropped quickly. Tomorrow morning a killer frost will blanket the lawns of Mecklenburg and Gaston Counties. I turn off the car radio; I've had enough crappy memories for one day.

I kept my promise, Alice. I never told you I stopped loving you because I never did.

You asked the wrong question.

You should have made me promise to tell you if I ever fell in love with someone else.

Meet the Wilkinses

"You'll like them. I know it."

I've never been a big one for socializing. Alice had to drag me out of the house kicking and screaming. This time she was insistent.

She was right. Why wouldn't I like them? They were probably lovely people, great folks, exactly the type of neighbors we were hoping for when we bought this splashily designed, poorly constructed, and wildly expensive town house in the most exclusive gated community in the Triad.

"Give them a chance," she said.

Alice wanted to cook dinner for them. No, I said, willing to give in only so far, we'll meet at a restaurant. She wasn't sure, wanting to avoid the awkward moment when the check was presented. No problem, I said, I'll give my card in advance and, at the end of the evening, I'll slip away from the table and discreetly sign. She finally conceded, knowing I really did not want to meet the Wilkinses.

I started to relax as the waiter uncorked the second bottle of wine. The evening was going well, better than expected. In fact, it was an unqualified success. The Wilkinses, unlike most of my professional acquaintances, gave every indication they knew how to read. There was plenty to talk about; there was a lot of laughter. Driving home, Alice asked what I'd thought of Nora. The question took me by surprise. I was having a hard time remembering her face.

"She seemed kind of quiet," I said, assuming shyness was the explanation for her failure to make an impression on me.

"Andy." Alice laughed. "She talked a blue streak all night!"

Hmmmmm.

"What did you think of Brian?" she asked.

I wondered if that was a trick question.

"Seems like a nice guy," I said, cautiously.

"You two really seemed to hit it off."

Did we? I felt a strange sensation in my chest. Good God, I thought, it sounds like an old cliché, but did my heart skip a beat?

"What did you talk about?" she asked.

"I dunno," I said, suddenly becoming inarticulate.

What did we talk about? Work, obviously. Our wives, certainly. It was easier to remember what we didn't talk about.

Golf.

Cars.

Power tools.

"Swimming," I finally said.

"He's a swimmer too?" she asked.

"Yes."

"You guys ought to swim together sometime."

"Yeah, he mentioned something like that," I said, sounding nonchalant and noncommittal. "He said he'd call to set something up."

Two days later, she was slipping on her Levi's while I cradled my foot, engrossed in a virgin blister on my heel. She asked if something was wrong. It must be the new shoes, I said. No, I don't mean that, she said. I'd thought she was blissfully unaware of my barely concealed agitation, of the nervous twitch

I'd developed whenever the phone rang, of my impatient inter-ruptions to ask who was on the line, and of my disappointment when the call was not the one I was so anxiously awaiting.

Wednesday night was close, but no cigar.

"It's Nora Wilkins," she said. "She wants to know if we're free for dinner Saturday night." She expressed our regrets, telling Nora we were visiting my parents this weekend.

"Wait, wait one minute, Nora. Andy's trying to tell me something."

I was waving my hands furiously to get her attention.

"Nora? Andy says they cancelled, that they're going out of town this weekend. Thanks for telling me, mister," she said, laughing. "We'd love to."

I needed to square this little white lie with my mother, pronto, before she called and told Alice they were looking for-ward to seeing us this weekend and she'd gotten tickets to the garden show for the two of them.

I got a fresh haircut Saturday afternoon and bought a new shirt that brought out the color in my eyes.

"I've been meaning to call you all week, Andy, and make a date to go swimming, but the days just got away from me," he said.

"Oh, I'd forgotten all about it, to tell you the truth," I lied.

"This week definitely."

"Not good for me. I've got a sales meeting with a distributor in Atlanta."

"Damn. Soon, then."

"I'll be back Wednesday night," I blurted.

Alice and Nora finished the house tour.

"Andy, you must see it," Alice said. "The Wilkinses have the most beautiful things."

If I hadn't known better, I would have thought Alice had a bit of a crush herself. Nora was so self-assured, a take-charge blonde, slightly butch in a female golf pro sort of way. I made it a point to be more conscious of her, notice her mannerisms, memorize one of her offhand remarks. She was bossy, but in a way that was more brisk and efficient than aggressive, as if she'd already considered and rejected all the alternatives to her way of doing things before you had an opportunity to propose them. She must have reminded Alice of her sisters, which explained why she was so immediately comfortable with her.

"Brian, it's time to light the grill. Andy, you go with him."

Aye, aye, sir . . . er, ma'am.

Central Casting would never have selected Brian Wilkins as the catalyst for my downfall. Hollywood's idea of a seducer was everything short, fair, and nearsighted Brian Wilkins was not. That's not to say Brian wasn't attractive. Years earlier, he might have been voted Cutest Boy by his high school graduating class. Best Looking would have been a classmate with a more classic profile, better bone structure, and features that would only improve with time, unlike Brian, whose chipmunk cheeks were thickening even before middle age.

A minor inferno erupted when Brian tossed a match on the charcoal. His hand flew up to my chest and he pushed me back from the flame.

"Someday I'll figure out how much lighter fluid is too much."

I drank a little too much that night, enough that Alice insisted on taking the wheel to drive home. And the more I drank, the less I'd cared that it was obvious our wives might have been dining in another solar system for all the attention we gave them.

"I told you you'd like them," Alice said triumphantly as I rolled into bed. "I knew it."

Brian called the next morning. He was wondering when we might get together for that swim. *Too bad this week didn't look so good. Hey, how about today? This afternoon. It's clear for me. How about you? We can burn off some of that alcohol. Let's make it two o'clock. Give me the directions. I'll find it.*

That's how easy it was. Alice's Sunday was committed to yet another shower—either bridal or, more often those days, baby. Her forced cheeriness at the breakfast table meant, yes, definitely, it was another celebration of the imminent arrival of Joshua, if it's a boy, Sarah, if it's a girl. She was genuinely delighted for Becca or Susan or Shelley, the glowing mothers-to-be, a happiness untainted by envy. Only once did her armor crack, when her friend Carolyn announced that she and her husband had settled on the name John for their son, after his father's father. Sure it was old-fashioned, but they were going to call him Jack. We still have lots of time, I consoled her. We can start trying to get pregnant again, as soon as she was ready. Yes, she agreed, soon, sometime soon. Little did we know that a low sperm count would turn out to be a minor obstacle compared to the events set in motion that perfectly ordinary Sunday afternoon.

I hadn't expected him to be so nervous. He dropped his lock twice, fumbling through the combination. He turned his back to me when he stepped out of his briefs and into his trunks. His shoulders were wide without being impressive. He coughed and bent down to swipe the soles of his bare feet. He finally turned to face me, red in the face and stammering.

"Andy, I'm really sorry about this."

"Sorry about what?" I asked, truly confused.

"I'm a terrible swimmer. I should have told you up front."

"Why didn't you?"

"Because I wanted to come swimming with you."

His forwardness made me self-conscious. I knew then why I had impulsively chosen to bring a pair of baggy gym shorts instead of my usual racing trunks. I was conscious of my naked chest and limbs as we walked to the pool. I took long strides, moving quickly, forcing him to keep pace, anxious for the protective cover of warm, chlorinated water. I chose my lane, dove quickly, and swam away.

He wasn't a bad swimmer; not in my league, but, of course, I was a former state high school champion in the breaststroke, the rare high point in an adolescence distinguished mainly by my ability to achieve new standards of awkwardness. He'd taken the next lane and I passed him many times, coming and going, always averting my eyes and immersing myself in my laps. Half an hour passed. When I pulled myself out of the pool, he was waiting on the deck, his arms wrapped around his knees and his toes inches from my nose. He had huge feet and, before I could censor my thoughts, I wondered if the old wives' tale was true—big hands, big feet, big everything.

"You've got a beautiful stroke," he said. "I could watch you all day."

Barely thirty, Brian Wilkins was progressing on his March to the Sea. He'd started in the tiny market of Rochester, Minnesota, fresh out of school, as associate producer of the ten o'clock news broadcast; he'd made his way south with an unbroken string of triumphs at small stations in the heart of the Midwest. The network had taken notice when he drove our local Greensboro affiliate's eleven o'clock newscast to first place in the ratings in nine short months by dumping the venerable local anchor for a former drum majorette with big tits and a blazing white smile of after-dinner-mint teeth. He knew it was his certain destiny to command network operations in the District of Columbia, finally capping his career in Manhattan as executive producer of a national broadcast.

Brian was self-effacing and falsely humble and always positioned himself so that his rivals and enemies would underestimate him. His work ethic was legendary. His instincts for what sold in the broadcast journalism market were remarkable. The fortress of his personal life was unassailable. His Valkyrie wife excelled at fulfilling the responsibilities of corporate wife and was willing to overlook his lack of interest in conjugal intimacy in exchange for a seat on the rocket launch to the top. They'd already accomplished one daughter, and a little brother or sister was scheduled to be in development in the near future. There was only one slight problem and a potential pitfall Brian Wilkins was determined to avoid. Brian had certain needs that none of his successes could satisfy. And so he chose me as the successor to my predecessors abandoned in Rochester and Springfield, Illinois, and Lincoln, Nebraska, all of us married men with too much at stake to risk indiscretion and potential exposure. Later, when he told me he'd accepted the network's offer for the number-one position at the Pittsburgh affiliate, I asked him how he'd known to pursue me.

"It was easy," he said, his smile almost a sneer. "You're smart. You figure it out."

I'd kept my mind a blank slate when it came to homoerotic attraction and proclivities. I would immediately extinguish the occasional, no, frequent, disturbing thoughts before they had an opportunity to reveal their nature, before they could identify themselves as *attraction* or *desire*. Brian Wilkins must have caught me in that split second before I put the fire out, my eye lingering a second too long before I blushed and looked away.

And so it began.

It was just waiting for the right opportunity, which was not, of course, going to be there and then, on the wet pool deck of my swim club, trunks around the ankles, writhing and moaning in the face of appalled exercise buffs. In the open shower, it was my turn to keep my back turned, feeling like I was back in high school and couldn't trust my defiant penis. We shook hands in the parking lot and I ignored it when he scratched my palm with his middle finger, not yet knowing the secret signals between closeted homosexuals.

"We should get together soon for drinks," he said, making it obvious that he meant alone, not with our wives.

"Give me a call," I said, hoping he couldn't hear the nerves in my voice.

"Didn't you say last night you'd be back Wednesday?"

I told him I had a late-afternoon flight out of Atlanta after my lunch meeting with the distributor. Great, he said, telling me where to meet him that evening.

That night I attacked Alice enthusiastically. Once wasn't enough. Twice didn't satisfy me. Long after midnight, Alice pulled the twisted sheets between her legs and sipped a glass of wine.

"You ought to exercise more often," she said.

A week later, she waited for a reprise. But that night I fell asleep during *60 Minutes*, not to awaken until seven the next morning. Everything had changed in those seven days.

I'd called home from the airport Wednesday afternoon and left a message on the machine, complaining that I'd missed my flight, that it was ridiculous to get routed through Columbus, Ohio, and the next nonstop didn't arrive until after midnight. *Don't wait up. Love you. Miss you.*

I thought his choice of a bar was a little odd. The Tara Lounge at a Holiday Inn on the outskirts of Winston-Salem? His briefcase was in plain view and he'd placed a thick ratings book on the table, evidence of a pure business purpose in the highly unlikely event someone who knew him stumbled upon us in a dark corner in the empty lounge in that tacky backwater. We started with beer and moved quickly to bourbon, straight up. It wasn't long before enough alcohol had flowed to excuse his shins touching mine under the table. I didn't pull my leg away and he pressed lightly, just enough to confirm it was intentional.

"How long have you and Alice been married?" he asked.

"Eight years."

"That's a long time."

"Longer, really. We met in college. Freshmen. Been together thirteen years."

"Hard, isn't it?"

"What?"

He went to the bar for another round, and, when he returned, he kept his legs tucked beneath the seat. I slid my foot across the floor until it nudged his shoe. He put his hands on the table and looked me in the eyes.

"What do you think?"

There was a key, Room 206, between us on the table. I panicked, admitting I'd lied to Alice, told her I'd missed my flight, she might call Nora and find out I was not far from home, meeting him for a beer. He laughed so hard the bartender looked away from the television.

"Are you fucking crazy? Nora thinks I'm in D.C. and won't be back until tomorrow night."

I called Alice at six in the morning, creating some preposterous explanation as to why I'd been forced to wait for a morning flight. *See you tonight. Let's go out to dinner. Your choice. Miss you. Love you.* I was never that careless again.

I learned a few things that night. First, big hands and big feet do not necessarily mean big everything. Just as well. Christ only knows how I would have reacted, what flashbacks would have overtaken me, if he'd unzipped his pants and pulled out a long red snake. As fate would have it, Brian Wilkins was the proud owner of a short brown snail. Second, I learned how my body could respond to a touch I truly desired. And, for the first time, I felt the fissures in the fault line of the life I'd created and the potential of my dry heart to crack and split.

Years of hindsight have taught me it wasn't love I felt for Brian Wilkins. I didn't know better at the time. What else but love could cause me to despair when I didn't hear from him for days, constantly debating the pros and cons of calling to break the silence? What else could explain the physical rush of elation whenever I picked up the phone and heard his voice? Only love could have inflated Brian Wilkins like a Macy's Thanksgiving Day balloon hovering over my every waking moment while shrinking Alice, like her namesake, to a two-dimensional shadow to be accommodated, gently, during the intervals between my secret rendezvous. Yes, hindsight brings wisdom. I know now it wasn't love. It was fear, an absolute, abject fear, that, without him, I'd be back in the box, snapped shut, sealed tight, labeled HUSBAND, and returned special delivery to WIFE.

He tried hard to appear sad the night he told me he'd got the transfer to Pittsburgh. But the sex was bad, hurried, obviously one more chore before departing, like registering a change of address with the post office. We had a last supper together, the four of us, their last weekend in North Carolina. I tried to make eye contact over the table, hoping to pass secret signals, looking for some sign of regret. But Brian was having none of it, never letting the conversation drift from market demographics, advertising revenue streams, and the necessity to adapt to survive against the threat of the cable news networks. I waited a week to call him at his new station. His secretary put me on hold for ten minutes after I gave her my name. Great to hear your voice, he said, sounding distracted and, worse, irritated. He told me he'd stay in touch. I never heard from him again.

The box couldn't hold me for long. It took a while, six months, until one night, alone in a hotel room in Dallas, the King of Unpainted Furniture safely snoring in a suite on a different floor, I called a cab and gave the driver the address of a bathhouse where many hands touched and stroked me before the sun came up.

The urge would lie dormant for weeks, months, only to rear its ugly head when I was stranded in a room in a budget motel, not because the King of Unpainted Furniture scrimped on the expense accounts but because moldy carpets and damp bedspreads were the best the town had to offer. The voices on the television at the foot of the bed sounded as distant as a conversation in a different state. I'd stand in the shower, listening to the eleven o'clock news, hoping the hot water would induce drowsiness and dreams.

Still wide awake, I'd log on to my laptop, find a chat room, and send my room number to aging lonely hearts, down-on-their-luck hustlers, even the occasional hunky college boy with too many hormones charging through his bloodstream. Or I would put on a clean shirt and navigate the rental car through the side streets of the seedy section of a town I didn't know. I'd debate myself—go back, stay here, go back—until a beat-up Honda or Toyota vacated a parking spot a stone's throw from the entrance to the "Buddies" or "Players" or "Side Traxx" in every town or small city with a dealer for Tar Heel Heritage pine furniture. I'd chug the first beer, chase it with a shot of tequila, drain another bottle, not relaxing until the room was in soft focus and I found the nerve to light the cigarette of the man sitting next to me. I'd struggle to make conversation, waiting for an indication of any possible interest. If I found it, I'd rush, growing anxious because the clock was ticking away, desperate to seal the deal, dreading driving back to my motel alone.

There was no turning back, not even when Nora Wilkins called to tell us that Brian had passed away, stricken by a pneumonia from which he never recovered. Nora had left Pittsburgh and was back home in Minnesota. She and Alice made a vague promise to see each other soon, a sentimental gesture appropriate to the moment.

"I don't think she was telling me everything," Alice said later that night. "At first she said yes, when I asked if he went quickly. Then later she said he hadn't been well for a while. I guess we'll never know."

I knew. Immediately. There's only one kind of pneumonia that would strike down a man in his prime. A man who was having sex, lots of it, with other men.

I wandered outside, needing a cigarette, my hand shaking when I tried to strike a match. Jesus, please God, I pleaded, sucking smoke deep into my lungs. Please, please let me be okay and I promise I'll do anything you want.

It was divine retribution for the baby. I deserved whatever I got. I could live with the consequences. Take me, I begged, trying to redeem myself through noble sacrifice. Just let Alice be okay. She doesn't deserve this. Don't punish her for little Jack. She'd be bouncing him on her knee today if it hadn't been for me.

I spoke to God on an hourly basis while I waited for the lab to report my results, promising, pleading, negotiating. And after the test came back negative, no nasty little HIV antibodies to report, the Good Lord must have sat by the phone like a jilted lover, incapable of accepting that my ardent pursuit and seduction could end so suddenly. I'd been ridiculous to worry. Leave it to me to turn the simplest story into a melodrama, infusing Puccini and Verdi into every nursery rhyme, creating a crisis out of every small problem. What the hell had I been so worried about? How many times had I been with him? Five, six at the most? But I'd learned my lesson.

"What do you think I am, some kind of fag?" he'd protested, insulted when I dared to question whether I should slip on a Trojan before I shoved it up his ass.

I'd never be so naïve again.

"I made a memorial contribution for Brian Wilkins today," Alice said a few weeks later over dinner.

I looked down at my plate, unnerved to hear that Brian Wilkins was still lingering in her thoughts.

"Oh yeah?" I asked. "These potatoes are awesome," I declared, trying to steer the conversation in different directions.

"Yeah, I really didn't know where to send it so I made it out to the Horticultural Society. Nora and I volunteered there together. I didn't really know him," she said. "Can I be honest? I didn't really like him."

"Really?" I said, squirming in my chair.

"You seemed to cool toward him at the end, didn't you?"

"Yeah," I said, feeling the tension in my shoulders.

"I don't know. There was something about him," she said. "Full of himself. I think he had a mean streak."

"I bet he could be a prick," I said, thinking back to the afternoon I locked myself in the john at Tar Heel Heritage, the water running full blast, crying my eyes out after I hung up the telephone, knowing I'd just finished my last conversation with the man I was sure that I loved.

"Are you going to finish your potatoes?" I asked, closing and locking the final door on Brian Wilkins.

Season's Greetings from the King of Unpainted Furniture

Everyone is titillated by the prospect of snow. Everyone has an opinion: It's definitely coming. It's not coming because it only happens when it's completely unexpected. Everyone's preparing, stockpiling toilet paper and milk. One school of thought says it would have been welcome two days ago. It would have been the first White Christmas in thirty-five years. Now it will just ruin the rest of the holidays. Another school of thought says better late than never and at least all those gruesome New Year's celebrations will have to be cancelled.

My window is open. It's definitely colder than last night. If it's coming, at least it waited until my sister packed her husband, two sons, and daughter into the SUV and headed south, back to the palm trees and tennis courts of Boca Raton. I finish knotting my tie and lick my palm to flatten my stubborn cowlick. Not so bad, I think. Why have I never seen a picture of myself where I resemble the man I see in the mirror? The camera never lies, they say. Out there, somewhere, my mug shots, full face and profile, are in the public record.

I pass my mother's bedroom on my way downstairs. She stands perfectly still, transfixed, as if stunned by her reflection in the mirror, gripping her pearl necklace, her yellow satin jacket burnished by the white winter sunlight.

My mother, by Vermeer.

She blinks like a startled bird and comes out of her trance. She seems puzzled, as if she doesn't recognize the brushes and combs and jewelry box on her dressing table. Feeling like an intruder, I go downstairs and wait for her to join me.

She disapproves when she sees me with a vodka and soda in hand. She usually doesn't comment on my drinking since she comes from the generation of women who nurse a single glass of wine or a very weak cocktail, if they partake at all, while their men drink themselves into oblivion. But this afternoon she reminds me the roads could be very hazardous in a few hours. I laugh and tell her it's bone dry out there and not a cloud in the sky. Nonetheless, she wins. I take one last long sip and pour it in the sink.

My mother and I are going on a date. I return from the kitchen, expecting to find her in the foyer, all buttoned up and pocketbook in hand. She isn't there. She's in the parlor, resting against the arm of the sofa, studying the Christmas tree, touching one of the glass balls, smiling at a memory of a long-ago holiday. Each and every ornament has a history. Only she knows all of them. After she's gone, they'll just be anonymous trinkets tucked in tissue paper.

I tell myself I'm overreacting, surrendering to my predilection for crepe hanging. It's probably just Christmas. She's just pushed herself too hard. My sister spent the past four days cataloguing every burner left lit, every door left open, every toilet unflushed, every pair of eyeglasses misplaced. She inventoried my mother's medicine cabinet and recorded the labels of every prescription bottle to look up in the *Physicians' Desk Reference*. If she doesn't understand the entry, she'll consult her gynecologist. My mother denies that anything is wrong. Regina has been insistent, a battering ram. There has to be a reasonable explanation for the pallor of our mother's skin and the dark pouches below her eyes. She's going to get to the bottom of this. There's nothing to get to the bottom of, I told her. She's getting older. It's what happens to people when they get older.

"Bullshit. She's not even sixty. My doubles partner is seventy-five years old and has a better backhand than me!"

Fucking Christmas. Thank God it's over for another year.

Hard to believe that, once upon a time, I started counting the days until December 25 on the October afternoon I came home from school to find the Spiegel catalogue had arrived in the morning mail. I'd sit at the breakfast table for weeks, thumbing through the well-worn pages, changing my mind two or three times a day, never settling on a present for Gina until my mother announced it was time to send in the order.

It didn't matter that by New Year's Eve, parts would be broken, pieces missing, instructions lost, pages ripped, because I knew that she loved every doll or game or book I ever gave her. She couldn't help that she was clumsy, awkward, and forgetful. Just the opposite of me, who carefully preserved the DC and Marvel superhero comic books she gave me every Christmas, reading each one carefully, no folds or tears, then slipping it in a plastic envelope for posterity.

"Do you like them? Do you really?" she asked every year, needing to be reassured she'd made all the right choices despite having tagged along on my weekly visits to Woolworth from January through November, watching me cherry-pick the same titles from the comic book rack.

Damn, we loved Christmas back then. Neither of us was ever disappointed after all the build up and anticipation. And Christmas night was the best—no Midnight Mass to attend, flannel pajamas instead of my bow tie and her tights, no limit on the number of Christmas cookies we could stuff in our mouths. Mama let us stay up until we were exhausted and longed for our beds, both of us already counting the days until Christmas rolled around again.

Her own kids could barely summon enough enthusiasm to crawl out of bed on Christmas morning. Michael, the oldest, had to be threatened with bodily injury to tear himself away from messaging his friends long enough to come to the table. Jennifer and Dustin rolled their eyes and sighed at every comment or question, mimicking the bratty "tween" queens of the Disney Channel. The only real pleasure the three of them seemed to get was taunting their father, a combustible sort like our old man, but without his redeeming qualities of fidelity and reliability. I suspect the rock he presented my sister on Christmas Eve is reparation for his latest flight attendant or Pilates instructor. Family honor says I should hate him, but he's a nice guy despite his philandering and occasional outbursts, unimpressed by his own Olympian status, someone to watch hoops with, arguing over who's the best point guard in the ACC while we ignore Regina's battle with her surly brood over the ridiculous "festive" holiday sweaters she bought them to wear for the video she wants of our happy Christmas dinner.

"These kids are too goddamn spoiled to appreciate anything," she complained last night. "Do you remember how you'd light up every time I gave you a pile of damn comic books on Christmas morning?"

Yeah, I do. What shocked me was that she did too.

The tension headache I'd been nursing for days started to fade as their SUV backed down the driveway. We got through the holiday, but only after endless hours of vigilance, waiting for Regina to bite through the tip of her tongue and violate the unspoken Nocera Family Agreement to rewrite history, erase the past, and expunge any trace of a major character from the story: *Have you heard from Alice? Alice? Alice who? I don't know any Alice. You must have me confused with somebody else.* Wonder of wonders, the moment never arrived, thwarted, no doubt, by my mother's steely gaze each time she saw temptation flicker across her daughter's face. *I don't know what you were so worried about. I told you I wouldn't bring it up,* I overheard Regina say as the SUV pulled away.

My mother takes a deep breath, fortifying herself for the afternoon ahead. I ask her if she really wants to go. Of course, she says. She's been looking forward to this all week.

"This" is the farewell reception for the bishop of the Diocese of Charlotte. On January first, he's being retired to a community for elderly prelates in New Mexico.

Maybe the forecasters are right. In just the few minutes since we've come downstairs, the sun has disappeared and the daylight has turned dishwater gray. The noisy winter birds have gone into hiding. The neighbor's cat streaks across the driveway, headed home to wait out the storm. My mother blesses herself as I back the car into the street.

I expect that she, like my sister and me, is desperately seeking a simple explanation for all the many ways her body is betraying her. She hopes all she needs is one good night's uninterrupted sleep. Maybe all it will take is the right combination of vitamin pills. Maybe her eyeglass prescription needs to be adjusted. Maybe, just maybe, tomorrow she'll spring out of bed, those heavy sacks of rocks she's been carrying for too long now tossed aside somewhere along the highway of her dreams, and she'll greet all the familiar little aches in her joints like old friends. My sister insinuates my "situation" is the reason our mother has taken up smoking after twenty years of abstinence. That's easier than accepting the fact that she suspects it can't hurt her anymore.

My mother and I drive in silence. We have to make a quick

stop at the cemetery. I insist she stay in the car, that it's too cold up on this bleak hill. I don't want her to see that the grave wreath, locked in the trunk over a week ago, has wilted. My mother's name and date of birth are already etched into the granite. The old man is biding his time, waiting for her to join him. The sky seems to brighten as we arrive at the bishop's residence. Maybe the forecasters are wrong.

The door opens before we have a chance to ring. Only a bishop can get away with having an ancient black man in *Gone with the Wind* livery greet his guests. He welcomes my mother as if she were visiting royalty. Merry Christmas, Nathaniel, she says, was Santa good to you? Oh, the best, Miz Nocera, he chuckles, the very best. I'm dumbfounded she knows his name and that she is a familiar face here. I'm shocked by what I don't know about her. We both have our secret lives, my mother and I.

Nudging my way to the punch bowl, I speculate there wouldn't be a wealthy Catholic left in all of North Carolina if a bomb fell on this place . . . and then it hits me, hard.

Good God, why hadn't I thought of it before I let a stranger spirit away our coats to the hidden recesses of this too-big house? A quick escape is out of the question now. Why hadn't *she* thought of it before accepting my offer to drive her here? Maybe she had. I hate being suspicious of my mother. No, obviously it hadn't occurred to her, otherwise she would have told me to stay home and relax in front of the tree and she would get a ride to the party with one of her cronies. She couldn't have an agenda. This wasn't a Saturday night dinner at the club where she could ever so genteelly force the truly disgusted or the downright amused or the blissfully unaware to acknowledge my ongoing existence. This was J. Curtis Mc-Dermott, Jr., the King of Unpainted Furniture himself. The largest donor to Catholic Charities in the entire state, certain to have received the coveted invitation, probably the first name on the list.

Two weeks ago, thumbing through the Christmas cards she'd received, I'd opened a reproduction of a Bellini Madonna and Child and was confronted by the printed salutation.

Season's Greetings from the King of Unpainted Furniture

Curtis maintained two Christmas mailing lists, one for the recipients of Italian Masters religious scenarios, the other for those who were sent the Currier and Ives seculars. After all, the King explained, Tar Heel Heritage, the world's largest manu-facturer of unfinished pine furniture, can't offend its Jewish friends, but we gotta remember that most of our Christian friends think, well, if it weren't for Christ there wouldn't be any goddamn *Christ*mas anyway. Curtis's staff could effort-lessly spit out catalogues, spreadsheets, and quarterly state-ments; certainly they should have been competent enough to hit the DELETE button and purge my mother's name from the Italian Masters mailing list.

This benign little outing is turning into a full-blown exercise in tactical maneuvers. The crowd looks harmless enough. A young man and woman, their first Christmas together as a mar-ried couple, giggle and spit hors d'oeuvres into paper napkins. An old man with hairy ears corners them to gloat over the American Civil Liberties Union's failure to persuade the Meck-lenburg County emergency judge to order the removal of the crèche from the entrance to City Hall. They feign interest, car-ing less about civil liberties and the Baby Jesus than in finding a trash can. A spinsterish woman in a Fair Isle sweater folds her arms and pretends to survey the cookie table, trying to make eye contact so she can strike up a conversation with me. A tired little girl in a velvet party dress skates across the hardwood floor on the soles of her patent leather Mary Janes. Braking with her toe, she looks up and asks me my name. Andy, I say, and ask hers to reinforce her lessons on good manners. Brandy, she answers. She must be the aftermath of an evening of one-hundred-proof induced lust, her name a commemoration, like winter babies named April or June. Our names rhyme, I say, making conversation. Whatever, she snorts, tossing her head.

Someone is tickling the ivories in the next room. The piano player runs through a few scales to loosen up his fingers. I recognize the opening bars of a Broadway show tune.

"You coax the blues right out of the horn . . ."

His booming voice crushes the weak harmonizing of the members of the chorus.

". . . MAME!"

J. Curtis McDermott. Having located ground zero, I can avoid him, escaping to the kitchen. A martinet caterer is bullying a platoon of exasperated college kids who persevere because she pays fifty bucks a night under the table. No one is permitted to leave the room without her approving the arrangement of toast points and smoked salmon on their serving trays. She dresses to intimidate, with short-cropped hair and a Chanel skirt under her kitchen smock. She's oblivious to the fact that people take one look and assume she's a lesbian, a creature to be pitied because she can't get a man.

An effeminate boy sweeps into the kitchen, tossing his empty tray aside: "It's snowing! It's really snowing!"

The college kids ignore their boss and rush to the kitchen windows. The pots stop rattling and voices are still. The windows are wide and high and someone hollers that everyone can see if we just squeeze a little closer and y'all in the back stand on tippytoes. A high girlish voice, probably the sissy boy's, starts singing "White Christmas" and everyone joins in.

The snow doesn't look like the big fluffy Hollywood downpour at the end of the movie. These snowflakes are aggressive. An advance attack secures the front line, melting on impact with the still-warm ground. The swift, hardy infantry assaults the rhododendrons and azaleas and chokes the lawn. A strong wind rattles the pine trees and slaps the power line, heralding the arrival of the cavalry. The final victory is swift, eerily quiet. The powder is accumulating.

Merriment dissolves into nervous apprehension as the snow starts to drift. Bing Crosby had snow tires; no one in North Carolina does. The caterer snaps at her crew, telling them to circulate, fast, before everyone deserts the party. She wants them to push the paté on melba.

I see one of the servers shooting her the finger behind her back. Caught red-handed, he gives me a bashful shrug. He's a tall, lanky boy, probably a track and field star, a Country Day School type. I wink to let him know I approve. She deserves worse than the finger. The track star offers me a piece of bruschetta. We're conspirators now. "Super cunt," he whispers, "what a lezzie."

Curtis and I spot each other at exactly the same time. He's slipped into the kitchen to be incognito since it's a dry party. He sees me when he looks up from the silver pocket flask tipped at his lips. I'm smiling at the obscenities the teenager is whispering in my ear. He couldn't have caught me at a worse moment. It's not the booze flushing his cheeks. His hatred of me has not diminished one bit in the six months since our last encounter.

Life is nothing more than a succession of *what-ifs?*

What if I had had more than ten bucks in my wallet when it came time to post the bond?

What if, having finally summoned up the courage to call Alice, fate hadn't intervened in the form of a malfunctioning automated teller that swallowed her one and only debit card?

What if I had thought to tell her the holding cell wasn't like the snake pits you saw in the movies, but was a spotlessly clean little corner I had all to myself, no bruising inmates to corrupt and abuse me?

What if her judgment hadn't been so clouded by worrying about my safety that she would have thought twice before calling her father and telling him she needed three hundred dollars, now?

He would have killed me if Alice hadn't jumped on his back, trying to pry his hands from my throat. He came close enough as it was. Those huge fists crushed my vocal cords and left me hoarse for weeks. But that was minor compared to the damage he wreaked on his own flesh and blood. She cracked her skull against the hard tile floor when he threw her off his back. The police arrived, summoned by a report of a domestic disturbance, the second time in twenty-four hours I found myself confronted by a badge and a blue shirt. Fire rescue was close behind.

Curtis insisted I'd tried to kill her. Alice, groggy from the concussion, refused to press charges. There's no charges to press, she insisted in her soft drawl. Daddy's wrong, she said, I fell. I remember the way "fell" tripped off her tongue, sounding more like "fill" or "feel." Most likely the effects of the concussion.

Her first instinct was to protect me. Given time, she might have learned to accept "it," "this." Someday, not right now, but maybe in the not-too-distant future, soon, once things got back to normal, we could come to *an understanding* over pinot grigio and Orange Milano cookies. She read about things like this in *Cosmopolitan*; she'd seen something like this in a movie of the week. It wasn't so unusual, was it? You don't pick up and leave if someone is paralyzed from the waist down in a car accident, do you? Was this really all that different?

Yes.

I knew it and Curtis knew it. It took Curtis to do what neither she nor I could: cut me out of her life.

Another man slips into the kitchen and accosts the King, wanting a sip from his flask. I take the opportunity to escape. Curtis reaches out to grab my arm. I manage to slip away from his fingers. He hates me not for betraying his daughter, but for betraying him.

I slither into the crush of bodies around the bishop, who's crouched over the keyboard, crooning "What I Did for Love." His dry voice resists the emotion he's straining to squeeze into every note. A fey young acolyte, most likely a seminarian, stands at attention, his long fingers ready to flip the sheet music at just the right moment. He seems to be the only person in the room who hears music in that voice. It's obvious to everyone in the room that His Excellency is sending a valentine to the boy. No one dares to wince, but one or two of the more irreverent stifle the clearing of throats, their amusement peeping from behind closed fists.

His Excellency is retiring at fifty-nine years of age. He doesn't just have the occasional binge anymore. He keeps himself permanently lubricated, which makes it easy for his predilections to slip into open view. The Vatican tolerated it longer than it should have in deference to his remarkable talent for fund-raising. Next week, he's being cashiered to an isolated outpost where he can drink himself to death in peace. The diocese is honoring him today with fruit punch and hors d'oeuvres and the announcement that the annual golf tournament for Catholic Charities will bear his name.

Curtis is not a man given to intrigue and stealth. His course of action is the full-frontal attack. But the bishop's audience is between us, making it impossible to make a direct charge. He has to maneuver through the bodies at the fringe to get to me. As he inches closer, I creep farther away. He's a little tipsy. Not a good sign. Curtis usually carefully measures his intake, believing drunkenness to be a liability. But the sight of me caused him to throw a little fuel from the flask on the fire of the rage that's been simmering on low heat since last summer.

His Excellency saves me, calling out to Curtis, insisting on a duet. The King isn't actually drunk, he's still in control and he gives the bishop a bear hug to compensate just in case it's apparent to anyone that he wants to tell the old fag to fuck off. Then he realizes he should have. He's mortified when he recognizes the first few measures of the song His Excellency has chosen. I take advantage of his temporary paralysis to slip away as the bishop sings the first few lines of "People Will Say We're in Love."

It's cold and quiet on the sun porch. The squealing radial tires, the sound of cars sliding on ice and snow, tell me I need to find my mother. I've neglected her. Actually, I've forgotten all about her. She is probably looking for me right now. The snow is the perfect excuse to get out of here. The nervous headlights of a caravan of fleeing automobiles creep down the drive. There's a loud outburst inside. Genuine laughter, not just polite mirth. I can imagine what's happened. The King has salvaged his dignity with a self-deprecating joke. But it doesn't douse his fury at being humiliated by His Excellency. He needs revenge more than ever. He's going to hunt me down.

Maybe I can wander off into one of the snowdrifts, disappear forever. At least until the big thaw which, this being North Carolina, will be the day after tomorrow at the latest. No. No more hiding. Let him find me. I deserve it anyway. The King has every reason to hate me. He's never liked me, not really. He'd suspected there was something slippery, untrustworthy, about me on first meeting, when I blew cigarette smoke in his face over the brunch table. But he'd let himself believe in the charade, made me his partner, the heir apparent, took me into his confidence and assumed I'd taken him into mine.

He thinks I'm malicious, venal, that I duped him. And now, his duet with the bishop over, he's found me. He's going to extract his pound of flesh. My resolve cracks and, coward that I am, I crash through the door and run into the snow. He follows like I knew he would. If I can only stay an arm's length ahead, at least until I can lock myself in the car and huddle in a corner until he is tired of banging his fists on the window.

Snow is a great equalizer and all the expensive sedans and coupes are fluffy marshmallows, one indistinguishable from the next. I slip and slide, swiping every hood, looking for metallic blue, until I stumble upon my mother's car. I hear him panting, he's that close. My fingers, trembling, drop the keys. They disappear, swallowed by the snow.

He intends to finish what he started months ago. He grabs me by the throat. I don't try to defend myself. His huge hands take him to the brink of breaking my neck, then he pushes me away. What makes him stop? He sees something in my face that won't let him smash me in a pique of anger. There's something he wants to say to me but my mother calls his name before he can speak.

The sight of this tiny frail woman high stepping through the drifts summons his innate chivalry. He wades toward her and wraps his arm around her shoulder, guiding her to the car. I hear them exchange pleasantries and polite inquiries about health and holidays. They don't acknowledge anything out of the ordinary though I'm gasping for breath. I find the keys while they talk about the snow. Curtis kisses my mother on the cheek after he helps her into the car. I close the door behind her and, by instinct, offer my hand to thank him for helping her. I break down when he accepts it.

My mother stares down at her hands to give me a little privacy. My father-in-law holds me upright, at arm's length, not knowing what to do with me, afraid I might collapse in the snow. It's awkward, standing face-to-face with him, my eyes red and snot dripping from my nose. He seems reticent, almost shy, his meat-and-potatoes mug more Ronnie Reagan than John Wayne. Maybe we're going to have a *moment*, a tipping point, a reconciliation.

"I knew there was something wrong with you the first time I laid eyes on you," he says, almost sympathetically, as if I were born with a birth defect for which the March of Dimes will never find a cure.

"I'm sorry," I say, though he's not the one who's owed an apology.

"You should be," he says, wiping his palms on his jacket as he releases me.

Let it go, I tell myself as I walk away. He stands, watching, as I open the car door and slip behind the wheel. I turn the key in the ignition and press the accelerator. The tires spin on the ice, going nowhere, proving once and for all my total incompetence. I'm completely emasculated by a few inches of snow.

"Put it in neutral and let it drift to a dry spot," Curtis shouts, his loud voice barely muffled by the windshield.

The King of Unpainted Furniture plants his size sixteen wingtips and grabs the hood with his powerful hands, drawing a deep breath as he rocks the car out of the ice rut. He stands in triumph, fists on his hips, as the tires gain traction on the gravel.

"I'll say it was an accident if you run over the son of a

bitch," my mother says, smiling sweetly as she waves good-bye.

"It's not worth it, Ma," I say, just wanting this day to be over.

"Ah, but think how good it would feel," she says. "I love this song. Turn up the volume," she insists, as the DJ on the AM band plays Anne Murray's "Snowbird" in honor of the blizzard.

Resolutions

It's a new year.

Time for auspicious beginnings.

Time to kick start my new life.

Ready, steady, go.

"Look, I really don't want to discourage you, but I'm not sure the timing's quite right," Matt says.

"What do you mean? It's perfect timing. It's January. When do you want me to make my resolutions? Sometime in the middle of March? Obviously you're not big on New Year's resolutions," I say.

"Quite the contrary," he laughs. "I took my last puff on a cigarette at eleven fifty-nine, December thirty-first. I broke my record this year. I was a nonsmoker for four and a half days."

"Maybe you're weak," I say, perfectly comfortable sounding smug and condescending.

"You're right. I probably am. Maybe you can do better. Go ahead. Tell me your resolutions."

I haven't come as prepared as I thought. But then how do I reduce *stop doing what I'm doing and start doing something different* to a laundry list of self-improvements?

"Well," I say, "first, I'm going to start getting more sleep."

"That sounds like a good idea."

"I think I'll look for an apartment," I announce, a sudden inspiration that catches me off guard.

"Are you ready for that?"

"For God's sake, I'm a lot closer to forty than thirty. I think I should be ready for that."

"How long has it been since you've lived alone?"

The answer's easy, but he doesn't need to know it. Never.

"Well, uh, I guess it's too many years to count."

"Look, Andy, I'm just concerned about setting unrealistic goals you can't achieve simply because the calendar's flipped to another year."

"You're a priest of little faith."

"No. Just a therapist with a lot of experience. By the way, you are taking your medications, aren't you?"

"Religiously."

"Secularly will suffice. So, getting back to your resolutions. What would you like to change?"

"Who says I want to change?"

"Do you want to continue on the same?"

"No."

"So what do you want to change first?"

Everything? I ask myself.

"Well, I don't want to be here."

"Not an option. But, just as a hypothetical, where do you want to be?"

"Home," I say, not hesitating.

"You just said you wanted to look for an apartment."

"No. *Home.* My home."

"You mean with Alice?"

"Yes."

"What would you do differently if you could go home to Alice tonight?"

Everything. I would be devoted, attentive, thoughtful, gentle, caring, committed, selfless, kind, affectionate . . . romantic . . . passionate . . . faithful. Am I being overly sentimental, insincere? Is that why I can't bring myself to actually utter this declaration in actual spoken words? Am I afraid that my trusted counselor will call my bluff?

"Were you happy living in Alice's house?"

"*Our* house," I correct him.

"Sorry."

"Sure, I was happy. I wasn't *unhappy*. Remember, I didn't leave. It wasn't my choice."

"Wasn't it?"

Of course not. The Green Goblin put a gun to my head and, finger on the trigger, marched me out of the house. He threatened to splatter my brains across the tile walls of that damn rest stop if I didn't drop to my knees and take that stranger's huge cock in my mouth. The King of Unpainted Furniture had set me up, paid the goddamn gremlin for the hit job, and, mission accomplished, booted me out on my ass. I had nothing to do with it.

"Do you think Alice was happy?"

"Yes."

"Why do you think that?"

"She never said she was unhappy."

"Has she tried to contact you?"

"She can't."

"Why not?"

"Curtis won't let her."

"How could he stop her?"

God, this priest can be obtuse. Curtis keeps the Green Goblin on retainer, a hired gun, muscle to enforce his will. Alice has been kidnapped, held against her will, chained in the basement, bound and gagged, threatened with starvation and dehydration if she even entertains the thought of attempting to contact me.

"You don't understand," I say.

"Do you?"

Maybe I don't want to. Maybe I'm not ready to accept the possibility that Alice, my wife, doesn't want to see or hear from me, not now, not just yet, maybe not ever.

"Have you considered the possibility she's trying to move on?" he asks.

Move on, go forward, proceed, progress, advance . . .

Why not . . . go back, retreat?

No, no way, that sounds too much like a military maneuver in the face of defeat.

How about . . . repatriate?

Yes! Repatriate, reclaim, restore, rebuild.

Has he considered the possibility that she's just called a time-out to consider her negotiating strategy, to finesse the conditions of the truce and draft the terms of the treaty?

I'll sign it. Unconditional surrender. I'll be the best goddamn fucking husband in history. As devoted as Winston to his Clementine, Ronnie to his Nancy, Edward to his Wallis.

One more chance. That's all I'm asking for, Alice. I'll be perfect, just wait and see.

"I would imagine she needs some distance to move on and she's trying to help you do the same."

"Isn't that your fucking job?" I say, sounding more hostile than I feel, suspecting he's placating me, sugarcoating the obvious fact that my wife hates me by deceiving me into thinking that her motives are altruistic, Saint Alice of the Little Flowers. Not that I need her help, or his for that matter, to *move on*. A raging success, a whopping triumph, a touchdown, a home run, no, a *grand slam* home run—how should I describe my remarkable achievements in the arts and sciences of relationships as I've scoured the lower forty-eight of Our Great Nation for Shelton/Murray over the past few months?

DATELINE: BOSTON, MASSACHUSETTS.
He takes me by the hand and leads me to a king-sized mattress and box spring. Unfolded laundry is tossed everywhere, underwear on stacks of yellowing newspaper, unpaired socks in open dresser drawers. His desktop is cluttered with broken pencils, twisted paper clips, dry felt tips of every imaginable hue, junk mail circulars, cheap plastic pens chewed nearly beyond recognition, invitations for credit cards with 6% interest and forgotten utility bills. Sneakers, wingtips, loafers, sandals—all creased by sweat and worn at the heel—collect dust at the foot of the bed. The nightstand's well stocked with a supply of lubricants and poppers and a pile of loose condoms he scooped up by the handful on his way out of the baths. The sheets are stained by his old enthusiasms. He makes love like he's starved, as if it's his first time, or his last.
Then he cums and shuts down in a flash.
"Should I leave?" I ask.
"Yeah," he says, a mocking smile on his lips, "I'm a real bitch in the morning."
I break a shoelace, racing against the stopwatch.
"Got everything?" he asks. "Wallet? Gloves?"
"Yeah."
"Good."
Meaning get out.
"I have no idea where I am."
"Just ask the doorman to turn on the cab light. You'll be back at your hotel in fifteen minutes."
And then I'm out on the street, shivering in the cold New England night, waiting for a taxi that never comes.

DATELINE: CHICAGO, ILLINOIS
The bar is packed, shoulder to shoulder, but the bodies miraculously part, allowing him to rocket by, swept along by the winds whistling off the whitecaps of Lake Michigan. Just as he's

about to disappear into the sea of flannel and black lambswool, he snaps to attention. He's picked up a scent. He grabs my elbow, peers into my face and says "hey." "Hey," I say back. He does a Popeye two step, mimicking my deep voice: "Hey."

"I can't believe this," he laughs. "You're too young for me."

We determine that I am sixteen, almost seventeen, years older than him.

"See," he says. "You're way too young for me."

"Are you wooing me, Rocket Boy?" I ask.

"Do you want to be wooed?"

More than he can ever know, for as long as he's been on this earth.

Four, five, is it six?, beers later, he tells me what he is seeking. Someone he enjoys being around, someone sweet and sincere. Sweet and sincere . . . Here! I know he's been waiting for me. Why don't I wrap him in my arms, squeeze the air out of him, fold him in a neat square, tuck him in my pocket, and carry him away?

Our romance ends as abruptly as it started. He announces he has to work in the morning. It's late. The alarm will go off soon enough. It's only nine o'clock, I protest. I need a lot of sleep, he says. I walk him to his bus stop, saying nothing as he climbs the steps and drops his coins. I see his paw clearing a circle on the frosty window. He presses his face against the glass, searching me out. I step back so he can't see me. The bus rumbles down the street, stealing a piece of me I can never retrieve. The exhaust pipe spits a black chunk of ice at me. It splatters on the street, missing my feet.

DATELINE: SAINT LOUIS, MISSOURI

He opens his eyes and snuggles against me, getting as close as he possibly can. He's purring, as coy as an irresistible and yielding French sex kitten. But cooing and mewing can't eroticize his prissy turned-up nose and thin lips and the pinched squint that

*makes him look as if he's sniffing a perpetual fart. It's embar-
rassing, this performance, like being forced to watch a middle-
aged maiden aunt do a striptease.*

*"Good morning, sunshine," he gurgles, his pale eyelashes
crusted with sleep.*

*He goes down on me, sucking like a Hoover, trying to get me
hard one last time.*

*"Mmmmm," he says, straddling my hips, his pencil stub of a
cock at full attention. His little titties jiggle on his soft pink chest,
reminding me of the piglet in Winnie-the-Pooh.*

"In the mood to get fucked?" I ask.

"Always," he murmurs.

Good. I want to drop this load quickly and get it over with.

*". . . but it's quarter to eight and I need to shower," he snaps
as he jumps off the bed, leaving Little Andy at full salute and
pointing at the ceiling.*

*What I'd give to wring his scrawny neck, wipe that smug lit-
tle smirk off his face, shove him through the window, see him
splatter on the sidewalk twenty-six floors below.*

"She's not coming back, Andy, and you know it."

"I know that. She hates me."

"I doubt that. But you've made it impossible. You realize it,
don't you."

"I made a mistake."

"You think it's as simple as that? You made a mistake? One
mistake? Which of the many was the fatal one?"

The one where I let her fall in love with me.

The one where I believed her love would save me.

Goddamn. Son of a bitch. Motherfuck.

The damn priest's got me crying.

Not really crying. More like "a little misty," red-eyed, maybe
a little tight in the throat. Not sobbing, not snot-nosed and

dripping. I do *not* need a tissue from the fucking box he's shoved in my face.

"You know, Andy, it's not a sin to be lonely."

"Who says I'm lonely? I knew we'd get to sin eventually," I say, trying to inject a little levity into this pathetic scene, anything to avoid to the bleak future I see in the crystal ball.

"Well then, it's not a sign of weakness."

"I suppose I better get used to being alone."

"Why?"

I snort, not believing I'm paying someone who is stupid enough to ask this question.

"You *can* have another relationship," he says.

"I'll just wait for Prince Charming to arrive and sweep me off my feet."

"Doesn't work that way."

I can't believe I'm getting advice for the lovelorn from Father Celibacy.

"Let's try one more resolution," he suggests.

"I'm all ears."

"We agree that these sexual encounters leave you feeling demoralized."

"No. You tell me that. I don't agree. Why do you insist on keep moralizing about it? It's just sex."

"That's exactly my point. It's just sex and you're looking for love. Or at least a little emotional intimacy. What you used to have with Alice."

"Sex. Love. What's the fucking difference?" I say, exasperated, aware that I'm making no sense.

"I'm surprised that you, of all people, would make that comment."

"What's that supposed to mean?"

"Well, your marriage, for one thing."

I start to protest, then surrender, unable to refute his professional observation.

"Not that they have to be mutually exclusive," he says.

"Yeah, well, good luck finding true love and happiness out there. Tell me how it goes," I snort.

He shrugs, conceding for once, he's not speaking from any vast experience of affairs of the heart.

"Well, I'll have to take your word for it. See you next week."

The Great DiMaggio

It's the second week of February. Pitchers and catchers have reported to Florida and Arizona. Position players are due in camp next week. The rituals of spring have begun. It's been a successful off-season for our Braves. The states of the old Confederacy are galvanized; Dixie will rise again. The wily general manager has won the lottery, signing the hottest bat on the free-agent market. He's completed a spectacular trade for a top-of-the-rotation pitcher and patched the leaks in the bullpen. *Sporting News* is predicting Atlanta will take the division and league championships, but go down in six to the reviled Yankees in the Series. What do those idiots know?

USA Today is reporting ice storms in the Plains and blizzard conditions in the Northeast. Even the Carolinas and Georgia are suffering through the deep freeze. But it's sunny and balmy in West Palm, perfect conditions, seventy-four degrees and no wind to speak of. It's too nice a day to waste kissing the ass of another leather-faced broad with flammable hair, pretending to be interested in increasing her sales volume per square foot by maximizing the display space for hideous porcelain figurines with ticket prices that could feed a family of four for a week.

Air traffic is snarled throughout the eastern half of the country and it's entirely plausible when I call to cancel the appointment, using the excuse that my flight's been cancelled, leaving me stranded in deepest, darkest Indiana. Yes, I'm disappointed too, I lie, remote control in hand, muting the volume on the television in my hotel room a half mile away. Let's e-mail tomorrow and reschedule next week. I decide to go for the extra point and call my sister. I've promised to spend tonight in her guest room in Boca Raton. I don't control the airlines, I tell her, there's nothing I can do about the weather. Do you really think I want to spend another night in Terra Haute? I check in with my mother, spreading the little white lie. She says she's not feeling any better. She can't seem to shake whatever it is that's got her down. She's lost more weight, she's exhausted, and the swelling has spread to her face. She has an appointment with her doctor next week. I'm sure it's nothing, I say. You've got the winter blues. Cabin fever. Just wait a few weeks until we're standing at the nursery, picking out annuals. You'll feel like a million bucks by then, I promise, still refusing to believe she's suffering from anything that can't be cured by a good multivitamin. Nothing bad seems possible on a beautiful day like today. Clearwater, the Gulf Coast, is only a few hours away. If I leave now I'll be there by happy hour.

Come on, Andy, try, Matt prodded last week, skeptical of my insistence of being unable to summon up even a single affectionate gesture by my father.

I arrive on the west coast of Florida at the peak of the afternoon rush hour. Urban growth has outpaced the ability of civil engineers and city planners to accommodate the army of refugees from the industrial wastelands up north. Traffic snarls along the new Tampa/St. Pete causeway, hundreds of SUVs and four-door sedans headed for Red Lobster and Hooters, Midas Mufflers and Walgreens. Clearwater's now just another Columbus, Ohio, or Arvada, Colorado, with palm trees growing in the traffic islands. But this town was probably never the place it has become in my memory. I remember the beach being wider, the sand whiter, the gulf warmer. Orange trees probably never lined the sidewalks, and that neon-lit Tastee Freez that glowed at night, where every gigantic swirl cone was dipped in chocolate sauce and sprinkled with jimmies, must have been a figment of my imagination. What made me think I'd find our pink and green L-shaped motel, the one with the huge pool that sparkled in the sunlight, where the old man and I competed to see who could make the biggest splash cannonballing off the diving board?

I go upscale—what the hell, it's only money—and check into a pricey "beach resort" with an ocean view. I flop on the bed, crack open a beer from the minibar, and scan the sports page of the local paper. Not a whole lot of news to report. The reigning MVP has arrived in camp five days early and twenty pounds lighter. The ace of the staff threw a bull-pen session this morning. I'll be at the retail furnishings expo in California by the time the first pitch is thrown at home field in Clearwater. In the morning I'll try to find that diner where the waitresses wear player jerseys and they call hot dogs Phillie Phrankfurters on the menu. There must be one happy memory that hasn't been bulldozed and redeveloped.

At least I'll be able to report back at Therapy Central I made the effort.

"All that boy wants is to be with you. Why can't you give him that?"

My mother's voice had a hard edge, bordering on confrontational. She was frustrated, angry, torn between divided loyalties, constantly running interference between the men in her life.

Didn't you promise him you'd take him for ice cream?
Weren't you going to let him help you paint the garage door?
I thought you said he could hold the ladder.
Would it hurt you to try to be enthusiastic when he wants to tell you something?
Can't you try to be a little patient?

She hadn't planned on spending my entire childhood playing umpire, but there she was once again, standing behind home plate, calling balls when my father's sure he's throwing strikes, awarding first base to her little boy.

"Why did you tell him you were going to take him to the movies if you were planning to play golf this afternoon?"

There was defeat and submission in my father's footsteps as he climbed the stairs. I turned my face to the wall when he opened the door. The mattress sank under his weight and he sighed, not knowing what to say. He reached over and patted my hip.

"Come on, come on," he said, his voice registering somewhere between irritation and resignation. "You're getting too old to cry. Come on, come on," he said, tugging gently at my shoulder. "I'm sorry. I'm really sorry."

I knew this was more than a half-baked act of contrition to get my mother off his back. This was the real thing. His deep voice rumbled and he spoke softly. He didn't say he was sorry often and he didn't want anyone to hear him, not even me. I knew I could get away with anything at that moment, even throwing my arms around his neck without him pushing me away.

Then he bounced me on the mattress and told me to put on my shoes. It's any movie I want to see. Just me and him. Gina's not invited and this time my father, who always surrendered whenever his little girl sulked or threatened to turn on the tears, was resolute, knowing it was less dangerous to disappoint his daughter than to upset his wife. I knew the old man didn't want to squirm through some stupid Disney cartoon and would agree to any horror movie I chose, the bloodier the better. My mother would lay into him good when I woke up screaming with nightmares. After the movie, we went for hamburgers and fries and I didn't even care when he chewed with his mouth open. And, that night, I went to sleep happy, believing every day was going to be like today, only to be crushed and defeated when he ignored me at breakfast in the morning.

I don't recall exactly when I began my guerilla campaign. My first acts of rebellion were benign enough, like leaving the new catcher's mitt out in the rain, then "losing" its replacement two days later. He assumed it was just carelessness, not yet recognizing outright defiance, and he hollered until he was red in the face. My efforts to capture his attention never failed to provoke paternal eruptions that fueled my courage and pushed me a little closer to the edge of outrageousness until, finally, one sunny afternoon when any true son of my father would be fielding ground balls, I burst out of my bedroom, shaking and twitching to the Original Cast Recording of *Hello, Dolly!*

Threats were useless, the situation hopeless, the conclusion obvious.

SOMETHING MUST BE DONE!

My parents—rather, more accurately my mother with my father reluctantly in tow—packed themselves in the Chrysler and drove the three and three-quarter miles to the Throne of Solomon. Father Gillen, the parish priest, steeped a pot of tea for my mother and brought out the bottle for my father. The good padre must have sat there, hands folded around his glass, while my mother groped for words to describe "the predicament," cautiously avoiding the obvious ones like "effeminate" and "sissified," finally settling on "different." They'd hoped I'd grow out of "it," that it was just a "stage," but I was almost ten years old and "the problem" wasn't going away. My father wouldn't have said more than ten words. Father Gillen had seen the world twice over through the bottom of his own whiskey glass and, clearing his throat, suggested the obvious solution.

And so it came to pass that arrangements were made with Harrison Park Elementary School to excuse one Andrew Nocera from five days of long division and the battles of the War Between the States. My father and I drove down the coast to spend an entire week, just the two of us, in Clearwater, Florida, spring training camp for the Philadelphia Phillies. He bought a pair of red baseball caps for the trip. His rested on his head like a crown; mine was too big and slid to my ears, the visor obstructing my line of vision.

God knows what that old priest expected to happen that week. I doubt that in his infinite wisdom he envisioned me propped on a bar stool until almost midnight, bribed with Coca-Colas and bags of potato chips, while my father relived Great Phillies Games of the Past, inning by inning, with assorted fanatics and hangers-on. During the day, we baked in the heat, my sunburn getting sunburned, staring at the field as my father read the tea leaves in the meaningless exhibition games that dragged on through the afternoon. My stomach revolted and I dropped my head and threw up the boiled hot dogs I had for lunch. The old man was flummoxed, staring helplessly as if he had never seen a sick child before, which, of course, he hadn't, having delegated all nursing duties to my mother. A butcher's wife from Allentown, Pennsylvania, took pity on me and wiped my mouth and cleaned my shoes.

At night, the old man snored and farted and woke up every two hours to piss. In the morning, I stared at the red puncture scars in his armpits while he dozed. I touched them gently, afraid of hurting him. The Army, he said, when I asked where he got them. Bullets? Shrapnel?

"No," he snorted. "Goddamn doctors."

He'd been a top prospect, signed by the Phillies out of high school in 1944 to a contract with a clause requiring him to report for assignment in the club's farm system within thirty days of military discharge. My father's war was played in innings. Assigned to Special Services, he attained the rank of center fielder and shipped out west, California first, then on to Hawaii. The marquee names of the Great American Pastime were serving their country playing ball for Uncle Sam; career minor-leaguers and promising young kids like my father filled any holes in the rosters. The homesick troops of the Pacific theater who packed Honolulu Stadium on R&R didn't seem to resent comrades in arms whose greatest risk was being hit by a wild pitch. A mosquito bite ended my father's baseball career. Stricken by malaria while touring the Philippines, he spent two years in a Veterans Administration hospital, his recovery, uncertain at first, complicated by juvenile diabetes.

"Wasn't meant to be. No use crying over spilt milk," he groused as he sat spread-eagled on the motel bed, injecting insulin in his thigh. Then he doctored his coffee with four packets of sugar and we split a half dozen doughnuts for breakfast before heading out for another afternoon under the blazing sun.

And finally it was Friday night. My father was nervous as we pulled into the high school parking lot, straightening the knot in his tie in the rearview mirror. He gripped my hand as we entered the auditorium. Grown men and women in baseball jerseys were milling around the tables, engaging in serious negotiations with crew-cut reps from the trading card companies. The old man nudged me as a gent ambled by, greeting fans calling his name. Whitey Ford, he said reverently. Hey, Whitey, he hollered and Whitey turned and shook his hand.

The line snaked around the auditorium. The old man and I took our place. A young woman with a sweet Florida drawl walked the line, issuing instructions to the faithful. No baseball cards, no bats, no gloves. Don't use your own balls. Only the official baseball, ten dollars each, will be signed. No photographs. Please don't try to start a conversation. Don't ask to shake his hand.

My father nodded obediently, memorizing the ground rules.

The line moved quickly, but he still fidgeted, his hand deep in his pocket, slapping his keys against his leg. He pulled out a crisp twenty, enough for two pristine, snow white baseballs. And then the fat woman ahead of us stepped aside and there he sat: crisp in his navy pinstriped suit, a silver pen in his long tapered fingers, diamond chip cuff links sparkling in the harsh auditorium lights.

"Hello," he said, not bothering to look up.

"Joe," the old man said, his voice cracking, "Tony Nocera."

"Nice to meet you, Tony," said the Great DiMaggio, brandishing the pen to etch his name into the first of my balls.

"We've met."

"We have?" he asked, uninterested.

"Special Services. Forty-four. Honolulu."

The Great DiMaggio looked up from the ball, mildly intrigued.

"I fielded your line drive. You complimented my arm."

The Great DiMaggio smiled, not pretending to remember.

"Your boy?" he asked, nodding at me.

"Yessir."

"Looks like a ball player. Name?"

I was speechless and the old man answered for me.

"Andy."

"Last name again, paisan?"

My father spelled it slowly and the Great DiMaggio inscribed the balls to me. We had ninety seconds to bask in the Presence before we were hustled away, the old man's hand still extended for the handshake that wasn't meant to be.

Saturday we would get up at dawn for an early start. The old man's sight wasn't what it used to be, fucking diabetes, and he wanted to be home before dark. But we had one last night away from the watchful eye of my mother. He heaped sour cream on his baked potato and ordered two scoops of ice cream and a slab of Black Forest cake, but he seemed to chew his food without tasting it. He was distracted, a million miles away, and when the waitress was slow to bring the change, he was irritated, mumbling under his breath. I was sure I'd done something to spoil his evening, that I'd slipped up, embarrassed him. I shrank when he reached for me in the parking lot, certain he was going to reward me with one of his harmless swats for some transgression. But all he wanted to do was rub his hand on my head.

"Tired?" he asked.

"No," I said, lying.

He wasn't interested in talking with his friends at the bar, dismissing the drunk who wanted to argue Ted Williams's claim as the Greatest Living Ball Player. He ordered another shot and a beer to chase it. "Asshole," he muttered. "Just another goddamn jerk running his goddamn mouth about things he doesn't know shit about."

"Your teachers think you're real smart," he said, firing up another smoke. "Father Gillen too."

He told the bartender to pull him another draft and bring another Coke for his son. I sat up straight on my stool and nodded at the bartender, making sure there was no mistaking I was that son and this was my dad.

"I bet you can be anything you want to be. A doctor. A lawyer. An engineer."

He ground his cigarette out in the ashtray.

"Don't ever let me see you pick up a baseball bat again or I'll break both your hands."

* * *

It's getting on for eleven Friday night and I'm sitting at the bar of the Carousel, again, nursing a beer, furious with Matt, angry with myself for telling him that goddamn story. I should have known that fucking priest would never understand, that he'd make some stupid comment.

"You must have been very frightened when your father threatened you like that," he said, expecting revelations and catharsis.

Frustrated, mad, rejected. Those were the emotions my father could arouse, not frightened. He could pop and sputter, his face a virtual pyrotechnic display while he bellowed like a wounded ox. He might give my backside a gentle whack or drop a soft knuckle rap on my skull. Once he grabbed me by the shoulders and shook me until my eyes rolled back in my head, not because he was angry, but because he was terrified when I absorbed a brutal shock after sticking a screwdriver into an electrical outlet. But he never hit me. Not once. Never. Corporal punishment was strictly a maternal duty.

I order another Heineken, wondering what ever happened to those goddamn baseballs. They sat on my bedside table until I left for college. I'm growing more tolerant of the ordained clergy as my blood alcohol level rises After all, Father Gillen had proven to be a sage counselor. The old man quickly forgot his prohibition when I begged to join the Gastonia Little Cherokees a few weeks after we returned from Clearwater. I threw like a girl, dropped every ball, and flailed at the plate, but not one of my teammates dared to taunt or mock me or even snicker behind my back, fearing the wrath of their fathers who gathered to watch the graceful arc of my old man's swing as he shagged fly balls to their sons. They were awestruck by his stillness at the plate, mesmerized by his power, spellbound by the sound of one ball after another being smacked into the outfield. Bullshit, he spat, his anger startling an admirer who told him he could have been another DiMaggio.

I never graduated to Pony League, moving on to solitary endeavors like the swimming pool and the speed bag. I grew bigger and stronger while my father slowly faded away. He looked odd in his new glasses, almost bookish; his face gradually seemed to shrink behind the ever-thickening lenses of stronger and stronger prescriptions. Eventually he couldn't go out in the daylight without sunglasses and, finally, his driver's license was revoked, making him dependent on my mother.

The last time I saw him wear dress shoes was when he danced at Regina's wedding. From then on, it was slippers and white socks until he lost his right foot to gangrene. He worked hard at his rehab, insisting he'd learn to walk without a limp or a hobble, but never succeeding before they told him they needed to take the leg below the knee. The procedure was a success. He was recovering nicely. His vital organs, battered by years of exposure to high glucose levels, had withstood the trauma better than had been expected. You'll be in skilled nursing when I come back next weekend, I promised, the crisis over, the obligations of Tar Heel Heritage beckoning. He was sitting up in bed, leaning forward, his gown dropped to his waist. I rubbed his bare shoulders, no muscle left to massage, just flaps of loose skin that yielded under the gentle pressure of my hands. Look at that, I said, as the Phillies All-Star lefty first baseman launched a magnificent opposite field three-run bomb, dooming the Braves to their fourth loss in a row. Turn it off, he said, I want to go home. Soon, I promised. Later that night, he was restless, unable to sleep, complaining he was cold, his gown damp with sweat. He insisted the staff turn up the lights in his room, trying to keep the dark at bay, and kept calling for my mother, who was standing beside him, unable to calm and reassure him. He struggled to crawl out of bed, resisting the efforts to restrain him, trying to escape the inevitable, if only for another hour or two. He coded just before midnight.

He was lying in the morgue when Alice and I arrived from High Point at five in the morning. My mother was about to sign the consent to the autopsy to confirm the obvious, postoperative cardiac arrest, when I ripped the form from her hands and tore it to shreds. *He's dead, he's fucking dead. Why do you want to cut him up again?* My wife and mother and sister, for once, were silent in the face of my ferocity. The night before he was buried, I wrote him a long letter, recording every minute of every day of that week in Florida. I'm sure most of it happened just as I remembered. I slipped it in the pocket of his jacket before the undertaker closed the coffin lid. When I think of him now, he's never old, feeble, broken. He's that magnificent animal he was when I was a boy, the man I'll never be, able to swat a baseball a hundred, thousand, million feet, then spit in his hands and do it again, never breaking a sweat.

"Hi. You remember me?"

He startles me, pulling me from my sentimental reverie.

He looks vaguely familiar. Ordinary. Could be a dozen different guys.

"I'm Harold. We met right before Thanksgiving."

"Sure . . . sure. Hey, how you doing?" I say, determined not to be my usual rude self.

"You're Andy, right?"

"Right."

"Can I buy you a beer?"

"That's great, but I really have to go. Someone's waiting up for me," I say.

"Your boyfriend?" he asks, his face sagging with disappointment.

"Believe it or not, my mother. I still have a curfew." I laugh, a too-subtle joke at the expense of a man who's way too old to be referring to anyone as a *boyfriend*.

"Next time, then," he says, obviously cheered by my revelation.

"Next time. It'll be on me."

Only once I'm in the car do I realize he was wearing a White Sox jersey. It comes back to me. He was the guy in the Tar Heels hoodie who gave me a chaste kiss last November. What a doofus, I think, smiling. Wonder what he'd think about my encounter with the Great DiMaggio? I'll have to remember to tell him if I ever see him again.

Another Diagnosis

It sounds beautiful, the way the oncologist describes it. A warm, pulsing, living thing. Organic. Almost musical. If I were an artist, I'd draw it on a field of blue. The lymph system. Thin, pliant tubes, the body's interstate system, a highway conveying precious lymph—colorless, watery—from spleen to tissue, from farm to market. Think of your nodes as pit stops along the way, bustling with activity, generating cells, an arsenal for the war against infection.

My mind wanders. Why haven't I ever seen lymph? Cut your finger, you get blood. What happens to lymph when that same paring knife severs a lymph vessel? Where does it go?

Blood also has a verb. Bleed.

Lymph is only a noun. No one ever asks if you're lymphing. I've never heard of anyone lymphing to death.

It's a mystery, this lymph. To you, to me, to my mother. But not to the trained eye of the pathologist peering into the microscope, classifying the node cells harvested in the biopsy into a familiar pattern.

The lymph node shows a diffuse lymphocytic infiltrate with occasional residual nonneoplastic germinal centers. The lympho-

cyctic infiltrate is composed of small cells with scant cytoplasm and irregular, cleaved nuclei (hematoxylin-eosin 40x, x 400 and Wright-Geimsa x 1000).

Wow. Dig that crazy medical lingo, Maynard G. Krebs. Sounds cool to me.

But not to the oncologist reading the report. Not from the look on her face, the slight knotting of her eyebrows.

Lymphoma, she says. Pretty word, I think, meant to be modified by adjectives like *languorous* or lazy, nice phonetic matches, synonyms of *indolent*. Indolent lymphoma. All we need to do is Watch and Wait. Odds are better of being killed in a car wreck or a terrorist attack than succumbing to your mutant cells. Right?

Sorry, the oncologist says, the cell pattern indicates adult lymphoblastic lymphoma.

I don't think I like what all those syllables imply.

An aggressive lymphoma, she explains.

Uh-oh. Aggressive. Rapid action. Carnivorous cells attacking poor, defenseless tissue with their sharp little teeth. Snip, bite, chew, spit. How much have they already eaten? What's left?

The oncologist asks the receptionist to bring in coffee. There's Danish left from the morning staff meeting. Please, help yourself. We're having a tea party, the oncologist, my mother, and me. The doctor slips her stockinged feet out of her pumps. It's all so cozy in here.

Staging. That's the next step, she says. Determine the spread. Let's start with some bloods, draw a little bone marrow, order a CT scan to get a peek inside the body. Now, depending on the results, we may have to consider a laparotomy to . . .

My mother twitches, a reflex. She must have misheard. She thinks the doctor said lobotomy. No, I assure her. Or maybe I misheard.

. . . that's actually a surgical procedure. We make an incision in the belly so we can get to the internal organs. We take little snips to view under the microscope. Not likely we'll have to go that far. The bloods and marrow hopefully will be sufficient and it won't be necessary.

The early reviews come in. It's necessary.

So we pack a little bag, just enough for a night or two, maybe three, and I whisk her away to the hospital.

Should I call my sister? She knows nothing yet. What if my mother dies on the table? What if she never wakes up from the anesthesia? Regina will never forgive me for denying her the opportunity to participate in the death watch, to share the ritual.

But wait a minute. It's just a test. Just a little exploration, just harvesting a few clippings for the laboratory. My mother will be home in a few days, her biggest worry being the new tinkle in her car engine and whether she remembered to turn off the sprinkler.

But she's got *it*.

That much we do know.

Non-Hodgkin's lymphoma.

It's just a question of how far it's gone.

And now we know it's gone far enough that they need to slice open her belly to determine the spread.

My sister has a right to know.

No, my mother says, no need for her to worry yet. Let's not give it to her in dribs and drabs. I'll tell her when I know everything there is to know.

Besides, I think, my sister would never appreciate the beauty of the lymph system. Its silent mysteries are beyond her comprehension. She's too literal minded. She's a real estate broker. Only hard facts are meaningful. Mortgage lending rates. Tax assessments. Comparables. There's plenty of time in the days ahead to reduce my mother's diagnosis to tangibles—treatments, side effects, diet, support groups—that Regina can grasp with her fist, bite down on, snap in two.

My mother absentmindedly scratches her freshly shaved belly. I tell her I'll be back in the morning, before they take her downstairs. I kiss her good night. Just a peck on the cheek. Nothing melodramatic. After all, it's just a test.

She scores four out of a possible four.

Great! That means she's won!

Sorry, it means she lost.

Stage IV.

The cancer has spread beyond the lymph system. Multiple organs are involved. An aggressive treatment regimen is recommended. Starting immediately. Yes, yes, I say before my mother can speak, answering for her, not allowing her any say in the matter, adamantly refusing to concede the possibility of a world without her.

Certain things are taken for granted; some basic assumptions go unquestioned. The sun will rise in the morning and set at night. The seasons will change. A year will pass and we'll all be older. My mother will be there, ready to catch me if I fall and lead the charge whenever I'm challenged.

Ma, someday I'll be ready to stand on my two feet. I promise. As soon as we get through this, all of this, cancer, divorce, scandal. I'm gonna stand by you, support you, be your rock. I can't say I'm a raging success, but I wouldn't have gotten even this far without you. And you, being who you are, will be kind and generous enough to pretend that all my efforts are for you when we both know you're really just the beneficiary of my own fear of being left alone. But my motives aren't important in the end; it doesn't matter that I'm not Mother Teresa because I'm going to be here with you, the whole way, right up until the day they tell us you've got a clean bill of health and you'll live to be ninety. I promise.

*　*　*

"It may not be a death sentence, Andy. Even the most aggressive lymphomas are responding to the newer treatment regimens. There's a little bit of God in medicine these days."

"That's weird," I say.

"Well, disease is a part of the natural order, but it always feels like a disruption of the natural order to those it affects."

"No. I didn't mean the disease is weird."

Matt waits for me to elaborate.

"You're a priest, you know," I say.

"Yes, I certainly know that," he says.

"And I've been seeing you since last summer."

"Right."

"And this is the first time you've brought up the subject of God."

"You want to go somewhere with that thought?" he asks.

I feel a professional pause coming on, one of those eyes-locked silences intended to draw me out.

"Do you believe in God?" I ask.

"Of course I do."

"You've never doubted?"

"Of course I have."

"But you still believe?"

"Yes. I do."

"I don't."

"I suspected as much."

"Doesn't that upset you?"

"Andy, I don't make judgments about my patients' religious beliefs or lack of them."

"But you're a priest!"

"Yes, I am. But that's incidental to our work together."

"How can that be?" I ask, not really certain why I'm so agitated. "How can you sit there and allow me to continue in my heathenish delusions? I thought it was your job to bring me back to God!"

"Andy, I'm not a missionary. I'm a shrink."

"I didn't think the Vatican let you compartmentalize," I say, laughing. "See, I *have* been paying attention. I'm getting pretty facile with the lingo, huh?"

"So does being an atheist bother you?" he asks.

"Aha! See! I knew you'd get around to converting me! A leopard doesn't change its spots!" I say, satisfied.

"Sorry, pal. It doesn't matter to me if you believe in God or Santa Claus or the Tooth Fairy. But I've got this funny feeling it matters to you."

"Think you know me pretty well, don't you?"

"I'm beginning to," he says.

"Maybe you are," I concede. "But you're wrong about this one. I'm not an atheist."

"So you do believe?"

"I suppose."

"What do you believe in?"

"I don't know. Maybe I'm just hedging my bets. Maybe I'm too much of a coward to make a commitment to heresy. I mean, maybe there is an Almighty Being and maybe there is a Saint Peter and I don't want to get turned away at the Pearly Gates because I made the stupid mistake of thinking there isn't a God."

"Covering all your bases, huh?"

"Right. Anything wrong with that?"

"Not necessarily."

"It's not all about me, you know."

Matt sits quietly, knowing where I'm headed.

"What if there aren't any medical miracles? What happens to my mother if she dies? I'd rather think of her flying around heaven with a harp than lying in a box in the ground."

"So you're saying your mother is the reason you haven't quite given up on God?"

"She's one of the reasons."

"Do you want to talk about your mother? About how you feel about this bad news?"

"No."

"Why not?"

"I don't want to think about it. I haven't thought about anything else. I just can't think about it anymore. At least not now. And you're right. Maybe it's not worth thinking about at all. Maybe there's a little bit of God in modern medicine after all. Maybe this time next year everything will be back to normal."

"Tell me about that."

"Tell you about what?"

"Tell me what it's going to be like when everything's back to normal."

Goddamn it. This priest sure has a talent for stumping me. Back to . . . what?

A Saturday night date with my mother at the club, then sleeping late in the morning while she putters in the kitchen, whipping up my favorite Sunday dinner?

Possible . . . but not normal.

Crawling into bed and drifting off to sleep while Alice rustles the pages of her novel?

Normal . . . but not possible.

"Andy, I think under the circumstances you need to concentrate on the present and not worry about the future. You need to focus on the positive to help you deal with the negative."

"The positive?" I sneer.

"You're a very lucky man, my friend."

I snort, laughing.

"It almost makes me angry, your willful refusal to acknowledge what you have," he says, his voice more measured than his words.

"And what would that be? A fat frequent flyer miles bank?"

"The knowledge that you are unconditionally loved. That's a gift not everyone is given."

"And now she's gonna die."

"That doesn't die with her. That you will keep for as long as you live."

I'm not taking a chance.

We're going to get through this, Mama, if it's the last thing we do.

The Most Beautiful Girl

It came disguised as a birthday present, but I know it's really penance, an offering, a bone to throw at the guilt that occasionally pricks the seamless rounds of closings, meetings, parties, tennis matches, all the comfortable routines of my sister's life. She's convinced herself that the distance between Charlotte and south Florida justifies why I've had to assume full responsibility for these endless rounds of hospitals and medical office buildings. She's willfully, blissfully ignorant of the six daily nonstop flights from West Palm. It's probably just as well. Patience is not one of my sister's virtues. To her, a waiting room is where people cool their heels until she is ready to receive them. She'd never be able to tolerate the slow drip of hours spent flipping through ancient copies of *Newsweek* and *Good Housekeeping*. Time doesn't exist in a doctor's waiting room, four beige walls and no window. It feels perfectly natural to study a recipe for the Perfect Plum Pudding for Your Holiday Table months after the twinkle lights have been packed away and the tree hauled away by the trash man.

"Mrs. Nocera, why don't you step this way."

I handed my mother over to the nurse and settled back to wait while they pumped her bloodstream full of chemicals.

Later, at home, I'll ask her how she feels. Fine, she'll say, when I can see she's doubled over with nausea. I'll pour her some flat ginger ale and she'll smoke a cigarette, saying it settles her stomach. My sister will call and my mother, exhausted, will try to sound interested in her tales. Then Regina will ask to speak to me and start haranguing, asking me the prognosis. I'll tell her I don't know. It's true. I've never asked. My sister needs something more definitive; she uses medical terms she doesn't understand like age-adjusted mortality and morbidity rates, primary and contributory diagnosis and cancer clusters, words she's picked up from the Internet. I tell her all of this doctor bullshit is nothing but educated guesses, something on which to base false hopes and unrealistic expectations. She needs to pick up the phone and call the oncologist if she's not satisfied with my reports from the field. Frustrated, she'll swear at me and slam the receiver in the cradle.

I'd brought the mail along, intending to pay household bills while I waited. My name was scrawled on one of the envelopes. I knew it was from Regina by the Florida postmark. It was just a birthday card, but I turned it over and over in my hands as if it were something rare and precious. Which, as the first piece of mail I'd received in months without the return address of a law firm, it was.

She's working hard, my sister, at trying to accept me. The last connection between us may be dying and she's afraid of losing her history once our mother is gone. Or maybe I'm just a bitter pill she has to swallow until Mama is six feet under and no longer needs care and attention. It could be she's doing it to spite her husband. Maybe she's preparing for the inevitable and using me as a dress rehearsal for the day her younger son comes to her in tears, terrified of rejection, with something he can't keep inside anymore, something he has to tell her.

I don't know why, but she's trying. It's just that it's hard to talk about. Gestures, even clumsy ones like this, are easier.

She'd taken a long time choosing the card, not knowing what I'd like, realizing she doesn't really know anything about me anymore. She remembers how I wailed and cried when she broke my Superman milk glass and how proud I was the day I finally figured out all the chords of "I'm a Believer" on my ten-dollar guitar. But it's been twenty years since she could tell you Colossal Boy was my favorite Legionnaire, followed by Lightning Lad and Timber Wolf. She doesn't know that Karloff and Lugosi had been replaced by De Niro and Pacino and that now, approaching middle age, Clint Eastwood's the only actor whose movies I never miss. If you asked her my favorite Beatle, she'd still get that one right. I've stayed loyal to George through a lifetime. But my obsession with Billy Davenport died many years ago and I don't like peanut butter cups anymore and competitive swimming cured me of my morbid fear of anyone seeing my bare feet. She'd barely recognize the boy she knew so well in the man I am today. We're strangers who once shared the same last name.

So she settled on something mildly risqué, probably bought two of the same card, one for me and one to titillate her overweight receptionist on her fortieth birthday. The messenger boy was chiseled down to his little toe, wearing nothing but a discreetly positioned beach ball. The Hallmark inscription said, "It's your Birthday! Have a Ball!" and the handwritten greeting from my sister said, ". . . on the beaches of Oahu. This card is good for one free first-class ticket to Honolulu. Love, Regina." The sweet old lady sitting across from me giggled, amused by the card.

My Born Again National Sales Manager wasn't too pleased when I asked for a week off. He's already perturbed about needing to schedule my trips to accommodate my mother's chemotherapy. But my sales are strong and it isn't easy to find someone willing to fly at the drop of the hat to every godforsaken outpost in the country. So we negotiated cordially and finally came to terms. He allowed me four work days off, book-ending a weekend. He walked away satisfied, having denied me the full work week.

Six days, five nights. About six days, five nights too long, as it turns out.

I haven't been able to breathe since the plane landed. The trade winds deserted Honolulu just in time for my arrival, highly unusual for the season, the hotel staff assures me, but in the meantime the city is wilting in high humidity. Even my Southern lungs, seasoned by a lifetime in the North Carolina Piedmont, are clogged by the tropical moisture. The fabled beach is more pebbles than white sand and no wider than a city sidewalk. I throw down a towel near the water. Japanese honey-mooners trip over my legs, filtering the Hawaiian experience through their Sony lenses. They back away from the rambunc-tious service boys on leave from Guam and Okinawa. The sol-diers, bellies all tight and ripped, goof off in the surf, throwing sucker punches and trying karate kicks, looking like perfect physical specimens cavorting in a beer commercial.

It's too fucking hot to lie here and fry. The air is oppressive and smells like the freon leaking from a million air-conditioning units. Even at the water's edge there's no escaping the endless pianos, guitars, accordions, organs, harps, even mandolins, all playing the Hawaiian theme song, that incessant tune that goes . . .

Kuluha luha, kala halaki, kaluha luha . . .

Or something like that.

I'm exhausted by paradise, but my return ticket isn't valid for four more days. I pick up my towel and head back to the room, deciding I need a nap though I'd slept until noon. I lie naked atop my bed, next to the open window, waiting for the trade winds to return. My room is damp and smells like co-conut suntan lotion and sweat. I sweep a collection of plastic bags off the bed with my left foot. Souvenirs, they're called, but it's the same shit from Bangkok to Miami to Rome to Addis Ababa. Cheap key chains, snow globes, T-shirts, shot glasses. Well, maybe the plastic leis are indigenous. I bought this crap out of boredom, lured by the sweet air-conditioning of the Honolulu shopping arcades.

I'll feel better if I eat. The choices at the hotel aren't appealing: the Terrace Luau, Fine Italian Dining in the Main Dining Room, or the oceanfront Sea Shack. One of the restaurants listed in *Fodor's* intrigues me.

Kiko's Thai Cuisine
Authentic Thai Dishes at Reasonable Prices
Cocktails, piano bar, dancing.
"My home away from home in Honolulu." —Jim Nabors

Gomer Pyle wouldn't lie. Kiko's is small—intimate, the guide calls it—with glossy photographs of smiling celebrities covering the walls. Movie stars, politicians, basketball and football and boxing legends, all posing with a genial Buddha I assume must be Kiko. He must have a great publicist because the limp noodles and rubber satay don't explain why the high and mighty have graced his tables. The waiter brings another bottle of Singha beer. He says I must stay for the show. (As if I have anywhere else to go.) I fiddle with my satay sticks while the band sets up their instruments. A blond with a shellacked bouffant and a clipped full beard watches their every move from the bar. He plays with a cigarette and chews the tip of his thumbnail, waiting to pounce at the slightest hint of a mistake, a fuckup. The instrumentalists finish setting up without incident and the drummer settles behind his instrument and looks towards the bar. He gets the thumbs up and hits the cymbals and the piano player leads off with the familiar intro to "Top of the World."

The blond leaps to his feet and grabs the microphone by the

throat. He shuffles to the music, a little sliding dance step. His hand gestures are only slightly more restrained than a drag queen's. He's good. He's really good. He knows his audience and his patter walks the fine line of risqué—salty enough to titillate, gentle enough to be flirtatious, too innocuous to offend. He races through a repertoire of rock and roll standards. The band plays nothing earlier than the Beatles (except for a show-stopping "Johnny B. Goode"). The set list is heavy on saccharine ballads and disco anthems from the seventies.

I sit back and stare, appreciating it, if at all, only as pure tackiness. But the middle-aged vacationers from the mainland and Australia don't know "irony" from "camp." Their bellies are full of beer and wine and they just want to get up and shake their booties to KC and the Sunshine Band and ABBA and forget about corporate downsizing and rebellious kids and stubborn prostates. The blond plays directly to them, encouraging a shy, awkward couple to "get down." A chubby fellow has a special request for the woman he's about to ask to become his bride. She sits rapt and open-faced, believing for a few precious minutes that she is, in fact, "The Most Beautiful Girl."

The song stirs the unpleasant, disoriented feeling that's been stalking me since I said good-bye to my mother. It comes as a complete shock when, sitting alone at my table, I realize I am homesick. How can I be homesick? I don't have a home. And why now? I travel every week for work. Maybe it's that here, without sales calls to distract me, the loneliness of my nights seeps into the void of the long and empty days. The blond announces the next number. Neil Diamond! And I suddenly know what's been eating at me, putting me out of sorts. How could I have forgotten? I was married on my birthday. It's my anniversary too.

A bottle of Cracklin' Rosie, then a second, what the hell, let's open another. Nothing on earth can make my croaking voice sound musical; nothing, that is, except absolute, total un-conditional love. Tonight is our first anniversary and I'm sere-nading Alice to make up for all the small disappointments of our twelve months of marital bliss. She's in awe of my encyclo-pedic knowledge of rock-and-roll trivia and I'm showing off, choosing just the right records, singing and playing three-minute musical tributes to the conjugal unions of babes in the woods.

She doesn't know I'm faking most of the lyrics of Buddy Holly's "Well . . . All Right" and nearly all of Chuck Berry's "You Never Can Tell." She doesn't mind that my guitar is out of tune and that I can't keep up with the Crickets. And hey, let's crack open another bottle of Rosie while we're at it.

Alice tosses the salad and slices the bread and I keep the vino flowing. The table is set, the candles are lit, and the mood is right for me to tell her how grateful I am she has rescued me. But then I would have to tell her what it is she has saved me from. I'm not even sure myself. I tell myself it's that long red snake in the cab of the tractor trailer. But I know that's not really true, that all the snake did was make me run faster, make me more desperate to find a place to hide.

I'm twenty-five years old today, too young yet to know that someday this sanctuary will feel like a prison, that I'll rattle the cage, that one day, before I'm even certain it's what I really want, the door will unlock and I'll be turned out. I think the unspeakable urges and desires have been banished forever by my perfect married life. I am a husband, her husband. She be-lieves in my kisses, my lovemaking, my devotion, and if she be-lieves, they must be real.

I make her happy. I know I do. I'm not sure that I want to know why. I don't want to confirm what I suspect, that she loves me for the things I hate about myself, that she loves me because I am weak and soft and need protecting. She's spent her life in the shadow of her overbearing father and her haughty older sisters, and the brash, the strong, and the self-reliant do not appeal to her. She wants someone to love like a puppy, someone who will lick her hand in gratitude when she scratches him under the chin. She is twenty-four years old, too young to understand the puppy is going to strain at its leash, snip at her ankles, and piss on her rugs.

But all of that is still years away.

Tonight it's time to get on board with Cracklin' Rosie, to thrill each other with our fantasies of how perfect it is all going to be.

A boy and a girl, I say. Buddy and Holly.

No, two boys and a girl, she insists.

There's one thing we agree on. Not yet. Not for a while. We'll wait until we're thirty.

I think, on her part, it's because she wants me all for herself for a while longer, at least all of me that's available to her. Maybe she already feels something missing, some small part of me just beyond her reach. Time and effort, she believes, without kids to distract her, will deliver the whole enchilada and a family can be deferred until she carries all of me in the palm of her hand.

Come on, sweetie, one more glass before we call it a night. You only have one anniversary. Sorry, sorry, you know what I mean, I say, trying to retract the slip of the tongue that threatens to ruin the night. You only have one *first* anniversary, one paper anniversary. She shyly hands me a small wrapped box that holds a sterling silver calling card case. It's too much, too extravagant, I protest because I'm embarrassed by the stationery I'd given her.

That's your birthday present. Your anniversary present is inside, she says.

The announcement is printed on pristine new cards of the highest-grade ivory paper.

TAR HEEL HERITAGE FURNITURE
ANDREW NOCERA
VICE PRESIDENT FOR NATIONAL SALES

It's really the King of Unpainted Furniture's anniversary gift to her, elevating me to a position undeserved by a failed graduate student in comparative literature who can't tell particle board from solid mahogany.

So, hey, let's drain the bottle in honor of the promotion and walk hand in hand to the bedroom. Yes, I may be a little drunk, okay, really drunk, but I love you, I really love you. I'm drunk enough that the ferocity of my erection surprises me, explainable only by the fact that tonight, maybe for the first time, maybe for the only time, I have complete and total faith that I am not who I am but who I want to be.

Pull over there, I order the cabbie.

The House of Pies: 101 Varieties.

I can't face the hotel yet, afraid of insomnia and of being alone. I can't bear the thought of cruising bars and looking for intimacy with a complete stranger. I'm so hungry I'll eat anything that doesn't come with chopsticks. A tired waitress leads me to a booth. She hands me a plastic menu and asks if I want coffee. She tries to be friendly, but her mind is elsewhere, probably with a sick kid at home. The dirty thumbprints on the menu kill my appetite. But there's a five-buck minimum per table and I order a grilled cheese and coffee. I realize I have no idea where I am. The hotel might be miles away or just around the block. I'm counting the cabs passing on the street when he slides into the booth.

"What did you think of the show?"

The furry blond singer from Kiko's flashes a Hollywood smile.

"Do you mind if I join you? I'm waiting on a friend."

I don't mind. I really do, but I don't. I don't want to talk to him, but I'm tired of sitting at tables alone. I tell him he was great, especially when he sat down at the piano and played a little boogie-woogie. He says that for what Daddy paid for four years at Juilliard, he ought to be able to fake a little cathouse ragtime for a . . .

"*. . . shall we say, less than discriminating audience.*"

I hear crape myrtle in that phrase. I say I'm from North Carolina, trying to bond. Why, you're practically a Yankee, he says. He asks if I'm traveling alone, if I'm married, if I have children. Yes, no, and no. So far so good, he thinks. And what brought you to Kiko's? he asks. Well, if it's good enough for Jim Nabors, I say. He reaches over to light my cigarette and lets his fingers brush mine. I don't back away.

Now that we've established that I am a homosexual, his flirtation becomes aggressive. He says he's thirty-two, an obvious lie. He's wearing light mascara and foundation. Well, he is in show business and works under the lights, I think, giving him the benefit of the doubt. He's from Mississippi, Old Mississippi, he emphasizes. He's setting the groundwork, establishing he is *somebody* and must not be mistaken for some piano player in a rinky-dink bar. *Somebody*, meaning somebody better than me. Daddy has been the Chief Justice of the Mississippi Supreme Court for over thirty years. Mother is old cotton money. I am appropriately impressed. He orders the California burger and a slab of lemon meringue pie and excuses himself. There's a trace of powder on the tip of his nose when he returns.

"Mother is a dilettante," he says, with a voice fueled by cocaine and bitterness, a modestly talented watercolorist who's shown in galleries as far away as Boston. She has a small but solid reputation. *Art in America* once called her an important regionalist. But her true vocation is reigning over the Gulf pan-handle arts scene.

"Oh, Mother is a cunt." He laughs. "A real card-carrying cunt," he says too loudly, drawing angry stares from other tables.

The thought of my own mother, insisting on driving me to the airport and waving good-bye at the gate as if she will never see me again, makes me want to grab my fork and stab him in his glassy eye. The waitress drops the grilled cheese on the table and warns us we'll have to leave if we can't behave ourselves. I want to protest, explain to her I'm here alone, that he's intruded on me just like he's intruding on the nearby tables. He rolls his eyes and zips his lips with his fingertips, mocking her prudery. He sees he's embarrassed me and reaches across the table to touch my hand. His apology sounds almost sincere.

"Please stay," he says. "I don't like sitting alone."

Why shouldn't you have to sit alone? I do. And I may not be *somebody*, but I'm somebody better than you. But instead I settle back in the booth and play at eating the greasy grilled cheese. He looks at his watch, then asks me the time. Whoever he's waiting for is late and probably not going to show. He asks why I'm in Hawaii.

"An anniversary gift," I say.

He looks addled. He must have heard me wrong. He says he thought I'd said I wasn't married. He's either done too many drugs or not enough. He doesn't understand.

I'm not going to confess what I've done to deserve spending my anniversary in a House of Pies six thousand miles from home, the captive of this nasty creature with tinted hair who's being stood up by someone who most likely charges by the hour.

"Excuse me for just a minute," he says, apparently having decided that the drugs he's already snorted aren't sufficient. I'm not going to play this one out. Not this time. Not anymore. I grab the waitress as soon as he is out of sight. I stuff a twenty in her hand, mutter a quick apology, and bolt. She calls after me, aloha, I think she's saying. I can't really hear her. The piped-in ukuleles crackling in the speaker over the door are too loud.

Kuluha luha, kala halaki, kaluha luha . . .

Or something like that.

Property under Contract

What God hath joined together, let no man put asunder.

Well, that's obviously one commandment the Bible-thumping legislators of the State of North Carolina neglected to codify. In fact, they've gone out of their way to make my divorce quick and easy, an exercise in politeness and consideration, a mediation, nothing like the messy marital battles you read about in the tabloids. No angry accusations of adultery from the witness stand. No tearful recriminations. No hostile exchanges under oath. No blame. No fault.

No-fault divorce. The lawyers have handled it briskly and efficiently and are polite enough to conceal their disappointment at not being able to run up the bills because I insisted she get everything. Needless to say, the King of Unpainted Furniture made short work of Alice's refusal to take it all.

The separation agreement and the property settlement were signed months ago. There's nothing left to do but wait. The divorce will be final one year and one day after the date we established separate residences; that is, one year and one day after Curtis kicked me out on my ass. The house went on the market the day the deed was transferred. Alice held out until she got her asking price, not because she needed the money, but, I suspect, out of a reluctance to let go. The message came through my lawyer. Everything had been packed and moved, everything but the clothes I'd left behind, a few boxes of books and records, my bicycle, and a set of weights. It was my responsibility to pick them up. The locks haven't been changed. Settlement is Monday, twelve noon.

I was up before dawn this morning, dreading the long drive to High Point. Thirty miles out of Gastonia, I realized it had never occurred to me I might need something larger than a two-door compact to haul away my few remaining material assets. Ah well, too late now. Maybe the new owner is athletic or has a kid who might appreciate a customized racing bike worth a few thousand bucks. Might as well throw in the dumbbells too. And I've read all the books. They can keep the ones they want and throw away the rest. And who really needs all those clothes? Not me. Maybe the husband is my size. If he isn't, they can call the Salvation Army and take the tax deduction. Come to think of it, there's no reason not turn the car around and head back home.

Except that I can't do that to Alice. She's the one who will have to go to settlement and face the pissed-off buyers who'd just come from the walk-through and found the last vestiges of my former life cluttering the rooms of their dream house. Besides, the time has slipped by and I'm almost there anyway.

REST STOP
TWO MILES AHEAD

I press the accelerator to the floor and fly past the scene of the crime at ninety miles an hour.

I'd prayed for rain and was rewarded with a beautiful, sunny Sunday, an unseasonably warm spring day full of the promise of summer. The kind of day to inspire my former friends and neighbors to turn on the spigots and slip into their flip-flops and spend the morning waxing and polishing their BMWs and Range Rovers. I can see the double takes at the sight of the notorious criminal pulling into the driveway.

What is he, honey, a pederast? Or is it a pedophile? A child abuser? Sodomite? Yeah, that's it, a sodomite. So how did he look, dear? Did he say anything to you? Did he look you in the eye? God, the nerve! If he had any decency, he'd never show his face around here again.

How could they forget my departure on that beautiful sunny day, much like this one except much hotter? The sirens and dome lights of the squad cars had alerted the entire neighborhood to the spectacle at 12 Virginia Dare Court. The whole cul-de-sac had a front-row seat and an unobstructed view of the King of Unpainted Furniture of late-night television fame ranting and raving in the flesh, threatening to break every bone in my body.

What the hell do I care what they think? Put it in perspective. It all happened months ago, almost forgotten now. If they think of it at all, it's only as a salacious little tale to reinforce their self-righteousness, threatening their complacency, the perfect order in their perfect worlds disturbed, if only momentarily. I pull into the cul-de-sac and am surprised to see that nothing's changed. I ask myself why I would have expected it to change since I've been gone. It must be because I've changed so drastically since then. How exactly, I'm not quite sure yet. I may never have been the man they thought I was, but I'm no longer the same man they didn't know.

There's not a soul in sight. No doubt the suspense on some putting green has them glued to their television sets. Thank you, God. Forgive me for doubting You exist. The lawyer was right. The keys still work. I put the car in the garage, not risking the unwanted attention a strange vehicle in the driveway would attract.

The boxes are stacked neatly in what used to be the dining

room. The bicycle is in the garage. The free weights are no-where to be found. I could just pack the car with as much as it can hold and take off, in and out in a few minutes. But some-thing is slowing me down, nostalgia perhaps, or maybe a nag-ging regret that I'd never had the opportunity to bid the rooms of this house a formal farewell.

I'll start on the top floor and work my way down. Climbing the stairs, I'm humming a tune I'd forgotten I remembered—a country and western weepy that's as much a part of my heritage as MoonPies and RC Cola.

"Step right up,
Come on in.
If you'd like to take the grand tour
Of a lonely house that once was home sweet home."

Life imitates art. Well, that might be stretching it. Life imi-tates the jukebox. The voice of Mr. George Jones follows me from room to room. I can't believe I know all the words.

"Straight ahead
That's the bed
Where we lay and love together
And Lord knows we had a good thing going here."

Well, George, maybe not. I've got another song about love-making for you, a duet, something you and Tammy would have taken to the top of the Country Hot 100.

Him: Distant and analytical—touch here and make her sigh; touch there and drive her crazy.

Her: Wary; sensitive of crossing the fine line between pas-sion and aggression.

Him: Rating his performance, keeping score, fretting over

the gradual slide in technical points as repetition and familiarity and, worst, lack of interest took its toll.

Her: Wanting more, getting less.

Him: Frustrated, angry, finally weary of trying to draw from a well of desire that was shallow to begin with, gone bone dry all too soon.

Her: Finally surrendering, conceding that he will not, cannot, respond to her touch the way she responds to his.

The End.

Ah, George and Tammy would have turned our sad story into poetry.

Our old bedroom, stripped of its contents, seems enormous. Sunlight falls on the large rectangle of clean, plush carpet where the bed used to be. I'm exhausted and the shadow of the queen-sized mattress makes sleep irresistible. I kick off my shoes and curl up on the floor. The pile scratches my cheek and my nose detects traces of factory glue in this unblemished section of rug. I'm sound asleep within a minute.

I don't know how long I've been dozing when I'm awakened by the sound of a car door. I jump up and look out the window. I panic, realizing I'm trapped in this room, unable to escape. It's too late to race down the stairs and slip out the door. Alice's key is already in the lock.

I have two choices. I can walk downstairs, announce my presence, hope that I don't startle her. But then I would have to look her in the eye. The alternative is to stay here and take a chance she won't feel the need to visit the garage or climb the stairs. I consider hiding in the closet and reject that strategy as too cowardly. Instead, I sink quietly to the floor to avoid any footfalls on the creaking floorboards. I hear the front door close and the quiet shuffle of leather soles on the parquet floor. Alice goes directly to the dining room.

Goddamn, I hear her say when she finds the boxes exactly

where she left them. She uses her cell phone to call someone, the real estate agent most likely, and bemoan the fact *he*—that would be me—*never showed up and the boxes are still stacked in the middle of the floor.* I hear her making arrangements for someone, the agent's teenage son apparently, to bring a van and haul it all away before the walk-through in the morning. She sounds more exasperated than angry.

No, no, she says, *he's not like that. He's got a lot on his mind right now. That's all. See you in the morning.*

Alice is still making excuses for me.

After all I've done to her, after everything I've put her through, she's still making excuses for me.

Yes, but sometimes he's a little absentminded.

He forgets things.

He didn't mean it the way it sounded.

He really is very sweet.

Everyone is a little cranky at times.

He's tired. He works so hard.

You don't know him the way I do.

No one knows him like I do.

Here in this empty house, I realize she's right.

No one knows me like she does. My mother maybe, certainly no one else.

But even Alice couldn't have imagined me down on my knees in front of the urinal, swallowing a stranger's semen. Or maybe I'm deluding myself and she knew all too well what I was capable of and turned a blind eye and a deaf ear, loving me anyway.

The house is so quiet I can hear her walking through the kitchen. I imagine she's opening the refrigerator door, checking for any ancient jelly or olive jars left behind. That's my Alice. Thorough to the end. Doing a little pre-inspection inspection. Making sure the faucets are working and the toilets still flush.

Oh, Sweet Jesus. The big, beautiful master bath, accessible only through this room in which I'm stranded, is sure to be on her punch list. I'm caught. There's nothing to do but get up off the floor and straighten my back, accept my fate, and stand face-to-face with the woman I betrayed. The words won't come easy. I can't ask her forgiveness. I'm afraid she would deny it, but am even more terrified she will offer it. Besides, I've asked enough of her over the years, more than enough, too much, more than I had a right to take. I can't ask her for anything ever again.

But what I can do is thank her.

Thank her for staying with me, for knowing I wasn't ready.

But this happy reconciliation will never come to pass if she goes into cardiac arrest when she unexpectedly comes face-to-face with this great ghost from the past. Just as I'm about to call down to her, her cell phone rings. *Hello?* she answers. *Okay. All right. I'll be there in fifteen minutes. I'm leaving now. Good-bye.*

She turns away from the staircase and closes the front door behind her. I hear her car backing down the driveway. She's probably singing along to the radio, her mind preoccupied with directions, blissfully unaware of me watching her from the window. She's let me off the hook again. I can walk away scot-free, without having hoisted anything heavier than my car keys. It's been a wasted trip. Hours of driving to accomplish nothing except a quick catnap. But I have a few moments before Zack or Tyler or Jason or whatever the most popular name for baby boys was sixteen or seventeen years ago comes bursting through the front door, still sweaty from lacrosse practice, to haul the last of this detritus from the house. I'm here, after all; it wouldn't hurt to take a quick peek at what's packed in that small pyramid of boxes downstairs.

Books, of course, as promised. Dozens of cheap paperbacks, their dry yellow pages crumbling, stuffed with bookmarks and receipts from long-shuttered bookshops, the underlined and highlighted passages revealing my impressionable undergraduate mind. I find what I'm looking for in the second box, the complete works of Faulkner, the Vintage editions, including a dog-eared copy of *Absalom, Absalom!* I carefully flip through it, astonished to find ancient petrified crumbs lodged between the pages. Is it possible they're from the bits of cookie I dusted off my lips when the bold little coed startled me in the Davidson dining hall? Not likely, but I'm not gonna let common sense stop me from believing they are.

Other boxes have books of a more recent vintage. Alice's book club selections are sandwiched between copies of *Ball Four* and the complete Henry Wiggen series. Along with the immortal volumes of Susan Moore Duncan and Lucy Patton Kline is her copy of *Wuthering Heights*, the tidy Everyman's Library edition with acid-free pages and slick red cloth place marker. Damn her, I spit, angry and hurt, my face stinging with rejection. She's jettisoned this very important artifact from our history, a critical key to deciphering the mysterious code that scripted the story of our marriage. I tear through the boxes, looking for more evidence of her callousness in her choice of what to keep and what to consign to the scrap heap of history.

It appears she's keeping those goddamn Dawn Powell books.

And, at last, in the heaviest boxes at the bottom of the stacks, I find hundreds of LPs in their faded and frayed jackets. Damn, it's the mother lode! These things are worth hundreds, maybe thousands, of dollars now that the warmth and beauty of the crackling imperfections of vinyl, once rejected in favor of unbreakable, unscratchable technology, has been rediscovered, championed by record store geeks, indie pop front men, and contrarians.

Not bad, I think as I shuffle the records, impressed by the range and depth of my musical knowledge and tastes. The collection spans generations and genres, from the most glittering, shimmering pop to chord-crunching R&B, from plaintive folk-songs to soul-crushing blues.

And *The Greatest Hits of George Jones and Tammy Wynette.*

Twelve three-minute masterpieces, each one a classic.

"Golden Ring."

"Two Story House."

"Near You."

Perfect harmonies, pierced by searing aches and throbs, transcending camp and kitsch to soar to that point in heaven where pain and desperation intersect with hope and optimism. Jesus, what chance was there for me and Alice to succeed where the two most glorious voices in Nashville had failed?

"We're Gonna Hold On."

And so we did, until it was time to give up the ghost and move on.

I debate for a minute, telling myself that, some day, I'm going to regret not exerting the small amount of energy I'd need to load the car with these boxes, the only evidence left of the union, imperfect as it was, between my wife and the man who loved her as best he could.

And so I compromise, taking *Absalom, Absalom!* and *Wuthering Heights* and *The Greatest Hits of George Jones and Tammy Wynette,* lock the door, and drive away.

Fumbled

I knew from the outset it was a mistake. The timing wasn't right. I wasn't ready. I was too inexperienced. Yes. Inexperienced. Not because I'd simply been away from the playing field for years and, with a little practice, could bring my skills back to championship form. The sorry truth was I'd never played the game at all. Alice hadn't merely rescued me from virginity. The wry little smart-ass with a studied, worldly demeanor eating alone in the Davidson College dining hall had never even been on a date. The closest I'd ever got to the prom was a fifth-aisle seat at *Carrie*. I had reached the brink of middle age without being issued the playbook on dating. I was totally ignorant of how to call a pass pattern, oblivious to the rushing offense, clueless about defensive positioning, incapable of running a punt return, stone deaf to the two-minute warning. All in all, it was the perfect scenario for a fumble.

I saw him in the shadows, standing near the dance floor. There were silver highlights in his close-cropped hair and he looked to be completely gray at the temples. But when he stepped into brighter light, I saw he had a baby's face, pink and healthy, without a crease, not a day over twenty-five. I walked away, seeking a beer and a quiet room. And then I looked up and he was standing directly in front of me. He caught my eye and smiled, pretending to be engaged in conversation with the friend next to him. Interested, obviously, expectant, but too shy, too inexperienced to speak first. A big boy. An overgrown cherub. Soft. Warm. The fine blond down on his cheeks was damp from either exertion or nerves. Probably nerves, since I hadn't seen him shaking his booty on the dance floor.

His name was Steve and he was a medical resident. Great, I assumed, he's older than I thought. Then he told me he'd done a five-year program, meaning he went straight from high school to anatomy and pharmacology without wasting four years on the Great Books and music appreciation. He was a first-year resident now, an intern, with a long haul until he's certified by the American Board of Emergency Medicine.

He said he lived close to the bar. Alone. In one room with a sleeper sofa. Don't expect too much, he told me, not wanting me to be disappointed. We opened the bed together, backs to opposite walls of the tiny room. The sheets didn't match and there was only one pillow. The blanket was rough as sandpaper. The first few moments were awkward and the night seemed destined to end in frustration and failure as he resisted the only plays I knew how to execute—quick rough jabs, poking his asshole with my fingers, grinding, pushing, racing to a quick, fierce conclusion.

"Slow down, we have all night." He laughed.

All night . . . with no eye cocked to the bedside clock or wristwatch, no ear pricked for the sound of a creaking door announcing the arrival of an intruder looking to empty a full bladder, no mind distracted by the need to compose an excuse for being late, again, or a reason for being called out of town on short notice, again.

"I really like your body," he said. "I want to get to know it."

How long had it been since I'd last heard a few simple words of affection? My restless, frantic assignations were always accompanied by a soundtrack of guttural grunts punctuated with harsh commands, *suck it, fuck me, yes, god, yes.* I flipped him on his back and pinned his wrists above his head, a clear message that he was my prisoner now and that it was useless to try to escape. He smiled and opened his mouth, his wagging tongue inviting, no, begging, me to kiss him. I slapped my hand over his lips when he tried to speak, expecting dreaded words like *daddy, sir.* But he shook my fingers away easily, insisting I hear what he wanted to tell me.

"You have a really nice face. Your eyes are incredible."

I'd never felt so completely possessed by another person before, never clung to anyone so greedily. Even the briefest bathroom break seemed like an eternity. There were no barriers, nothing I wasn't willing to do, even allowing him to go where no one had been since the long red snake many years ago.

In the morning he asked me to wait so we could leave together. He wore his scrubs proudly, certain that they gave him an air of authority, but, to me, he looked like a happy toddler in a comfy playsuit. We exchanged phone numbers. He gave me his home number, but told me to try the cell first. He's a busy guy, he said, on the move. He was young and having a romance with the commitments of grown-up life. The phone was his sweetheart. He wouldn't have believed me if I had told him the day would come when he would be exhausted by its demands.

I waited a respectable three days, calling his home number from a different time zone, in midday, when I knew I'd reach his machine and avoid any possibility of awkward pauses, flimsy excuses, maybe even hostility. I couldn't blame him. He wouldn't remember anything about my face except the lines in my forehead and the bags under around my eyes.

Hi. It's Andy. Just wanted to let you know I had a great time the other night. Hope you're doing well. Stay in touch.

That's it, I thought, I'll never hear from him again. C'est la vie. He was a nice kid. I really liked him. I felt a kick to the stomach. My cell phone rang two hours later. I was finishing a sales call and let it roll into voice mail.

Hi. It's Steve. Nice to hear your voice. Where are you? Texas? Right? When do you get back? Call me. I'll be home tonight doing some reading. Bye.

He answered on the second ring. I told him about my late flight; he told me about the broken bone he'd set on a little boy. The dreaded awkward pauses never came. He asked when I would be home. We made a date for hamburgers and beer later in the week.

I was a few minutes early; he was right on time. He was still wearing his scrubs. His forehead was peppered with beads of perspiration. He'd rushed, afraid of being late. I extended my right palm for a handshake. He leaned forward and kissed me, not on the cheek, but smack on the lips. The hostess was too startled to ask smoking or nonsmoking.

The beer settled the butterflies in my belly. The hamburgers were eaten, the last fry dredged through the ketchup. We split the check. I only had a twenty and he had to make change for me. He had a question to ask before he handed over the ones. Did I bring my own toothbrush? No, I lied, not wanting to sound presumptuous. He laughed and handed over the bills. Good, he said, now I know I didn't waste three bucks when I picked one up for you this afternoon. He slept in my arms that night; I lay awake, enchanted by his snoring. Don't forget me this week, he said in the morning, kissing me good-bye at the door.

He called me in Salt Lake City and said he wanted to make me dinner in his tiny bed-sitter when I got home from my trip. Four nights later, I sat on the bed in my underwear, listening to him chatter as he chopped and minced. He was eager to share his history, insisting I know him, or at least his romanticized view of himself.

I like you. I like you. I like you so much.

He kept repeating the words as we made love that night. Why couldn't I respond? Didn't I like him too? No. I realized my feelings ran deeper than that. I couldn't explain them without sounding crazy, obsessive. He couldn't know the impact of his words; he wouldn't understand I'd waited my entire life to hear another man speak them but had made conscious, deliberate choices to ensure I never would. And all that careful planning—compartmentalizing, rationalizing, justifying, avoiding, excusing, lying—where had it gotten me in the end? Locked in a fucking jail cell and kicked out on the street. But somehow I'd survived to make it here, at long last, to this tiny apartment, at the brink of an auspicious beginning. But my fear of the risks of intimacy, the possibility of rejection, still held me back. The only thing more terrifying than losing my home, my job, my good name, was the very real possibility of losing my heart.

I felt him squirming in his sleep. He rolled on his side, turning his back to me. I finally fell into a light sleep as the sun was coming up. He threw his arm across my chest, reaching for the alarm, then flopped on his back. I waited for him to touch me, to stroke my chest, to dawdle a few minutes, reluctant to leave the warm bed. He scratched his armpit and yawned. I rolled toward him, pretending to be asleep. He slipped out from under my arm. Then I heard the water running.

He seemed to spend an hour in the shower, but it couldn't have been more than ten minutes. I hoped he would crawl back into the bed, all warm and damp. But he went directly to his closet and pulled on his scrubs. I opened my eyes and yawned. He noticed I was awake and smiled.

"Rise and shine," he said, sounding like my mother.

He offered me a bowl of Cheerios. I declined and ducked into the bathroom for a long piss. I came out and dressed without speaking.

"Last chance for oats," he said, tipping the bowl to his mouth. He wiped the milk from his chin with his sleeve.

"Where do ya live?" he asked, maybe realizing that last night he'd shared deep, dark family secrets and I'd volunteered nothing.

"Far suburbs, Gastonia actually."

He looked puzzled. Local geography meant nothing to him.

"You married?" he asked.

"No. No." I laughed, nervous. "Why?"

"I dunno. Sometimes you seem married."

"I was once," I admitted.

I broke down and told him the truth. At least part of the truth. That I lived with my mother, quickly qualifying it with the explanation that she had cancer. Someone needed to be with her, I said, afraid of sounding like a boastful knight.

"Hey, we gotta get going," he said, obviously unimpressed by my dutiful sacrifice. I couldn't find my watch. He seemed frustrated as he tossed aside the bedsheets and ran his palm under the bed. I read rejection in his helpfulness. He could have, should have, said, don't worry, it'll turn up, you can pick it up next week. But he didn't. It meant that he was sick of me. He woke up this morning and stared at my unguarded sleeping face; everything changed once he saw me for what I am. I'm old. I'm puffy. I drink too much and smoke. There's something shady about me. I'm dishonest. Or at least not forthcoming. I've gotten too comfortable around him. Let down my guard. He'd heard the occasional squeaky pitch that betrays my practiced baritone. He'd seen the unmanly flinch as he described some particularly gory medical procedure. He'd picked up the slip of the tongue that revealed an unhealthy interest in Rodgers and Hammerstein. He'd pierced the façade and exposed the little sissy Bride of Frankenstein. He was repelled, disgusted, horrified by his own bad judgment and he wasn't going to give me the sorry excuse of a mysteriously missing watch to force him to call me now that he'd decided he was done with me.

"Ta-dah!"

He dangled the watch in front of my face. It was under the mattress. I looked back at the unmade bed as we left, wondering if I'd ever lie there again.

He asked where I was headed for the week. I gave him my itinerary, telling him I'd be back on Friday. He told me he was on the ER schedule for the weekend. We'll talk, he said. Yep, we'll talk, I answered.

My mother's nurse caught me sneaking into the kitchen. You look like hell, she said. I went to the mirror and saw what he had seen this morning. I should have had a haircut last week. I should have clipped the hairs in my nostrils. I should have gotten more sleep in Utah. I watched the clock all day, imagining his routine at the hospital. Twelve-thirty. Lunchtime. He'd be sitting in the hospital cafeteria, talking excitedly about procedures I can't even pronounce and crushing an empty milk carton to emphasize a point. I was the furthest thing from his mind.

Seven o'clock. He'd be having another hospital meal. Less conversation, more exhaustion. Maybe he would call to say hello. The cell phone stared up from the armrest, silent.

Eleven o'clock. He'd be trudging through the parking lot and driving home. He would be crawling into the unmade bed, falling into a deep sleep. I jumped out of bed to respond to the moans coming from my mother's room. I wanted to call him but knew I couldn't.

I awoke in the dark to make an early-morning flight. The morning paper wouldn't be delivered until six, so I spread the Sunday magazine supplement beside the cereal bowl. Cheerios. The cover article was about something called the Cosmic Dark Age before the Big Bang that created the universe. The *Charlotte Observer* reported with firm certitude that the Dark Age extended "a billion years until the stars emerged to light the universe." How do you measure a billion years? I looked out the window into the pitch-black morning. I panted, panicking over the brevity of life.

I wanted to call him, then and there at four-thirty in the morning, but I forced myself to wait until I landed in Denver, with two hours' time difference. What was he doing while I was in flight? Sleeping? Alone? He didn't answer. I couldn't remember his schedule. Was he at work or was he at home, avoiding me? I left a message and regretted it immediately because putting the ball in his court forced me to wait for his return call.

An hour later my cell phone rang. He sounded relaxed, casual.

"I got Saturday night off. Wanna go to a party?" he asked.

I was distracted through my session Friday night, far less interested than Matt in probing the cause of my anxiety.

"How much are you drinking these days?" he asked.

"Not much."

Compared to Dino Martin and Mickey Mantle.

"Are you smoking pot?"

"No."

Well, only for religious purposes. Did I forget to tell you I joined the Rastafarians?

"Are you taking your medication?"

"Yes."

When I remember to fill the prescription.

He flipped through my record. My hated *medical* record. He tapped the pages with the tip of his very expensive pen.

"Well . . . we adjusted the doses six weeks ago."

"It makes me groggy."

"Are you sleeping well?"

"Like a baby."

Just like a baby. Waking up two, three, times a night. Thrashing on the mattress. "If we don't see some improvement soon, I want to try a different class of antidepressants."

Whatever you say, Doctor.

Steve's face was puffy and his eyes watery when he answered the door Saturday night. His forehead was clammy and warm.

He'd told me to wear a coat and tie. He was wearing a suit. A knubby gray worsted with too few natural fibers. His shoes were poorly made and warped from many seasons of puddles. His outfit made me want to protect him. I was sure I loved him.

It was an engagement party for one of his colleagues. Cocktails and a buffet supper at the chief resident's new town house. There was one other obvious gay there, a nurse from the hospital, the only guest who arrived alone. It was obvious Steve had told his friends about me, apparent that he had spoken of me with affection. They sized me up, seeing how I would fit in their group. Steve was quiet, smiling but not very animated. I must have embarrassed him. He stayed on the sofa, nursing a beer. I made eye contact with him but no sparks flew. I felt out of place. The outsider. An intruder making his one and only appearance. I walked over to the sofa and sat at his feet. His dress socks were too short and a band of white skin peeked beneath his cuffs. He touched me on the head. He took my hand and our fingers intertwined. I berated myself for being so insecure.

He persevered through the evening. We were among the last to leave. Soon I would have my arms around him and feel his deep breaths against my chest. But in the parking lot of his apartment building, he turned sheepishly, red-eyed and sweaty, and asked sweetly if I minded if he went upstairs alone tonight. I spoke without thinking, blurting out we didn't need to do anything. He was gentle, but firm. He needed to sleep this off. He couldn't risk missing work. Of course, I said, back in control. He asked if I was free tomorrow night. Can't, I said, my sister's in town for a funeral and I have a family dinner to attend. Maybe we can meet at the Carousel afterward, he suggested. Yeah, maybe, I said. He called in the morning to tell me he was feeling great. He would be at the bar with a friend after his shift. Who? The potbellied nurse from the party?

The family dinner was a tense little pas de deux, Gina and me, our mother having begged off with the excuse that she didn't want to miss that new Patty Duke movie on the *Hallmark Hall of Fame*. But my sister and I knew it was an excuse to force us to spend time together alone. Decisions loom in the near future that we will need to agree on; best to get it settled now at a nice, quiet dinner at the golf club when we're both calm and rational. No one but my mother would ever consider the possibility that her two children might act calmly and rationally.

"I just can't get over Randall Jarvis," Regina announced, pushing the iceberg lettuce through a sludge of bright orange salad dressing. "You know, Andy, we didn't have to come to this shithole if she wanted to stay home and watch television."

My sister's life in Florida has made her contemptuous of the frayed provincial charms of Gastonia country club dining.

"Maybe you would have preferred the Waffle House?"

"I don't know how you can live here. I'd lose my goddamn mind."

Then get on the next fucking plane back to Boca Raton. Go back to fucking paradise. Tomorrow morning you can jump in the Benz and drive over to the strip mall for a quick Botox injection before you meet up with some bony, bleached, tanned bitch for a Caesar salad at the Palm, flaunting your new tennis bracelet and pretending your hound-dog husband fucks you more than once a year on your anniversary. Your goddamn cell phone will ring and you'll say you need to race back to the office for a big closing when you've actually been summoned to your oldest son's middle school because security found marijuana in his locker. And don't forget to stop at the pharmacy on the way home because you need a refill of your Ativan and you won't be able to fall asleep without it since the bastard called to tell you he won't be home until after midnight again.

But I wasn't in the mood to be kind and said something I knew would inflict far more damage than a full-frontal assault on her life.

"Well, I won't have to live here much longer."

She dropped her head and whimpered quietly.

"Gina," I said, feeling like a complete shit and reaching across the table for her hand.

I was startled by how soft and vulnerable she looked when her eyes were wet with tears. For a brief moment she was the lovely little doe she'd been not so very long ago, the girl who strangers stopped in restaurants and airport terminals, remarking on her resemblance to Princess Diana. But she quickly composed herself, her face once again the tense mask she's worn these past few years.

"I'm sorry," she apologized. "You don't need me dumping on you. I can't believe how much this Randall Jarvis thing has upset me. I wish you were going to the funeral with me, but I know you didn't like him."

How could I have disliked Randall Jarvis when I'd seen him only once since her wedding, and then only briefly, in the incontinence aisle of Walgreens several months ago, so gaunt and sallow I didn't recognize him when he called my name. I'd hemmed and hawed, promising to call, knowing that I wouldn't since the last thing I wanted to do at this sorry juncture of my life was relive old times with a man who'd obviously come home to die.

"Regina, that's not fair. What do you think that fucking asshole boss of mine would say if I asked for more time off? He'd have fired me already if he wasn't afraid I'd sue Shelton/Murray because it wouldn't give me my family medical leave. Thank you, Bill Clinton."

Actually, it might have been worth getting fired to see the look on the Born Again National Sales Manager's face if I had cancelled my appointment with a VIP prospect in Connecticut so I could attend the funeral of a flamboyant fashion designer now known as Randy Sainte-Villaneuve, a man who had once danced with supermodels in the pages of *People*.

"Besides, he was your friend anyway," I said.

"That's not true," she insisted, insulted by my casual rewrite of Nocera family history. "Don't tell me you've forgotten how close the three of us were."

You bet your ass I've forgotten. I wouldn't admit it under the pain of death. Not a bit of it. Not that he was "Barbie," sloe-eyed, his face all cut glass angles and deep shadows, and she was "Midge," the "best friend," a natural born sidekick in corrective shoes with a half-moon pee stain on the seat of her pants. They spent days, weeks, entire summers, playing out his extravagant fantasies of Hollywood movie sets and European castles with her Barbie collection, all resplendent in outfits designed and stitched by a precocious little boy that were far more beautiful and elegant than the cheap costumes packaged by Mattel. And me? I was "Ken," the man in the henhouse, sometimes fussed and fought over by the "women" in my life, other times so infuriated at being excluded from their nasty secrets that I tore up the bridal gown Randall had spent a week sewing for Redhead Ponytail Barbie and etched *fuck* and *me* into Blonde Bubble Cut Barbie's tits with a ballpoint pen.

"I'll never understand why you turned against him," she sighed. "He was always such a sweet boy who loved you so much."

My sister can be almost willfully obtuse at times. But that's not fair to her. How could she know what happened whenever Randall Jarvis and I were alone? And what would she say if I were to tell her about all the times he talked me into putting my dick into his mouth or sticking my finger up his bum or persuaded me into lying on top of him, rubbing our naked weenies together until they were raw and chafed? All of which I was willing to do, wanted to do, even looked forward to doing, until the day he made the mistake of assuming he could confide in me.

"I wish I was a girl so I could be your girlfriend."

Years later, he'd returned in triumph for my sister's wedding, already famous beyond a small town's ability to comprehend, his gift her wedding gown. He seemed lost at the reception, self-conscious, the wretched town of Gastonia still able to intimidate a man who'd conquered the world. Tipsy on champagne cocktails, he approached me shyly, thinking he'd found a friendly face. His accent revived by alcohol, he said I looked wonderful, that he'd always known I'd become a handsome man, a son of the South.

I responded like any respectable Vice President of National Sales would have been expected to, like a true son of the South.

"Well, I hope you're proud of yourself, Randall, or whatever you call yourself these days."

My wife refused to speak to me the rest of the evening and well into the next day.

"You know, you still look like Princess Di," I assured my sister, changing the subject and wanting to make some long-overdue amends to her and to Randall Jarvis for my despicable behavior.

She snorted, dismissing the compliment.

"Right, with this damn nose and my dago skin."

"Well, she looked her best with a good suntan."

She's far too self-critical to accept a compliment, but I knew I'd pleased her and could end the dinner with a clear conscience.

"Oh, what the hell," she said, happy, if only for the briefest moment. "You only live once. I'm gonna order the mousse, even though I know it's probably Jell-O Instant Pudding in a champagne glass."

The dinner finally over, I got to the Carousel twenty minutes before closing. He wasn't there. I described him to the bartender. He shrugged, disinterested. I wouldn't give up. He would have been wearing hospital scrubs or an East Carolina School of Medicine sweatshirt. Oh yeah, the bar man said, he left over an hour ago. Yes, alone, as far as I know, he said when

I persisted. I wanted to call, to ask if I could come over, to confess I wanted to see him, but knew I would sound desperate.
The next morning I was scheduled to fly to Hartford for a five-
day swing through New England. I called from the boarding
area. He answered on the first ring, sounding annoyed. What's
wrong? he asked. I'd gotten him out of the shower; he was
dripping and shivering. I could tell he wanted to get off the telephone, to get dressed, to get to work on time. Was that a voice
in the background? Was he wildly gesticulating to the man he'd
brought home from the bar until he could get rid of me? Had
the bartender lied? No, it was only the perky chirp of the morning news anchor. I'll see you Saturday, he said, anxious to get
off the phone. *Don't forget me this week.* It seemed like forever
since he'd said those words. The tables had turned; he was slipping through my fingers, this confident, cheerful boy.

I had too much on my mind. Airline schedules. Hotel reser-
vations. Sales appointments. Doctor's appointments. Oncolo-
gists. A pharmacopoeia of goodies for my mother needing to be
picked up. And now Steve. No wonder I was always exhausted,
wanting to do nothing but sprawl across the roomy bed in the
Sheraton, and flush everything away with Budweiser and
Johnny Walker and the crummy homegrown weed I get from
the lawn boy at my mother's club. What's the difference if I
slept through the wake-up call as long as I was up by noon?

"I'm so very sorry," I said sheepishly. "I must be confused.
I'm sure the appointment is for two."

Meaning . . . what's the big deal? I'm here now. Let's go to
work.

The honest mistake routine had worked in Buckhead, Georgia, and Bryn Mawr, Pennsylvania, before that.

But not in Darien, Connecticut, where I was four hours late
for my appointment with the proprietor of an upscale kitchen-
ware shop in the wealthiest zip code in the United States of
America. Yes, I understand time is money and, yes, I under-

stand that like everything else, time is more expensive within the boundaries of Darien, Connecticut.

"The appointment was for nine A.M. I verified it this morning with Shelton/Murray."

I could almost hear that sniveling Born Again National Sales Manager licking this asshole's balls, appeasing him with promises of discounts.

"Well, perhaps if it wouldn't be inconvenient we could—"

He cut me dead.

"It would be very inconvenient."

The thought of facing the Born Again National Sales Manager made me cringe. This wasn't just some shopkeeper I'd alienated or a sale I'd lost. I'd managed to anger a Walking Endorsement, the author of a best-selling manual on grill techniques and a monthly column on cookware and utensils for the largest-circulation food and wine magazine. A man with an audience. A man with sufficient connections and influence to snare a design magazine spread on the expansion of his destination-point store. An article which would have prominently featured Shelton/Murray fixtures. In a nutshell, I'd fucked up.

But not fatally.

At least not this time.

The National Sales Manager forced himself to practice a little Born Again forgiveness.

But, going forward, he insisted I confirm every appointment by telephone twenty-four hours in advance.

Or else.

Finally, it was Saturday night. I met Steve at a cheap Italian restaurant near the hospital. I ordered a carafe of the house red and he asked the waitress for a Coke. No vino for me tonight, he announced. He'd picked up a night shift starting at eleven. I was dumbstruck. He was able to make a last-minute switch with a friend and patched together his three-day weekend. He'd scored a great airfare on the Internet and was flying to

Pompano Beach to spend Easter with his family. I couldn't even offer to drive him to the airport; it was all arranged. He was really looking forward to the break. He needed to decompress. Shit, the last month had been stressful, he sighed. (My fault? I wondered.) I pushed the spaghetti around my plate, choking at the sight of it.

He kissed me in the parking lot, seeming surprised when I didn't kiss him back. He shrugged it off, his mind already back at the hospital, already on its way to Florida. By the way, he said, there's a new movie he really wants to see. Maybe we could go together when he gets back if he doesn't catch it while he's in Florida.

"Happy Easter," I said as we parted.

"But I'll talk to you before Easter," he said.

"But I won't see you before Easter," I answered.

He shrugged and turned away, his backpack jiggling on his shoulder.

Driving home, I stared beyond the road and into the horizon, past the warm starlight and into the frigid black of the Cosmic Dark Age. Only the clinically depressed despair over the infinity of eternity. Well, wasn't I clinically depressed? Hadn't I been diagnosed? Was I not suitably medicated? Don't I have a right to chronic melancholy? My mother, the only human connection I have left, is dying. I will be even more alone than I am right now. How could she do this to me, abandon me at the time I need her most? I felt my heart racing, panic gripping me at the thought of her dying before I can thank her for her fierce and passionate loyalty, the gift of unconditional love my counselor assures me is rare and precious. But we're not talkers, she and I, not really. It's never been necessary. And just like it's always been enough for me to know she is there, ready to attack or defend as necessity demanded, now it's my physical presence, a somnambulant blob snoring and farting in the bedroom down the hallway, that reassures her during the long sleepless, painful nights. We don't need words, the two of us.

I swerved to miss a rabbit. The car buckled, smearing the poor bunny across the asphalt.

My mother. I'd barely thought of her since I met him. Even when I was listening to her complaints, answering her questions, playacting at having a conversation, my thoughts were in a bed-sitter on a pull-out mattress under an itchy blanket. I loved him and he was trying to escape without confrontation, without any ugly scenes. Why should he bother with those? It wasn't as if he loved me. I was a diversion, a release. The hospital was more important. So, of course, were his parents. His young and healthy parents who weren't even dying. Me. I would snap to attention when wanted and keep at a safe distance when not.

I made the decision quickly and dialed his machine before I could change my mind. I knew how I wanted to sound. Sad, but not hurt. Fond, but not in love. Not paternal, but maybe a bit avuncular.

Hi. Look. I understand how you feel. You didn't have to make up an excuse about having to work tonight. You could have just told me it's over. It would have been all right. I'll make this easy for you so you can enjoy your trip and not have to dread coming home to face me. I don't want to see you anymore. You can call if you like. So I'll talk to you if I talk to you.

I didn't know how to end the message. I couldn't find the right words to compel him to call. Words that would make him pick up the phone to tell me I had it all wrong. I checked my voice mail every hour for the next two days. It's Friday night, almost a week later, and I've accepted he'll never call. His silence means either his feelings for me were small and easily abandoned or deep enough to need protecting. I'll never know. Someday I will see him at the bar. It will be awkward. Maybe we will speak. Maybe I'll see him at the hospital during my mother's next inevitable admission.

"I'm shaping up," I swear to Matt. "No more missed appointments. I promise. My sales are good, better than good, great."

"You look like hell," he says. "Let's try this," Matt says, interrupting my patter to write me a script. "I've seen some good, relatively quick results with this medication."

I've got a better idea. Let's build a time machine and set the clock back ten, twelve, months ago. I don't need drugs. I need another chance. An opportunity to do things right this time. The days are getting longer, but the sky is growing darker all the time. Look ahead. Nasty-looking clouds are hovering on the horizon. The forecast is calling for storms.

Robert

Smelling your mother's farts feels uncomfortably close to incest. Disease does many ugly things, but this is the worst, this stripping away of dignity. She controls the things she can, observing the rituals, big and small, that mark her days. Sunday Mass at ten. Tuesday bridge nights. Friday mornings devoted to Forrest, who whips her new chemo wig into a facsimile of her old familiar hair. She accepts the things she can't control, like flatulence and the other rude outbursts of a body in revolt. She and I have learned to ignore them. She doesn't beg my pardon and I don't crinkle my nose and crack the car window. We sit tight, waiting for the not-altogether-unpleasant smell to atomize and disappear.

It's too cold to open the window anyway. Spring is in full bloom in the Piedmont, but winter still clings to these ancient hills. Columns of gray smoke rise from the bonfires of last season's field debris burning in the valleys below. The towns on the distant ridges all look the same, a dozen or so low-pitched tar-paper roofs clustered around the steeple of a white wood-frame church. Most of these buildings are older than my mother. There's no new construction in these hamlets. Their

200 / *Tom Mendicino*

citizens are all dying off. Only the valiant still force a living out of the exhausted fields.

My mother, the youngest of ten, escaped over forty years ago after being orphaned at sixteen. My grandfather went first, losing a slow, ugly battle with colon cancer. My grandmother followed eight months later, quickly, from a heart attack, leaving my mother, only a high school girl, to keep house for the two bachelor sons who'd stayed behind to run the farm. The other boys had fled Watauga County for the machine shops of Johnson City and Knoxville; Buster, my mother's favorite brother, made it all the way to occupied Japan, courtesy of the United States Army. Her sisters had left the farm when they'd married, following their husbands to Cleveland and Detroit, where union jobs in steel and construction paid good money. The house where she was born seemed strange, unwelcoming, after her parents died. She felt she was a burden on her brothers even though she washed their clothes and cooked their meals.

One Friday assembly during the fall of her junior year, the principal of her high school introduced a special guest from a brand-new factory up north. Mr. Yarnell, a gentleman in a black suit and heavy steel-frame glasses, had been dispatched to the backwaters to seduce the daughters of the harsh subsistence farms and dying towns of Appalachia with promises of adventure and excitement. The gray eyes behind the thick lenses saw the spark in my mother's eyes as he described the lush truck farms of New Jersey, bursting with sweet corn and beans and especially tomatoes. Trucks and trucks of huge, red tomatoes so ripe they split at the seams. My mother jumped at the opportunity to enlist in the army he was recruiting to bottle and label the rivers of ketchup flooding the Garden State.

Her oldest brother resisted signing the consent forms. But the principal was a kind man who intervened and gently persuaded my uncles to allow her to follow her dream. He came to the bus station to see her off a week later. They corresponded until he died of lung cancer ten years later. His letters are tied together with a blue ribbon and kept in a box with her photo albums. His name was Andrew Miller and I am his namesake.

My uncle Buster, his wanderlust cured by two tours of duty in the Pacific, inherited the Calhoun homestead when his bachelor brothers died. He went to his grave ten years ago leaving my cousin Bobby to fight the noble fight. After Bobby's gone, the farm most likely will be sold. His son JR spends his days staring at his computer screen, making contact with the world beyond this county, counting the days until, like my mother, he can escape.

We're close now, almost there. The scrub brush, still gray and bare, grows right up to the edge of the county road, hiding the ancient fence of stacked railroad ties that stakes out Calhoun territory. I make a sharp left and the car crawls up the rutted path to the barn. I help my mother to her feet. It's a long walk to the farmhouse and the stone path, worn smooth over the years, must be negotiated with care. The door to the barn is open. Inside, someone—my cousin Bobby most likely—is banging milk buckets and listening to the Power Country station on a portable radio. If he heard our car and our voices, and he must have, he is ignoring them.

My parents used the farm as a summer camp, sending me to Watauga County every July. The landmarks of my childhood are aging and precarious, but still extant. The barn, of course, never changes, reeking, as always, of damp straw and shit. I spent long afternoons as a kid shucking field corn in the mesh crib until blood blisters bubbled on my fingertips. The muddy pen, empty now, is where Uncle Buster performed a brutal autopsy on a sow that turned up dead one morning. The small slaughterhouse, garage to a new pickup truck these days, is where, laughing and drunk on beer, he pointed a fat kidney at us kids, threatening to squeeze piss in our faces. Ahead, closer to the house, is the chicken coop where I would trail my aunt as she gathered freshly laid eggs. But the old oak tree has lost the branch where the ruined tractor tire used to hang. I still have faint scars above my eyebrow and upper lip where its crusty bark tore up my face when I swung too high and lost control. Beyond the house are fields, and farther yet, the boarded-up entrance to a small, abandoned mine, the black hole in the earth where Bobby claimed to have killed a vampire bat, no, ten vampire bats as the story was embellished, that tried to suck the blood from his neck.

My aunt has been watching for us at the kitchen window and comes outside to greet us, her arms open to embrace my mother. They have known each other for more than half a century, their entire lives, and no words are necessary between them. My aunt tries to hide her shock and concern. She knows my mother has been sick, but is unprepared for the fragile creature she has become.

There's no affection in the hug she bestows on me. She's never been fond of me. My aunt is a tough old bird, broad and squat, butch despite the bleached French twist she's worn since the sixties. Almost seventy, she still walks like a shot-putter. Her one concession to the cool weather is not going barefoot and her little toes peek out of the frayed edges of her old, unlaced Keds. She loves boys, had three of them, and spent her life happily refereeing their roughhousing. My reticence as a child irritated her. She had no patience for any boy who feared bruises and pain.

I feel ten years old again.

I'm really nothing but a bystander, a spectator, to this weekend. I've finished my role, driving my mother, and have no other part to play. I have nothing to contribute to any conversations. My mother and aunt will take pleasure in each other's company, both thankful the other is alive, the last survivors of their generation. My cousin and his family will go about their routines as if we aren't here. I'll find a quiet place to read, maybe slip into the living room and stare at the television. There are no Catholic churches in this corner of the world and I can't even look forward to driving my mother to Mass to break the monotony. It will be an eternity until Sunday night when I will pack my mother into the car and head back down the hills, leaving this place behind.

Bobby's wife is cheerful enough. She doesn't mind the extra mouths to feed and enjoys the company. She knows we'll keep out of the way and out from under her feet. Damn, she says, staring at an Easter Bunny cake with coconut frosting fur and jelly-bean eyes. She forgot to buy licorice whips for its whiskers. The cake seems odd, a little out of place. JR is a teenager, too old for Peter Rabbit. She frets that Bobby will be sure to notice if the whiskers are missing. She needs to make a quick run to the drugstore. I offer to go for her. It's the least I can do. After all, there's sweet satisfaction in learning that the Fearless Vampire Killer might break down in tears if his Easter Bunny's missing his whiskers.

Up in Watauga County you can't simply jump in the car and drive five minutes to the local superstore. This mission could take me the entire afternoon. The local convenience store only sells candy bars; the drugstore in the nearest town sold the last bag of licorice whips an hour ago. Too bad. I suppose I'll have to drive all the way into Boone, to the Wal-Mart strip center or maybe to that little mall a few miles on the other side of the town. I'll hang around, nothing better to do.

The mall is grim. Bottom-of-the-line chain stores, bad lighting, high vacancy rate. The man lingering at the entertainment shelf of Waldenbooks wouldn't be my first or even second choice in a lineup of possibilities. He's slightly effeminate, puffy, and wearing a shabby Members Only jacket. He flips through a picture book, *The Films of Joan Crawford*, his eyes darting quickly between the page and me until we establish there is an understanding, an attraction, a chemistry. I decide he's not so bad after all. He's got a pleasant smile and a dimpled chin, and his gold wedding band is a powerful aphrodisiac. He clears his throat and slips Joan back on the shelf.

I tell myself I'm not really going to do this. But I know that I am. No one will ever know. I'll be careful. I won't do it unless I'm absolutely certain it's safe. I'm not really going to do it. It's just a fantasy and I'm bored. I already have an erection. The fact that I'm nervous, very nervous, makes it more exciting. I'm on autopilot as I follow him. He walks slowly, looking back over his shoulder, not trusting he won't lose me in a nearly empty mall deserted by everyone except a few elderly power walkers. He nods at the door marked Men and disappears inside. I steel myself for the inevitable: *Just do it! There's not another soul in sight. Do the deed, zip up, no harm, no foul.*

"Hi, Andy."

I'm speechless, confronted by my cousin Bobby's son as he emerges from the restroom.

"Be out in a minute, really got to go," I manage to say, flustered by this completely unexpected encounter.

He steps aside and I rush by. I'm so shaken I can barely locate my zipper. I fumble inside my shorts and try to find my dick. It's shriveled into my body cavity. It's not as if I had to piss anyway and I'm conscious of every passing second. I run my hands under the faucet, barely wetting them. My confused would-be paramour is peeping over the stall. I'm in and out in two minutes flat. No reason for anyone to be suspicious.

JR is standing at the door to Women, waiting for his girlfriend.

"Weird," he says, "running into you here."

He seems a bit embarrassed. Maybe he suspects something. I tell myself I'm being paranoid.

"Your mother sent me on a mission," I say.

"Oh yeah?"

"Licorice whips."

His eyebrows form a question mark.

"For the bunny cake."

I'm spared further explanation by the appearance of his girlfriend. Amanda, I think he says her name is, Mandy.

"You had lunch yet? We're going to grab something to eat."

Mandy doesn't look too pleased by his invitation. I tell him I've eaten and that I'll catch up with him back at the house.

"Well, have coffee then. You can have a cup of coffee."

She squeezes his arm, signaling him to not encourage me. She doesn't attempt subtlety, doesn't care I can see. Fuck the little slut. I say yes to spite her.

Mandy orders fries and a Diet Coke. She won't take off her cheap leather jacket even though the mall is overheated. Her magenta nail polish is chipped. She affects the Gothic look, her hair dyed black, parted in the middle and breaking at her shoulder, trying to project sensitivity through fashion. I feel hopelessly middle aged in my pastel polo shirt.

Bobby's son has changed since the last time I saw him. He's always had a face that hinted at masculine beauty. Now, at the verge of manhood, it's fulfilled its promise. He could pass for a heartthrob on one of those television teenage soap operas. *Watauga County 90210.* He has deep blue eyes and a perfect nose. His thick, shiny hair is a testimonial to the miracle qualities of his conditioner. He looks exactly like Bobby at his age except he didn't inherit the cruel streak that cast in cold stone those same perfect features in his father.

I congratulate him on his big news. He's headed for Chapel Hill come fall. It's a couple hundred miles away and on the other side of the moon. He's already shed the clothes of Watauga County. Gone are the dirty sneakers and down jackets, replaced by black T-shirts and boots, the look of MTV. A thrift-shop overcoat is slung over his chair. But none of these accoutrements, intended to make him look dark and ominous, can dampen his sunny disposition. He's a terrible mismatch

206 / *Tom Mendicino*

with this scrawny vulture who's licking the ketchup off a greasy limp fry.

We talk about college. He tries to appear world weary, but can't hide his eager giddiness at escaping this pit. He says he's sure that no one on campus will be cool, but it's just a show of bravado. He's already worried he's going to come off as a country bumpkin. We talk about pop music. He's amazed at how familiar I, a dinosaur, am with his favorites from the college radio station. I ask Mandy where she's going to college. She responds with a look of sheer hatred. I've picked at a scab.

"Mandy's thinking of going to nursing school," JR interjects.

It's impossible to imagine this harsh, brittle creature in the healing professions. Then I think back to all the snide and abrupt registered nurses I've encountered in the past few months and decide she'll probably graduate first in her class. She doesn't bother to thank me for picking up the check and her good-bye smile has a sarcastic undertone. JR thanks me profusely and promises me we'll catch up later.

I buy a bag of licorice whips. I try to kill time in the record store but the aisles of Nashville hitmakers depress me. The toilet is off-limits now. To go back would make me feel dirty, diseased, a polluter desecrating public places where nice, trusting kids like Bobby's son go to empty their bladders. I have nowhere to go but back to the farm. I hand over the candy and ask Bobby's wife where she wants me to bunk. She says she hasn't given it much thought. She's got a full house this weekend. Would I mind sharing? JR's got a double mattress and hasn't wet the bed in ten years, she laughs. It's either that or the couch.

That's fine, I say, and excuse myself to take a nap. I want to sleep until dinner, through dinner if I can get away with it.

The nap doesn't refresh me. After dinner, I collapse, staring at the television as the Braves lose to the Phillies in an early season series while Bobby snores in his lounge chair. I can barely keep my eyes open. It's all of ten o'clock and I'm exhausted. I head off to bed.

I strip to my underwear and crawl between the sheets. Bobby's wife hasn't bothered with fresh linen. I worry I'm sleeping on his side of the bed. He's in for a big surprise when he comes home, maybe a little tipsy, Mandy on his fingertips, if, in fact, he comes home at all. I haven't slept in this room, a stuffy dormer, right below the roof beams, for twenty-five years. The old mattress is full of peaks and valleys. It's probably the same bed where I slept as a boy. Bobby always had a double, even as a kid, a place for my aunt to exile Uncle Buster when he drank too much beer and farted in bed and tried to take a poke at her. Maybe that explains why she never liked me. When I was here, she had nowhere to send him and had to endure his dick.

The door opens and JR lowers himself on the bed. One shoe drops, then the other. The bed shifts as he shucks off his jeans and pulls off his socks. My muscles stiffen, resisting gravity when the bed sags as he lies down. He smells like soap and pizza, no trace of beer or Mandy. He yawns and his elbow grazes my back when he reaches up to scratch his head. Then he flops to his side, shaking the bed, and is asleep in a minute.

I grip the edge of the mattress, determined no part of my body will touch any part of his. But, in his sleep, he drops his hand on my waist. What next? Is he going to start stroking my ribs while he dreams of Mandy? It takes me hours to fall asleep.

He's up and gone before I wake. It's nearly eleven, an unconscionable time to rise on a farm. I pull on my pants and shoes and guiltily make my way to the kitchen, hoping to find some dregs in the coffeepot.

My mother is working at the kitchen table. Her perky wig contrasts with her exhausted face. She soldiers on cheerfully, rolling the dough and cutting it into perfect squares. My aunt stands behind her, hovering, playing backfield, ready to catch her if she collapses. She thinks she is being discreet and my mother is careful not to let her irritation show. My mother and I know a tornado couldn't bring her down, let alone a little chronic fatigue. She's been up since dawn. The tomatoes on the stove have already cooked down to a thick sauce. The Calhouns will have one more Ravioli Easter. It's my mother's contribution to the family reunion. Up here in the hills, pizza chains with guaranteed thirty-minute delivery and Al Pacino in *The Godfather* are the sum and substance of things Italian. The Calhouns wait each year for their homemade pasta.

My mother insists on brewing a fresh pot of coffee for me. My aunt grudgingly pulls the can of Maxwell House from the refrigerator and carefully spoons out just enough for a two-cup pot. I've won a small victory and don't bother to suppress a smug smile. My mother stuffs and folds and pinches the corners of her ravioli while the coffee perks in the background. She looks up and sees me staring at her. She smiles, letting me know she appreciates what drudgery this weekend is for me, promising that, in a day, it will be over. Her smile is an apology, not asked for, unearned. Why she loves me so much I will never understand. If I don't leave the kitchen I might start to cry.

I want to go back to sleep, to crawl back into bed and not leave the room until Sunday evening. The day ahead, or what's left of it, stretches and yawns, mocking me with its leisurely pace. The coffee does the job. I have to shit. It's inevitable.

I'd hoped to get through the weekend without the need to take a crap in this tiny bathroom. It's an add-on, its walls nothing more than drywall partitions. The family still goes to the outhouse for privacy when the weather is warm. There's one advantage to sleeping late. At least I'm not spurting while foot traffic passes outside the door. While I'm at it, I might as well shower and shave. The water is tepid and keeps me from lingering. I wrap a towel around my waist and walk back to the bedroom, surprising JR. He slaps shut the book he's holding between his legs and self-consciously covers the title with his broad hand.

He smiles and tries to act nonchalant, telling me I can have the room to myself, now that he's found what he was looking for. Mildly intrigued by the kid's odd behavior, I scan the paperbacks on the shelf by the bed. Nothing out the ordinary for a seventeen-year-old boy, certainly not anything that raises any red flags. *Franny and Zooey. Stranger in a Strange Land* and *Dune. Silas Marner* and *The Mayor of Casterbridge* (neither spine creased, required reading, no doubt), the mandatory Tolkien and Orwell. A bottom-of-the-line Taylor acoustic is propped in the corner. There's a chord book with leaves of loose sheet music. Some pretty hip stuff. Old Velvet Underground songs—"Sweet Jane," "Head Held High." A stack of printed e-mail messages slips out of the book.

Jesus H. Christ! Holy shit!

I've stumbled across the mother lode. I read them once, then again, letting it sink in. It's hard, no, impossible, to believe the clean-cut kid I just shared a bed with has a secret identity as WrestlerJoc2071. Bobby's son is maintaining a heavy correspondence with some unsavory characters. Mongoloids, probably, who can't string a coherent English sentence together, but who demonstrate a definite affinity for constructing pithy screen names trumpeting physical attributes and sexual predilections.

Leantight8.

NCbtm4U.

JOBuddy.

NCtop4U.

Sukitall.

Once I get over the shock, I feel almost giddy discovering another aberration in the family tree. A little twinge of guilt for invading his privacy doesn't keep me from reading his e-mails. WrestlerJoc2071 tries hard to go mano a mano with the hardcore sexualists, peppering his talk with descriptions of throbbing cocks and quivering assholes. But his phrases have a tentative cadence that reveals his tender, young heart. He's naïve enough to believe the love and acceptance he's seeking can be found in this miasma of pornography pecked onto a screen by sticky, dirty fingers. The object of his affection calls himself OnMiKnees4U. They're embarking on a romance, one so deep and real and full of promise and undying devotion they actually share their names, their first ones at least.

> *Dear Cary,*
> *Thanks for the pic. I hope you aren't too disappointed by mine. Some people tell me I'm handsome, but I don't believe it. If I had seen your pic first, I wouldn't have had the nerve to send mine. I hope you will still write back now that you know what I look like.*
> *I can't believe we found each other online. I can't believe that in only five months I will be at Chapel Hill too. I know there's so many things you can teach me. I am reading the book you suggested. It kind of scares me. But I like it very much.*
> *And I love you very much.*
> *Robert*

Robert? He's already begun his double life, taking a new name. But then again, who really expected him to go through life answering to JR, called that only to distinguish him from his father?

And this Cary? Why do I expect it isn't a real name? Why do I suspect JR is fated to spend many lonely evenings in September, wandering the streets of the campus, looking up at windows and wondering if the boy sitting, reading, writing, staring at a computer screen, is the Cary who disappeared into cyber-space without a last name or address or telephone number?

I rifle through the papers looking for the picture of Cary. But JR hasn't printed it. It's safe in his program file, secured by his password. What would it mean anyway? The face in the picture probably doesn't even belong to "Cary." JR is too young, too trusting, to even imagine such duplicity.

Who is this predator? Some ancient, overweight tenured faculty troll, belching after indulging in rich meals and glasses of port, sublimating his sexual frustrations? Some scrawny graduate student in Birkenstocks with clove cigarettes on his breath and an ass that smells like macrobiotic rice? Whoever this creature is, he's putting JR at risk, laying the foundation for a lifetime of heartaches.

And what the hell was JR doing in that notorious toilet at the mall? Did he have an agenda more sinister than taking a piss and washing his hands? I have to find him and warn him. He's starting down the wrong road, one that could lead to a dead end on the interstate on a sticky summer night, to arrest and probation (if he's lucky).

Neither my mother nor his knows where he is. Bobby's wife looks out the window and says his car is gone.

"He'll be back, probably with that girlfriend of his. Wait till you see her, hard as nails and looks like she's been around the block a few times. Bobby has a fit every time he brings her around. But I tell him to calm down. JR's at that age that it would only throw gasoline on the flame if we started bitching about her. Let it go and it'll die out. Hope I'm right or Bobby's gonna put me six feet under." She laughs.

I ought to tell her not to bother measuring the shroud, but keep my mouth shut.

He's back home in time for dinner, the notorious Mandy in tow. She doesn't disappoint the low expectations of her. The leather jacket must be a second skin. Again, she refuses to take it off despite, or maybe because of, Bobby's wife's many gentle suggestions and Bobby's very apparent irritation. Me, I'm feeling a little sympathy for Mandy, much to my surprise. Each little grunt, each shrug of her shoulders, each toss of her stringy hair betrays the feelings of inadequacy stirred by the big, beautiful boy sitting next to her. He's unfailingly polite despite his juvenile delinquent gear and engages my mother in conversation almost to the point of flirting with her. He tells Mandy to just wait until tomorrow, she's never tasted anything like Aunt Ruth's ravioli. Bobby almost chokes on the unexpected invitation.

Mandy has heard my mother is very sick and manages a smile in her direction. You have lovely eyes, my mother says, finding the silver lining in every cloud. Thank you. Mandy blushes, immediately turning to JR to see if he agrees.

I've seen that look a thousand times before on Alice, abashed by compliments on her hair, her skin, her waist, her dress. Like Mandy, she'd look to me, seeking confirmation by the only one who really mattered, the only one who seemed oblivious to her wonders and mysteries. I've seen that same expectation in her eyes, never giving up hope that, suddenly, the scales would fall from my own and I would see her as the world saw her.

But JR's attention is fully on me. He wants me to join them tonight. They're going to the movies. A "chick flick," he says, rolling his eyes, thinking Mandy can't see him. She tells him the name of the movie. They're all the same, he says.

"It's Julia Roberts," Mandy says. "She's really beautiful."

Even Bobby's interest is piqued by Julia Roberts. Everyone at the table has an opinion about her eyes, her lips, her hair, her body, and, of course, her smile. I wait for JR's turn, curious to hear his remarks.

"She can't act her way out of a paper bag," he says.

I laugh, agreeing.

"Then you gotta come," he pleads. "Misery loves company."

Once again Mandy must accept the inevitable. She's counting the hours until I leave and she has JR to herself again. She hasn't given up yet. Someday soon she's going to prod him beyond soul kisses and titty squeezing. She's going to get her hands on that thing in his pants and put it inside her. But time's running out. Only a few months until he disappears. She's desperate, knowing he'll never return except for the occasional holiday, which she'll spend sitting by a phone that never rings.

I take him up on the offer. Why not? The alternative is another night listening to Bobby snore in front of the television, sprawled in his Barcalounger, erection rising in his pants, dreaming of Julia Roberts.

Good old Julia works her movie magic and cracks the crust of Mandy's heavy makeup. She's sobbing by the time the credits roll, the prince having swept Julia to his Manhattan penthouse where they live happily ever after. JR feigns studied indifference but his eyes are a little red when the lights go up. I barely remember anything about the movie. I'd expected Mandy to sit between us, but JR stepped aside, letting her in the aisle first, leaving him and me knee to knee the entire two hours.

A whirlwind had raced through my mind as Julia cavorted across the screen. What should I say to him? How would I even broach the subject? I could tell him about myself, not the disgusting, dirty details, just enough to highlight my mistakes, warning him about paths not to take. We could talk about love. I could assure him a sweet and gentle soul awaits him. I could tell him not to throw himself away, not to let himself get bitter and callous and unable to trust love when it finally appears. I would promise him it will happen. If not for me, at least for him.

And that's why, when the lights go up, my eyes are red too.

Mandy's pimples need feeding. Over another plate of french fries, she quizzes JR about his reaction to every twist and turn in the plot of the movie, seeking the passionate soul she knows he's hiding behind his placid demeanor. JR is distracted, lost in his own fantasies of Prince Charming. He insists on picking up the tab tonight. After all, I bought lunch.

Without thinking, I say . . .

"Thanks, Robert."

I might have just handed him the crown jewels of Russia. He beams, ecstatic. A look of absolute delight lights up his face. He knows I understand him, at what level he's not sure, but I know he is Robert now, that JR will be left behind for good when he finally escapes Watauga County.

We never have that soul-to-soul chat. This is Watauga County, after all, not a Julia Roberts movie. I wait in the car while he walks Mandy to her door and gives her a chaste kiss on the cheek. We listen to the car radio as we drive home. He can't wait to get to Chapel Hill and hear *real* radio. WXYC is totally cool. The disc jockey plays an oldie we both love. "Kiss Me on the Bus." I tell him I saw the band years ago; they played at a roller rink in Raleigh and got so drunk they fell off the stage. They're his all-time favorite group, he says; he wishes he could have seen them.

"Yeah, then you'd be as old as me." I laugh.

"You're not that old," he answers.

Home, we go directly to bed. We undress shyly, careful not to look at each other, and crawl under the covers. Long minutes pass in the dark and I think he has fallen asleep. Then, sounding younger than he has all night, he asks me a question.

"Andy?"

"Yeah?"

"Are you happy?"

Something about his tender solicitousness compels me to lie.

"Happy enough."

"Good."

My answer seems to satisfy him and he rolls over on his side. He's soon swept up in the arms of Morpheus, transported to a big, fluffy bed in a penthouse in the sky and Prince Cary is swearing his eternal love and the credits roll and they live happily ever after.

Calling Dunkin' Donuts

I know better than to call from the phone at my mother's house. The King of Unpainted Furniture is certain to have caller ID. He'll have a stroke if the name Anthony Nocera pops up. (The phone is still listed in my father's name even though he's been dead for years.) I'm sure the King is screening her calls. Particularly today, traditionally an occasion for greetings and best wishes. I know how he thinks: *Wouldn't it be just like that little worm, that little piece of shit, to pick a day like today, when she's even a bit more vulnerable than usual, to come sniveling around, tail between his legs, with promises of how he's changed, how it was all just a bad dream.*

Over his dead body. No, more likely, over *my* dead body.

He's sure to have taken precautions. He's probably thrown every single Catholic in the state of North Carolina at his daughter. He wouldn't even bother to check out the portfolios of the older ones or the prospects of the young. What the fuck would he care? He'd floated me for years. Nothing he couldn't do again. The screening wouldn't be rigorous. Alcoholics, deadbeat dads, suspects under indictment, numerous cases of halitosis and body odor, countless fashion victims in polycotton blend khakis: they'd all pass with flying colors. There was only one qualification.

None of them could be me.

A shot of bourbon will bolster my confidence. A small one, just enough to give me a backbone. What if she hangs up on me? What if she tells me she doesn't want to hear from me and threatens dire consequences if I try to contact her again? Worse yet, what if she laughs at me? That would be the cruelest response of all, more terrifying than a vicious, angry attack. Stop making excuses, I think. That's not your Alice, she's incapable of hate. How do I know? I know because she wrote me a letter after the house was sold. The sentences were so perfectly straight I could almost see the invisible ruler guiding the pen across the stationery. Her wastebasket probably overflowed with balls of expensive writing paper, discarded if the pen went an eyelash astray. The perfection of the handwriting and the symmetry of the pages affected me as much as the words themselves.

No prosecutor could have drafted a more damning indictment of my indefensible betrayal and her humiliation.

I finally found the courage to ask my gynecologist for the test. Knowing the questions she would ask didn't prepare me for the shock of hearing her words. What are your risk factors, Alice? How often did you and your husband have unprotected sex?

No judge or jury would have shown me such undeserved mercy.

I would have preferred to say all this in person, but I knew I couldn't. For too many years, I was willing to close my eyes to everything, ignoring the obvious, not because I thought things

218 / *Tom Mendicino*

would change, but because I wanted them to stay the same. Living without a husband is easy. But every day I miss my best friend.

I've read and reread it more times than I can count. I wanted to, meant to, reply. One epistle, carefully crafted in my head over several days in Denver, came close to being committed to posterity. It was apologetic, empathic. I wanted her to know I wished I were different. I'd change if I could. That even if I ever found someone to love, I'd never love anyone more. I should have scribbled it onto paper while I was euphoric and light-headed in the thin air of the Mile-High City. But my best intentions sank in the oppressive humidity of North Carolina. I never set pen to paper.

Nothing has changed. I'm still rejecting her, sending her to the mailbox day after day, expectantly at first, certain I would respond, despondent when, after a few weeks, she realized I wouldn't. Why doesn't she curse me as the bastard I am and hate me with a blazing white passion? No, she still finds some excuse to exonerate my bad behavior, excoriating herself for the unpardonable transgression of making a small, kind effort to reach out to me. Drink me, I say, and she drinks and she keeps on shrinking, Tiny Alice in our little Southern Gothic melodrama.

Tonight I'm going to make amends. I pull out my cell phone and dial the number. She answers on the second ring.

"Dunkin' Donuts!"

Alice sounds happy and giddy, a little tipsy. I ought to try something witty, something half-witted, like "a dozen chocolate glazed to go." But my mouth is too dry and my voice is cracking. "Happy Birthday" is all I can manage.

"Oh my God!"

Oh my God good or Oh my God bad?

"Oh my God. I'm so glad you called."

Oh my God good.

I hear the clatter of dishes, chatter, glasses clinking. She's on the kitchen phone.

"Sounds like quite a bash going on there."

"Yeah."

She sounds a little hesitant, nervous, as if her deeply rooted Southern conscience is stricken. How impolite. Caught red-handed. She's having a party and I'm not invited.

Hold on a minute, she says.

I hear her talking to someone. *Just an old girlfriend,* she says, *calling to wish me a happy birthday. Who? Susie. You remember her. I'll remind you later. I'll just be a minute.*

I hear a door open and close as she steps outside, into the quiet evening.

"That's better. I'm so glad you called," she says again as if she doesn't know what else to say.

"Hey, I'm sorry I never wrote back."

"That's okay. I shouldn't have written you."

"Stop apologizing."

"Sorry. How is Ruth? I heard about the cancer."

"Not too good."

"I've wanted to call, but I didn't know if . . ."

"She'd really like that."

"I'd like to see her. I miss her."

"That would be real nice."

"Are you sure?"

"I'm sure. I'll tell her you're gonna call. She'll look forward to it."

"I'll call tomorrow."

"Okay."

I ask after her sisters, her mother. She catches herself before she asks if I want to say hello to them.

"Look, don't tell them I called."

"No. I won't."

It's a nice, comfortable feeling to share a secret with her again.

"Are you all right?" she asks.

"Sure."

"I mean, I just mean with Ruth and all. It has to be hard on you. That's all I meant."

"I know that."

"So how are you?" she asks.

"I'm okay. Really."

"I worry about you," she says.

You shouldn't. You shouldn't even think about me. And if you do, it should be to hate me. Don't let your mind drift across the years, skipping from memory to memory, skimming the surface of our life together. The Turnbull & Asser shirt and the tie from Pink you gave me on my thirtieth birthday. Our first night in our first home. A hot Fourth of July in Rome, drunk on Sambuca, celebrating ten years of marriage, promising each other to return to this same little place to celebrate our twentieth. You holding my head as I vomited in the toilet, devastated by the call telling me my father was dead. Small, insignificant events and the important landmarks of our life, now all equalized by the passage of time, none able to evoke any emotion stronger than nostalgia for the past.

"I worry about you too," I say.

"Andy, I'm so glad you called."

"That's the fourth time you've said that." I laugh. "I'm starting to think you're trying to convince yourself."

"Well, I was thinking of calling you anyway. I just . . . well . . . Andy, I'm pregnant."

I barely hear the rest of the conversation. It's a double celebration—a birthday and engagement party. Her fiancé is so sweet. He has a thirteen-year-old son. He's so nervous about starting a new family. He's this. He's that. She knows I would like him.

I'm only half conscious of her voice. I'm more a detached observer, someone overhearing a conversation in a dream and recognizing a familiar voice responding with the polite niceties. I'm so happy for you. No one deserves to be happier. I know the baby's going to be beautiful. Have you thought of any names?

"Andy, are you okay?"

"Of course I'm okay."

I need to let her go, send her back into the kitchen, back to her new life.

"I'm glad I called."

"It was a great birthday surprise."

Not as great as the one you've given me.

"Andy?"

"Yeah."

"You know this doesn't mean I don't love you. I'll always love you. In some way."

In some way. At long last, a level playing field. Now the love going both ways has qualifications, conditions.

She bursts out laughing. At first, I think she is mocking me. No. Someone has come up from behind and grabbed her by the waist. She giggles, says bye-bye, and hangs up the phone. And ninety-some miles to the north, the scene continues without me, the not-so-young lovers, still enchanted by the newness of their attraction, swaying to music that only they can hear, a favorite song, its lyrics known only to them.

Who wrote this ending to my story, the one that started on a night like this, hot and sticky, when I looked up to the constellations and instead saw my neighbor's son stepping out of his underpants? The night that ended with me in the back of a squad car, too stunned to even cry? The Brothers Grimm have given her a knight in shining armor, a Prince Charming to rescue her, and a house full of people applauding her happily ever after. I'm not sure I like the way this has turned out, not that

222 / Tom Mendicino

she doesn't deserve the happiness a new life and a baby can bring her. I refill my glass and stroll barefoot out into the backyard, uneasy, consumed by a strange, unprecedented fit of jealousy, agitated by the only conclusion to be drawn from the life growing inside her.

Someone, someone who is not me, has stuck his fucking dick in her and got her pregnant.

You're an idiot, I say out loud, pacing across the lawn. Did you expect her to remain untouched, unsoiled, shrouded in the veil of celibacy, faithful beyond the legal bonds of the marriage, until death did us part?

Yes, I admit, in a rare moment of honesty, too devastated by the knowledge that I've been completely and irrevocably replaced to have the strength to lie.

Rolex

Her words aren't explicit. But her body language, her moods, tell me, tell the world, what she can't quite bring herself to say. She's scared. Things aren't going well. She's not responding to the treatment as well as was hoped. She's cranky, irritable, prone to snapping. Not at me. Never at me. She's very careful how she handles me. Just yesterday she bit her tongue so sharply I'm sure she drew blood. A single harsh syllable managed to escape before she clamped down. The pitch, the tone of her voice, indicated criticism. Of what? My inattentive driving? My distracted grunts at the latest updates from Florida? The volume of the radio? The station? I turned off the music, cleared my throat, and asked a question about my niece Jennifer, defusing the tension, if only temporarily.

But today, I am sitting across from my mother, and the table between us feels as wide as the Sahara. I feel small, horrible actually, at my reaction when she hands a gift-wrapped box to me. My mother laughs, asking if I remember my father's rule book for life. The three simple laws all men must obey. Of course I remember.

No jewelry but a watch.

Boxers, not briefs.

Men don't wear sandals.

I've never broken a single one, even refusing to wear a wedding ring. Did him proud on that one. But the gift in the box meets rule one only by a technicality. Calling it a watch is like calling the mansions of Newport cottages. *Functional* is not a word I'd use to describe it. Uncomfortable, queasy actually, is how it makes me feel.

"You don't like it."

"No. Of course I do."

"No. You sniffed it."

"What?"

"You sniffed it. Ever since you were a little boy, I could always tell if you liked something by your face. If you didn't like it, you sniffed. It always reminded me of a cat."

"That's not true."

"Why are you arguing with me?"

"I'm not arguing with you."

"It's Mother's Day and I'm your mother and no one knows you as well as I do."

My counselor accuses me of describing my mother as if she were an ethereal spirit, rarely engaged, a benign, but remote, presence. He says I romanticize her, speaking of her like she's Cinderella, content in her life of servitude. He says he senses conflict between us, deeper and more painful to admit than that with my father. Bullshit, I tell him.

No one knows you as well as I do.

It brings the blood rushing to my cheeks. I call the waiter over and order a drink, a real drink, muddy hundred-proof swill, no ice. And much to my surprise, my mother asks him to bring her another glass of wine, no, make that a highball please, with ginger ale, on the weak side. She takes a cigarette from the package and asks for an ashtray. It's a nonsmoking section but some strange authority in her voice compels him to obey.

My mother, by Bette Davis.

I wish my counselor were here to witness this little scene. See, Matt. My mother's not the Pollyanna you say I make her out to be. I know she's not perfect. But why should I share that with you? Why should I give you the opportunity to pick her apart? She's at least earned my loyalty, hasn't she? She's never done anything to hurt me. And I really resent you implying she has. All right, all right, I'm inferring that, you didn't imply it. Thank you for correcting my word usage once again.

"Well, you're wrong," I inform her. "I love it."

"Then why are you sniffing it?"

"I don't know. It's just . . . well, I don't know. I mean, it's Mother's Day and I take you to dinner and give you a dozen roses and you drop five grand on a fucking watch."

"Watch your language."

"Sorry."

"Well, it's Mother's Day and I'm allowed to do what I want and I wanted to celebrate being a mother."

"What about Gina?"

"Taken care of. Diamond earrings."

"Why are you doing this?"

She takes a deep drag on her cigarette and blows the smoke across the table, annoyed.

"You know why."

No, Matt. You're wrong. There's no conflict between my mother and me. There can't be. Just the opposite. It's been her mission in life to protect me, keep me safe, and make sure the world has righted all the wrongs it has inflicted on me.

All that boy wants is to be with you. Why can't you give him that?

That voice is so clear in my memory it's as if I'm back in my bedroom, listening to my parents argue downstairs. That voice, quiet but persistent, insistent, repeated over and over, throughout my life. The voice of the iron fist in the velvet glove.

My mother, insisting she be put through to the commander

226 / *Tom Mendicino*

of the Army base, persuading him to punish his vicious brat of a son for bloodying my mouth and calling me an unspeakable name.

My mother, demanding an audience with the school principal, making it clear that it was in my swim coach's best interest to deliver me a heartfelt apology for calling me "Anita" after a dismal showing—second place—at an invitational meet.

My mother, intimidating my father with her steely gaze, forcing him to confront the neighborhood asshole who was mimicking my high-pitched voice. *Yeah, and when your kid's digging ditches, my kid will be doing brain surgery and making six figures a year.* He sounds almost convincing. I remember him looking back over his shoulder, making sure my mother had seen and heard him doing the right thing.

My mother, speaking to my lawyer, telling him she'd take care of everything, the judge would be more than satisfied with the arrangements she would make.

My mother's voice, always fighting for me, as if I were incapable of fighting for myself.

"It's beautiful, it really is," I say.

My mother does this quirky thing when she smokes. She flicks the tip of her tongue against her lips, chasing phantom pieces of tobacco, a habit ingrained from all those years dragging on unfiltered cigarettes. Only she hasn't smoked cigarettes without filters for decades.

"Good."

"What's that?" I ask, forever and always distracted.

"It's good."

She means the chicken she's sawing away at. I'm ashamed of myself for not paying attention and, worse yet, for being irritated by her voice. *Good.* She stills slings a diphthong across those vowels. What's she saying? Gud? G'wood? That's it. *G'wood.* Why does she still speak with that hillbilly twang after all these years? It's not like she's some fucking Queen of Country Music who has to market her "authenticity." And what's so *g'wood* about that dry stuffed chicken breast on her plate? How many times has she ordered the same goddamn thing in this same goddamn Gastonia-elegant club dining room with its linen napkins and a dusty silk rose in the lead crystal bud vase? It isn't *g'wood*. It's bland and tasteless, seasoned with nothing but salt and pepper and McCormick's all-purpose spice blend. She reads the critical glint in my eyes and, not quite certain why she's earned my disapproval, puts down her fork and wipes her mouth with that linen napkin.

I feel like a piece of shit. Why am I so carelessly cruel? What am I doing? She's been nauseous for weeks; the antiemetics are finally working. Why am I denying her the small pleasure of her Sunday dinner? I'd apologize, but there's really nothing to apologize for. After all, nothing hurtful has been said, it's all just been a misunderstanding, a misinterpretation, a misreading of signals. I want to talk to her, but I can't. I want to talk about this morning, tell her I heard it all. She thought I was asleep upstairs when I was lying in bed, hiding, tugging on my dick, jacking off twice, three times, until I got nothing but dry heaves for my efforts. I heard the familiar kitchen sounds, cake pans rattling in the cabinet, the whir of the mixer, the cling and clang of spoon on bowl, the oven bell, followed by the unfamiliar, a wail, tears and curses, then a deep sigh before getting on with it, rinsing, washing, cleaning up.

When my sister and I were kids, my mother always baked a cake for Mother's Day. Red velvet layer cake for me in odd years, coconut sheet cake for my sister in even years. It was supposed to be red velvet this morning, even though it's an even year. All she got for her time and effort was two thick puddles to be flushed down the disposal. Later, when I finally made my appearance, she made a joke of it. Imagine. Forgetting the baking soda. But what she was really thinking was how the malignancy is chewing up her sticky brain cells, digging deep holes into which things disappear, never to be retrieved.

What time is it? she'll ask. Ten minutes later than the last time you asked, I'll think. Two twenty, I'll say.

She's sentimental these days; the past has acquired a warm, fuzzy glow. Did I know she wanted to be a stewardess? No, I say, resigned to hearing the story again, knowing the pleasure she gets from telling it. She still has a letter from Mr. Peter van Hussell, Recruiter, telling her the airline was growing and encouraging her to apply again when she was eighteen.

My mother, by TWA, in a perfectly tailored suit and jaunty cap, silk scarf knotted at her throat and immaculate white gloves on her hands, dispatching her duties, maybe catching the appreciative eye of the captain.

Coffee, tea, or milk?

She might have traveled the world, had adventures, met people earthbound girls would never have an opportunity to encounter, had songs and stories written about her. But first, she wanted to see the ocean. The Jersey shore was only an hour away from the ketchup factory and her roommate Betty had a car. Every man should be as fortunate as my father and first appear as an object of desire backlit by a blazing sun. She was on her back, her arm slung across her face to protect her eyes from the sun. The voice, gravelly, with a harsh accent, light-years from the familiar rhythms of the Carolina hills, made her turn her head in the sand. She opened her eyes and saw his flat, strong feet, inches from her face. My mother's eyes wandered up his calves, his thighs, passed quickly over the wet jersey trunks, and settled on the black thicket covering his chest. Her eyes played a silly trick on her and created a halo effect around his head. He could never have been born in her mountains, not with his thick black brows and crooked nose and eyes such a deep brown they seemed black. He belonged to another world.

He had big white teeth and a smile that made her believe he could see through her modest swimsuit. And when he knelt beside her, she was thrilled and mortified at the same time.

He smiled and told her what a pretty voice she had. He made her repeat his name over and over.

Anthony.

Again . . .

Anthony.

What's my name?

Anthony.

He persuaded her to wade into the water. She was too shy to tell him she couldn't swim, had never even stood in water deeper than her knees. And when she wobbled in the surf, frightened and tentative, he stood behind her. His reflexes were quick and, when a wave knocked her off her feet, he caught her before she fell.

My father, too restless to settle for a union manufacturing job and frustrated by the limited opportunities for a journeyman machinist, was rebuilding his life on the G.I. Bill the summer he met my mother, focusing his ferocious energy on mastering the intricacies of heating and air-conditioning. She was not quite twenty and he was thirty-one when they married in a civil ceremony at City Hall in Philadelphia the following year. She didn't write her brothers; a few of the girls from the factory were her only family at the ceremony. She spent her wedding night and the first year of her married life in his bedroom in his mother's house. One year after the civil ceremony, after my mother converted, she and my father were married again, properly, in Saint Mary Magdalen de Pazzi Parish. My mother was three months pregnant with me on her second wedding day.

I might have grown up on the streets of South Philadelphia, nourished on cheesesteaks and Italian water ice, but my father had dreams and a wanderlust that would take him far from the neighborhood where he was born. On an unseasonably warm October morning, he helped his expectant wife into a used Oldsmobile packed with their few belongings and drove away, leaving his weeping family behind on the stoops of Montrose Street. He had five hundred dollars and the president of Pennco Technical School's letter of introduction to an alumnus who was looking for an apprentice in small city in the South. When he asked my mother, a native of North Carolina, about Gastonia, she looked at him as if he had asked her to describe Jupiter or Mars. And so, within three years of leaving the farm, my mother was back in North Carolina, never to leave again.

He could be demanding. He could be thoughtless. He had a temper and sometimes lashed out, frustrated by the world. She wished he could be more patient with me. But he never hit her or her kids and didn't get drunk and didn't run around with other women. He was better than a good provider. And, once upon a time, he had washed her hair and crooned Sinatra tunes in her ear while they swayed to the radio. A lifetime later, on what would be their last anniversary, he told her the day she married him was the happiest day of his life and she held and comforted him while he cried, ashamed because diabetes had left him incapable of making love to her. She told him she didn't mind, and she didn't because, after his body failed him, he started to woo her again, kissing her gently first thing in the morning and the last thing at night, just before she spooned her body into his and he fell asleep. If you asked her, she'd tell you she's had a good life. The world has surprised her by letting her be happy.

My mother, by June Allyson.

But that was the past, and what terrifies her is the future. The holes are getting bigger, and one day, soon maybe, she'll blithely emerge from the bedroom, her wig on backward, lipstick smeared like a clown, her blouse unbuttoned, her slip mistaken for a skirt. She'll be smiling, unaware she's an object of ridicule, no, worse, an object of pity. Poor thing, they'll say, re-member how meticulous she was about her appearance? Today it's baking soda. Tomorrow she might be wandering naked into the street.

She'd let me sleep this morning, knowing how hard it is to work all week and be at her beck and call all weekend. I need my rest so I can turn her over to Rent-A-Nurse tomorrow morning and hop a flight to escape. And no sooner will I board the plane than I'll start to miss her, regretting all these days spent away from her, the dwindling opportunities to let her know what she's meant to me. But if I stay she'll drive me crazy. *G'wood*, she'll say over and over again until it pushes me past the breaking point and I'll want to smash her against the wall.

"Finish your drink," she says when the waiter offers coffee. She stares at me, wondering whether this human detritus sitting across the table is her fault. I look away, down at my new watch.

"You shouldn't have done this," I say, looking at my watch.

"You're right, maybe I shouldn't have," she says, sipping her coffee. "But I did."

That's my mother. Are you happy now, Matt?

Casta diva

Another Kennedy is dead.

The talk show host says we measure our lives by their tragedies.

The sunlight pierces the dark lenses of my Ray-Bans. I need coffee and aspirin and water. Especially water. My mouth feels like I gargled with sand. The flight from New York to Charlotte was torture. Barely navigating on two hours of sleep, I got to the gate just as they were closing the door. The flight attendant eyed me warily. Unshaven, agitated, a little wild eyed, sweaty, I was a perfect match for the airline's suspicious passenger profile. Inebriate? Schizophrenic? Terrorist? Fortunately US Airways decided I was harmless enough to board the plane. We circled Charlotte for thirty minutes, waiting for clearance. I forgot where I parked the car and took a wrong turn out of the lot, driving three miles in the wrong direction before I could turn around. I don't have enough energy to turn the radio to another station.

The host welcomes a caller from Worcester, Massachusetts. She feels like she's lost a member of her family. She's reliving that dark moment decades ago when she heard that Jack had been shot.

Last night was a classic, a new low. Hard to believe the evening had such auspicious beginnings. The exhibit space closed at five to give the exhibitors time to grab a bite before heading off to see *Les Miz* or *Phantom*. I showered and put on fresh clothes. The sun hovered over the rooftops of Madison Avenue. A couple approached. The man was wearing reflecting aviators, but there was no mistaking who he was. My boyhood idol, his name synonymous with New York rock and roll, a onetime junkie who's eased into a graceful middle age. His fingers punctuated his comments to the willowy blonde beside him. As they passed, I heard him talking about the dead Kennedy.

Many hours later I ended my procession through the bars of Manhattan at an East Village dump where the floor show was winding up for the big finale. The mistress of ceremonies, a famous drag queen porn director, snarled a nasty play-by-play as her latest discovery strutted for the last stragglers nursing their nightcaps. *He may be straight, honey, but he likes a little surprise up his ass now and then.* In a dark corner in the back of the room, a stripper was getting a hundred-dollar blow job, counting his tips while an old man sucked him off. A couple of bills were twisted in his G-string.

I found my way downstairs to the toilet, each step confirming I was drunk. Drunker than I'd been for a long time, too drunk to stand and piss. I would never have squatted on that filthy bowl if I were sober. Someone kicked the bathroom door open. I heard tears and a sissy's voice, pleading, as he was slammed and shoved across the room. A deeper voice threatened. *What did I tell you? What did I fucking tell you?* The mistress of ceremonies had her protégé pinned to the wall by his wrists. Sobbing, scared, his face red and wet, he looked younger than he had on stage, much younger, just out of high school. The drag queen smashed the boy's right hand against the wall and a syringe fell to the floor. *Get the fuck out of here, asshole*, she hissed at me, crushing the hypodermic with her heel.

What a fucking night. Threatened by the scum of the earth. I ordered one for the road, one to help me sleep. The guy standing next to me at the bar was flipping through yesterday's *Post*, studying the pictures of the dead Kennedy. He turned to me and smiled. It was the blow-job stripper in his street clothes, denim shorts and a white button-down with the sleeves cut away. The wire-rim glasses threw me off. Now that he wasn't squinting, he looked like a puppy, relaxed and friendly. No one ever sees a stripper wearing glasses. Maybe because they have to fly blind to do what they do. When I spoke he said I sounded like home. He was from a town not far from Fayetteville. I saw his whole story in his face. A boy from a tobacco farm down east. He never expected to end up here when he enlisted in the Navy. He wanted to buy me a beer. I told him I'd never make it home. Don't worry about that, he said, I'll get you home. I apologized for not having any money left, not even enough for a cab. He said he had a pocket full of small bills. They smelt like his balls, he laughed, but they were still legal tender. In the cab, he stroked my knee as the driver stared at us in the rearview mirror, disgusted, the black eyes of Islam uncomprehending. The boy didn't care I was too drunk to perform. He was homesick and wanted someone to lie beside in bed, a man to kiss and snuggle with, someone who didn't laugh when he shared his dream of saving enough tips to buy a convenience store back in Carolina. He bought me a coffee in the morning and stood with me as I waited for a cab to the airport.

Whew! Who opened a can of peas and spiked it with vinegar? That sharp cider smell can't be my armpits, can it? Is it my feet? My crotch? It was either shower or make my flight this morning, and I must be a little ripe. My pants are dirty and my shirt belongs in the laundry pile. All I want is to scald myself in the shower and crawl into bed for thirty-six hours. I'll be lucky to steal a few hours' sleep; my mother's expecting a nice evening tonight. A hair of the dog will help. There's one last swig left in the flask in the glove compartment. It tears a hole in my throat when I swallow it.

Clete from Oklahoma City is unmoved by the Legacy of Camelot. He doesn't understand what all the fuss is about. Just another kid born with a silver spoon in his mouth. The country has lost its mind, weeping and wailing over this spoiled brat because of his last name. The talk show host is indignant, cutting off the naysayer, enraged by his heresy. The caller from Oklahoma has created a firestorm. Patty from Pittsburgh is leading the lynch mob. The Kennedys have given us so much, she insists. They've earned our respect. Tom from Tioga challenges the apostate to a fist fight. Even Merrill from Provo, Utah, a militant Republican, is calling for the blasphemer's head.

Distracted by the funeral choir, I nearly rear-end a BMW sedan parked in the driveway of the Monument to Heat and Air. How much are we paying these private-duty nurses that they can afford to indulge their appetite for luxury imports? The car is a beauty, right off the showroom floor, probably less than three thousand miles on the odometer. There's a Princeton decal in the rear window. What a racket, I swear as I grab my bag from the trunk of my sorry little Toyota compact. I'm subsidizing the German auto industry *and* paying Ivy League tuition. I take the long march to the back door. The overgrown lawn is a rebuke to my commitment to my domestic duties. I'll call a lawn maintenance company tomorrow, conceding that assuming any responsibility for the upkeep of our house is beyond my capabilities. I'll hire a painter and a contractor to replace the gutters while I'm at it. The Monument to Heat and Air is starting to look like the residence of the Addams Family.

"I'm home, Ma," I shout, praying for no response, hoping

she's in her bedroom, resting, exhausted by the chemical cocktails racing through her bloodstream. But she calls out immediately, not answering me, but announcing my arrival.

"He's home! You're not going to miss him!"

And as I step in the kitchen, a familiar figure rises to greet me.

Ambushed! I'm in shock, denial. This can't be happening. I must be further gone than I think since the only possible explanation for this hallucination is end-stage delirium tremens. My soon-to-be-ex-wife, the woman I haven't seen since I was kicked out on my ass, is rising from her chair. Our one brief telephone conversation was deceptively easy. This unexpected face-to-face encounter is awkward, worse than awkward, painful. Alice could never play poker: it's obvious, to me at least, she'd called ahead, knew I was out of town. Running late this morning, she didn't want to disappoint my mother by canceling; she's been sitting anxiously, too polite to cut the visit short, trying not to be distracted by her watch and dreading the possibility of this uncomfortable moment. How do you greet a woman you've lived with for nearly twenty years, who vowed to stay with you through better or worse unless the worst meant being rescued from a police station, no toothbrush or mouthwash available and the smell of cock still on your breath? A handshake is too formal; even a chaste kiss on the cheek is too intimate.

"Please, please, sit down," I say.

"Barry's family is from Charlotte. They're down visiting his folks for the weekend," my mother says, as if this reunion is as casual and relaxed as an old chamois shirt.

"Who's Barry?" I ask.

The uncomfortable look they exchange answers the question. Barry is obviously the individual responsible for this insult to Alice's once robust and healthy body. She's the exception to the old adage that all pregnant women glow. She looks exhausted, with an unhealthy pallor, and the pouches under her eyes are as dark as mine. Her feet and ankles are swollen. Most shocking of all are the gray roots of her still stylishly cut hair. How long had she been coloring it before her obstetrician banned tints and rinses for the duration? Had she kept it a secret from me or had I simply not noticed?

"I really have lost track of the time," she says to my mother with forced cheerfulness. "It's good to see you," she tells me. "Call when you can."

Why? So we can chat about Barry?

"I'm so glad you came by," my mother says as she and Alice embrace. I can see Alice is shaken. By me? By my mother's condition? "I just know you're going to have a beautiful baby," she promises.

My mother has defected to the other side! She's a pom-pom girl for Alice and her wonderful new life with beautiful, perfect Barry who would never be caught dead showing up like me, scruffy, rumpled, not quite clean, Jack Daniel's on his breath. Beautiful Perfect Barry wakes up clean-shaven, rinsed, gargled, armpits shellacked, hair stylishly spiked. Beautiful Perfect Barry, the Princeton Man, has accomplished in record time the achievement my feeble sperm were incapable of producing. Alice must have pulled his photo out of her wallet so they could coo over this paragon of manhood with the piercing eyes and the Clark Kent cleft in his chin, her ultimate triumph, her reward for the years of humiliation and perseverance.

See, Ruth, this is my Beautiful Perfect Barry, my vindication, proof at last I wasn't to blame for the failure of my marriage, none of it was my fault.

"I'll be in touch," she says to my mother. "We'll be back in Charlotte planning the . . ." Her voice trails off, avoiding mentioning the sacred ceremony.

"I can't wait to see the baby," my mother says.

I've stumbled upon a conspiracy of estrogen! Why don't we

plan a big Sunday dinner together? My mother, Alice, Barry, the baby. How about inviting Barry's parents? I bet they're lovely people. While we're at it we should ask Curtis to join us. Time heals all wounds. The two of us can bury the hatchet.

"I need to move the car," I say, impatient for her to leave. "I'm blocking you."

I leave the two of them alone for one last embrace and an opportunity to whisper their concern over the wreck I've become. *He's just not adjusting*, they commiserate, *we wish there was something more we could do than hope and pray it all works out.*

"I'm glad I came," Alice says, emerging from the house.

"Yeah, thanks. It meant a lot to her. I know this can't be easy for you."

My instinct is to hold her when she starts to cry; her instinct is to be held. We take one step toward each other and stop.

"Andy, she looks terrible."

I refrain from commenting she's doesn't look so hot herself.

"They're considering a bone marrow transplant," I say instead.

"That doesn't sound good."

"No. No, it doesn't."

"It's hard to believe that this time last year . . ."

This time last year. Is she rubbing salt in the wound?

". . . she was so full of life."

This time last year.

"I'd really like to help," she says. "I can, you know."

Last summer. The very recent past. Practically yesterday.

"You didn't waste any time, did you?" I say abruptly, the words sounding harsher than I'd meant.

"What do you mean?"

"You know what I'm talking about. It hasn't even been a year and you show up here pregnant."

She stares at me, not responding, not backing down, her body language challenging me to keep going until I go too far.

"You're already knocked up by some guy you didn't even know a year ago."

"I knew him," she says, quietly, deliberately.

She's not even kind enough to look away. Her face is a mask, impassive, refusing to confirm or deny the awful, unbearable possibility of her infidelity and betrayal, her secret life. I regret the words before I can spit them out.

"You fucking bitch."

She opens the car door, tosses her purse on the seat, and crawls behind the wheel. A blast of music assaults me as the engine turns over. "Girlfriend." She's playing my fucking CD in Beautiful Perfect Barry's Princeton-mobile. She wouldn't even know who Matthew Sweet is if it weren't for me. She turns off the music, pauses, then looks up, mocking me with an indulgent smile.

"Andy, I feel sorry for you. I really do."

"Don't. Don't feel sorry for me. I don't want your fucking sympathy," I shout, slamming my car door. The radials squeal as I back into the street. I press the accelerator, hitting the mailbox and crushing the post.

Thank you, thank you, God, thank you, Jesus, for sending me to that fucking interstate shithouse that oppressively hot summer night! Thank you for clapping on the cuffs, booking me, setting my bail, forcing me to call my loving wife and forcing her to rescue me. The poor little thing must have been torturing herself, trying to find a painless way to break the news to me, how to gently announce that she was ending our marriage. Of course, in the midst of all this angst, she still found plenty of time to call Beautiful Perfect Barry to invite him to my house while I was out of town, sharing a bottle of my champagne while they listened to her favorite bel canto recordings on my sound system. Chaste Goddess my ass, holding hands on my sofa, a roaring fire in my fireplace, making out in my great room. I wonder if she felt the slightest twinge of guilt when she took his hand in hers, led him to my bedroom, and fell back on my mattress, lifting her legs so he could slip off the lace panties I bought her, begging him to stick his fucking dick into her unfaithful pussy. She did it with him in my bed. My fucking bed. I know it.

It was poetic justice, you goddamn fucking bitch. The Lord has not forsaken me. All your best-laid plans torn asunder by that one phone call, denying you the opportunity to humiliate me, hurt me, reject me, pity me, cast me as the victim in our marital melodrama. I got there first and I have just one regret. I wish I had a photograph, irrefutable evidence of my insatiable hunger as I sucked that enormous musky cock with a look of pure and unconditional pleasure that you never, not once, saw on my face.

The voices on the radio are still babbling about the dead Kennedy. The host is repeating himself. The subject's exhausted. There's nothing left to say but no one wants to talk about anything else. I drive aimlessly for an hour, turning left, then right. I lived in this town for eighteen years. It's impossible to get lost. I've got nowhere to go but back to my mother's house.

Case Study

Adios!
 Aloha!
 Au revoir!
 Arrivederci!
 No, make that . . .
 Addio!
 Sayonara, Mothra!
 Bring out the cake! Blow out the candle! Give me my present! It's almost our anniversary. Our first and last. We'll crack open the Veuve Clicquot and celebrate!
 "I just assumed you'd be continuing in therapy," Matt says, sounding disappointed, almost dejected.
 Why would he assume that?
 "You've got a lot going on, what with your mother and all."
 "I can handle it."
 "And there's the question of medication."
 Can't he just call in refills as needed?
 Each of his arguments is swept aside, inconsequential, and he's forced to accept my decision and concede he can't hold me here any longer. Our work is nearly finished as far as the State of North Carolina is concerned. And I'm tired of not having a

level playing field. I'm tired of not being able to ask questions or, more accurately, tired of asking questions he never answers.

This evening, I had a chance encounter with one of the priests who share the house. The front door was open and Matt wasn't in his office. I wandered into the kitchen, looking for a glass of water. A radio in the backyard was playing dance music, ancient and out of style or maybe so retrograde as to be fashionable once again. An emaciated blond in floppy shorts and a muscle shirt was slumped in a lawn chair, one long thin bare foot twitching to the beat as his bony fingers tapped the arm rest.

"Ohhhhhhhhhhhh. Love to love you, baby."

"Can I help you?" he asked, using his sermon voice, a deep rumble resonating from that scrawny chest.

"I'm here to see Matt . . . Father McGinley."

"His office is at the front of the house. You passed it on your way back here."

He held a pair of glasses up to his eyes and squinted, assessing whether I was one of Matt's juvenile delinquent sociopaths, on the prowl, compulsively pilfering small objects. He saw I was nothing more than a garden-variety neurotic who, once chastised, would pad sheepishly back through the house. He dropped his glasses and turned his attention back to Donna Summer.

All I'm able to squeeze out of Matt is the blond's a Jesuit from Wisconsin on loan to UNC–Charlotte for the academic year. He's teaching a course on the French Deconstructionists for the comparative literature department. Matt studiously deflects any further questions, but I persist.

"Why is this so important to you?" he asks.

"It isn't."

"Then why so many questions?"

"I'm just curious."

"Curious about what?" he asks.

About that priest, about you, about whether you are what you seem to be, controlled, engaged in life yet detached, distant enough to remain objective, not a prisoner to whims and urges, highs and lows. I'm curious about whether it's all a façade and, just like me, you toss and turn in your spartan single bed, your beefy, hairy legs twisted in the sheets, kicking at the hobgoblins crawling out of the woodwork. Where do you hide from your demons? What's the antidote for desire? Dropping to your knees for a rosary and a pair of novenas for the strength to resist temptation or a quick jack-off and a week without candy as penance?

"Nothing . . . actually, I am curious about something."

"What?"

"How do we end this?"

"Haven't you talked with your lawyer?"

"Right. We show up before the judge. No arrests. Completion of counseling verified. Listen to a word or two of wisdom. Look abashed, no, look reformed, like I couldn't even conceive of fucking up again, like I'm a whole different person than the loser who stood there a year ago. Record expunged and I rejoin the ranks of solid citizens."

"So there you are."

"But I'm still curious. What's your role in all this?"

"I submit a final report to the Court."

"Have you started it?"

"Yes."

"Is it finished?"

"No."

"When do I read it?"

"You don't."

"What does it say?"

This line of questioning makes Matt uncomfortable.

"I'm afraid I can't disclose that."

I nearly jump out of my seat. One more question he won't answer, one more secret he's hiding.

"Whoa, calm down."

"What do you mean you can't disclose it?"

"It's a confidential report to the Court. It belongs to the State. That's how it works. It's not mine to give you. It's the judge's decision whether to share it. Your lawyer will have to file a motion to get a copy."

"Wait a minute!"

"What?"

"Who the fuck are you working for here?"

"Well . . ."

"Haven't you been preaching to me for months that I'm your *patient*?"

"Yes."

"Then give me the report. I have a fucking right to see it. I've spent too much time in hospitals and doctors' offices. I know about patients' rights. You *have* to let me see it."

"Andy, it's not that simple."

"It's not that fucking complicated," I shout.

"Andy, if you want to see your medical record, fine, but this is different. It's a report that . . ."

I realize I'm crying and reach for the box of tissue on the low table between us. They're oily and they stink, scented to suggest floral bouquets. It's nothing but frustration, this outburst. I'm tired of him shutting me out, blocking me off. He watches, silently, and the longer he observes, the harder I cry. I point to the closed door. He understands, knowing I don't want to be humiliated.

"Don't worry. No one can hear you."

He waits until the tears have stopped and I'm dabbing my nose obsessively, worried about stray strings of snot.

"I really wish you'd reconsider your decision," he says.

I shrug and mumble.

"We have one more session. And you can do something for me."

"What?"

"Write your own evaluation and report. We'll see how it compares to mine."

I agree. I work on it all week. On planes, in hotels, at counters, in my little book where the customer thinks I'm scribbling measurements. I edit, revise, tinker until it's perfect. The honest, unvarnished portrait of the salesman as a no-longer-young man. This is what I write:

Subject: Caucasian male homosexual floating through his late thirties. Divorced, no children. Above-average intelligence and uninvolved in current occupation. Pleasant, unremarkable appearance. Average social skills, but no friends at present time and emotionally detached from family members despite current residence with mother with end-stage lymphoma for whom he acts as primary caregiver.

Pathology: Subject demonstrates certain narcissistic qualities and exhibits tendency for self-obsession without self-awareness. Subject has difficulty forming intimate emotional relationships and his resultant isolation is further exacerbated by a fear of exposure. Subject's prime motivation in personal interactions is to avoid reviving residual sense of shame created by paternal disapproval of his childhood mannerisms and conduct.

Subject is currently in thrall to deepening depression over recent dissolution of his long-term marriage and the anticipated adverse outcome of mother's treatment. Subject's current medication regimen is yielding diminishing results. Subject has difficulty sleeping and self-medicates by increasing alcohol intake and using marijuana when available. Sleep, when finally achieved, is unsatisfactory, coming in fits and starts, seldom extending beyond four hours and often accompanied by hallucinatory images *that force his eyes open and render him unable to fall back into unconsciousness.*

Subject is morbidly preoccupied, no, obsessed, with death and disease. His current personal situation requires him to spend endless hours in hospital cancer centers where he is constantly confronted with, no, assaulted by, evidence of the precariousness of life. Subject cannot differentiate himself from the fragile creatures surrounding him. Broken things, crumbling, shattered by disease, shriveling to dust, noses plugged with tubes and clamps, lips too dry and cracked to form words, they must rely on their hollow, bruised eyes to communicate their message: Now it's our turn, soon it will be yours.

Subject experiences panic attacks, hyperventilating as he compulsively calculates and recalculates the ever-dwindling pool of days and the shrinking distance between himself and the intubated and catheterized population of the hospital. Subject responds by seeking temporary relief and gratification in sexual contact. Subject's panic intensifies at the recognition that his impulsive conduct could be accelerating his projected arrival time at his final destination.

<u>*Prognosis:*</u> *Poor. Subject's few remaining meaningful contacts are falling away like fish scales. Subject is becoming delusional, with fantasies of drifting away, a Dowager Empress in Splendid Isolation, freeze-dried in the lotus position, afloat, miles above the chaos and cacophony of human interaction. Subject has conversations, dialogues with himself, as there is no one else to listen and respond. The sound of subject's own voice assaults his eardrums. Subject is exhausted by the endlessly repetitive content. Me. Me. Me. Subject has reached the end of the journey, there's no fresh laundry in his baggage.*

Subject is not, repeat not, *planning anything dramatic or irreversible, being, after all, at his deepest core, a good Catholic boy.*

<u>*Recommendation:*</u> *Ignore all of the above. Subject has not*

dropped to his knees in a public place in a year. Ergo, Subject has been cured of what ails him and should be set free.

"Why do you insist on being so hard on yourself?" Matt asks after reading my assignment.

"I think I'm letting myself off pretty easily."

I light a cigarette, self-conscious about my shaking hand, a side effect of drinking too much, secretly, alone with the lights off. Matt doesn't comment on the slight tremor.

"I'm going to break the rules for you. I trust you'll keep this between you and me."

At last, a secret he's willing to share!

I race through the document and, astonished, reread his conclusions:

The therapeutic regimen has been successful with the patient exerting appropriate impulse control. His sexual habits are unremarkable in the sense that that there has been no reoccurrence of public sexual activity. It is this observer's professional opinion that the patient is unlikely to revert to prior behavioral patterns. Further therapeutic treatment is recommended to facilitate his successfully achieving his self-realization goals, but such further treatment should be voluntary and not imposed as a condition of any further court-ordered program.

"Thank you."

"You're welcome."

"Why did you do that, break the rules?"

"I thought it needed to be done to reestablish your trust in our relationship."

"Do you like me?"

"Yes."

"Why couldn't you just say you did it because you like me?"

"Because that's not why I did it. I did it because I didn't want to risk invalidating the work we've done together over the last year."

"But you do like me?"

"Yes, Andy. I like you."

"Well, would you sleep with . . . no, let's not use euphemisms here, would you fuck me if you weren't a priest?"

"No. I'd still be your doctor."

"Would you fuck me if you weren't my doctor?"

"No, I'd still be a priest."

"Fuck you."

"Go ahead and ask."

"Ask what?" I say, playing dumb.

"Would I fuck you if I weren't a priest or your doctor?"

Does he really think I'm going to give him the opportunity to reject me?

"Why does a fucking priest become a fucking doctor?"

"He doesn't. At least, I didn't. I was a doctor who became a priest."

I've learned that meaningful silence can elicit more information than the most probing questions. He recites his curriculum vitae. College (Loyola, summa) and medical school (Georgetown, with highest honors). Residency training program (Penn, selection as chief resident, of course, let no one mistakenly believe these Jesuits take a vow of modesty). Board certification. Novitiate. Dual master's in theology and health care ethics (Georgetown again). Ordination. Practice. Ministry. All black and white, clinical, just the facts.

"Very impressive. But you haven't answered my question. Why?"

"Because I believe I have two callings."

"How did you know that?"

"I didn't, at first."

"When did you learn it? I mean, how did it happen? Was it

like Saul on the road to Damascus, were you knocked off your horse?"

"Very funny."

"I didn't mean it to be. Really."

"No. It was a decision I made after much thought and prayer and spiritual counseling, not unlike what we do here together."

"If you had to give one up, which would it be?"

He shakes his head, signaling he's done answering questions, and smiles.

"Would you struggle with it?"

"Everyone struggles."

"Even you."

It's an affirmation, not a question.

"Even me."

What is it you struggle with? I know I can't ask you that question. Well, I can ask, but you'll never answer. You'll turn the tables, ask why it's so important to me. And I would tell you I need to know if you and I struggle with the same thing, if you use that Roman collar the way I used Alice. Why would that matter? you'd ask, crossing your legs as you settle back in your chair. Because I need to know if, unlike me, you've kept your vows. I hope you have. In fact, I need you to. I need someone to be winning their battles.

"Do you ever preach?" I ask.

"Most weeks," he says, telling me he's an assistant weekend pastor of a small parish just over the state line.

"Can I come hear your sermon?"

"You don't need an invitation to come to Mass."

"I'd like that."

"Fine."

"Then maybe we could have breakfast. Go to the Country Buffet and pig out. My treat."

He smiles, neither encouraging nor discouraging me.

It's a pathetic scene, this needy little boy, begging his father for friendship, affirmation.

"Can I come back next week?" I ask.

"Of course."

"Would you like that?"

"Yes, I would like that."

"God, what I must sound like."

"You're hurting."

So are you. So are we all. But at least one hour a week I don't need to do it alone.

Bone Marrow Transplant

I've got a hole in my hip.

Sounds like a lyric from an old standard by Cole Porter or Rodgers and Hart.

I've got a hole in my heart.

I've got a hole where my heart used to be.

It's the kind of song you'd hear in a piano bar, a wrinkled old pixie with Vaseline teeth crooning away. I'll write down the lyrics and send them to my furry blond friend in Honolulu.

Anyway, playing here tonight . . .

I've got a hole in my hip.

My sister returns bearing gifts, a towel and ice. The last pack melted on my leg and all over the sofa and my boxers are dripping wet. She offers to go upstairs and fetch a dry pair, but I decline, saying they'd just be soaked in a few minutes. Then I relent, knowing I'm selfishly depriving her of the opportunity to play Big Nurse in the Nocera family medical melodrama.

I reach for the remote and change channels. It's late afternoon, the Day After. I'm exhausted. The oncologist says I should be feeling better tomorrow. I hope not. This provides the only acceptable excuse for dropping out. Soon enough, the routine will start all over again. . . .

. . . Up before seven, a quick j.o., swallow coffee from a paper container (blue, with a frieze of Greek soldiers, like the Parthenon) and chew on a powdered doughnut, sing along, loudly, to the car radio, find a parking space, take the "shortcut" through the ER ("Hey, Steve." "Hey." "Sorry, gotta run."), squeeze into the elevator (chattering nurses in soft, blowsy smocks; young orderlies, all hard muscles beneath those loose green scrubs; octogenarians, beyond gender, being wheeled to MRI), stop at the nurse's station, ask if she's awake, ask what kind of night she had, ask when the oncologist is making rounds, remember forgetting something, take the elevator back down, hang around the locked door to the Gift Patch, wait another five minutes until it opens at nine, buy a couple dollars' worth of peppermint patties, stall a little longer leafing through the tabloids (Oprah's Diet Secrets!: she has a personal trainer and private chef on call twenty-four hours a day. William and Harry's Secret Anguish: fading memories of their mother), stop for a pee then back up the elevator, give my mother a good morning kiss and ask how she's feeling, unwrap one of the peppermint patties, watch her place it on her tongue, squirm at the dry sucking sounds she makes, hope that it relieves the rancid metallic taste of the chemicals battling the tumors in her body, fall into the chair beside her bed, the day all but done by nine twenty in the morning, nothing to do but stare at the four walls, the television, my mother struggling to stay alive. . . .

I never thought I'd miss having to make a six A.M. flight to Dayton or the eleven P.M. red-eye from Denver. But the situation has become desperate, necessitating THE LAST BEST HOPE, and I'm on leave begrudgingly approved by my Born Again National Sales Manager under mandate of federal law. I've appeased him by promising to be back in time to work the show at the Chicago Merchandise Mart.

Ouch. Stupid of me to roll over on the goddamn hole in my hip.

My sister is hovering in the corner of the room.

"Are you all right?"

"Yeah, sure."

"Do you need anything?"

"No. Yes. Can you bring me a beer?"

She screws her face into a question mark.

"Are you allowed?"

"Of course I'm allowed. The treatment regimen is two Tylenol, as needed," I say, exasperated.

I could have told the oncologist the preliminary blood work wasn't necessary. There was only one possible donor, the results were inevitable, the conclusion foregone.

My mother and I are A Perfect Match.

My bone marrow is being transplanted in a sterile room in the hospital in Charlotte. I've got a hole in my hip where they drilled for oil. Now my mother and I are closer than ever, not simply a Match anymore, but One and the Same, the very cells of our blood generated from a single source.

"You ought to head back to the hospital," I say as Regina hands me a can of beer. "I'll be fine."

"Do you need anything else before I go?" she asks.

"No."

"Do you want me to bring anything back for you?"

"No."

Once she's gone I hobble around the kitchen looking for something to eat. I settle on another beer. It's oppressively hot, even for Gastonia in early summer. I flop on the couch. It's almost four o'clock, Oprah time. She's my new best friend. My mother and I both love her. I don't even begrudge her the ability to summon exercise gurus and gourmet chefs with the snap

of her fingers. Those big cow eyes and her nonjudgmental attitude are irresistible. But I'm beyond tired or fatigued. I feel
crushed, sinking, with pains in my joints and the sinews of my
muscles. A team of sled dogs couldn't drag me to my bed upstairs. So long, Oprah, I mutter, plunging into a coma, dead to
the world . . .

. . . only to be rudely awakened hours later by a loud crack
and the sound of a metal bowl spinning across the tile floor. I
wander into the kitchen to investigate. My sister is standing on
a kitchen stool, back toward me, head and hands deep inside a
cabinet, muttering, swearing. I'm careful not to startle her since
her balance is precarious. Dishes and glasses, canned goods and
spices, boxes and jars clutter the counter.

"What are you doing?" I ask when her footing seems sturdy
and she's not likely to topple and break her neck.

"What does it look like I'm doing?"

"Relining the cabinets."

"Bingo. You were always the smart one."

"It's half past eleven."

"So?"

She steps down from the stool, trying to hide the half-empty
wine bottle on the counter.

"Have you had anything to eat?" I ask, trying to gauge the
effect of two glasses of wine.

"Yeah, a piece of cheese."

"You want me to call for take-out?"

"It's too late," she says.

"Want me to make something?"

"I just want to get this done. You can tell she's been sick by
the condition of these cabinets. I bet she hasn't relined them in
two years. She never used to let things get this bad."

The crumpled, torn paper on the floor doesn't look so bad
to me. A few blemishes, a ring here and there, certainly not the

grease-smeared, dust-coated mess you'd assume from my sister's comments.

"Is that some type of criticism?" I ask.

She looks up, clearly perplexed.

"I mean, are you saying if I'd only paid a little more attention to the shelf paper I would have realized she was sick and could have gotten her to the doctor earlier, on time, before it was too late?"

"No. Of course not. No criticism intended. For God's sake . . ." She reaches for the bottle and pours another glass of wine without offering any. "Why would you think that . . . What do you . . . Why do you hate me so much?"

What kind of question is that?

I don't hate her. How could I hate my little sister? My buddy, my pal, the one person on earth who knows things about me that would still smart and sting if she were to fling them in my face. Which, remarkably, she hasn't, despite numerous provocations, still protecting me, God knows why, never mocking me, knowing how deep a wound she would inflict just by reminding me . . .

. . . that I would creep down the hallway and crawl into her bed after another bloody nightmare roused me from a deep sleep.

. . . that I kept silent, allowing her to take the blame for the ruined lipstick, knowing the consequences would be far more severe if it were ever discovered it had been me that smeared it across my mouth.

. . . that I would talk Randall Jarvis into pulling down his pants and letting Gina and me touch his thing whenever we played *General Hospital*.

. . . that the real reason Billy Cunningham split my lip was because I tried to kiss him on the mouth.

How could I hate the woman who once was such a tough

little kid, who spat when my mouth was dry from fear, punching and swinging when I was unable to make a fist, screaming and cursing when I choked on the words. *Don't cry, Andy,* she would console me as she prepared for battle, grabbing a brick, a bat, a board, her arms flailing, threatening to draw blood from the Billy Cunninghams and Richard Tricketts, never backing down when they taunted her with names like Fatty, Blimpie, Whale Girl.

Fuck you, she shouted at our tormentors. *Fuck you, assholes.*

No one, she insisted as our mother pinched her mouth with her thumb and forefinger, threatening to insert a bar of Fels-Naptha laundry soap if she didn't confess who taught her such terrible, terrible words. Brave little Gina, always standing up for the men in her life, her foul-mouthed daddy and me.

Of course I don't hate you, baby sister. If I did, I'd free you to tell the world all my dirty little secrets.

She finally gets around to offering me a glass of wine, which I decline, getting a beer instead. I let her question drift away, refusing to answer. I go out on the porch for a smoke, leaving her to her cabinets. But she follows me, using the excuse she'd like a cigarette too. I remind her she quit (not to preserve her pulmonary functions but to halt the erosion of the fine skin around her face and eyes).

"Why do you have to be such a prick?" she asks. "What have I ever done to you?"

She thinks she deserves an explanation why I refuse to acknowledge the bond that existed between us before I erected a barrier more permanent than the Berlin Wall. Truth is, I'm straining to think of some way to respond, a bone to throw her, some reason that justifies my slow intractable retreat over the decades. I could tell her I resent her for outgrowing me.

Do you remember when no one was more fun or fascinating than me, your older brother, whose vivid imagination cast you as Robin to my Batman, Becky Thatcher to my Tom Sawyer, Joe to my Frank Hardy (and, yes, I'll admit it to you but no one else, sometimes Ethel to my Lucy or Mary Ann to my Ginger)?

I could blame her for losing her baby fat and growing into a beauty, for making friends with the girls who'd taunted her when she was big and clumsy, not simply forgiving them, but sharing her secrets and confiding her dreams in them.

When did you realize you wanted a brother like their brothers instead of one who was interested in your crushes and jealousies and rivalries?

But both of those ring a bit a hollow. They're excuses, neither of them completely true. Anyway, my impatient little sister would never understand concepts like erosion and accretion and evolution. She needs a moment, an instant that changed everything, a gunshot, an explosion, a confrontation, the Big Bang. She needs a wound we can lance so we can move on with the healing. Except I can't think of any single cruel act she's ever perpetrated that deserves such unrelenting hostility. Well, maybe one.

"You are such a faggot," I say.

"What?" she asks, taken back, her suspicions confirmed. I have lost my mind.

"Not you. Me," I say.

"What are you talking about?"

"You are such a faggot."

"You aren't making sense. Sometimes I think you're crazy," she says, her voice getting in pitch for the argument that's beginning. This is the stuff she's made for. In ten minutes, she wants us sobbing, collapsing in each other's arms, competing in contriteness for all our past mistakes, pledging undying fealty.

I repeat the mantra again, frustrating any attempts at quick angry retorts. She needs to serve and volley. I keep hitting junk balls, soft lobs she can't swing at.

"What's your point? I have no idea what you're talking about."

"Yes, you do."

"No. I do not."

I search for a few facts for backdrop, but my recall betrays me, coming up short. All I can retrieve is a stray moment, isolated, stripped of context. I'm standing at the open refrigerator door, poking around loosely wrapped moldy cheese, disgusted, whining, probably squealing, and sounding like a bratty little girl.

You are such a faggot, my sister, behind me, says.

I hid my face in the ketchup bottles and milk containers until she walked away. Five little words that branded me, irrevocably. How old was she? Who knows? I can't remember anything else about that day, not the month, not the year, not if it was summer or winter, not if it was dark or light. All that survives is that one blazing minute, seared into my memory, the act of betrayal, the sharp kick in the guts, completely unexpected, by my loyal ally, the girl who had always put her thick orthopedic saddle shoes to good use, bruising the shins of our enemies.

I should have pulled my head out of that refrigerator and punched or slapped her, taking a lesson from her book. One gesture to ensure she would never forget what she did to me that day. Some violent act to teach her the consequences of turning against me, abandoning me, leaving me with nothing left to rely on but the benevolent protection of my mother. But I let her walk away with her bowl of chocolate ice cream, and today she has no recollection of this life-changing event. It's as lost to her as a single grain of sand tossed back on the beach, indistinguishable and irretrievable.

"I don't know what you are talking about. I really don't."

"Yes, you do," I repeat, halfhearted, unwilling to concede the insignificance of the remark.

"How old was I?" she asks.

"Old enough. I can't remember. Ten. Eleven. Twelve. I don't know. It doesn't matter."

"So you hate me because of some stupid remark I made twenty-five years ago. Do you think I even knew what the word meant at that age? Maybe *you* did. Remember, you were the smart one."

She pours the last of the wine into her glass, drains it, and opens another bottle. I anticipate a head-on assault, a blistering attack, anything but unconditional surrender.

"I give up. You win. I don't care anymore. How many times have I tried to reach out to you? For years, I blamed that wife of yours. Oh, sorry. I forgot. We're not supposed to mention the perfect Alice. I guess I can tell you now I never liked her, hated the way you were when you were with her, the two of you in your own little world, laughing over some private joke you thought everyone else was too stupid to get. I suppose I should feel sorry for her now for putting up with you all those years. You're a coldhearted bastard, you know that, don't you?"

Yes, Gina, I know that.

I've got a hole where my heart used to be.

"You wouldn't understand" is my feeble response. I could ask her how she would have felt if I had called her a fatty or teased her about peeing her pants. But I know that I did—many times—and she's either forgotten or forgiven the careless cruelties of childhood.

"You're right," she says, stubbing out her cigarette. "I don't understand, you asshole."

But you'd understand even less if I followed you back to the kitchen and tried to explain that I don't hate you. You're being punished for all those things you know about me that I want to forget, for having a front-row seat to all the humiliations, usually self-inflicted, I endured. Sorry, Regina, I hate that little boy you loved and you're collateral damage. You try to talk to me about your sad little son, thinking I'll understand, maybe offer some insight or at least some friendly support. Why would you think I have any insight into that pathetic kid? Don't you remember your wedding day, how you confronted me about my reprehensible behavior, not understanding how or why I could be so mean to Randall Jarvis? He'd gotten shamefully drunk, reeling from my cruel remark, intended to wound.

"Come on, he's rich. He's famous. He's a big boy," I said, defending myself.

"Yeah, but he remembers what it meant to be the little boy he was back then," she said, the one and only time she went for the kill. "Obviously, you've forgotten."

Not if you won't let me, Regina. And you're not getting another chance, I think, retreating to the sofa and my television, remote control in hand, ready to crank up the volume in the all-too-likely event my sister has some further afterthought she feels compelled to share.

Help!

"Gina!" I scream, jumping to my feet, forgetting until it's too late the hole in my hip.

"What? What?" she shouts, panicking, running in from the kitchen and stopping dead in her tracks to gasp at the unexpected sight of the Fab Four cutting up on the Alpine slopes in their goofy cloaks and funny hats.

"Oh my God," she says.

We've seen it a dozen times. A hundred. Maybe a thousand. No, a million!

"Oh, Paul," she says, swooning like a little girl again.

I love cable. Thank God there's plenty of beer and wine in

the house. It's a Beatles marathon. After *Help!*, *A Hard Day's Night*.

"It's the better movie."

"It's black and white," she argues.

"So?"

"Why couldn't they have made it in color?"

"Black and white is better. It's more expressive."

"No, it's not."

"Yes, it is. Color is too literal."

"Oh just shut up. I love this song," she says, still insisting, despite the visual evidence otherwise, it's Paul, not John, singing lead vocals on "If I Fell."

"I do too," I say, not wanting to argue.

Suddenly it's four in the morning and I'm up in the attic, tearing through boxes, not bothering to reseal them when I don't find what I'm looking for. I won't be deterred. I know they're up here somewhere.

"Ta-dah!" I shout.

"Did you find them?"

"Yep."

And, praise God, they aren't warped after decades of hibernation in this sweatbox of an attic. Leave it to my mother to pack them so tightly, so expertly, that moisture and heat hasn't destroyed them. I have a moment of drunken insight. This is what she preserved them for. Tonight.

My sister and I argue over which record to play first. Finally we compromise and drop a stack on the spindle.

"Oh, God, do you remember . . ."

As my mother would say, no pun intended, we sound like a broken record.

Do you remember this?

Do you remember that?

Do you remember him?

Do you remember her?

And so the night passes, nothing resolved, nothing settled. But for a few hours, we blast *Rubber Soul* and *Revolver* loud enough to wake the dead and stay pleasantly smashed and I am the ten-year-old she loved and she is eight and I can love her back and all the years of polite estrangement still lie in the future.

Cancellation Policy

By noon the heat will be blistering. The county's on crisis alert. The scorched earth is a fire hazard and Smokey the Bear has orders to arrest anyone tossing a lit butt to the ground. The Department of Public Works is rationing water and the drought guidelines recommend flushing only "when necessary." I turn the dial to news radio. The death toll is nineteen and rising. Luxury imports speed by me in the passing lane, tinted windows protecting their pampered passengers from the intense sun, while some poor old lady suffocates in an airless room because she can't afford a cheap electric fan. Robin Hood ought to loot the aisles of Kmart and Wal-Mart and bring relief to the needy and deserving.

The overnight low was a record ninety-four degrees. My sister has summoned her husband from Florida and they've moved to the best hotel in Charlotte: twenty-four-hour room service and fresh towels and bed linen feel more like necessities than extravagances under current conditions. Alone now in my mother's house, I turned off the thermostat and let the Monument to Heat and Air bake all day in the sun. I couldn't sleep, tossing and turning on my stripped bed. I'm exhausted and fight the urge to doze at the wheel. Exhaust fumes caress my face and carbon and sulfur char my nostrils and throat. My bare legs are branded with grill marks, seared by the vinyl upholstery. I could close the car windows and crank up the air, but the heat is a respite from interminable waiting with no end in sight. The vigil goes on. I don't measure time in days and weeks, but by hot and cold.

I park the car and enter the deep freeze of the hospital. The frigid air creeps into my loose shorts. The cold keeps me awake. My phone is vibrating. I don't recognize the number. Sabotaged! My counselor is calling from his cell. I tell him I just arrived at the hospital and can't talk. Surprise, surprise! He's at the hospital too, only three floors away. He insists that I meet him. Now.

"You did get my message, didn't you?" he asks, bounding out of the elevator as if it's a matter of some urgency.

"Yes. I did."

Hello, Andy. It's Matt McGinley. I'm sorry for the short notice but I need to reschedule Friday's appointment. I know this is a difficult time for you, so please call me. Perhaps we can find some time before my flight on Thursday. I'm back late Saturday morning. I can do Saturday afternoon or evening. I can even try for Sunday. Call me.

"Why didn't you call?" he asks.

"I forgot."

He looks skeptical.

"Four times? I've tried you four times since Monday afternoon."

"Seriously, Matt. I forgot. I just plain forgot."

He tries to put his arm around my shoulder, but I push him away.

"Sorry, sorry," I say. "I don't need to start crying."

"Nothing wrong with that."

"Not now. Not here."

"Here" is the harshly lit Critical Care Unit, a place designed for observation and expediency, not privacy. I ask why he's chasing after me. He says he was in the hospital anyway. There'd been a little problem with one of his admissions to the psych unit. I thank him for taking the time to check on me, tell him he shouldn't have bothered. He should go back to the psych ward, the kid's problems seem more important.

"No. Not more important, just more emergent," he says. Little does he know.

"Why did you cancel?" I ask.

"I told you. I need to go out of town. It was unexpected."

"Where are you going?"

"Washington."

"Why?"

He's clearly uncomfortable being questioned.

"We can talk about that when I get back. If it's necessary."

"I think it's necessary."

"It may not be."

"Is it an emergency?"

"No. It's not an emergency."

"Then why couldn't you have planned ahead?" I'm surprised by how shrill I sound. "You know you've violated the cancellation policy, don't you? Payment in full for cancellations with less than forty-eight hours' notice. I'm enforcing it. It's only fair. Here's my price. You have to tell me why you're going. Tell me what's so—how did you say it?—important but not emergent. You cancelled too late. Now you have to pay."

"Andy, I gave you plenty of notice and tried to reschedule."

"I'm a very busy man, Matt. Can't you see that? Take a look around. You think I don't have anything better to do than sit around and watch the monitors? *Hey, nurse, what's a flat line mean?* Well, maybe you're right. Maybe I don't have anything better to do. That doesn't mean I'm not very busy."

This time he forces me to accept the arm around my shoulder.

"Come on," he says. "I can take a later flight."

He knows the shortest route to the nondenominational chapel where the anxious can seek comfort in the Crucifix, the Star of David, or the Crescent Moon. Hindus are shit out of luck. The room is spartan and austere and feels about as devotional as an interfaith public service announcement on late-night television.

"Thanks for coming today," I say.

"Sure."

"You still owe me, though."

"Come on, Andy."

"I'm not letting you off the hook."

"Technically I am off the hook. But because I've inconvenienced you, I'm waiving the fee for this session."

"I'll pay. Now tell me."

"Look Andy, it's a bit premature. There's no point discussing it until, no, unless and until, it's necessary. I don't want to risk upsetting you for no reason."

I don't like the sound of this.

"Now you really have to tell me."

"I'm in discussions with Georgetown. They've made me an offer. They need an answer by next week. I'm meeting other members of the department tomorrow, then dinner with the chair and the dean and the president of the hospital. I don't know if we'll be able to come to an agreement."

This is perfect. Just what I need. Probably what I deserve. The final, gratuitous kick in the stomach. You fucker. Three weeks ago I was ready to walk out the door. Adios, amigo. These boots were made for walkin'. Up and over. Out from under. I would have ended it in a heartbeat if you hadn't duped me with your silver tongue, hadn't pacified me with your fucking case study. I see your agenda now.

Can't take being rejected, huh? Keep me dangling a few

more weeks, just long enough for you to be the one who walks away.

Fucking priest.

"Congratulations" is all I say.

"Like I said, Andy, it's a little premature."

I stand up quickly and extend my hand. "Well, good luck."

"Andy, sit down. We were going to talk."

"Matt, I have to go. I really do. My sister's waiting for me. I'm late."

I find the closest toilet, bolt the door, and vomit. I try lifting my head, but I'm dizzy, too dizzy to stand. I thought I could at least count on him. I thought I could at least rely on paying someone to keep me from being completely alone. Everything's collapsing around me. Even my money's no good anymore.

Regina is furious. She looks at her watch and hisses. She doesn't understand why the unit is freezing. It's like a meat locker in here, she says. What do you expect, I want to ask, where do you think you are? Don't you see all these limp bodies, all these lives hovering just above the baseline, a weak pulse the only line of defense against the onset of bloat and rot? Face facts, kiddo, you're in an abattoir.

Good morning, folks.

The army is descending on the Critical Care Unit. They've come to hear the announcement of my final decision.

Do not resuscitate.

DNR.

They're sensitive to the palpable tension.

Pardon me, Mr. Nocera, Mrs. Gallagher? Are you in agreement? We like to have consensus within the family. Of course, Mr. Nocera, you have the power of attorney. The law says the decision is yours. However, it's our experience that it's better if everyone's in agreement.

The pulmonologist has determined my mother is to be transferred from critical care. Other patients, ones with some hope of survival, deserve this bed. All of this expertise, this attention, cannot be wasted on comfort care. The hospice unit is perfectly capable of ensuring she feels no pain. The hospital has summoned the troops. They've been kind enough to provide us with our very own social worker, right out of Central Casting. She's thin, tremulous, horse-faced. Why is her lower lip quivering? It's not her mother lying there with her face covered by a thick plastic breathing cup. She oozes empathy and compassion, compensating for the let's-get-on-with-it demeanor of the pulmonologist.

Regina and I retire to a small waiting room. We've been through this twenty times in the past week. She knows I won't change my mind. She knows my mother's last wishes. So she fixates on the oncologist, accusing her of having an attitude. She mistakes the good doctor's dog-tiredness for lack of concern and impatience. I tell her she's not being fair, that the woman could have chosen the safety and distance of communication by telephone line instead of a face-to-face confrontation with the consequences of the failure of the transplant.

My bone marrow has been swept away by an avalanche of white blood cells.

All further treatment to be limited to keeping her comfortable.

Do not resuscitate.

No mechanical respiration.

No tube feeding or invasive form of nutrition or hydration.

No blood or blood products.

No form of surgery nor any invasive diagnostic procedures.

No kidney dialysis.

No antibiotics.

No codes.

No extraordinary efforts to sustain life.

Do whatever you like, my sister shrieks, running out of the

room, battered and defeated, only to reappear seconds later. She insists on a feeding tube. Memories of *National Geographic* and the bloated babies of sub-Saharan Africa haunt her. She can't bear the thought of our mother starving to death. I agree and put my arms around her, letting her sob into my chest. I can always change my mind later, if this misguided act of mercy prolongs the agony.

The oncologist hugs me when I tell her our decision. She doesn't offer any bromides, no it's-for-the-best, it's-what-she-would-have-wanted. She leaves that for the social worker. I thank her for being here, tell her it means a lot to us. She wishes she could have done more. She lets me comfort her, knowing the soothing effect my own kind words have on me.

The social worker says my mother should be settled in her new room in an hour. She suggests we get something to eat, we need to keep up our strength. My sister and I trudge down to the cafeteria and forage the steam tables. We carry our plastic trays, scratched and pocked from a thousand forks and knives, and find a table where we sit, silently. I squeeze a dry scoop of mashed potatoes through the prongs of my fork. My sister watches, disgusted. She drinks bottomless cups of black coffee and plays with the salt shaker. Then she starts tapping the tabletop with her lacquered fingernails. She knows the rat-a-tat-tat is driving me crazy. I push my plate away from me and set down the fork. She stops drumming the table.

Truce.

"Sorry," I say.

"Same here," she says.

I need to piss and she needs to call her husband. Duties finished, we meet at the elevator and ride to the fifth floor. Gina pauses before she enters the room and our eyes lock. We share the same thought: our mother will never leave this room alive. She lies perfectly still on the bed, asleep, no, something deeper, more profound than sleep.

"Mom? Mama?" my sister says.

She pulls a chair close to the bed and holds one of my mother's hands, talking to her in a low voice, sharing the latest news of the grandkids back in Florida. I don't recognize the three model citizens in this family update. Neither would my mother if she could hear. My sister will not concede our mother is far beyond the sound of her voice. She's read a half dozen paperbacks on death and dying and every pamphlet and brochure in the social worker's arsenal. *Mama? Mom? Can you hear me?* She swears by the reflexive twitch in my mother's fingers. *See, Andy, she knows we're here.*

My feet are sweating despite this freezing room. I slip out of my sneakers and press my toes against the cool tile. The funky scent corrupts the antiseptic sterility of disinfectant. I look down and see my father's feet. Middle age, decades of pavement pounding, years of being bound in tight leather wingtips, have taken their toll. When did the tiny nails on my little piggies splinter and crack? I tuck them under the chair, out of sight. My mother, lying prone an arm's length away, is confirmation enough of my mortality. The blinds are drawn so the sun can't penetrate the room. The only light is electric and is kept as dim as possible, the darkness perpetuating the illusion she's just asleep. We keep our voices low and step softly so we don't disturb her. She needs her rest. We don't acknowledge an explosion wouldn't rouse her now.

My mother, by Caravaggio, dark tones suffused with mortuary light, anguish revealed, humanity triumphant.

My legs are stiff and I need to stretch. The staff doesn't mind my pacing so long as I stay out of their way. It's three o'clock. The shifts are changing. Bloods are being drawn. Doctors are rounding. One last flurry of activity before evening. Barring a code, the only crisis will be the late arrival of a cold dinner tray. I hear conversations, actual and televised, in the other patient rooms. I reminisce, thinking back to the many Oprah hours my mother and I have shared during this ordeal, comforted and re-assured by the tragedies of others. Please, the nurse says, point-ing at my bare feet. I apologize, embarrassed. She smiles and says she understands my mind's elsewhere.

Yes, it is. Where, though, I don't know. Anywhere but here. I want to leave. I want to stay. Time seems to drag, yet races away. I look at my watch. Almost seven o'clock now. It might be seven in the evening or seven in the morning. It's all the same, night and day, nothing to do but wait. Thank God for the cold. I feel it, so I must still be alive.

Snap out of it. It's mashed potato time again. My sister asks me to bring her something from the cafeteria, tuna on white toast, maybe some skim milk.

The cashier is bored and passes the time watching the clock, counting down the ninety minutes until the cafeteria closes. She knows me well by now and smiles. We've never spoken, not even hello, not once in the past many weeks. She's never asked why I'm here or how the patient's doing. She knows one day I'll disappear and never return, replaced by another just like me. She and I are familiar, intimate even, and totally anony-mous. Like all my relationships. Perfect. Right? That's what I want. Isn't it?

I sit in the cafeteria, alone, staring at a roomful of tabletops, counting the napkin dispensers, the salt and pepper shakers. I should have brought a newspaper so I could disappear into the world outside the hospital, where skirmishes break out in unfa-miliar parts of the globe, Republicans and Democrats argue, scandals erupt, celebrities mate and separate, box scores are tabulated, highs and lows are recorded, barometers fall. What if someone walks in here? What would they think if they saw me in this far corner, alone, mashed potatoes untouched, gazing into space? They'd grab their coffees and doughnuts and hustle out the door. There's something terrifying about a man sitting alone. People avoid him, run and hide, spooked, afraid, not because he's a psychopath or pervert, but because he's ordinary, just like them, an unwelcome reminder of how alone we all are.

I jump up, nearly knocking over the chair, and walk away quickly, with purpose. I leave the tray and the tuna-to-go on the table. I don't hesitate as I pass the elevator and pick up the pace as I enter the main lobby. The automatic doors open and I run smack into a brick wall of heat. It kisses my bare skin, taunts me, starts an erection stirring in my pants. The temperature's a cock tease. I stink. My clothes are dirty. My hair is sticky and matted. I don't care. I need people. I run a red light. Thank God the cross street is empty and no patrol cars are lurking nearby.

Buck Moon

I turn left at the interstate bypass. Gastonia and home are to the right. The sun is dying; the last blue streaks of light are fading to black. The radio announcer predicts a break in the heat, expect more typical seasonal temperatures tomorrow. Ahead, nearly at eye level, a full moon is emerging. In a few minutes, its bright light will dominate the heavens.

Buck Moon. I remember its name from Boy Scout Indian lore. It's the first full moon of summer, the full moon after young bucks sprout their antlers. A lunar celebration of raging hormones, impulsive behavior, and the excesses of youth. The moon's power controls the sweep of the tides. How can a puny thing like me resist it? It's the only possible explanation for my abandoning my mother and sister tonight.

I'm entitled to one night's dispensation. After all, I'm the one who's been here throughout the whole ordeal, phoning in reports to my sister poolside in Boca Raton. I'm the one who's had to make all the decisions, be second-guessed, have my judgment challenged, be resented. I deserve one night out. But why didn't I tell Gina I was leaving? She wouldn't have begrudged me one night. Of course she would have. She doesn't realize this has been really hard on me. No one realizes how hard this has been on me. I'll call her as soon as I get home. First thing. I'll tell her I felt sick. It's true. I think I've swallowed a tarantula. My throat is scratchy and the glands behind my ears are hard as rocks. I'm infectious. I'm sure of it. The flu maybe. Can't risk contaminating my mother's room.

Thank God it's dark and no one can see me babbling to myself. An hour or two reprieve is all I need. A Thursday night at the Carousel in the dog days of summer. I don't expect more than a couple of lonely drunks nursing drinks, waiting to get flagged, maybe a hairdresser or two who couldn't swing a cheap beach share. What a shock to walk through the door and find the place is packed to the rafters! Maybe the buck moon's raised the testosterone levels of Mecklenburg County. Maybe it's the heat, all that prickly rash needing to be scratched. Or maybe all of Charlotte has turned out in full force for Elvis Karaoke (full costume encouraged, but not mandatory).

The crowd is middle aged, overweight, attached. Everyone's out to have fun, more interested in singing than cruising, no reason to feel self-conscious about big bellies, no need to monitor a partner's wandering eye. The costumes keep it camp; no one's taking it seriously. I don't see any Hillbilly Cats, but there are at least three Vegas Legends in white sequins and tinted aviator glasses. The final contestant in the Dueling "Don't Be Cruel" Competition is wailing away. Our hostess, Miss Priscilla, vintage 1966, dressed for her wedding day with mascara-drawn Cleopatra eyes, asks the finalists to join her on stage. Contestant Number Two must have come with a group, his softball team or bowling league. They scream and whistle and stomp their feet until Miss Priscilla declares him the winner. The Grand Prize is a toilet brush and a bottle of bathroom bowl cleanser, presented on a velvet pillow by Little Miss Lisa Marie.

I drain my beer and order another. I'll nurse it, then leave.

This is fun enough for tables of friends who cheer the talented and make snide remarks about the shrill and off-key. But alone, I feel as sad and pathetic and obvious as in the cafeteria. And then, an aging choir boy steps up to the mike and sings "Love Me Tender" in an achingly beautiful tenor. It's one of my mother's favorites and she'll never hear it again. Maybe I made a mistake, pulling the plug. I must be a heathen, not believing in miracles. The bartender is staring, wondering if I'm drunker than I appear. I should down a large black coffee, suck a pack of Pep-O-Mint Life Savers, head back to the hospital, and fall asleep in a chair in my mother's room.

Which is what I decide to do. But first, I need to hit the head before I hit the road, Jack. Standing at the urinal, shaking the last dribble of piss, I feel a surge of energy next to me. He's shuck-and-jiving, trying to find his pecker in his baggy nylon warm-up pants. Hey, he says, looking up at me. He's got a broad, friendly face and just enough baby fat to make him cuddly. He grins like a naughty schoolboy and leans over the modesty panel to check me out. I'm a grower, not a show-er, I say, embarrassed by the sorry state of my flaccid penis. We'll see about that, he says. He steps back, proud to be a show-er. He shoves himself back into his noisy pants and says, excited, that he's up next.

"Promise you'll clap for me," he pleads. "Promise!"

"What're you singing?" I ask.

"It's a surprise. Promise you'll clap!"

"Okay, I promise."

He's on stage when I get back to the bar. I order another beer, all best intentions postponed for the time being.

"By special request, the King's gonna leave the building for our next performer," Miss Priscilla announces. "But don't any of you tired old queens get any ideas and ask to sing 'Over the Rainbow.' Y'all ain't as cute as Douglas, and he's promised to massage my feet when I ditch these fucking heels." She shoots the boy a lascivious grin and growls into the microphone. "Grrrrrrrr . . ." The kid blushes, dissolving into giggles.

"Okay, let's have a big hand for Douglas!" she shouts.

A drumroll rumbles, followed by a three-chord progression. Douglas grabs the mike and dances along.

> *"I saw him standing there by the record machine,*
> *Knew he must have been around seventeen."*

He's got rhythm and enthusiasm to burn. His joy is contagious.

> *"The beat was going strong, playing my favorite song*
> *And I could tell it wouldn't be long,*
> *till he was with me, yeah, me.*
> *Singing . . ."*

Everyone knows the words to the chorus. Everyone sings along, even the shy and self-conscious. Even me.

> *"I love rock 'n roll.*
> *So put another dime in the jukebox, baby."*

Douglas jumps off the stage and dances around the tables, doing a funky little backstep and waving his free hand above his head. It doesn't hurt he's a little drunk, maybe a little stoned. He goes from table to table, pointing, challenging everyone to sing *louder, louder!* The queens are out of their seats, pumping their fists in the air.

> *"I love rock 'n roll,*
> *So come on and take your time and dance with me!"*

People are pounding the tabletops. The bartender has stopped serving and is singing along. Douglas rips open his shirt, freeing his little belly and budding love handles to bounce along to the beat. The boys are going wild, shoving dollar bills in the elastic waistband of his pants as he builds to his climax.

"I love rock 'n roll,
So put another dime in the jukebox, baby.
I love rock 'n roll,
So come on and take your time and dance with me!"

The Carousel goes crazy. Wolf calls and whistles and cries of Encore! Encore! Douglas's an astute showman. He smiles shyly and shakes his head no. He leaves them begging for more.

"Did you clap? You promised!" he gushes, flushed and happy to find me still at the bar.

"Naw," I say, acting coy, "you didn't need my measly claps."

He looks crestfallen.

"But you promised!"

Disappointed, he looks even younger, jailbait almost.

"Lemme make it up to you," I say, ordering him a beer.

"Yeah, but you still broke your promise."

He recovers quickly, seeing he hasn't lost my interest.

"You were great!" I say.

"Think so?"

"Know so! You ought to go on tour."

"I do!"

"Huh?"

Is there a tour for pudgy Joan Jett imitators?

"I mean, I used to before I got my new job."

Douglas tells me he used to tour with bands as a gofer, the lowest rung on the roadie ladder. He spent a year on the road with the Dead, right before Garcia died. He loves rock'n roll. Put another dime in the jukebox, baby. He pulls off his baseball cap and his thick, sandy hair falls over his face.

"I'm sweating," he says. "I must smell gross."

He smells like a boy, all keyed up, racing through his youth. He could talk for hours about his days with the Dead. Garcia was a god, aloof and quiet, usually on some other planet in a distant solar system. Jerry never actually spoke to him. No one in the band bothered to learn his name. Everything he needed to know the other roadies told him. They'd call him over, give him a list—guitar strings, picks, amp fuses, all the little essentials that constantly needed to be replaced—and make sure he wrote it down, send him off with a pocket of cash, tell him not to return until he'd collected everything they needed, and, for Christ's sake, don't dawdle and don't call to say he's lost.

He ran for cigarettes and rolling papers and herbal essences. But mostly he made calls from pay phones, dialing numbers the head roadie passed him on matchbooks and hotel message pads, getting an address and scribbling it in ink on his wrist while he juggled the receiver, hailing a cab, ringing the buzzer of some tenement flophouse, exchanging thick rolls of hundreds for a discreet-looking package. He had to be very careful. The head roadie threatened to break his neck and dump his body in a landfill if the tour manager, who was paying a small fortune to a Zen master watchdog to keep you-know-who clean and sober on the road, ever discovered their little operation. I tell him it sounds dangerous and ask if he ever got scared.

"Naw," he said, puffed up with bravado. He was terrified, probably pissed his pants more than once, until, like everything, it became dull, a routine, just like any other job.

I ask where he grew up. The question makes him uncomfortable and he winces. He says his father is an ordained minister with a small fundamentalist congregation in the Florida panhandle. He left home after his mother died. He went back last year, thought maybe he'd stay a while this time. He lasted six weeks. The old man accused him of terrible things, of being a criminal, just because his friends would call and he'd have to go out in the middle of the night. He left in tears at three in the morning. The preacher's not his real father anyway. Douglas is adopted.

"So, you gotta work tomorrow?" he asks.

"No. Naw. I have to be somewhere, though. I can be a little late."

"Good. I'm gonna set us up here for another round. Let's get real drunk!"

"What about you? You have to work tomorrow?"

"Hey, man, I'm working all the time!" he says.

"So you're working now?" I ask, skeptical.

"Always!"

He fishes in the pocket of his warm-up suit and snags a ball of rumpled bills. He flattens them on the bar with his fist, scowling at all the George Washingtons. But, hey, bingo, hello, President Jackson, jackpot!

"Hey, another pair of shots this way!" he calls out to the bartender.

"Lemme buy this round," I say.

"Naw, my treat." He sees me looking at the bills on the bar. "Plenty more where that came from," he insists. "Cheers!" he shouts, downing a shot.

"So this job must pay pretty well," I say, trying not to sound facetious.

"You bet!" he swears. He's says he's working for a major recording label. On the creative side.

"Artist and repertory?" I ask, skeptical.

"Wow!" he shouts, slapping the bar with the palm of his hand. "Cool. How did you know that?" he asks, impressed.

"Come on," I say, teasing him, urging him to come clean. I'm hard-pressed to accept that any major label would entrust the nurturing of its precious investments, its stable of artists, to a baby-faced kid in warm-up pants and a baseball cap.

"Okay. Okay. You got me," he says. "I'm a college rep."

Douglas swears Columbia Records is paying him a living wage and a car allowance and an expense account to hit every tiny club on every campus across Tennessee and the Carolinas. He says it's his job to learn the names of every new band as they emerge from suburban basements and garages, to schmooze local radio marketers and program directors, to hit frat parties with live music, to collect "alternative" weekly presses and clip every review of a Columbia record, to make the scene, listen to the buzz, to funnel leads to the real A&R people desperate to sign the Next Big Thing.

Sounds plausible enough. Only one way for me to be sure.

"So how much do they pay you for all that?" I ask.

The figure is too high, confirming my suspicions. The label could offer peanuts, or no pay at all, and still turn away hundreds of kids for a job like this, if it exists at all. Maybe he knows a connection or two at the label from his touring days and maybe, at best, Columbia Records picks up an occasional bar tab and reimburses him for show tickets. I'm pretty sure those bills on the bar are going to have to last him a while.

Yeah, it's a great job, he says, not so enthusiastic now, but not throwing in the towel either. He's looking for a place to live. He thinks he'll be able to cover a thou a month, maybe twelve hundred. Maybe I know a place? He's going to lease a car. Something with a little muscle. A Mustang. Red.

Elvis has returned to the building. The queen on stage is singing "Suspicious Minds." Thanks for the warning, buddy, but I'll have none of that tonight. I like the boy, appreciate his fumbling, guileless attempt to impress me. The fibs, the little white lies, they're harmless, easy to swallow, warm honey to soothe my scratchy throat. It feels good to have someone care about what I think, to talk to someone who likes me.

"So Columbia must think there's a market out there for fat fruits who look like Elvis the day after he bit the bullet?" I ask, sitting back down and dropping a twenty on the bar.

"Huh?" he asks, confused.

"You said you're working now," I say, pointing at the stage. "Guess you're here to check out the talent."

He bursts out laughing. I order another round and offer him a Camel filter.

"Naw, I came with a friend."

"So where's your friend?"

"Dunno," he says. "Ain't seen him for hours."

"So you're stranded?" I ask, knowing he doesn't have a car.

"Nope. I'll ask them to call me a cab."

There's two sorry Georges left on the bar.

I ask where he's staying. He tells me the name of a cheap budget chain motel famous for its coin televisions and scruffy sheets and tiny soaps that cause skin rash.

"Only temporary," he assures me.

Last call for alcohol.

Where did this evening go? What time did I get here? Am I drunk? Can I drive? Well, one more won't make a difference. I'll slow down. Another shot and a beer for Douglas; just a beer for me.

He's evasive when I try to nail down his age. I try some simple arithmetic. Garcia's been dead how long? Douglas was with the band a year. He must have been a high school kid when he took off on the road. He asks if he can give me a kiss. Sure, I say, laughing. He leans forward and gives me an awkward, affectionate buss on the lips, a peck without erotic undertones, like the kisses my oldest nephew used to give me before he turned into a self-conscious adolescent.

The bar's closed. You don't have to go home, but you can't stay here, the bartender shouts to the stragglers. I excuse myself for a last piss. Douglas is gone when I return. Fucking little hustler probably found a better john. Naw, I think, choosing to be benign. The kid was *working, always working*. Must have got called in. Probably has a delivery to make. It's a few steps down from his heyday in pharmaceuticals on the road with the Dead, but, what the hell, it's a living. I step out into the heat and see him pacing the empty parking lot, cell phone at his ear, a duffel bag in the other hand.

"Who are you talking to at this hour of the night?" I ask.

He looks up, startled, frightened at first, then relieved, happy, when he sees it's only me.

"Hey. Hey," he says, letting himself breathe.

"Who are you calling?"

I see the wheels turning as he searches for a plausible answer, one credible enough to not prompt another question.

"The program director at the radio station. She left me a message. I need to get back to her."

"It's late."

"She's open all night," he says.

"Always working too?" I ask, not too sarcastically.

"Yeah, right. Uh, she found an apartment for me. I have to get back to her."

The cell phone rings. He hits the answer pad, then, having a change of heart, smacks the OFF button. He looks up at me, trying hard not to cry.

"Can I come with you?" he asks.

This boy is as alone as I am.

I can't leave him here. He insists we put the duffel bag in the trunk. In case we're stopped, he says. I wonder what the contents of the bag are worth. This is fucking crazy, I tell myself. But I want him to be safe. I want him to be with me. I want to leave quickly. Somewhere in the city, an engine is turning over, a determined foot is flooring the accelerator, a cigarette's being lit in anger, Douglas's number is being punched into a cell phone.

I reach for the ignition and he attacks, knocking my head against the window. I panic, certain I'm being robbed. But what Douglas wants isn't money. He bears down, smashing his mouth into mine, his teeth clipping my tongue, drawing blood, a kiss too furious and aggressive to be mistaken for affection.

"Come on," he says, pulling at my arm as he crawls over the seat. "Come on. Hurry."

Twisted and contorted in this jack-in-a-box backseat, he manages to wriggle out of his crackling running suit and kick off his sneakers. The car stinks of sweat and dirty socks. He feels like a plush toy, soft and furry. He crushes my face with his damp armpit and squeezes my head with his arm. His other hand grabs my cock through my pants. "I hope it's big." It's big enough, but smaller than his fat firecracker with its thick, padded cushion of pink flesh.

"Oh yeah," he says as he frees me from my pants. Something much fiercer than desire compels him. "Please," he begs, actually tearing my shirt from my chest. "Fuck me. Fuck me really hard." He's too impatient to waste time on foreplay. He doesn't want me to stroke his body, tease his balls, and take his enormous cock down my throat. I reach between his legs, thinking I'll have to finger him to get him loose. But his ass yields without resistance, threatening to swallow my entire hand. He's wet, maybe not entirely clean.

"No. No. Not like that," he says, wiggling away. "Fuck me with that big cock."

284 / *Tom Mendicino*

I tell him I can't. I don't have a condom and I'm certain without asking that he doesn't either.

"I'm okay. I promise," he pleads.

I have no reason to believe him. All things considered, I shouldn't. But I do.

I lower my hips and push inside. It's thrilling, feeling this alive. He grabs me by the waist, challenging me to ride him harder. He bears down, squeezing my cock. He says he can feel me shooting inside him. Don't stop, he begs, not yet. I stay hard enough to keep pumping until he splatters a huge load on his chest. He flashes his most wicked smile as he licks his cum from his fingertips. My heart is racing and my pulse is pounding. For the first time in months, years maybe, I've made someone happy.

"It'll be better when we're in bed," he promises. "I want to show you what a good bottom I can be."

Cleaned up and on the road, he tells me his rock and roll dreams. He claims he's the cousin of the bass player in a famous band. They share the same last name. I ask if they're close. Very, he says, crossing his fingers to emphasize how tight. He squirms when I ask why he's not on the road with the band. Well, your cousin must have helped you get the job with the label, I say, trying to bolster his fantasy. Right, he says, and changes the subject.

"I love you, man," he says, grabbing my hand.

He feels safe now and he knows I'm his savior. He's escaped another scrap, another ugly confrontation, and he has me to thank. He knows only one word to describe how he feels. And tonight, when he says he loves me, he means it.

"Where we going?" he asks, smiling.

"Next town over."

"Cool," he says, feeling completely at home in the car now. There's an endless string of cheap motels between Charlotte and Gastonia. Free cable. Pool. In-room coffee. Vacancy. I have enough cash in my pocket to front a week in any one of these dumps. I should pull over, check in, wear him out with another bout of sex, then sneak away when he's in a deep sleep. But something keeps the car on course, the autopilot set, destination home. I'll spend the night watching over him, feeling his chest expanding and deflating until dawn. Maybe I love him back. It's a vague enough word to describe how I feel.

"Cool," he says again. "What's your name?"

I tell him.

"Sorry, I must have forgot. Sorry."

I tell him not to worry. I'd never told him.

"Look, man!" he says, pointing at the big white moon looming ahead.

He listens, enraptured, while I tell him the old Indian legend of the buck moon.

"You know a lot about a lot of things," he says, impressed.

"Not really."

"I know something too," he says, self-conscious.

"What's that?"

"I know I'm glad I met you."

For the first time in weeks, months, a year, since the arrest, years before that even, I am exactly where I want to be. Not ten minutes, three hours, a month, a year in the future. Not yesterday, last week, five years ago, not revisiting every crossroad, taking a different turn this time. And then, on the radio, a drum roll and a power chord and Joan Jett is singing about loving rock'n roll.

"Hey, it's our song!" he says. He tightens his grip on my hand. "Let's just keep going."

"Where?"

"Anywhere. Just keep going. Drive through to Tennessee. Let's go to Gatlinburg."

"What's in Gatlinburg?" I ask, laughing.

"You'll be there."

I pull my hand away to downshift, tapping his gently to re-assure him.

"But I'm right here in Gastonia," I say.

"Can I stay with you in Gastonia?"

"Tonight. Sure."

"Only tonight?" he asks, heartbroken.

I think ahead to tomorrow, the morning call to the hospital, the status report, and, then, hours and hours of sitting and staring into space. Tomorrow at least I'll have him to think about, after he's disappeared into time and space, nothing left of him but a first and last name, maybe real, maybe not. For a week, maybe two, I'll obsess over him, an object desired because it's inaccessible. I'll imagine him going about his mundane routines, brushing his teeth, yawning, scratching an itch, charmed as if they were something magical. I'll coast on these pleasant fantasies until they're exhausted, stale. In the months to come I'll think of him now and then. I'll never know how it all turned out, his story, never know if he's checked out of this world, a victim of a collision or gunfire. I'll tell myself I loved him and mean it since it's easy to love someone who touches your body once and disappears in the morning.

"We'll see," I say.

"I love you," he says, taking my hand again.

I pull the car into the drive and turn off the engine. We're home, I say. He likes my choice of words. I hold the car door for him, as if it was 1957 and this was the prom. He asks for his duffel, the precious bag.

"Hey, this is nice," he says, impressed by the big house, lots of rooms to get lost in, "real nice." I lead him to the kitchen and find a couple of beers.

"You live here alone?" he asks.

"Yes," I say, shocked by my answer. It's true. She's never coming back. Her clothes are still in the closets. Intimate items—combs, pins, sprays—are scattered on her dresser. Her magazines, manuals on *Good Housekeeping* and *Better Homes and Gardens*, are stacked in her bathroom. Her collectible porcelain dolls stare wide-eyed, thinking she's going to return. But the hospital bed is gone, shipped back to the rental company. The medications have been flushed down the toilet. The milk in the refrigerator has a later expiration date than my mother. Yes, I live here alone.

"Ever get lonely?" he asks.

Wait a minute. Back down. He's playing with me, trying to manipulate a one-night stand into an extended visit. Do I ever get lonely? How could I possibly get lonely when intimacy's so cheap, no more than the price of a few beers? How can I be lonely when there's always someone like him, charming me with sincere endearments that don't have to be accounted for in the bright light of day?

"No. Not really," I say, lying.

"I do," he says. "I wish I didn't."

He asks if he can kiss me, for real this time, not like in the bar. I'm ashamed of myself. This kid, this overgrown boy who's in way over his head, is incapable of guile. His wet lips roam the contours of my face, grazing my cheeks, eyelids, nose, finally settling on my mouth. His tongue is tentative, not sure how it will be received, and when it finds a warm welcome, he whimpers as if he's in pain.

"Wow!" he says when he comes up for air. "Need to cool off," he says, fanning himself. "Break time!"

We take our beers out back. He looks up at me, thick bangs falling over his eyes, Dennis the Menace shit-eating grin on his face.

"You know what?" he asks.

"What?"

"There's nothing I like better than to do some blow and suck a big dick. Back in a minute," he says and disappears, leaving me alone in the dark.

The buck moon casts a silver sheen on the damp, neglected lawn. Deep in the night, between midnight and dawn, when each dark hour is the same as the last, it's impossible to tell time without a watch. Mine has stopped, suspended at 11:17. I shake my wrist, trying to revive it. The battery's dead. Weird. How can it be? My Rolex isn't three months old. Douglas returns and drops to his haunches, squatting like an Asian as he carefully packs a little metal pipe with powdery granules. He strikes a long kitchen match against the rough concrete patio and, guiding the wild flame with a steady hand, lights a small fire, all crispy crackles, in the bowl. He rocks on his heels, back and forth, striking a second match, then a third, drawing the harsh smoke into his lungs.

I look up to the kitchen window, expecting to see my mother's face, frowning at backyard crimes and misdemeanors, ready to toss the dish towel in the sink and rush outside to make everything right. But there's no one there. I touch his shoulder and he grabs my leg, clinging to me like I'm the last piece of flotsam in the raging sea.

"How long can I stay here?"

"You need a place to stay?"

"Yes. Yes." And he starts crying, really sobbing.

"Hey. Hey," I say, sitting beside him on the concrete. "What's going on? Who are you afraid of?"

He doesn't answer.

Then a hoarse, tired voice is calling my name.

I tell Douglas to hide in the yard, lie flat on the grass, away from the light of the windows. Keep quiet, be still, everything will be all right. He's terrified, not certain he can trust me, but doesn't have a choice. He dashes into the yard and throws himself facedown in the grass. Prone, he's well hidden, out of sight.

"Out here," I shout. "I'm coming."

My sister's husband, exhausted and agitated and reeking of cigarettes, is standing at the glass door. His arms are crossed accusingly, his thick chest is heaving, and there are sweat circles under his armpits.

"What are you doing?" he asks.

"Looking at the moon."

His anger and frustration escalates. Indignation gives way to murderous impulses.

"Where the fuck have you been?" he hisses, spraying spit across my face.

Who is this prick? Who does he think he is, confronting me? I don't owe him any explanations, any answers. I open my mouth to tell him to get out of this house, this sanctuary where my sister and I grew into the miserable, pathetic creatures we are today.

"Your sister had to be sedated," he shouts, not giving me a chance to speak. "No one could find you. Where have you been, you irresponsible little fuck?"

Lucky man. Lucky for him I don't have a gun or a knife or brick in my hand.

"Your mother's dead. No one could find you."

"When?" I ask.

"Eleven. Quarter after eleven. Hours ago. I'm sorry, man," he says, his anger exhausted, relieved he's found me, mission accomplished. "Come on. I'll drive."

Douglas, his voice, tight, high pitched, scared, calls out to me, startling my brother-in-law.

"Jesus. Jesus Christ," my brother-in-law says, realizing he's barged into some sordid little assignation, disgusted, looking at me as if I'm an insect to be crushed under the sole of his size thirteen shoe. "Fucking Jesus. Unbelievable!"

"Go," I say, my voice calm, under control. "Leave now."

He doesn't know whether to take a stand for all that's decent or escape while he can, absolved of any further responsibility.

"Let Gina sleep in the morning. The arrangements have all been made. Everything's taken care of. Just go."

He pauses, straining to see beyond me, needing to have his worst suspicions confirmed.

"You sure? You okay?" he asks, wary, stalling.

"Yes, thanks for asking."

I don't move until I hear the front door close behind him. Douglas is fumbling around in the dark, afraid to come out where he can be seen. I wait for grief, pain, shock, some emotion to overwhelm me. I've spent months preparing for this moment, to gird myself for the kick in the stomach, the sharp blow to the throat, the lead pipes across my knees that would follow the final pronouncement. But the minutes pass and nothing. I say the words aloud, sure they'll trigger an appropriate response. My mother's dead. But here I stand, unchanged, feeling no different than five, ten minutes ago. I try to summon up an image of my mother. Her features are already vague, hazy, indistinct. I can't remember the color of her eyes. Definitely not brown. But gray, green, hazel, pale blue? I thought I'd seared them into my memory, but they're gone, lost forever. The next time I see her they'll be sewn shut, never to be pried open again.

My thoughts wander back to the stoned boy stumbling in the grass. In a few hours, it will be morning and the sun will burn away the haze, the fog in my mind. There'll be enough time to despair. But tonight, at least, I'm not alone.

"Douglas," I call out. "Doug. It's okay to come out."

He emerges from the dark, backlit by the moon, shoes in hand, hesitant, afraid to throw caution to the wind.

"Can I stay here with you?" he asks again.

"Yes."

I mean tonight. He thinks I mean longer. I'll wait and break it to him in the morning. The bogeyman won't be so scary then.

He follows me into the house and up the stairs. My twin bed can't accommodate both of us and I lead him to my mother's big queen bed, the one she shared with my father. He slumps on the mattress and smiles at me.

"I'm so tired," he says.

"So am I."

"I'm sorry."

"Don't worry. We'll just sleep."

"I wanted to give you the best blow job ever."

He's slurring his words, fumbling with his buttons. I turn back the sheets and help him wiggle out of his pants and pull off his socks. He lies on his back and watches me undress. He drapes his arm across my chest when I crawl in beside him. His head droops and he is asleep. I touch the port wine stain on his shoulder and count the birthmarks on his neck.

He's far away, safe in Never Never Land, where lost boys live forever and never have to grow up. He doesn't hear the angry little cell phone shrieking in the duffel bag downstairs. Somewhere out there, a driver is cruising the streets of Charlotte, searching for a boy in a nylon warm-up suit. I'm afraid Douglas's not as lucky as Peter Pan and that his story won't have a happy ending. Tomorrow night, the warm body next to me may be lying in an emergency room, beyond repair, just a few heartbeats away from being rolled to the morgue on a gurney.

Do not resuscitate.

No mechanical respiration.

No tube feeding or invasive form of nutrition or hydration.

No blood or blood products.

No form of surgery nor any invasive diagnostic procedures.

No kidney dialysis.

No antibiotics.

No codes.

No extraordinary efforts to sustain life.

But that's a day away. Tonight he will sleep like a baby, the inevitable postponed until the sun rises. I'll lie awake, haunted by my mother, with his warm body spooned into mine in the bed she shared with my father. We've both earned another precious day, and that's as much as any of us can expect.

Mary, Queen of Heaven

The forecast was on the mark. It's still reasonably hot, it being summer in North Carolina, after all. But the temperature feels surprisingly comfortable after the Old Testament scourge of the past week. I've spoken to Regina and she's agreed, begrudgingly, but without argument, to respect my wish to do this alone. I'm showered, shaved, gelled, deodorized, fortified with black coffee and a piece of rye toast before climbing the stairs to the bedroom. I lower myself on the mattress as Douglas, this perfect stranger, sleeps contentedly in my mother's bed. Rise and shine, I say, sounding like her, gently waking him. I find a way to slip my name into my greeting, assuming he doesn't remember it. He looks forlorn, like he was hoping to hide under the covers all day, when I tell him we need to be going. I've got to be somewhere, I apologize, I can't drive him back to Charlotte. I insist he accept whatever's in my wallet, a couple hundred, more than enough for the taxi to take him wherever he wants to go. He had a really great time, he says. He wants my number so he can call me when he gets a phone. The one he's been using belongs to a friend. He gives me a friendly kiss and hops into the cab, his precious duffel bag held tight, talking excitedly on the cell, concocting some wild and improbable tale to explain going AWOL last night.

I'm wearing a blue suit and white shirt, dressed for the occasion this time, hoping to avoid the withering disapproval and arched eyebrows of M. Sweeney of M. Sweeney & Son. But it seems M. Sweeney is now resting comfortably in one of his top-of-the-line models. Sweeney the Son greets me in "business casual": shirtsleeves, khakis, and boat shoes. The tables have turned, and Sweeney the Son, surprised by my gabardine and tie in these less formal times, is embarrassed and excuses himself, returning in a gold-buttoned navy blazer. Add epaulets and a visored cap and he'd pass for the majordomo of a yacht club.

The times, they are a-changing. Solemnity is outdated, even at a funeral parlor. The M. Sweeneys of tradition, dour and elegiac, church bells ringing out with every footstep, are asleep in the graveyard. Sweeney the Son has a difficult time repressing his cheerful good nature. Try as he might, gravity does not come easily to him. He bounces from casket to casket on the balls of his feet. He bubbles with enthusiasm as he describes the luxury extras of the better models, their plush interiors padded with creamy fabrics, with lifetime warranties against seepage and moisture.

Whose lifetime?

Mine?

Certainly not my mother's.

Is there a money-back guarantee?

How would I collect? Do I pick up the phone in twenty years and schedule an exhumation to check on the state of preservation? Pay up, Sweeney! My mother doesn't look as fresh as a daisy anymore!

Just a simple pine box. Nothing fancy. Nothing garish. Just plain and simple. That's what I asked for back when I was a novice at this, touring the "showroom" in shorts and sneakers, not knowing if I was expected to rap the casket lids with my knuckles like I'd kick the tires of a new car. In the end, my father drove to heaven in the Lincoln Town Car of coffins. This time I have no delusions that a simple pine box will suffice.

I can't tell M. Sweeney I want a container and nothing more. I don't want to seem cheap and callow. I don't want him thinking I'm mocking the dead. I won't insist on the simple pine box. But I won't be duped this time. I'm a savvy consumer now and won't be bulldozed into squandering ten thousand dollars on the Mary, Queen of Heaven model. He's wasting his time extolling its virtues, rhapsodizing over the craftsmanship, explaining the silkscreen technique used to imprint an image of the blue-veiled Virgin on the thick cushion inside the lid.

"No thank you," I say politely. "I don't think my mother envisioned spending eternity with the Mother of God's nose planted in her belly button."

Sweeney the Son can't help laughing, but, afraid of appearing disrespectful, composes himself quickly. He relaxes when I laugh too.

"I have just what you're looking for," he says.

We settle on the Michelangelo, solid mahogany, with gold leaf trim and Pieta miniatures carved into the four corners of the lid. It's dignified, beautiful even, a few steps above the middle of the line. A perfectly adequate container.

It's barbaric, this ritual, dressing my mother in her Sunday best, tucking a rosary in her hands, slipping some precious object—a stuffed animal or a photo in a heart-shaped frame—under the blanket. I'd prefer cremation, but it isn't an option. My mother suffered from a morbid fear of death by fire. My sister says she would come back to haunt me if I were to perpetrate the transgression of popping her into the toaster oven. I doubt it, but don't see any reason to assume the risk. Anyway, it's my own claustrophobia that makes me panic at the thought of the Michelangelo being slammed shut, sealed tight, and covered with earth.

Why can't I just tie helium balloons to her ankles and wrists and let her float high in the blue skies? Why can't she just drift until a strong wind comes along to sweep her into the stratosphere where a shroud of ice crystals will preserve her for all eternity in the deep freeze of space? Then I could spend my evenings studying the night skies, seeking my mother, Queen of Heaven, as she orbits the earth.

But no, it has to be into the ground where, the miracles of engineering and lifetime guarantees notwithstanding, she's destined to rot. Fungus will cover her face and hungry microbes will strip her flesh to the white bone, leaving nothing but an anonymous, toothy grin, a memento mori, a prop for a cheesy horror movie.

The worms crawl in, the worms crawl out. . . .

"Are you all right?" Sweeney the Son asks, drawing me out of my reverie. "Would you like water, an iced tea?"

"Water would be good," I say.

"Maybe something a little stronger on the side?" he suggests.

The whiskey burns my throat, bringing tears to my eyes. Time to get back to business. The coffin is only the first item on the list. Her favorite dress, navy worsted with delicate red piping, waits in the garment bag. The pearls my father gave her on their thirtieth anniversary are in a small silk pouch in my pocket. Only for the viewing, I instruct. Certainly, he assures me. I've brought a recent photograph, taken just before the ravages of lymphoma became apparent. I tell him Forrest, my mother's devoted Pekingese of a hairdresser, will be preparing her wig. We can't bear the thought of my mother lying in state sporting a careless comb-over by some overweight matron with club hands. Of course, Sweeney the Son says, always willing to accommodate.

And the viewing, he asks, one night or two? Open or closed casket? Of course, immediate family will have an opportunity to view the deceased regardless of the decision.

Open? Closed? My claustrophobia dictates my decision. Open, of course. Don't cheat her of any precious moments of air and light.

The death notice needs to be placed. The *Gaston Gazette*, of course. What about the Charlotte papers?

I think back to Christmas and my amazement at learning how many lives she touched.

Merry Christmas, Nathaniel. Was Santa good to you?

Oh, the best, Miz Nocera, the very best.

Yes, the *Charlotte Observer* too.

Sweeney the Son is every bit as efficient as his late father. He takes me in hand and walks me through every detail, answers every question, resolves every problem. Gratitude and exhaustion and the whiskey overwhelm me. Without thinking, I embrace him, thanking him for making this so easy. It's impossible to imagine such intimacy with his austere father. Sweeney the Son, being a different breed, pats my back. He doesn't need to speak; his touch conveys his empathy and sympathy. For one fleeting second, I consider burying my face in his neck and sobbing. But I resist. This is professional intimacy, with definite limitations and boundaries that cannot be crossed.

"Were you close?" he asks, withdrawing from my bear hug, careful not to convey discomfort and rejection.

"Yes," I say, sounding uncertain.

I think so.

Were we?

Did she still feel close to me or did my selfishness and self-absorption, my unwillingness to feign interest in her anxiety and fears, disappoint her? I kept my distance, letting her words drop in the space between us, depriving her of the easy, intimate conversations of my childhood and youth. I couldn't comfort her. I was constitutionally incapable of thinking of anything but my own misery. And worse yet, what will be impossible to live with, is that I made her last months more difficult, that I compounded the strain. My mother, bravely facing painful therapies and bleak outcomes, feared only one thing in the end.

Me.

I'm afraid to speak to him anymore. He gets angry at everything I say.

I assume it's a lie, another pathetic effort by my sister to hurt me, revenge taken for my mother's unconditional love for me. But there was no satisfaction in my sister's eyes when she betrayed my mother's confidence and broke her solemn promise to say nothing to me.

My sister is telling the truth.

Some essential part is missing in me. I know I have a heart, but it seems incapable of kindness. Sweeney the Son steps forward again, anticipating tears. He's ready to offer a clean handkerchief and a palm on the shoulder. How easy it comes to him. I'd like to strap him to the embalming table behind those thick doors. I'd crack open his breastplate and search and probe until I found the little generator that pumps empathy and compassion into his soul. I'd snip it with the scalpel and bury it in ice and race to the emergency room, demanding a transplant. And when the sutures healed, I'd emerge a different person, whole, able to experience a full range of emotions.

"May I have the dress?" he asks.

"Yes, here," I say, handing him the garment bag.

"Can I see her?" I ask.

"She's not prepared," he says.

"Please. I wasn't with her when she died."

He relents and, against his professional wisdom, agrees to allow me a few moments alone in the embalming room. He hovers on the other side of the door, wary, ready to spring into action at the first sign of rage or inconsolable grief. So I stand quietly, barely whispering, telling my mother I love her and begging for one last gift, mercy.

Maybe it's lack of sleep. Maybe it's the whiskey. Maybe my eyes are playing tricks on me. Maybe it's a miracle. I can never tell anyone. They'd think I was crazy. But my mother hears me and takes my hand and squeezes it, telling me to make my peace with the world.

Antibiotic

LAURA WAY BREWER, M.D.
PRACTICE LIMITED TO PSYCHIATRY

The address is smack in the heart of one of those leafy suburbs where the oak trees are older than the nation. So private, so quiet. Volvos for daytime errands and a Mercedes for a night on the town. Two children . . . no, no, it would be highly irresponsible of Laura Way Brewer, M.D., to contribute to the global overpopulation straining our exhausted planet. One-point-five children. A son and half-a-daughter, eviscerated at the midsection.

There'll be a discreet side entrance. Dr. Brewer? I presume. So stylishly unstylish. A simple haircut with a light rinse that set you back a cool hundred fifty after tip. A silk blouse, single strand of pearls, wool crepe skirt, and European leather pumps, softer than skin. Bric-a-brac from the Asian continent scattered around the office, booty from her journeys. (God knows Dr. Brewer would never deign to do something as mundane as *vacation*.) Plush oriental carpets and ethnic wall hangings to soak up the interminable silences that are broken only by the sound of the half-a-daughter several rooms away, practicing piano. Pardon me, Dr. Brewer. Can you spare me your undivided attention? I'm not paying you to be distracted by your darling child as she fumbles her way through "Für Elise." Don't you want to know how salty a mechanic's cock tastes at three in the morning in a shit-stinking rest stop on the interstate?

I made the appointment but didn't keep it.

And God knows how I hate you. Sorry, not you, Dr. Brewer. We've never even met.

You, Reverend Matthew McGinley, S.J., M.D.

Or is it M.D., S.J.?

We never did get that sorted out.

How's tricks up in the good old D. of C.? Hail the conquering hero. The whole town must have turned out to celebrate your triumphant return from exile in Mayberry and your liberation from us po' bucktooth yokels with bad haircuts and cornmeal between our toes.

Oh, God, did I forget to tell you I've accepted the academic appointment at Georgetown? I'm referring you to Dr. Brewer. I'm sure you'll enjoy working with her.

Maybe your announcement wasn't that harsh, but it felt that way.

Adios, amigo. Yeah, you got your problems, but the chairman of the Department of Psychiatry is wheezing close to seventy and they're searching for young blood and there's no blood younger and fresher and more deserving than mine.

Maybe those weren't your exact words, but it's exactly what you meant.

That's terrific, Matt. I'm so happy for you. Maybe we can do dinner some night when I'm in D.C. We'll catch up. You can ask me how things are going.

Great. Things are going great. You know my mother's dead. My sister's a bitch. She's selling the house. I'm a gentleman of leisure now. My throat has been sore for weeks now, since the night my mother died. Staph, strep, gonorrhea, syphilis, maybe just postnasal drip? Who knows? Maybe I should get it checked out, but I refuse to set foot in one more doctor's office, flipping through ancient copies of *People* and reading about forgotten celebrities whose moment has passed. Not that I don't have time to spare. I haven't worked since my mother died. I got fired or quit. I'm not sure which. My Born Again National Sales Manager sent flowers and a sugary sympathy note and left a holier-than-thou condolence on the answering machine. He waited a respectable seven days and left another message with my itinerary along the California coast. He sounded so pleased with himself, telling me how he'd chosen the trip with the *gorgeous* weather in mind, knowing how much I'd appreciate a break after the past few months. I never returned the call or any of the others he made in the following days. Finally, he left an angry message, demanding I return the company laptop, calling me irresponsible and threatening me with ugly references.

The estate is divided equally between Regina and me. She's anxious to sell the house. She says we should capitalize on the hot real estate market. What she means is she's afraid the ash from one of my cigarettes will ignite the carpet and burn her security to the ground. She's not unsympathetic to my plight, but money is money and, as she points out, I need my share more than she needs hers. You need a change of scenery, she says, you need to get on with your life. She says she doesn't think my antidepressants are working. I haven't told her I've stopped filling my prescriptions, except for the anti-anxiety pills, of course, which I swallow religiously to put me to sleep, washed down with a six-pack and a couple of shots.

But I am getting on with it. Three days ago I dragged myself out of bed before noon and ran a razor over my face for the first time in weeks. My hangover tasted like spearmint mouthwash and my pants were spotted with coffee rings, but I looked respectable enough to the manager of the Charlotte outpost of the Barnes and Noble empire. He hired me on the spot, sales associate at minimum wage, and asked me to start the next morning. Startled, I backtracked and told him I wasn't available for two weeks. I wouldn't bet the ranch on me showing up.

My new landlord certainly didn't seem to mind the Crown Royal blended on my breath. He was eager enough to take the check. In two or three days—or is it four or five?—I begin my new life as an inmate in one of his $600-a-month cells, complete with barred windows and chipped enamel sinks. I'm looking forward to meeting the other prisoners and spending time with their screaming babies and drunken spouses. We'll all shout to be heard over the shrieking televisions. My sister offered to loan me the down payment to buy, but I'd rather serve my sentence at the Magnolia Towne Courte than in a luxury condominium with ceiling fans and hardwood floors and a wide balcony.

The contents of the Monument to Heat and Air are being put in storage. The move is scheduled. The movers are coming to pack everything into boxes and cartons and haul it off to a cinderblock storage compound near the airport. Regina says the charms of the listing—the crown moldings, actual plaster on the walls—will show better stripped to essentials and slapped with a fresh coat of paint. I've got my instructions to tag the few bits and pieces my prison cell can accommodate. She's called and left several messages, not confident of my ability to accomplish even this one small duty. She's right. I haven't lifted a finger yet. The movers are coming . . . when? Tomorrow? I'm confused, uncertain when she left the message.

My mother's bed, a dresser, an upholstered chair, and a television are all I need. I suppose I ought to poke around the kitchen and toss a coffeepot and bottle opener into a box. I need to pack my clothes. Everything else can collect dust in the storage compound.

It's one o'clock. Not too late for an early start. I've had two cups of coffee and a half pack of cigarettes. Time to crack open a beer and get to work. The phone rings and I let it spill into the answering machine. It's just my sister again, asking me to pick up, please. I ignore her and go to the front door to retrieve the morning paper. I keep forgetting to stop delivery. Need to put it on my to-do list. I skim the pages, looking for a headline about a body found in a city Dumpster, young white male, identity unknown, sandy hair, dressed in a nylon warm-up suit. Nothing. Somewhere out there, Douglas is still "working," singing "I Love Rock 'N Roll," dodging his angry supplier, finding refuge for the night.

Why didn't you believe me when I told you I loved him, Matt? You told me you were concerned about my state of mind. You urged me to follow up with Dr. Brewer and gave me a prescription for Ativan. I promised I wouldn't take them with alcohol. You gave me a number in Washington where you can be reached twenty-four/seven. Your messages are more and more frequent, pleading with me to call. Dr. Brewer has told you I didn't show for the appointment. You're threatening to call my sister if I don't respond by ten o'clock. I'm not sure when you left that last message.

I should go upstairs and throw my underwear and socks and shirts in a suitcase. Maybe the movers will never come. Maybe they'll come, but they'll take pity on me and refuse to pack and haul, their consciences unwilling to let them throw me out on the street. I need a little nap. I can't drag myself farther than the sofa. I close my eyes and my thoughts drift to a packed church, filled to capacity. I feel the heat of the bodies in the pews behind me. An ancient crone is pumping away and the organ is groaning. My sister sits beside me, whimpering and dabbing her eyes. Her husband puts his arm around her shoulder. Her sons stare at the casket resting before the altar. Dustin, her younger boy, tries to comfort his sister, sweet and awkward and self-conscious as he rises to the occasion. My heart is racing. All these people and the church feels empty, just me and the coffin.

Then a warm body slides into the pew. A small hand takes my larger one and gives it a soft kiss. My wife—no, my ex-wife, my friend—has taken pity and rescues me from my solitude. She stays with me through the interminable service and the long ride to the cemetery. She's obviously pregnant and Sweeney the Son fetches a folding chair, setting it at the graveside. She ignores his kindness and stands by my side in the oppressive heat. She presses her left hand against my back to steady me. I feel her wedding band, not the one I slipped on her finger, through my damp jacket.

Later that night, I sit on the patio, drinking and smoking and counting the moths fluttering in the porch lights, while my sister and her husband, who've re-occupied the Monument to Heat and Air since my mother died, eat pizza and watch *Die Hard* with their kids. Little Dustin, looking younger than his years in his Tweety Bird nightshirt, comes seeking quieter companionship, an old board game under his arm.

"Sure, I'll play with you," I say, grateful for the company. "You can be Miss Scarlet if you want. I promise I won't tell."

I lie on my back, dozing, debating whether to pop another pill to put me under for the afternoon. I think that tarantula might be tearing my throat apart. I can't swallow and drool is dribbling from my mouth. Perspiration drips from my eyebrows. I stumble to the kitchen but cold water from the faucet doesn't soothe my burning eyes. I trip over my feet and fall face first into the sink, splitting my lip. My blood tastes like roast beef, rare. I wrestle with an ancient ice tray, spilling the cubes on the floor. I pick up the one closest to my foot and press it against my throbbing lip. I feel a long hair dangling on the tip of my tongue. I try to flick it away, but it has a will of its own, clinging to my bloody finger by its steel gray root.

I go upstairs, searching for an aspirin to dull the pain. My medicine cabinet's empty except for my trusty Ativan, an exhausted tube of toothpaste, and a used Band-Aid. I'll try my mother's. Surely one lonely Bayer survived the wholesale disposal of her pharmacopoeia. The last of the prednisone, Compazine, and Lomotil has been flushed down the toilet. The septic tank's probably developing muscles from all the steroids it's swallowed. What's left? Tweezers, cotton balls, and cuticle scissors. And one lonely hidden prescription bottle, dated over a year ago, when the word *lymphoma* was only a Latinate obscurity in the *Family Medical Dictionary,* when my mother's sore throat meant nothing more than a bacterial infection brought on by the change of seasons. A simple cephalosporin, a ten-day regimen, *Take Until Completed.* My poor mother, usually so compliant, ignored the instructions on the label and stopped taking the pills when the pain subsided. Maybe it upset her tummy, maybe she felt like being defiant just once in her life. Six little striped capsules are left. Not too old, probably still effective. If one works, two will work even faster.

I swallow one, then another. I should start packing, but my mother's rumpled bed is more appealing. I crawl under the covers, wishing I had a beer, but I'm too tired to walk downstairs. The label said *Take Until Completed.* She didn't, leaving six in the bottle. Maybe that was her fatal mistake. The causes of cancer are a mystery, that is, beyond the obvious things like cigarettes and charred meat and Three Mile Island. Maybe that innocent sore throat started a chain reaction that eventually consumed her body.

It could have been what killed her. That or a million other things. It doesn't make much difference. All that's left of her is her bed. And even here, it's hard to find any trace of her. I've slept in this bed every night since my sister left and spent most of my days propped against the pillows. There's no television in the bedroom, just a small clock radio still tuned to her favorite station. I listen to happy talk, armchair psychologists and financial advisors and brand-name chefs and celebrity interviewers more famous than the celebrities they interview. It's all white noise filtering any intrusions from the world.

My mother would hardly know this bed anymore. I haven't

changed the sheets. I prefer body smells to fabric softener; they're rich and warm, fecund like the good earth. Like the boxers I haven't changed in days. No wonder my crotch is itching like hell. Scratching just makes it worse. I should be ashamed of myself. What would my mother think if she saw me wallowing in her bed in this condition?

But she's not coming back. And if she could, she'd probably just pull the covers up to my shoulders and tell me to try to sleep. Or maybe she would haul me out by the ankles, yank me by the hair, deliver a swift kick to the ass, and tell me to shape up.

I kick aside the bedsheets and stick my hand in my boxers, lazily scratching my balls. A rash is spreading beyond my crotch, across my belly, over my chest, up to my head. I sit up in bed, pawing myself like a bipolar chimpanzee on a manic swing. A shower might help. The water is tepid, as cold as it ever gets in the dying days of a Southern summer, and relief lasts only while the water is running.

I turn off the water and reach for a towel. I'm red, a bright flaming scarlet. My body is a lunar landscape of angry hives. I drop the towel on the floor, barely recognizing the monster in the bathroom mirror. Huge welts creep across my face. My body is going haywire. Alarm bells are ringing inside my ears. No, it's just the doorbell. No, it's too shrill for the doorbell. Can't be the doorbell. Only the Jehovah's Witnesses come calling these days, trying to rescue my soul with copies of *Watchtower*.

What the hell were those pills? They look harmless enough, sitting here on the sink. What are these fucking things? I pop the lid and flush them down the toilet. The whirlpool makes me dizzy. One little capsule clings to the porcelain bowl, defying me. I fill a glass with water and try to swallow, hoping to restore my body to a state of grace.

The phone is screeching again. The answering machine picks

up and my sister begs me to answer. She sounds as if she's crying. Don't cry. Don't cry. I'm all right. It's nothing. She keeps calling my name. Andy. Andy. Andy? She can't hear me answering.

Where's the phone? Where's the fucking phone? I weave and stumble toward the bed, trying to catch my breath. Aha! There you are, you naughty little glow-in-the-dark princess. My awkward foot kicks the receiver across the floor.

Are you there? Please, are you there?

Gina's voice is tiny, tinny, muffled by the thick carpet.

I'm all right . . . all right, I want to tell her, but I can't speak now, can't waste the effort. It takes every bit of strength I have to breathe. I can only look at the phone and gasp and heave. My throat is collapsing; my lungs are screaming for oxygen. I want to tell her bye, bye, kiddo, sweet dreams, don't let the bed bugs bite.

Go ahead and close your eyes, I think. Sleep tight. Don't be afraid. It doesn't matter anyway. I'm scared, but not as much as I should be. Some part of me believes this is only a dream and I'll wake before I stop breathing.

Fuck Jesus!

I feel strong arms pick me up and carry me down the stairs.

Call 911!

I hear another voice at the far end of the tunnel.

What you say?

Call fucking 911! This man ain't breathing so good!

What?

911! Call now, motherfucker! This man gonna die!

But I don't.

Hours later, I'm lying in an observation bed in the emergency department. The nurse says two gentlemen would like to visit. Jerome and Nate, Bekins Moving and Hauling, stand over me, smiling, basking in the warm glow of playing God. Their names are embroidered above their shirt pockets. Nate. Nathaniel.

Merry Christmas, Nathaniel. Was Santa good to you?

I try to thank them, but it's too painful to speak. The breathing tube bruised my throat. My hands and thighs are tethered by lines and needles. Benadryl and steroids and adrenaline have worked their miracle and brought me back to life.

Take it easy, little buddy, Nate says, *thought we'd lost you.*

I shake my head and doze off, comforted by his voice.

"You're a very lucky fellow," the nurse says as she hands me my discharge instructions. I don't disagree even though it's been a long time since I would have chosen that word to describe myself.

So I check into a hotel, seeking room service and clean sheets until Nate and Ben can deliver my mother's bed to Magnolia Towne Courte. I decline the key to the minibar, not completely trusting my ability to resist temptation. I call my sister, then Matt. I give them my room number and assure them I'm fine, that I just need to get some sleep.

Which is what I do for three days. Real sleep without pills or booze, relying only on my own circadian rhythm. I order cheeseburgers and fries and chocolate milk for breakfast, lunch, and dinner. When you're paying top dollar, the staff accommodates your every need. I stare at the television between bouts of sleep. I start to feel better, stronger, almost content.

Anaphylactic shock didn't transform me. Maybe it's just that I'd sunk as low as I could go. Not that my little tale of woe was anything special, nothing for the record books. I'll never experience the horrors and epiphanies of true addiction. A little heavy drinking and a few sour sexual liaisons and a chance encounter with an antibiotic with a four to five percent cross-reaction with penicillin are the sum and substance of the drama of my life.

I wish I could say that I'm seeking redemption through meditation and prayer. But the reality is I'm lying on the bed burping ground beef and onions and dozing while my Psychic Friends promise Great Revelations on the television screen.

Your loved ones are waiting to speak to you. . . .

The Celebrity Spokesperson, all bright and shiny with red lacquer lips and shoe polish hair, speaks directly to the camera, sending a not-so-subliminal message to call the number crawling across the bottom of the screen. Apparently, my mother is beating down the fourth wall separating those who have passed and those of us still encumbered by mortal flesh and blood. And she has a message for me! All for the small investment of two dollars and fifty cents a minute.

Curiosity killed the cat and, after validating my card, a lazy voice thanks me for calling the Zodiac Hotline. The Celebrity Spokesperson, of course, is too busy with her sales pitch to channel my mother's spirit herself. My minimum-wage clairvoyant sounds barely out of high school. Her questions are peppered with teenage slang.

So, um, like, your mom . . . like, when did she pass?

After twenty dollars of preparatory interrogation, my mother is ready to make her Grand Entrance. The message is simple and, though delivered in an unfamiliar voice, can only have come from her.

Get out of bed. Shower. Check out. Move on.

Good boy that I am, I obey.

Intervention

She hadn't needed Nancy Drew to track me down. She'd dialed my mother's number and an automated voice provided the forwarding number, repeating it twice in case she didn't have a pencil in hand. What's surprising isn't that she's found me, but that she's come looking.

Bobby's wife sounds shy and awkward when I answer the telephone, introducing herself as if she were a stranger, as if I couldn't possibly have any recollection of having spent the past Easter in her home. She apologizes for intruding; she feels terrible about bothering me. She's calling from the Pride of Carolina Motor Lodge on the strip highway outside Chapel Hill. Her voice is tired and raspy. She says Bobby refused to come down from Watauga County; his son is dead as far as he's concerned. The doctors told her the cuts were deep and plastic surgery might not hide the scars. She's worried JR will have to wear long sleeves, even in the heat of summer. The television bleats in the background, noise to keep her company.

"JR asked me to call you," she says, assuming, incorrectly, the boy and I have struck a special friendship, that I'd been sought after and my advice solicited as his only flesh-and-blood relative who'd been to college. She has it all wrong.

Robert, not JR, has asked her to call. That much I know. What I don't know is how Robert knew to ask for me. Did he figure it out on his own? How? Had someone told him? I ask what she wants me to do. Can you come to the hospital? she asks. I'll meet you in the lobby tomorrow at two, I say.

The hospital is like every other, with walls painted neutral colors and spit-polished floors. The simplest question—room, please, of Robert Calhoun—seems to overwhelm the red-smocked old woman volunteering at the reception desk. The computer denied access to any information, referring her to confidentiality protocols. Flustered, she excuses herself and dashes off to find help.

"Andy."

I spin on my heels and stand face-to-face with my cousin Bobby's wife. She's aged since my mother's funeral. She's missed her appointment with Lady Clairol and hasn't slapped on any makeup to brighten her dull pallor. She's not making any efforts to put a best face on things. Meeting is even more awkward than the phone conversation. She asks if I've eaten. I lie and say yes since hospital food still haunts my dreams. We walk to the locked unit. She introduces me to the unit clerk, then excuses herself. She'll meet me in the lobby after visiting hours, knowing we "boys" want to talk. I listen for subtext, insinuation, innuendo, in her comment, and hear none. All she cares about is that her damaged son has asked for me and I have come.

Robert is embarrassed by his circumstances, but happy, genuinely happy, to see me. He doesn't seem so different from the boy I shared a bed with last spring. He hardly looks to be a danger to himself, bandaged wrists notwithstanding, and no one would ever believe he's a threat to others. He doesn't seem to belong here, locked away with the agitated, the obsessed, the haunted, the irredeemable. After hello, I grope for words, appalled by the question that finally tumbles off my lips.

"What have you been up to?" I ask.

"Oh, not a lot," he answers.

We sit knee to knee, talking about inconsequential things. I stumble from one faux pas to another. He squirms when I ask how he likes school. He wants to talk about me, wants to ask about when I was eighteen, his age.

"Did you ever do anything crazy? Really crazy?"

I tell him about hitchhiking alone to D.C. to see the Stones. He's impressed. "Yeah, they were great, it was great, best night of my life," I say, lying.

A hip-hop psych tech, not much older than Robert, announces that visiting hours are over. Robert grabs my arm and asks if I'll come back tomorrow. He doesn't tell me why he wants to see me. I don't have to ask.

"If you like."

"I'd like," he says. When I shake his hand, he grabs and squeezes me, then breaks away quickly, not knowing how I might react, not trusting that I won't push him away. He's unsure of the world these days.

He's quiet when I return the next day, absorbed in a television movie. But when I stand up to stretch, he grabs my elbow, not letting me wander from the sofa. At the end of visiting hours, he asks if I'll be back tomorrow. Maybe, I say. My minimum-wage obligations back in Charlotte are looming. Please, he says, hopefully. Sure, okay, I assure him. If Barnes and Noble won't accommodate me, I'll take my skills across the street to Borders.

Bobby's wife isn't the type of woman comfortable with tears, but the events of the past few weeks have broken her down. I'm not that comfortable with emotional outbursts either and, if truth be told, I would rather she not start crying when I tell her I'll hang around a little longer. She's overwhelmed by what she thinks is my kindness and generosity. I let her believe my motives are selfless. Why should I tell her the truth, that I've failed everyone around me, my wife, my father?

Christ, I couldn't even be at my mother's bedside when she died. Now they are all gone and I'm alone and, if not entirely unloved, then, at least, unneeded. What twist of fate has dropped this kid in my lap? Why now? Bobby's wife has it all wrong. Kindness and generosity have nothing to do with it. I'm doing this for me.

Besides, I genuinely like the kid. I knew the bare bones of the story. He's eager to talk, but reluctant to be the first to speak. On my third visit, the charge nurse makes a special dispensation so Robert and I can have a little privacy. We sit quietly in his tiny room. He fidgets on his mattress and offers to change places with me.

"That's okay. The chair's fine," I say. He looks at me and sighs. I'm going to have to make the first move. I make it easy for him to open his heart and pour out his soul. I confess I know all about WrestlerJoc and OnMiKnees4U, about Cary, about whom I had been both wrong and right.

"Cary, Cary, Cary," he repeats, feeling a rush of liberation just being able to speak the forbidden name.

Cary wasn't the dreaded predator I feared and ended up being pretty much the package presented over cyberspace— twenty years old, in the throes of first love and infatuation, the type of boy on whom Robert had harbored secret crushes since junior high. Still, just like I predicted, he ended up smashing Robert against the rocks of reality by abruptly announcing he really was straight, was only really comfortable with girls, that being around Robert now made him feel a little creepy. Maybe Robert shouldn't call or hang around his dorm, and probably he shouldn't acknowledge him if they happened to run into each other on campus.

This sudden change of heart happened after (and, as he will realize when he's a little older and wiser, because) Robert, emboldened by the power of true love, placed a classified ad in *The Daily Tar Heel*, participating in some phenomenon called

National Coming Out Day by sending a public mash note using his *real name* to the Love of His Life, a man, yes, a man, he identified only by the initials CAL. In a gentler, kinder world, Robert would have been allowed to quietly retreat to lick the wounds of rejection, and, over time, learn to love Cary less and less.

But, of course, fate would intervene in the form of Mandy's older brother, the beneficiary of a UNC wrestling scholarship, who clipped the disgusting announcement from the paper, folded it, and tucked it in his wallet, saving it to share with his bitter little sister when he went home for Thanksgiving. Little sister, drunk and betrayed, threw the crumpled piece of paper in the face of my cousin Bobby when he answered the door.

To say he beat the boy to a pulp wouldn't be much of an exaggeration. Robert crawled back to Chapel Hill that night with a black eye and facial abrasions and a sharp pain in his rib cage where his father kicked him for good measure after knocking him to the floor. The dormitory was empty except for a couple of Chinese kids who didn't speak much English and kept to themselves anyway. By the time halls started to fill up again on Sunday, the swelling had gone down and he told anyone who asked about his eye he'd been in a car wreck, nothing broken, just knocked around a bit.

"Have you ever felt as if you were living in someone else's body?" Robert asks me. "Did you ever touch your skin and couldn't feel it?"

"All the time," I admitted. "Not so much now. But it hasn't been so long ago since I felt that way."

He called his mother, told her not to worry, he was all right, they'd talk about it later, decide what to do, where he'd go, after exams. He stared at the open book on his desk, unable to read, not even seeing the print on the page, finally closing it. It was pointless, his father was cutting off the money and he wouldn't be returning, at least not until he could earn some cash. Barely eating, unable to sleep, not bathing, he wandered the streets until daylight, talking to himself, he counted down the days—twenty, nineteen, eighteen—until they closed the dorm for winter break, leaving him nowhere to go.

He paced outside the library, open all night during exams, arguing with himself, swearing he wasn't going to give in to temptation, finally losing the battle and ending up in the men's room deep in the bowels of the building. Locking himself in a stall, he waited, not wanting sex actually but needing to feel something warm—a belly or a crotch—against his face, hoping someone would slip into the next stall and a foot would slide across the tile and nudge his, the blossoming of romance.

He sat for hours, his ass and thighs turning to cold lead, hearing nothing but piss against porcelain, an occasional turd plopping in water, flush and run. Just when he was about to give up, go home and pull the sheets over his head, he heard the sounds of procrastination at the sink, hands being washed and dried, then washed again, a brief, hushed conversation, and then belt buckles slapping the floor in the next stall. Robert leaned forward and saw suede bucks and familiar red sneakers with black racing stripes. His knees buckled and his stomach heaved when he stood to pull up his pants. He tripped over his own feet, cutting his chin on the edge of the door, and, bleeding, ran as fast as he could, away from the banging and thumping and hands slapping the stall, from the grunting and groaning, from Cary's voice, begging the boy in the suede bucks to do it harder, go deeper, harder.

He waited until nine in the morning when the dorm was empty. Then, alone in his room, he slipped a pocketknife in the pocket of his robe and walked the corridor to the shower room. Once the water was scalding hot, he pulled the shower curtain behind him and slashed first his left wrist, and then, before he passed out from shock, gouged his right, not as prettily, but effectively. The blood came in spurts and the last thing he remembered was it swirling around his feet and disappearing down the drain.

"I didn't think about killing myself. I just wanted to feel something, something that hurt. But I didn't want to kill myself, you've gotta understand," he says, shaking my arm, pleading with me.

"Why?" I ask him. "Why is it so important I understand you?"

"Because no one else does."

"Why are you so sure I do?"

"Mandy told me," he says. "She said you were a fag. I thought about you all the time after that. I wanted to talk to you so bad. I almost called you, but I was afraid."

The shrink thinks Robert would benefit from intensive therapy and the medications might need to be adjusted, but the insurance won't approve any further inpatient treatment. Bobby's wife panics. Robert cannot go home. The hospital can't keep him just because he has nowhere to go.

I haven't finished making the offer before he accepts. I explain my spartan existence and warn him his feet will hang off the couch. More permanent plans can wait until after the holiday. Who will follow his case? Who will make the doctor's appointment? What about school? What about the lost semester? How he will pay his tuition? And the dormitory. Will they take him back? How can he face all those well-scrubbed little Tar Heels who last saw him being carried out the door by paramedics? It's not my problem. After the new year, I'll send him packing, bus ticket in hand, destination unknown.

Much to my surprise, my prison cell at Magnolia Towne Courte seems larger, not smaller, when he takes up residence. It's strange, how much we have to talk about, this eighteen-year-old kid and me. He wants to know everything about me. No, not everything. He's not interested in my life with Alice.

He's only curious about the life he and I share. He assumes I was always what I am today. Which I was. Only I didn't know it. No, more accurately, I didn't *want* to know it. He wants to know about my first time. *What did he look like? Was he nice? Did you love him?* No, I certainly wasn't in love with a long red snake. But I don't share that with Robert. He's still a boy, impressionable, and, after Cary, his faith in his fellow travelers is too precarious to withstand the sordid little tale of my rape by a nicotine-stained stranger in the cab of a tractor trailer. So, instead, he's enthralled by the tall tale of the First Time I wished I'd had. Like Baron Frankenstein, I assemble this chimera from bits and pieces—part Randy T, part Brian Wilkins, a dash of the Rocket Boy, a bit of Steve, even a trace of Douglas. I christen my fantasy first love "Nick," inspired by the Beach Boys Christmas song on the radio. *Surely, you've got a picture of him? Somewhere,* I lie, *I'll look around.* I dig out an old photo album I hadn't put in storage and chose some long-forgotten young Nocera Heat and Air technician captured for posterity at the annual summer picnic to cast in the role of Nick.

He uses me as his sounding board for his theories and opinions about everything and anything. The debate between genetics and environment. The theory of dominant mother/absent father. Why Lou Reed, despite overwhelming evidence of his heterosexuality, is a better role model for gays than Elton John. I make mental notes, checklists, of all the things I want to tell him in our short time together. Soon enough, it will be time for him to be thrown back into the harsh world. He puts up a good show of bravado, but I know he's afraid to venture out there alone. He reminds me of a boy I once knew, a kid who dreamed of conquering the world, but chose safety and security over Chicago. I don't want Robert to retreat like I had; I want him to be strong and fearless.

Gina calls on Christmas Eve to wish me a Merry Christmas and to inflict a ration of guilt for declining her invitation to spend the holidays in Boca Raton. The family's making progress, she reports. Dustin's father got him the Original Cast Recordings of *Annie* and *Rent* for Christmas, and Dustin is over the moon about the Stowe father-and-son ski trip the two of them are planning. She wants to talk about our mother, to rhapsodize about our last tortuous Noel, remembering it as a glorious Technicolor MGM musical. You really are a selfish bastard, she says, do you know how much it would have meant to me to spend this first Christmas without her together? That goddamn minimum-wage job is a pretty lame excuse. We both knew I hardly need the money now. But she says all of this affectionately, without rancor.

I tell her it would have been impossible anyway. I have a houseguest. I can't really talk. He's sitting a few feet away. Robert. JR. You know, I say, Bobby's kid. No, he's eighteen now. Yeah, how time flies. Stop being so suspicious. He got into a little trouble and needed a place to stay. No, not that kind of trouble. Of course his mother knows he's here. She's the one who asked me to help. Look, I said, I'll tell you about it later. Merry Christmas. I love you too. Yes, I got it. Yes, I love it. No, I haven't read it yet. But Robert has spent hours poring over the Beatles coffee table book she sent me for Christmas.

Christmas is a clear, sunny day. The forecast is calling for a high in the upper sixties, chance of precipitation nil. I let the kid sleep in the morning; it's almost noon before the smell of brewing coffee, my second pot of the day, lures him off the couch. He chews on a Pop-Tart, crumbs falling to the floor, and asks what we're doing to celebrate. I invite him to take a ride with me. Sure, he says, not asking where we were going. A couple miles from home I curse myself for forgetting my sunglasses. He insists I borrow his.

The gas tank is nearly empty as I pull into a station—*We Never Close*—just over the Gastonia city limits. I pump while Robert, always hungry, goes in search of a bean burrito and a microwave oven. As I wait to pay, I realize I'm going empty-handed. I grab a pale, wilted poinsettia on the counter and ask the Pakistani behind the register to add it to the bill. Take it, take it, no charge, free, Merry Christmas, mister, he says, bobbing his head and smiling like a lunatic.

The cemetery isn't far, another mile or two. We pass the crumbling headstones and the granite pylon dedicated by the Daughters of the Confederacy and drive up the hill where the grave markers are flat and the lawn kept neat and trim with riding mowers. I set the flowerpot on a small pink slab that marks the final resting spot of Anthony (Nunzio) and Ruth Calhoun Nocera. Later that night, the weather will turn more seasonable and a strong wind will tip the pot, mercifully finishing off the already half-dead flower. Robert takes pity on me and stares at his feet when I start to cry.

The temperature plummets as soon as the sun goes down. Robert and I, neither of us wearing coats, make a quick dash through the truck stop parking lot. The waitress is in a good mood, dropping quarters in the jukebox, playing Elvis's "Blue Christmas" six times in a row. Robert, a smudge of yellow omelet on his chin, calls out the chord progression. Wrong, I say, correcting a major to a minor chord. Right, perfect, we really need to play together, as soon as these are off, he says, waving his bandaged wrists. The waitress brings refills, wincing and trying not to stare. Sure, I say, we'll play some day.

Eleven O'clock Number

What goes around comes around?

Things have come full circle?

There must be a one-size-fits-all cliché for this final chapter of my belated bildungsroman.

A leopard doesn't change its spots?

When all is said and done, it's been easier to embrace my new "lifestyle" than to accept the fact that I'm a natural born salesman. After all, my style of life seems remarkably unchanged. I live in a brand-spanking-new town house that, except for a difference of, say, a thousand square feet, could be mistaken for 12 Virginia Dare Court—not surprising since the elves in the Toll Brothers workshop are more renowned for their productivity than their originality. The Toyota's been upgraded to an SUV, same make, later model year, same color as the vehicle I'd signed over to Alice. Maybe I dress a little better. No, not really, but my clothes fit better because I hit the pool five mornings a week, determined not to concede to the fullfrontal assault of early middle age. Then I guzzle a cup of coffee, premium blend of course, and resist (usually) the Krispy Kremes, fortifying myself for another day on the front lines. You could say I'm an evangelist of sorts, spreading the Gospel of Nocera/Olsson Climate Control Systems, formerly known by the more quotidian moniker Nocera Heat and Air. What could have persuaded me to walk away from the promising career opportunities at Barnes and Noble? Randy T had been running the business since the old man died. My mother had been generous, paying him a substantial salary and a hefty percentage of the ever-increasing construction boomtown revenues. He'd lost his hair, but still had his athlete's body and charm and animal magnetism, expanding Nocera Heat and Air into commercial construction and exclusive distribution rights. After years of being unfettered by our mother and anticipating a future under the scrutiny of the ungrateful heirs, he was about to accept an offer to jump to a competitor. Regina and I engaged a broker to value the business and summoned Randy T to Boca Raton. He left Florida an equal partner, owner of one-third equity interest with the title of President and CEO.

Randy T has a vision for the company's future. The old man installed and serviced HVAC units; Randy T toils in "thermal control design and construction." He didn't need a Wharton MBA to know that Nocera/Olsson needed a Director of Sales and Marketing to take it to the next level. The title was a compromise because family pride, which I graciously allowed my sister to defend, would not permit the son and heir of the Founding Father to agree to be called a "Vice" anything. It wasn't a hard decision to make. Lying awake in my bed at Magnolia Towne Courte, full of midnight courage, I'd plotted my escape to Atlanta or south Florida. But when I gazed into the crystal ball in the harsh light of day, the future was daunting: the anxious interview, the entry-level sales position, the young and hungry competition, difficulties closing the deal, the sweet temptation of bourbon as an antidote for loneliness. Fearlessness isn't one of my virtues. I'm still the boy who opted for the comfort and safety of Sweet Home Carolina when I hit a speed bump on the yellow brick road to Chicago.

A leopard doesn't change its spots.

The time had arrived to step forward and embrace my legacy. I'd been preparing for this since I withdrew from Duke. Selling thermal control systems is a step up from persuading gullible retailers that Shelton/Murray design solutions will turn their pumpkins into Cinderella's coach and it's a whole other league from hawking cheap pieces of glued fiberboard for the King of Unpainted Furniture. I could even say it's a noble endeavor, preserving the Nocera in Nocera/Olsson, carrying on the family name.

Besides, supporting Robert has turned out to be an expensive proposition. There's tuition, room and board, spending money. Robert couldn't sleep on the sofa forever; a boy needs the privacy of his own room. He knows there is a place he can call home during school breaks or the occasional weekend when Chapel Hill doesn't feel so friendly. He's taken up residence for the summer and tries to act enthusiastic about spending ten weeks on the Nocera/Olsson payroll, spending eight hours a day trying not to look totally useless. Randy T's son has taken him under his wing.

Things have come full circle.

"Andy, uh, there's someone here to see you," Randy T says, standing awkwardly at my office door, looking a little flustered.

Goddamn it. It's Friday afternoon and if there's any chance of making Durham by the first pitch we need to be on the road in an hour. The Charlotte Knights are playing the Bulls tonight and rumor has it that Josh Strickland, the ace of the Triple-A pitching staff, is going to be called up to the majors after the game. Harold says he's a highly prized prospect, the jewel of the White Sox farm system. Every general manager in the majors would like to hold his rights, and the Sox, desperate to trade one of their aging superstars to strengthen their bull pen, can't close a deal because all of the potential trade partners insist that Josh be part of the package. Harold is a repository of useless sports trivia. Not trivial, not useless, he protests, since this is knowledge he needs to defend his championship of his fantasy baseball league.

Somewhere up there my father is smiling.

Harold's a sweet kid, although Robert is quick to remind me he's barely ten years younger than I am. It's just that he seems like a kid with his floppy hair and his aversion to any Gillette products and his wardrobe that consists almost entirely of Official NCAA and MLB Sanctioned UNC and White Sox gear. He manages a Charlotte branch of an office supply chain but he's only twenty-six credits away from his bachelor's degree in secondary education. He wants to teach American history and coach high school hoops, an ambition I caution him he's not likely to achieve if he keeps on spending happy hour at the Carousel and insists on broadcasting his lifestyle with that ridiculous rainbow bumper sticker. He says he's not worried about stuff like that, that people don't care who you sleep with so long as you don't rub it in their face. Maybe he knows something I don't, but I doubt it.

Anyway, I won't have to comfort and console him when he smacks into a brick wall of disappointment. It's not like I expect him to still be around when he discovers that the good Christian people of Mecklenburg and Gaston counties have no intention of giving him an opportunity to pat their impressionable young sons on the ass when they make a free throw. Harold is a temporary thing, no doubt about it. It's hard to believe it's sustained itself for three months. It's still surprises me that he wakes up in my bed most mornings, brushes his teeth (with his own toothbrush, nestled in the cup beside mine), chugs a glass of orange juice, and says "call you later" as he walks out the door. He calls by noon, every day, for no reason at all, not because he has to, only to ask "how's it going" and we decide where and when to meet after work. And every morning at 11:45 I start to fidget, growing irritable, because I'm certain that this is the day he's not going to call, then the phone rings and by 12:15 I'm content and satisfied, a man with plans and someone to be with. Someone whose odd little tics are more endearing than irritating.

Usually.

Harold can barely carry a tune, but he loves to sing. Actually, his taste in music isn't bad, even if he refuses to concede that his beloved Jesus and Mary Chain ought to pay the Velvets royalties for ripping off their songbook. He says it wouldn't hurt for me to try to appreciate music recorded after the invention of the compact disc. Robert says it's all very romantic. I think it's preposterous, this thing with Harold. Robert asks what's so preposterous about falling in love? God, he's so young. Where does he get these ideas?

I'm about to call Harold to warn him we might run a little late. But I drop the phone, dumbfounded, not knowing how to greet my surprise guest.

"Fucking Jesus, I don't fucking believe it! Oh Jesus, I'm sorry, damn, I wasn't thinking!"

"It's okay, Andy." Alice laughs. "I think Bradley is a little young to be permanently scarred by your dirty mouth."

"What are you doing here?" I ask, forgetting my manners. "I mean, I'm glad to see you. It's just, well, I don't understand. What are you doing here?"

The baby is fussing, demanding her undivided attention. Alice looks like a suburban sherpa, saddled with her infant and an overstuffed, oversize canvas bag.

"Here, let me take that," I offer.

"You can call him Bradley."

"No. No. I mean the bag, not the baby," I say as I roll my chair from behind my desk.

"Thanks," she says. "Can you get the bottle out of the bag? Is there a microwave around here?"

"I'm not sure."

"Ah well, we'll make do, won't we, kiddo?" she asks.

I start to answer, then realize she's talking to her son. Baby Bradley is soon sucking away, drifting into sleep.

My wife, by Bellini, Madonna and Bambino, placid, content, destiny fulfilled at last.

"He's beautiful," I say.

"Don't forget we were together for twenty years. I know you think all babies look parboiled."

"Other people's babies," I say. "Not yours," I add quickly so there's no room for misinterpretation. "But what are you doing in Gastonia? You didn't make the trip to our fair city just to see me."

"We came to Charlotte to spend the weekend with Barry's parents. I drove over to Gastonia to see you."

"Well," I say, embarrassed. "It's good to see you."

"Thank you again for the baby gift. It was lovely."

"It was nothing."

"Well, it was a lovely nothing."

"Your thank-you card was sweet."

"You look much better than the last time I saw you."

"I was a mess. I don't think I ever thanked you for coming to the funeral. I wouldn't have made it through the day if you hadn't been with me."

"I wanted to be there."

The baby is squirming again.

"Would you like to hold him?"

"No. I mean, it's not that I don't want to hold him, but what if I drop him? I'm not very experienced."

"You're not going to drop him," she says as she lays him in my arms.

"He smells like a baby," I say, amazed by the sweet powdery scent of his pink skin.

"Enjoy it." She laughs. "Sometimes he smells like a goat. I'm warning you. He can turn in a second."

I squeeze him gently and tell him what a lucky, lucky boy he is.

"You would have made a wonderful father," she says. Knowing her as well as I do, I detect the slight hint of regret in her voice, the what-if, the if only.

"I hope I would have been a better father than I was a husband."

"You were a good husband," she says firmly, leaving no question her opinion is not open to discussion.

"I doubt Curtis would agree with you on that subject."

"What my father thinks is beside the point."

And now I know. The obvious can no longer be denied. Curtis hadn't ended my marriage. Neither had Barry. It was my wife.

"You may not believe it, but you're back in my father's good graces."

"You can't be serious."

She lowers her voice several octaves. Her impersonation of the King of Unpainted Furniture is still pitch-perfect.

Goddamn it, not one of these cocksuckers is half the salesman that little cocksucker was.

We're laughing, tears in our eyes, and Baby Bradley is protesting at having his nap disturbed. I don't know how long Harold has been standing at the door to my office. He looks a bit forlorn, like he's just stumbled across a party to which he hadn't been invited.

"Oh, hey," I say. It's awkward being stranded between Alice's curiosity and Harold's self-consciousness. A moment passes, then two. I can't seem to kick-start the introductions.

This is . . . the woman who shared my life for twenty years. Sorry I can't be more specific. "Wife" isn't accurate. "Ex-wife" sounds harsh, too full of bitterness and regret. "Friend" would be an insult to our history; it can't describe the bond between us, even now.

328 / *Tom Mendicino*

This is . . . a pal, a buddy, the man who's been falling asleep beside me for the past few months. "Boyfriend" is too juvenile; we're not in high school and he hasn't asked me to go steady. He's definitely not a "partner" or "lover."

A half million words in the Oxford English Dictionary and I can't find two that fit.

"Alice, this is Harold. Harold, this is Alice."

"Nice to meet you," she says.

"Nice to meet you," he mumbles, shyly approaching her and extending his hand. "Sorry, I didn't mean to interrupt."

"No, please, it's okay," Alice and I say in unison.

"I'll call you later," he says as he backs out the door.

"No, no. We'll just be a minute."

"Really, I was just getting ready to leave," Alice says.

"We're driving to Durham. We need to be there by seven," I explain, offering a reason for his palpable anxiousness.

"Durham?" she asks. Harold doesn't know the subtext to her question.

"Alice and I used to live in Durham," I explain.

"I thought you lived in High Point?"

"Before that, when I was at Duke."

Another fact in my personal history Harold doesn't know.

"It was nice to meet you," he repeats, excluded, the odd man out. "I'll wait downstairs."

"I'll meet you there in a few minutes."

"He seems very nice," she says after he's gone.

"He is."

"How did you meet?"

"Believe it or not, he pursued me." I laugh. "Harold has very low expectations."

She rocks little Bradley in her arms, saying nothing, knowing her silence will compel me to babble on.

"He's more persistent than he looks. He kept buying me beers at the local watering hole and I kept blowing him off.

Then one night I was eating dinner alone at Cracker Barrel—go ahead and laugh—and he plopped in my booth uninvited. That's how I learned the man pours ketchup on macaroni and cheese."

"Love is blind." She laughs.

"It's not what you think."

The reflex is still there, the need to disavow the blatantly apparent.

"How do you know what I'm thinking?" she asks.

"For the same reason you always know what I'm thinking."

"So you're suggesting we can read each other's minds?" she asks.

"Yes."

"Not always," she says, bringing me back to earth. "I shouldn't have surprised you, Andy. But I figured if I called ahead you'd make an excuse."

"See, you can read my mind."

"I have something of yours I know you'd want and I didn't want to send it by mail. It's there. In the bag. Can you get it? I don't want to wake him."

I set the bag on my lap.

"Go ahead. It won't bite you," she says, encouraging me to fish through the pacifiers and baby spoons in plastic baggies, the disposable diapers, the jars of applesauce and the stuffed sock monkey. I know what it is as soon as I touch the plastic cube. I'd resigned myself to accepting it was gone forever, tossed away with the detritus of my former life. It's preserved in its pristine state, protected from the elements, snowy white, the ink as fresh as the day it was etched into the cow leather a lifetime ago.

To Andy Nocera, Joe DiMaggio.

"Damn, I don't believe it. Where did you find it?" I ask.

"It was never lost. It just got forgotten in the . . . the confusion."

"There were two of these," I say wistfully. Forgive me for plagiarizing the great Nabokov this once. There's no way to describe the effect of a ten-dollar baseball except to admit I'm easily intoxicated by the impossible past.

She blushes and clears her throat, not once, twice—the sure sign she's embarrassed.

"I have it. I'll send it to you when I get home."

"No, no, I want you to keep it," I say, happier than I should be, thrilled actually, to know she keeps a small reminder of me in the house she shares with her husband and son.

"Are you sure?"

"Of course I'm sure. The least I can do is give you one of my balls."

She laughs (I knew she would) and the dreaded moment arrives when the violins swell and the lens goes soft focus and we're meant to fall in each other's arms and declare eternal love despite the impossible circumstances. But Baby Bradley has an impeccable sense of timing. He knows exactly when to strike up the band.

"Someone's cranky," she says, rising from her chair. "I'd give you a hug but I'm a bit encumbered."

Instead we settle on a chaste kiss on the cheek and a thank-you. I'm sure it's my imagination but I swear Baby Bradley is giving me the evil eye, warning me to back off.

"I'll walk you to the car," I say, hoisting her bag on my shoulder. We make small talk about the weather, comparing last year's blistering temperatures with the pleasant balminess of this July. A real Mayberry summer we're having, I observe.

"What is it with men and that show?" She laughs. Obviously Barry and I have something in common.

"Men are only allowed to be sentimental about two things. Their own ten-year-old selves and dead athletes. Them's the rules," I say, explaining the Opie factor.

"I can't believe you're forty." She sighs, strapping the baby in his car seat.

"You're not far behind."

"Surreal, isn't it?" she says. "Do you remember when we thought we had all the time in the world?"

"I do."

"He seems really nice, Andy. I can tell he really loves you."

I shrug my shoulders, neither admitting nor denying it, and now we do hug, an embrace no different than one I'd share with my mother or sister.

"Don't fuck this one up," she says, turning the key in the ignition. "You deserve to be happy."

My Rolex says it's 1:45 as her car rolls out of the parking lot and disappears in the traffic. Alice is right: time is slipping away. I find Harold and tell him we need to hit the road if he's going to see young Mr. Strickland one last time in a Charlotte uniform.

He's quiet in the car, unusual for him. The radio is off and he doesn't reach for one of his discs to slip in the player. I know exactly how to cheer him up.

"Hey, I've got something to show you. You're going to love this," I promise, handing him the baseball cube.

"Is this for real?" he asks, his natural giddiness bubbling through the gloom.

"Absolutely."

"How did you know Joe DiMaggio?"

"My dad played ball with him once."

He hands the cube back gingerly as if it's fragile porcelain that would shatter if he sneezed.

"No shit," he says, amazed.

"No shit."

He stares at the road beyond the windshield. He shakes his shoulders and cracks his neck, loosening up, preparing for the crushing disappointment of losing the son of a man who played ball with Joe DiMaggio.

"So," he says, unable to control the tremor in his voice. "Are you guys getting back together?"

I suppress my natural instinct to laugh because now I finally see what Alice recognized at first glance. Harold really loves me.

"No. No. That's impossible."

I can leave it at that or I can remind him that the bundle of joy on Alice's knee didn't arrive by FedEx, purchased on eBay. Or I can take the opportunity to make him happy.

"You see, I'm already taken," I say, squeezing his knee. "So you know where we're going?"

"Durham," he says, reaching down to grab my hand.

"And then?"

"What do you mean?"

"After Durham?"

"Home?"

"You know how to get there?"

"The same way we came."

"Last star to the left, then straight on to Neverland."

"What?"

"Didn't you ever read *Peter Pan?*"

"I saw the movie. You wanna hear some music?"

"Sure."

He pops in a Weezer disc, the Blue Album, fast-forwarding to his favorite track. He picks up my hand again, pleading, come on, sing it for me, just the chorus, please, pretty please. What choice do I have but to surrender?

"Woo-ee-oo, I look just like Buddy Holly."

Yep, things have come full circle.

He plays the track a second time, then a third. He wants to

harmonize, but it's been a long, strange afternoon with hours ahead of us before we roll into Durham. The sun is shining, bugs are splattering on the windshield, and I'm losing a battle with the Sandman as the pine trees and blue skies of North Carolina race by in a blur.

Acknowledgments

The late Mark Harris and the late Jerre Mangione were the first writers to encourage me to follow in their footsteps. Elaine Scarry was exceptionally generous and supportive and deserves all the accolades she has gone on to achieve.

Nick Street, Joe Pittman, and Lawrence Schimel were willing to put me into print.

Judith Stern, since 1994 and counting.

Brian Corbett, Mark McCloud, L.W.B., Sharon Sorokin James, Lori Biondi, and Cheryl Radenz all contributed to making this possible.

Mitchell Waters has been steadfast throughout, and John Scognamiglio ought to be on a Publisher's Row Mount Rushmore with Perkins and Robbins and Maxwell.

The family in this work of fiction are pikers compared to my parents and sister when it comes to unconditional love.

And, finally, to Nick Ifft, for better or worse, for richer and poorer, in sickness and in health and, thirty years later, till death do us part.

PROBATION

Tom Mendicino

ABOUT THIS GUIDE

The suggested questions are included
to enhance your group's reading of
Tom Mendicino's *Probation*!

DISCUSSION QUESTIONS

1. How would you describe Andy and Alice's relationship? What do you think their marriage meant to each of them?

2. What qualities of Andy do you think attracted Alice at the beginning of their relationship? What did she continue to see in him that sustained their relationship both throughout their marriage and after their separation and divorce? In the closing chapter, Alice tells Andy he was "a good husband." Why do you think she would say that?

3. Do you think Alice suspected Andy's infidelities? Was she aware of his attraction to men? Why would she remain in the relationship if she suspected he was gay?

4. What would you identify as the critical moment in their marriage?

5. In the chapter "Casta diva," Andy becomes suspicious that Alice began an affair while they were married. Considering his own transgressions, why is Andy so angry at the thought of his wife cheating? Do you think Alice was unfaithful to her husband? Why do you think Alice was willing to forgive Andy? How would you explain her surprising lack of bitterness and anger?

6. Why does Andy seem so hostile to his sister at times?

7. What are Andy's mother's and father's strengths and weaknesses as parents? How did each of them affect his development?

8. How different do you think Andy's life would have been if he'd gone to college in Chicago?

9. Andy is both frustrated and intrigued by the boundaries of his therapeutic relationship with Matt McGinley. Do you think Matt's being a priest hinders or enhances his ability to break through Andy's resistance to therapy? Are you curious about the details of Matt's personal life? Do you think Matt is gay too?

10. Why do you think Andy is such a successful salesman— a career he fell into and a job he doesn't enjoy and seems to disdain?

11. Why did Andy intervene in Robert's crisis? What was his motivation?

12. Has Andy fully accepted himself as a gay man by the end of the novel? Does he seem reluctant or hesitant to fully commit to his relationship with Harold? Describe Andy's life ten years in the future.